CHECK THE GATE!

Movie-Making in the Amazon
While Dodging The Alligators in Hollywood

A Novel By
MICHAEL DRYHURST

ISBN: 9798614816568

First Edition: February 2020.

TRIVIA

Within the following story, there is a considerable amount of movie technical terms, English rhyming slang and snippets of foreign languages. To help the reader understand much of this, at the rear of the book is a glossary, wherein hopefully all is explained.

Author Michael Dryhurst was born into a movie family. When his parents met, the gent who became his father was an assistant director, while his soon-to-be mother was a screen extra. Father Edward Dryhurst later became the first independent producer in the U.K., in addition scriptwriting many of the movies he produced. Also, Michael's late brother Christopher was an assistant director.

Michael Dryhurst himself entered the industry at the age of seventeen (the Pa had gone belly-up), as a clapper-loader, in these politically-correct times known now as a 2nd assistant cameraman. After five years in the camera department, he transferred to production as a third assistant director, progressing as a 2nd A.D., 1st A.D., unit production manager, associate producer and producer/director. In total, he spent 52+ years in movies, and is married to Karen Gordon, a one-time high-profile Hollywood production accountant. They live in rural Arkansas.

In truth, Michael's ambition was to be a bus driver, so to fulfil that dream, he bought himself a double-decker. Here he is seen at the wheel of his baby, while location shooting *Hope and Glory* at London's Marylebone railway station.

Thank you for buying the book; all concerned hope you enjoy reading a different view of the movie industry.

"Movies are an art form which is a business, and a business which is an art form."

Dalton Trumbo, Screenwriter.

"Film is frivolous."

Abel Gance, Movie Director and Cinematic Visionary.

"Films will not be an art until the materials to make them are as cheap as paper and a pencil."

Jean Cocteau, Movie Director

"Film is a battleground. Love, Hate, Action, Death. In a word . . . Emotion."

Samuel Fuller, Movie Director

"The movie business is the deal business."

Francesco Delli Tonnini, Movie Producer

He was being tapped on the shoulder gently, very gently, yet firmly. It was the perfume aroma which aroused him. Clive Christian's 'Imperial Majesty.' Someone had a sugar-daddy, but Cooper had a better sense of scent than Lt. Colonel Frank Slade.

"Mr. Cooper?"

He stirred. His mouth both felt and tasted like a sewer in *The Third Man*. He blinked several times and saw the blurred face of a cabin-crew member. Adjusting gently his seat-back, she lowered the tray-table.

"We'll be landing in about one hour, sir. What can I get you for breakfast?"

"Coffee."

"Cream and sugar?"

"*Schwarz, bitte.*"

"Cereal, fruit?"

"Just the coffee, thank you. Oh, and eh, what's the current time?"

"It is . . ." She checked her watch. "Zero six-thirty B.S.T., Tuesday 19th May, 1987."

The car pulled away from Heathrow Terminal Three. Wearily, Cooper relaxed into the rear-seat comfort of the Humber Hawk, smiling as he shook his head. "You know Len, the motor industry has brought out newer designs."

"Foreign crap! This motor's built like a tank. It'll still be around longer than you and me. And, it's got a lot more airport trips in it, I can tell you!" Emphasizing the point, Len adjusted his chauffeur's cap. Firmly.

Cooper looked around the interior of the sedan, rather as one studies a house long-since vacated. Gently, he ran his hand over the dubbinladen leather upholstery. "I was a second assistant director when I first saw this car." He looked up. "You were driving actors to the studios then." He sighed. "Gawd, that's the best part of twenty years ago."

Len looked in the rear-view mirror. "It never is?"

"Bloody well is, and I used to call you 'sir'."

"Yeah, well, times change, don't they?"

After stopping to buy some basic and much-needed provisions—milk, coffee, tea, the favored brand of biscuits and a six-pack of Guinness—the black Humber arrived at no.46, Priory Gardens, Barnes S.W.13. A bijou Edwardian red-brick terraced house with a small, neat front garden, the type of residence much-favored by the yuppies of the late sixties and early seventies. Close to the River Thames and Richmond Park, easy to get into Town, marred only by the fact that it was underneath the incoming flight-path for London Heathrow, the world's busiest international airport.

As Len unloaded the luggage, an airliner roared overhead. There would be another within three minutes, and another a minute after that, *ad infinitum*. Entering the house, Len left the baggage at the foot of the stairs.

A shout roared from the kitchen. "Cuppa?"

"Love one. And some of those chocolate digestives you just bought."

Cooper entered, tray in hand. Gesturing to a chair, he handed Len a mug of tea and a plate of biscuits. "Make yourself at home." He himself poured a drink. A very large one.

"What's that?"

"V and T. Duty-free vodka, local tonic."

"Blimey, with that measure it looks more like a tonic and vodka." He supped his tea, accompanied by the munching of a biscuit.

Cooper raised the glass and took a deep gulp.

Watched by Len. "Y'know, James, alcohol's a great friend but it's a lousy master."

A wan smile creased Cooper's visage. "But a great comforter and, a

2

great relaxer."

Len studied Cooper. "Christ, James . . ."

"What?"

"You look like death warmed up. I reckon you could do with some relaxing. Where was it this time?"

"India." Cooper drank. "Thirteen God awful months."

"Then tonight's dinner won't be from the Taj Mahal Tandoori Take Away, right?"

"More likely junket and semolina. But you're right, I should, should have a nice long relaxing period."

Glancing at the mantlepiece clock, Len stood. "Thanks for the *rosy*. Best be off." Crossing the room, he paused at the door. "Take it easy."

Having refilled his glass, his libation was interrupted by the phone. " Two three-four-three."

"I call on the off-chance, and bingo!"

"Seth! Big brother, how are you?"

"Fine. Yourself?"

"Surviving."

"Fancy a Ploughman's?"

"A Ploughman's? For sure!"

"Meet you at The Sun? Say . . . forty minutes?"

They sat at one of the tables on the forecourt of the pub. While Seth got the drinks and food, Cooper watched the antics of the ducks on the pond across the road. His reverie was broken by the noise of crockery, cutlery and drinks. A Guinness for Seth, and for his brother, given the paucity of the English measurement of spirits, a triple V and a T. Plus, a Ploughman's for each of them.

Seth raised his glass. "Good to see you again. Good to have you back."

"It's good to be back." Cooper smiled at his elder brother. "Cheers."

Clinking glasses, they drank.

"You look knackered." Seth stared at his sibling. "This producing lark. Is it worth it, I mean, *really* worth it?"

Cooper looked over at the frolicking ducks. "It's lucrative. You get to

3

sit in the front cabin of the plane, first class hotels, etcetera." He turned to his brother. "But. There's the alimony payments, the mortgage and as you well know, the film industry doesn't pay pensions so as a freelance, I have to save for that rainy day when the phone stops ringing." Breaking off a chunk of French bread, he buttered it, adding a wedge of cheddar cheese plus a copious layer of branston pickle.

"Reckon you'll last that long?"

"Well, I couldn't work solely on commercials like you do. And Seth, why *do* you? You had a great future in features as a first A.D. And what about that Cambridge masters degree. All gone to waste?"

"Commercials are a no brainer. I only need a minimum of three a week, the money's good, no 'all-in' deals, a straight eight hours and then it's overtime, and most commercials go into overtime. Often exotic locations and I can take holidays when I want, when *I* like. It's a comfortable living and no ties, not like you, where you *marry* a movie. Besides, unlike you, I've never had that degree of ambition."

Cooper's brow furrowed. "Ambition? *Moi*? I've never thought of myself as ambitious. Added to which, that has to it the ring of . . . ruthlessness? Do I want to better myself, my career, advance step-by-step?" He nodded at his brother. "Yes. But doesn't the leader of an orchestra aspire to be the conductor?"

"And you don't think that's ambitious, ambition?" He nudged Cooper. "Semantics, little bro, semantics." His brother stood. "Same again?"

"Seth, it's my shout."

"No, my welcome home drinks." Collecting the glasses, he headed for the bar.

Sitting, Cooper pondered. He'd never ever thought of himself as ambitious, his ascending of the career ladder being in his judgment a simple yet natural progression. Like his move to producing. He'd been the unit production manager on a movie, the director had his next show lined-up already, they'd got on exceptionally well, and he asked Cooper if he'd be interested in producing it. Natural progression . . .

Fresh drinks were on the table. Seth raised his glass. "To commercials."

"Cheers." Cooper smiled. "Here's to your next tampons ad."

4

As he drank, Seth gazed at his younger brother. "James, why don't you just take a break?"

"Like I just said bro, there are financial commitments so, at my level you can't afford to let go, even professionally. There's too many others out there like me, doing the same job, waiting for that same Hollywood movie to land at Pinewood or Shepperton. And then, there's always the rejection factor."

"What's that? A TV reality show?"

"Seth, it's the movie industry. Irrespective of how good you are at your job, first and foremost your face has to fit and often you're answering to three masters. The studio, the director and or a film finance company. One wrong word, move, gesture, however well-intentioned but made at the wrong moment." He shrugged. "You're out, period. Blackballed."

Seth chuckled. "And you wonder why *I* stick to commercials?" Nodding his head good-humorously, Seth finished his stout. "Tell me brother, to brother-in-law. What *really* happened with you and Judy?"

At the mention of his ex-wife, Cooper sighed. "A location too far. Australia, ten months, then two in New Zealand followed by one in Tasmania. She got lonely. She met somebody else." Shrugging, he looked at his brother. " I could hardly blame her?"

Seth shook his head. "Another reason I'm happy. Never married, no guilt, nor alimony payments. Plus plenty of chances to play the field."

They laughed.

"As you've obviously walked here, why didn't you bring the dog?"

"Jesus! The dog! He's still in the bloody kennels! I forgot the poor little bugger."

"Drink up. I'll run you home."

Seth looked around the room, in so doing noticing the flashing red light on the answering machine.

"James! You've have a phone message."

Cooper arrived with drinks. Guinness for his brother plus for himself the inevitable V and T. With ice and slice.

Seth nodded to the machine. "Answer that and then I'll run you round to pick-up the dog."

Cooper played the message. *"James Cooper? This is Tonnini International Pictures in Los Angeles. Would you please call Mr. Don Seidelman collect, at this number. Thank you and have a nice day."* He wrote down the number and dialed the international operator. After a few minutes he was connected. "Don? James Cooper."

"James, hi. Busy?"

He looked at his brother. "Just finished one."

"So you're free, available?"

His brother was staring at him. Their eyes met.

"James, you there?"

"Eh, yes. Available."

"Then here's the deal."

Cooper wrote feverishly, taking down everything said to him by Seidelman. The call lasted eleven minutes. Resting the phone, he looked at his brother. "No point in collecting the dog."

"Oh?"

"I leave tomorrow morning for South America. Imperio."

In the bedroom, he looked at his unpacked luggage. Everything was laundered clean, and . . . tropical. No need to unpack? He rummaged in a drawer for some pyjamas. Which is when he saw it.

The framed photograph.

He stared at it. A snap of himself with his arm around a very attractive young lady, taken some years earlier on a sightseeing boat against the Manhattan skyline. The frame he held closer. Cooper racked his brain, speaking aloud to the photo while rolling his eyes. "Now what. What *was* your name?"

Removing the pyjamas, he propped the photo against the table-lamp. Facing the bed.

Ready to go, they stood on the hall floor. His talisman, the location bag, presented to him by the crew of an enjoyable movie shoot in Hong Kong, and the 'wheelie' suitcase.

Cooper answered the doorbell.

"S'truth, James. What happened to that bloody long relaxing break?"

Cooper looked sheepish. "Len, the phone rang. Just can't afford to look a gifthorse in the mouth."

"Y'know sunbeam, you ought to rest-up before you crack-up." Len loaded the luggage. "Terminal Three?"

Cooper breathed-in deeply. "Terminal Three."

SCENE 1. TAKE 1.

Smoke drifted languidly across the sun-baked and scarred landscape, obscuring fitfully the dross of battle, the wrecked tanks and trucks lying amid the innumerable craters and scarecrow-like trees, while the stretch limousine made its way tortuously along the rutted track. Looking out, Tonnini sighed deeply. How many hours, he asked himself, how many man-hours, how many broken lunch breaks and how much construction overtime had it cost to create this, this . . . *mess*?

Now aged sixty-two, Francesco Delli Tonnini was one of a group of Italian producers who had migrated to Los Angeles and although at five-feet five-inches (or as he preferred, *one-point-six-six meters)* small in stature, he was big in ambition, being cultured, creative and, street wise, and thus armored he had beaten Hollywood at its own game. A proud native of Rome, Tonnini used his considerable Lazio charm unashamedly, manipulatively and without discrimination.

De Laurentiis, De Sica, Ponti, Tonnini, all had made their mark in the U.S.A. as respected and trusted producers, Tonnini with his long-established Tonnini International Pictures, known readily by its acronym, T.I.P. On this, as on every day, from suit-to-shirt-to-tie, Tonnini was dressed immaculately in timeless and classical Italian style, he returning to Rome at least once a year to be fitted for new tailored suits and custom-made silk shirts, his hand-made shoes being crafted in London. He turned his gaze from the window and looked across the broad expanse of the rear seat, to where sat his executive vice-president business affairs Tonnini International Pictures, and, as usual, buried in paperwork, and as usual, oblivious to all around him. Don Seidelman.

Seeing in the young man a great deal of talent, he was lured by Tonnini from a Beverly Hills law firm and rose rapidly within T.I.P. and although Seidelman wasn't Italian, hadn't Mama said always that '*After Catholics, Jews are the next best!*' And in this case, it was true, especially as Seidelman was fluent in Italian, in business meetings giving the two men an added edge and tactical advantage, allowing them to converse openly and yet privately, much to the frustration of their American and British movie business rivals.

In his late forties now, Seidelman dressed in the manner of his mentor, a sort of Men's Wearhouse meets Lungotevere Dei Cenci and while Tonnini was more-than satisfied with Seidelman's running of the company, the Italian felt his protégé lacked that buccaneering spirit, sensing it had been chiseled away by U.S. corporate sculpting. The Seidelman forte of business-insight, legal knowledge and loyalty was countered by a total lack of imagination and sensitivity.

The limo hit a severe rut, causing her to be jolted out of her seat. Leaning forward, Tonnini offered a helping hand. "*Stia attento.*"

Nessa Preiss was no less susceptible to that Lazio charm, but by way of thanks was able to give Tonnini that incredible yet calculatedly-modulated sensual smile. Yes, that smile, that facial expression guaranteed to break-down effortlessly the guard of any man.

"It the first thing I ever notice about you."

"What was?"

"Your smile."

"*My* smile?"

"*Si.*" He fidgeted. "You no remember?"

Feigning non-recollection, Nessa shook her head. "No."

"Churubusco Studios, Mexico City. One of my movies. I come into the accounts office, an' you, you were buried in a ledger. No air-con. You look up an' you look terrible, terrible! Then you smile. It like the sun rising, the Mona Lisa, but sweating, in tee shirt and jeans."

8

Seidelman looked-up briefly, at the Ferragamo shoes, the charcoal grey silk stockings, the cream silk blouse, the Chanel suit tailored so perfectly to show but the slightest of knee, yet teasingly so. "She is Venus when she smiles . . ." He continued his work.

"You right, Don. Nessa *is* Venus when she smile."

Seidelman nodded. "But she's Juno when she walks and Minerva when she talks." Resuming his work, he failed to see Nessa poke-out her tongue, mouthing "Slydelman."

The limo arrived at the location site. The chauffeur opened a door and Nessa alighted. Seidelman snapped-shut the files on which he'd been working.

Tonnini eyed him. "So?"

Seidleman gestured to the files. "*Redmayne West*?"

"*Si, Redmayne West.*"

"When?"

Shrugging, Tonnini looked into space. "Whenever."

Experience told Seidelman this wasn't the moment to pursue the matter, knowing that in the fullness of time, returned to would be the question of *Redmayne West*. He followed Tonnini out of the limo.

Abruptly, Tonnini halted. "What we doing here?"

Seidelman's eyes went up into their lids. "Franco, as producer of this movie, you're here to welcome on his first day of shooting Mr. Bjorn Neilsen, our new Troy Donohue."

As Tonnini surveyed the location, the five-feet seven tall Nessa stood back slightly, knowing how sensitive was the Italian about his height. She nudged Seidelman to do the same. Frowning, he shuffled to one side, as Tonnini stood, shaking his head in bewilderment. He contemplated the location activity. "Always, always it like a circus, a circus! All these trucks, lighting equipment, camera equipment, an' food . . . an' more food! These people, they eat like locusts!" Tonnini shook his head, exasperated.

"Even so Franco, there is an excitement about it all, eh? It gets you . . ." Seidelman shook his head in wonderment, a clenched fist thumping the left side of his chest. "Right . . . here!"

"No, Don. It get me here, right here!" Tonnini stabbed the visible outline of his wallet. "*Here*! Every time!" He sighed deeply, exhaling loudly. "Why? Why I still amazed by movies? One a hundred sixty people doing the work of . . . of twelve an' make it look like it need one a hundred an' sixty!" Tonnini shook his head. "I guess it the magic of cinema, no?"

Nessa inclined her head towards Tonnini. "Franco, d'you know how you can tell a dead Teamster?"

Turning, Tonnini eyed her expressionlessly. "How?"

"When the doughnut rolls out of his hand."

Turning his head to one side, Tonnini raised an eyebrow.

It was Seidelman's turn. "Franco, don't you know why the Teamsters have a horse as their logo?"

"Tell me."

"Because it's the only animal that sleeps while standing up."

Tonnini raised his eyebrows. Glancing at Nessa, he studied Seidelman. "What you know about South America?"

Seidelman grinned, weakly. "Eh, this a latin Teamster joke?"

"No. It a serious *Redmayne West* question"

"*Redmayne West*? But it's set in Canada?"

Nodding, Tonnini studied his fingernails. "But no set in cement?"

Seideleman stared at his boss. "What's in that Lazio mind of yours?" He gave a poor imitation of Don Corleone. "Somebody make you an offer you couldn't refuse?"

Tonnini gestured to Seidelman, who joined the Italian in a leisurely stroll. "Don, you an' me, we both know the movie industry is a really the deal industry, no?" As he turned to Seidelman, Nessa moved closer, much closer, as she regarded these dissertations as an invaluable learning process in her quest, that quest to be a producer.

As they walked, Tonnini gestured to the battlefield set. "From a deal comes a piece of celluloid thirty-five millimeters wide, maybe three-thousand meters long, born out of a play-or-pay deal, tax shelter, lease back, negative pick up, agency packaging, first look, overheads and development or, maybe just a favor owed, who knows, but—"

"Franco," said Nessa quietly, but firmly. "I know some of this stuff but if I'm to function as a . . ."

"*Cara bella Nessa*, they all mean the same thing." He gestured to

Seidelman. "Tell her."

"Money. They all mean money. Production money. To finance a movie."

Nodding, Tonnini smiled at Nessa. "How you guys say it, there more than one way to skin a cat?"

"Franco," Seidelman was impatient. "What's in it for us, for T.I.P.?"

Hands behind his back, and flanked by Nessa and Seidelman, Tonnini continued his in-thought amble. "In most South American countries there many multinational conglomerates accruing vast profits, profits they prevented by law from remitting to their parent company overseas."

Seidelman frowned. "What's that to do with *Redmayne West*?"

Emphasis was made with a Tonnini pointed finger. "These foreign companies sit on mountains of what to them is dead money. Australs, pesos, reals, bolivas, cruzeiros, cruzados, escudos." Coming to a stop, Tonnini regarded Seidelman. "If these companies take out their profit, they pay anything up to thirty-five percent remittance tax." He shook his head. "Thirty-five percent." Turning to both Nessa and Seidelman he continued. "But, there is a way to get their profit out." He raised a warning hand. "Sure, it cost, but not thirty-five percent."

Nodding, Seidelman digested what had been said. "So where does *Redmayne* fit in?"

Tonnini pondered. "Simple. We pay a U.S. corporation discounted cash dollar in New York an' in return that company make available to us funds in the relevant currency via its South American subsidiary, funds to make a movie. Funds we get cheaper, no black market, no insider trading, all above board an' they get hard currency for their South American profits. All . . . legal."

Not convinced, Seidelman looked about him, stroking his chin. "Sooooo, we buy *all* of our currency up front?"

'*Si!*' Tonnini nodded eagerly. "To maximize the discount." His hands opened out. "If we spread the purchase . . ." The arms were widened to their fullest extent. "It reduce the discount. *Si?*"

Deep in thought, with his right foot Seidelman tapped pebbles to and fro. "Franco, every South American country suffers from raging inflation and you know the time frame of a movie. With prep and principal, our money would melt quicker than an Arctic ice flow. From inflation?"

"No, Don, not if you do an accurate cash flow. Then, we draw down only *what* we need, *when* we need it?"

Seidelman nodded understanding. "Okay, but what about the rest of the money?"

"That? We put it on the overnights markets, in Sao Paolo, Rio. The interest made on those overnights more than cope with inflation, no?"

Scratching his head, Seidelman was still less-than-convinced. "Okay, but what about the tax liability on the interest?"

Sighing, Tonnini looked obliquely at Seidelman. "Don, you thinking of making *more* than one movie in South America?" He paced a circle and returned to confront his Executive V.P. Business Affairs. "Look, get a rewrite done. Move Canada to . . . to anywhere in South America, who care?" Tonnini punched a palm with a clenched a fist. "An' I find a U.S. corporation that want to get out profits, okay?"

Absorbing all that Tonnini had said, Seidelman was ready for the challenge. "We'll need some up-front money. For a rewrite, budget, line producer?"

"Don, no, no. No American!" He smiled. "We all know that more than twenty miles from Hollywood an' Vine, they get lost. They think Athens is in Georgia, Paris is in Texas an' London in Canada. You no hear about the American location manager sent to scout Venice? He take one look and fire off a fax to the studio back in Hollywood. *'Streets full of water, stop. Please advise. Stop.'*" Both Nessa and Seidelman chuckled.

"Don, Americans no travel well. They worry about whether the water safe to drink an' if they be put up in a Marriott. Get a European."

"Franco, I'm two steps ahead of you. I got him already." He gestured a thumb at Nessa. "The guy she suggested."

Tonnini frowned. "The Brit? Eh, what his name?"

"Cooper," replied Nessa. "James Cooper." Annoyed, she addressed Seidelman. "Bit premature, weren't you?" And turned to Tonnini. "The movie's not green lit yet?"

"Nessa right. Why the rush, an' the cost?"

"He was the first choice. He was free, but, I only gave him a five-week guarantee. If you give the get-go, he comes on full time, but until then he's on a short string."

"Okay. But next time, Don, don't jump the gun. *I* say when we take people on, *comprendere*?"

Tonnini and Nessa wandered closer to the filming area, to catch the end of a take involving his 'new' Troy Donohue. The director yelled, "Cut! That's a print."

"Check the gate!", ordered the first assistant director.

Shaking his head, Tonnini turned to Nessa. "A star . . . is not Bjorn."

SCENE 2. TAKE 1.

"So we sailed, off into the sun, until we found, a sea of green . . ."

The song was running through Cooper's mind as he looked-out of the cockpit of the single-engined Cessna and down to the awe-inspiring spread of the Amazonian rain forest, a sea of green mass over which one could fly for up to five hours and see nothing but the canopy of green, it fighting upwards to seek the life-giving rays of the sun, the ocean of green being relieved here-and-there by the occasional river, a slash-and-burn site, or, the intermittent landing strip.

To Cooper, humbling was the immensity of the rain forest. He studied the map spread on his knees and without looking up, Cooper nudged the pilot. "Pepe, where are we now?" The pilot did not respond. Folding his arms and sitting-back, Cooper looked at the pilot. "*Onde?*"

Begrudgingly, Pepe leaned to his right, an index finger hovering. Then it speared the map. "*Aqui,*" returning immediately his attention to flying.

Cooper studied him. "Who, who in this wide wide world and in this country of Imperio, who can tell me why *I* have the misfortune to have a pilot who is A, Argentinian, B, speaks only dago dialects and C, lost a brother in the Falklands war, for which he holds responsible every Brit, including mostly me? And when spoken to in English replies always with that one monotonous word '*Malvinas*', which is what I know you Argies call the Falklands and, like Gibraltar, have been ours, British, since before mother was a boy." Cooper nodded to himself. "Still, was my Portuguese '*onde*' the catalyst for an '*aqui*,' instead of the ubiquitous response of '*Malvinas*'? Pepe, are you listening? Am I a Claude Rains to your Bogart? Is this the beginning of a beautiful friendship?"

"*Malvinas*."

"And bollocks to you too." Cooper sighed. '*Ah, plus ça change*.' Returning to the map, Cooper noted their position and checked his watch. "Okay, that's it, Pepe. Scarper, vamoose. Pepe. *Casa!*"

The lugubrious Pepe Babenco set the new course. "*Malvinas*."

Within two hours could be seen the high-rise buildings of Santa Mosquiero, the capital city of the Imperio State of Boa Vista, beside the vast River Amazon, all sitting now under the anemic sky of the daily tropical downpour. Watched by Cooper, Pepe studied the instruments nervously, particularly the fuel gauges, of which the needles were flickering frenziedly. To allow him to look towards the ground, Pepe banked the aircraft slightly.

"Eh, problems, *problemas*? And don't bloody well give me that Malvinas crap!"

"*Chuva*."

"Yes, Pepe. Rain."

"*Chuva violenta!*"

"Yes, yes, heavy rain."

Suddenly, Pepe released the controls and then forced one hand over the other, to convey the effect the tropical downpour would have on the small Cessna. "*Muito pesada!*"

Cooper studied the Argentinian. "Pepe, this is no time for charades."

It had become dark, extremely dark. As Pepe banked the aircraft, it was caught by the full-force of the storm's up-current, causing the plane to lose height abruptly and despite their harnesses, throwing-around the two men as if they were toys.

Cooper closed his eyes, thinking, *Is this it? After twenty-nine groveling fucking years, just this?* While in the tossing plane and hanging-on to all and anything he could grip, he visualized the minimal obituary in *Daily Variety, The Hollywood Reporter . . . The Barnes & Mortlake Monitor? James Cooper, aged 43, killed in an Amazonian plane crash while scouting locations for a Tonnini International pic. Survived by his accountant and a Corgi dog named Taff. Asked for a comment, T.I.P. Business Affairs V.P. Don Seidelman answered. "Jason was a great guy. He will be sorely missed. We already have someone in Imperio to carry on Jacob's legacy. The Tonnini offices will be closed for three days of mourning in Jake's remembrance."*

Cooper was startled out of his reverie as the plane was tossed around constantly, surrounded by vicious lightning strikes. Pepe was blessing himself continually as if confronted by the Madonna at Fatima but in fact terrified by his reading of the dials. Cooper joined him at the dashboard. Pepe pointed to the dials. "*Gasolino?*" They looked at each other, in sync muttering, "*Nada.*"

A break in the clouds. Pepe pushed-forward on the stick and as the aircraft nose-dived, it vibrated violently for what seemed an eternity.

Cooper closed his eyes, asking his Corgi dog Taff isn't this how Nigel Patrick bought it in *Breaking the Sound Barrier*? His eyes were closed tighter than a new-born babe's. He was scared, scared more than he could recall, more terrified even than when filming in Austria and he was trapped atop an immobile cable-car, dangling hundreds of feet above a mountain chasm, and like then, he had no control over his screaming voice. "Pepe, Pepe, why did you have to take flying lessons from a bloody kamiikaze pilot!"

"*Malvinas.*"

Finally, Pepe got below the turbulence and leveled-off, flying above the wide river, which was speckled with many jungle-covered islands, none of which offered any sort of a landing spot, and all the time the engines were coughing and spluttering. Frantically, both Pepe and Cooper searched for somewhere to land, somewhere, anywhere! Which is when a sudden up-draught carried the plane back over the verdant ocean. And then, the engines. The engines? They just died . . .

Eerie. Eerie was the whistling wind noise created by the stricken, uncontrolled and completely silent Cessna. By sheer flying skill Pepe managed to keep the plane in the air but a fact of aeronautics is that for every three-feet flying horizontally, they were descending by one. Vertically. And fast.

Suddenly, Pepe pointed. "*Está ahí, ahí!*"

Cooper followed his gaze. In the distance, like a mirage, and cut out of the jungle like an arrow, Pepe was pointing to a landing-strip. Of a paved runway.

SCENE 3. TAKE 4.

In the darkened main room of the hacienda that served as the operations hub, Roberto Cirla sat dressed in his usual fatigues, his homage to Fidel Castro, watching on the radar screen the blip which in fact identified the aircraft carrying Cooper and Pepe. Beside him and watching the screen also, stood Antonio Rubio, dressed in tailored casual clothes more befitting Rodeo Drive than the isolated Colombian rain forest.

Cirla pointed to the screen, speaking in his native Spanish. "Either the pilot's drunk, blind or both? In any event, I think he and his plane are a threat." He glanced at Rubio.

Rubio studied the blip. "Drunk, or simply off course? Either could explain why he's crossed the border?" Rubio stood, pointing at the radar screen. "And the storm? The pilot may have not realized he's even *over* the border?"

"*Federales*?" asked Cirla.

Rubio shook his head. "At this time of day?" He picked up a walkie-talkie. "Topete? Radar shows an unidentified aircraft. Could be heading this way but we've nothing scheduled. If it lands you know what to do, a few men but *no* killing, you understand? *No. Killing.* I need to know who they are, and where they're from but don't give them any chance, not one, to actually see this place. Understood?"

The runway was paved perfectly. While there was a pole, no wind-sock was flying nor was there any other landing aid. Pepe hadn't a clue as to wind direction. Looking at the runway, he blessed himself and then kissed the crucifix hanging on the chain around his neck, an action not un-noticed by Cooper.

"You ever hear about the dyslectic atheist who didn't believe in Dog?"

"*Malvinas.*"

With some one-hundred yards to spare, Pepe made a text-book touchdown, managing to stop the powerless Cessna before running out of paved strip. He slumped over the controls. Cooper put an arm around him. "*Gracias amigo, mucho gracias.*"

Cooper climbed out of the aircraft, followed by Pepe, who produced a bottle of pinga, the local moonshine. He took a gulp and offered it to Cooper, who raised it, saying "*Malvinas.*" Which is the last thing they remembered as each man's world went black.

All of their personal belongings had been removed from the plane and were spread-out now on a table. All that Pepe possessed was a plastic folder containing maps, which was dealt with quickly by Rubio. He picked-up Cooper's camcorder, replaying the tapes and viewing them through the eyepiece. "Whatever they were looking for, it's nowhere around here."

Cirla looked at the map marked-up by Cooper. "Neither is this." He held it aloft. "None of the places circled here are on this side of the border. They're all in Imperio.

Rubio delved further into Cooper's *location* bag, removing and glancing at the Nikon camera, and handling the cassettes of 35mm exposed Kodacolor film. He studied the cassettes.

Cirla moved to take them. "I'll destroy these, okay?"

Rubio shook his head. "Roberto, it's cost too much to set up this place and its profit potential is so fantastic in no way can we afford to endanger it. We must be *extra* careful in the way we protect it and the one thing we must not do is attract attention, *any* attention." Looking at the cassettes, Rubio bounced them in his hand. "Now, *what* do we know?"

He studied Cirla. "We know they were out of fuel, therefore probably off course, probably lost and probably shit scared. So, all they wanted was a place to land and providence showed them our runway." Rubio pointed to the collective belongings of both Cooper and Pepe. "Nothing here indicates they were *Federales*, Cartel competitors, U.S. snoopers, you know, A.T.F., F.B.I., C.I.A. but just lost?"

"Lost?" Cirla lit a cigarette, inhaling deeply. "Lost? Then why were they up here, this far? They must have been looking for *something*? Just look at all the cameras, and film? Tourists? I say we risk nothing. We get rid of them, and destroy their plane." He nodded to the cassettes. "And, burn that stuff, all of it."

Ever the pragmatist, Rubio thought for a moment. "Roberto, somewhere these guys will have filed a flight plan. Someone knows about them, where they were heading. So, whatever we do, it must be planned and not be a knee-jerk reaction. For all we know, there may be a search on for them right now?" Picking-up the cassettes, he handed them to Cirla. "Have these processed. We need to see what's on them, and, if there's any shots of this place . . ." He looked at Cirla, meaningfully. "Imperio's a small country. If they pose a threat, we can find them in no time, and dealt with even quicker. No fuss," Rubio eyed Cirla. "And, no trace?"

Cirla smiled. "No. No trace."

Rubio studied a large-scale wall map. "In the meantime, have their plane refueled and have one of Topete's men fly it to . . ." He pointed out a particular spot. "Here. Valdivia. Just this side of the Imperio border. Leave them there to wake up. If nothing else, it'll give them a surprise."

The Cessna stood under some trees. In the coolness of the shade, Cooper finally came-to, opening his eyes slowly, to see nothing but branches and the cloud-speckled sky. He sat-up. Sitting on the ground with his back against a landing wheel was Pepe, quietly smoking a cigarette. He smiled. "*Bom dia.*"

"*Bueno dias*, Pepe." Cooper combed fingers through his hair, frowning as he did so, focusing and re-focusing . "Jesus, that pinga . . ."

Shaking his head, Pepe murmured, quietly. "*No pinga.*

"Okay." Blinking and squinting in sync, Cooper focused once more. "Then where's the bloody runway?" Easing himself into a standing position, he looked pointedly at Pepe, as if the pilot had on his person a mile-or-so of tarmac runway. Shaking his befuddled head, Cooper asked himself aloud "Did we, or did we not, land on a paved runway?"

Pepe gave an uncomprehending look. He gestured Cooper to the cockpit.

The pilot activated the ignition, pointing excitedly to the two fuel gauges, the needles of which indicated 'full'. Studying them closer, Cooper turned to Pepe.

"*Pinga?*"

Pepe laughed. "*No, no pinga. Gasolino!*"

"And we got the Green Shield stamps?"

Which is when they heard an approaching vehicle, the unmistakable sound of a 1200c.c. air-cooled engine. A Volkswagen Beetle. A taxi.

The two men looked-on in amazement. "I thought we agreed we'd take the subway into town?"

The cab stopped, the driver adjusting the meter flag to '*libre.*' With a luxuriant head of silver hair and a matching mustache, a tall, tanned man in his late seventiess eased himself out of the little car.

Cooper glanced at the license plate, '*OO8*'. "Did 'M' send you?"

"*Bueno dias.*"

Cooper frowned. "What happened to Portuguese?"

Pointing to the ground, Pepe addressed the driver. "*Imperio, si?*"

The driver laughed, shaking his head. "*No, no. Esta Colombia!*"

Pepe frowned. "*Eh, donde esta Imperio?*"

The driver indicated south-eastwards. Cooper pointed to the dirt landing strip. "Ask him *donde esta* the bloody paved runway we bloody well landed on?" Cooper held-open his location bag. "And while you're at it, ask him *donde esta* my bloody Kodachrome every-frame-a-Rembrandt films?" He showed the bag for Pepe's inspection.

Pepe looked at Cooper, bemused, while the driver tugged at an elbow of the pilot. "*Había dos aviones.*" He pointed at the Cessna."*Este, y el otro.*"

Cooper frowned. "*Dos aviones*? Has he been at the pinga?"

"No, *Señor*. Two. Definitely two."

Cooper looked aghast. "*Su habla Inglês?*"

While Pepe appeared stunned by Cooper's Spanish, little did he know it was one of only two such Iberian phrases the Englishman could muster.

"Little." The driver proffered his hand. "Me, Joao Calixto, parachuter, nineteen forty-four, with a Brasilian brigade, with Americanos, Canadianos and British. I was one of the lucky ones. At Arnhem."

"Then you must know Dickie Attenborough?"

Calixto shrugged, as he shook hands with Pepe.

Cooper looked about him. "Listen, guys, we've got to get out of here and back to Santa Mosquiero. I know no one knows what the hell I'm talking about but what I *am* saying is, time and tide wait for no man, *comprenez?*" He glanced at each man, who were equally baffled. Which is when Cooper checked his watch. He held it up to his ear. It ticked efficiently. "I don't bloody *Adam and Eve* it!" He held out the watch to Pepe. "Look!" Cooper indicated the date. "It's Thursday! We've been away for two days, *dos*, two bloody days!" Cooper pushed Pepe to the plane as the pilot checked his own watch, with stunned realization.

Standing by the door of the already-revving aircraft, Cooper shouted to Calixto. "If my films turn up at the local One Hour, order jumbo, glossy, borderless."

Calixto waved, shaking his head and muttering, "*Americanos . . .*"

This time, the sky was clear over Santa Mosqueiro.

Pepe made an uneventful landing, uneventful that is until roared up the red lights-flashing yellow-painted Volkswagen, with atop the large sign in English, 'Follow Me.' The car took up a position in front of the taxiing plane.

Cooper looked questionably at Pepe, who shrugged. The VW passed the taxiway to Pepe's hanger, at which Pepe frowned, as the Cessna was led off the runway to the Terminal Building. To see awaiting their arrival two police cars and six police officers.

"See what happens when you overspend in the duty free?"

Noting the reception committee, Pepe eyed Cooper, putting an index finger over his closed lips. "Shhh . . ."

Before the aircraft had been chocked and the propeller stilled, the door was yanked open by a gun-toting policeman. As Cooper clambered out, another policeman snatched away his location bag while yet another held-open the door of a car, signaling Cooper to get in; Pepe was put into the other car. Both men were seated in the rear, with a policeman either side of each of them. The two vehicles sped-off, lights flashing, sirens blaring.

Similar misfortune had befallen Cooper on previous occasions, being an occupational hazard of Third World locations movie-making, although at one time he had even been arrested in London by the Metropolitan Police when, at the height of the morning rush hour and without any permissions whatsoever, cavalier director Michael Winner ordered towed into Piccadilly Circus a vintage car which was loaded with special effects charges, with stunt doubles representing the principal actors. The towing-vehicle released the vintage car which then was exploded by remote detonation, with flames, smoke and flying stuntmen everywhere. Passers-by were terrified and within seconds the area was a cacophony of flashing lights and sirens, as it was filled with ambulances, fire engines and police cars. A senior police officer demanded to know who was in charge and instantly director Michael Winner pointed at the lowly third assistant director, shouting "Him, sir, him over there, James Cooper!"

But this arrest, Cooper knew, this was very different. On those previous occasions when arrested, he'd been on home turf and had the back-up of a studio to smooth-over things and have him released quickly. But here? Who knew him here? His only contact in the whole country was Pepe, hardly the stuff that is made of being sprung from police custody? Running through his mind the options, he knew he had to be cool, courteous and co-operative, none of that Cooper flippant self-defence stuff. He knew this was his only option, his only course; after all, anything could be done to him and nobody would ever be the wiser?

Cooper was shown into an interrogation room. Despite the barred window, it was bright and cheerful. In the centre stood a table, with three chairs, two one side, one facing. Cooper sat at the single chair, convinced his heartbeat could be seen thumping beneath his shirt.

He waited.

Some thirty-five minutes later, the door was opened briskly and in strode a tall police officer, his shirt and epaulettes awash with decorations and medals. His short hair was slicked back and his mustache was trimmed perfectly. He spoke to Cooper rapidly, in Portuguese. The Englishman raised a hand, but the officer took no notice and carried on his questioning.

Eventually, Cooper shouted. "*Me no fala Português!*"

Eyeing Cooper, the officer stopped mid-sentence. "*Español?*"

Cooper shook his head. "*Inglês.*"

"*Americano?*"

"No." Cooper sighed. "*Inglês.*"

The officer held-out his hand. "*Passeport.*"

Dutifully, Cooper put the document into the outstretched palm, whereupon the officer left the room immediately. Cooper spoke aloud. "Great move, Cooper, ace. Now they can wipe you off the face of the planet, no witnesses, no passport, no trace. Not even two lines in the *Reporter* or *Variety*. Brilliant, bloody brilliant!"

Another two hours passed. To Cooper, it seemed an eternity. Then, he was escorted into another room where on a table was laid-out neatly all of his possessions. He inspected his location bag.

"Everything there?"

Cooper spun around, to be confronted by a very tall, thin pale-complexioned man, in his late thirties, dressed in a baggy linen suit so creased that Cooper figured the man must have been sleeping on park benches. Under the suit was a blue cotton shirt and a regimental tie. Walking forward, he extended to Cooper a limp, sweaty hand-shake. "Pitt-Miller, British Consul General's office." He gave Cooper the once over. "Mr. Cooper, you do realize, do you not, that *you* are in trouble, very *serious* trouble?"

"Mr. Miller—"

"*Pitt*-Miller! *That,* is my correct name"

"Sorry, but d'you really think I haven't twigged it? I've been incarcerated here for God knows how long now, during which time my whole life has flashed before me a thousand times."

"And, you and your companion entered Imperio illegally." Pitt-Miller flicked a peppermint into his mouth.

"Illegally? Bullshit! We'd filed a flight plan."

"There's nothing on record."

Raising his eyes heavenwards, Cooper spoke slowly. "I . . . I have a visa to be in Imperio, and my pilot, Pepe Babenco, he's a national."

"Of Argentina. And, furthermore, the two of you entered from Colombia, not in an authorized air traffic corridor and without a filed flight plan!" Pitt-Miller held-up in one hand the camcorder, and in the other the videotapes. "As with most countries, in Imperio it is illegal to photograph its territory from the air." Pitt-Miller replaced the video equipment on the table. "As I said Mr. Cooper, you are in a very serious position."

"What about outbound? A flight plan has to be on record?"

"Indeed it is. Which shows that all travel would be within Imperio, with return the same day." Another mint was popped into the Pitt-Miller *north-and-south.* "Which, as we both know, was two days ago. Correct?"

Cooper nodded.

"Mr. Cooper, it really is in your best interests to tell me, tell me what you were doing on those two missing days in Colombia? Also, what are you actually doing here in Imperio and why, why haven't you registered your stay with the British Embassy in the capital? Oh, and let me remind you also about Imperio's laws concerning drugs trafficking."

Cooper's head snapped-up. "Drugs trafficking?"

"Drugs trafficking in this country is a most serious crime." Pitt-Miller stared at Cooper. "Conviction can result in the death penalty."

Cooper returned the stare, thinking perhaps a more appropriate name would be 'Twit-Miller,' but steady Cooper, this is the only lifeline you're going to be thrown, and drugs? Shit. *Not* funny.

He omitted nothing. The storm, the loss of fuel, being blown off course and finding the perfect runway except when he saw it next, it was a dirt strip cut-out of the jungle. Cooper told the purpose of his presence in Imperio for Tonnini International, and the proposed shooting of the movie *Redmayne West*.

Pitt-Miller fiddled with his breast pocket dress handkerchief. "Bit far-fetched, what?"

By way of resignation, Cooper raised his hands. "As far-fetched as it may sound to you, nevertheless, it does happen to be the truth."

"Can it be substantiated, verified?"

"Sure, just ask Pepe."

"I already have," replied a different, accented voice. Cooper turned, to see standing in the doorway the same tall police officer.

"You didn't say you could speak English?"

"You didn't ask." As he walked into the room, Pitt-Miller almost assumed a military bearing, standing erect. "Colonel Mendoza. *Bom dia*."

Hardly acknowledging Pitt-Miller, Mendoza concerned himself with Cooper. "Far-fetched, but possible, even plausible, seemingly."

Cooper relaxed, visibly.

"Your companion hardly speaks two words of English, so it's unlikely the two of you could have concocted such a fanciful story." He pointed to Cooper's bag. "You'll find everything's there, but . . ." Reaching into the bag, he held aloft a small clear plastic sachet containing a white powder. "We will keep this."

So surprised was Pitt-Miller that he nearly choked on a peppermint.

The sachet. Mendoza swung it to-and-fro in front of Cooper's face. "I will overlook this for now, but I warn you, I will not forget it, nor, *you*."

Swallowing hard, Cooper whispered a 'thank you,' then managed to regain his voice. "What about Pepe, officer?"

"*Colonel* . . . Mendoza." He twirled the sachet, gazing at it. "Mr. Cooper, you're in a very precarious position." He looked at the Englishman. "If I were you, I'd concern myself *only* with myself. Anyway, since when did any Brit care about an Argie? Isn't that what you call them?" Nodding perfunctorily at Pitt-Miller, Mendoza crossed to the door, and paused, looking at Cooper. "You may go. But we keep the passport." He exited.

Peppermints were shoveled into Pitt-Miller's mouth. "My God man, talk about being caught red-handed?"

Cooper straightened. "How well d'you know Colonel Mendoza?"

"We're both members of the local polo club. We play together."

Cooper pondered how a polo-playing diplomat could look so ashen, so un-tanned? Figured he must have the largest pith helmet in Imperio. "Socialize?"

"As a matter-of-fact, yes, we do, but what's that to do with you?"

"Mr. Pitt-Miller, police forces are known to fabricate evidence right, *fabricate*?"

Pitt-Miller looked puzzled. "You're not suggesting that—"

"Mendoza put the sachet in my bag? Of course not, not him personally. But it was put there on his orders."

"I find that hard to believe. Colonel Mendoza's a gentleman."

"Which in your book puts him above such things?" Cooper shook his head at the naïvety of Pitt-Miller. "In the twenty-nine years I've spent in an industry of coke heads, I've never sniffed, snorted nor injected. Never smoked, the only drug to which I've ever succumbed is alcohol, and right now I need a drink, a long cool drink, and some fresh air."

Pitt-Miller fidgeted. "The air pollution level in Santa Mosqueiro is worse than Mexico City."

Cooper picked-up his belongings. "I'll take my chances."

"Not too many chances, Cooper. You're on borrowed time."

Coffee cup in hand, Colonel Mendoza stood away from the window, as he watched Cooper depart State Police H.Q.

"What do you think, Colonel?" Asked his aide, Captain Possi.

"Rubio and Circla did a good job." He continued to watch Cooper. "A fine job. They didn't panic, do anything stupid, they used their heads and our magnificent men in their flying machine, Cooper and Babenco, neither know where they were nor what happened to them." Mendoza shrugged. "All's well that ends well. But, we'll keep an eye on them, especially the gringo." He drank the coffee. "Jesus, Possi! How many damned times do I have to remind you? Four sugars!" From Mendoza's desk Possi picked-up the plastic sachet, the sachet of white powdered *sugar*, emptying the contents into Mendoza's cup. "Better?"

Mendoza drank. "Much. '*Brigade*.'"

Out on the street, Cooper looked around him. He detested disorder, thus he disliked intensely Santa Mosqueiro, with its teeming streets full of people, of which many were limbless, scooting by on hand-propelled skateboards, streets full of horn-honking traffic, streets full of fumes, noise and with fetid, untreated sewage running down the gutters below what passed for sidewalks, a full symphony of disorder. His disdain for this he attributed to his northern-European heritage, that Anglo sense of order. But he acknowledged those who saw such disarray as an expression of freedom, a *joie de vivre*, an eschewing of those supposedly creatively-inhibiting traits such as cleanliness, orderliness and tidiness. Life is for living, for carnival, samba, expression, work to live, not live to work! Not for repairing pot-holes and ruptured sewer lines, providing potable water for all-and-sundry, hell no! But to Cooper, it translated simply as laziness, period. He was all for creativity much as anybody, but felt such expression was more pure, unadulterated if born out of an aura free of distractions, in other words, neat, tidy, disciplined. Hadn't one of mother's many pronouncements been *Cleanliness is next to Godliness*? Cooper thought to himself, how do people live like this?

He pivoted slowly, sighing as was recognized the once-orderliness of the colonizing power now flooded in a tide of indifference. Sighing, it dawned on him he should refuse work in Third World countries of which the initial letter was 'I'–India, Imperio, Indonesia, but he reminded himself that in his opinion, the most civilized country in the world had the initial 'I'. Italy.

Thirst was overcoming him. He espied a sign. 'Bar Piccadilly.' He thought it a good omen.

Sitting at the counter, the first gentle swallow reminded him of the finale of *Ice Cold in Alex*. But on looking around, the bar was empty. No Johnnie Mills, Sylvia Syms, Harry Andrews nor Anthony Quayle. He shivered, feeling as if enveloped in a gossamer cloak of ice. In that moment, Cooper felt as lonely as he did on that day in February 1955 when he walked into the lobby of London's St. Mary's Hospital, to be confronted by a sad looking Seth and a stern-faced father.

"As usual, you're too late. Your mother died forty minutes ago." Cooper looked at his brother, who nodded resignedly.

Scene 6. Take 4.

The projector beam dimmed, the house lights illuminated.

Tonnini gestured to the screen. "What you think?"

Seidelman pondered. "Well, I guess it'll get good critical reviews, y'know, Siskel and Ebert, Shickel, it's their kind of movie, but a wider audience? I dunno." He looked at Tonnini. "Word of mouth?"

The Italian grunted. "Then we need a lot of mouths . . ."

As a short man loathe to look-up at people, Tonnini's desk rested on a dais, allowing him to look down on others. In front of him was laid out lunch; sandwiches, fruit, Italian cheese, Italian mineral water and, strong espresso coffee. For Seidelman, the same menu; although his coffee was decaffeinated.

Without warning, Tonnini spluttered, spitting out a mouthful of food, holding-up the offending sandwich. "What this, eh?"

Seidelman glanced at his boss. "When I ate processed red meat, it was called pastrami."

Tonnini continued to pull-apart the distasteful sandwich. "Why, why in a country full of Italians, why it so difficult to get a decent pastrami sandwich? Why?"

"Franco, you know if you want something done properly, you do it yourself?"

Tonnini studied the sandwich. "Maybe you right."

Seidelman returned the gaze. "We going into the food business now?"

"Why not?"

Seidelman scoffed. "We're a movie company."

"So was Coca-Cola."

Seidelman munched. "We've enough on our plate."

"But maybe room for more, *si*?" Pushing away his food, Tonnini peeled an apple. "What word from, where it . . . eh, Imperio?"

Seidelman looked-up, slowly. "Now you mention it, *niente*."

The paring knife was waved directly at Seidelman. "Don! If we wan' make this blocked currency deal work for us, *Redmayne West* must be delivered before the end of the corporate, fiscal year. *Capis*?"

Seidelman shifted, uncomfortably. "Sure, I understand. But we haven't even got a director yet?"

Tonnini chomped on the apple. "Directors? Huh!" He discarded the apple core and leaned on the desk. "Don, say you casting the male lead in *Itatchia*? Who you choose?"

"Franco . . ." Seidelman disliked intensely these sort of questions, feeling much more at home negotiating contracts. "I *don't* know," he replied testily.

"Don, come now, try. For me?"

Seidelman frowned. "Jeez . . ." He sighed. "Ummm . . . Robert Eden?"

"An' you think you no creative?" Tonnini beamed. "The only man for the part."

"Franco, our budget and Robert Eden's going-rate are poles apart."

Tonnini swung his chair through ninety degrees and leaned back, his hands clasped behind his neck. After a pause, he addressed the ceiling, speaking quietly, slowly and unequivocally. "Leef. Anthony . . . Leef."

Seidelman sat bolt upright. "Leef? Director? The guy's unemployable! He can't direct traffic up a one-way street!"

Tonnini continued his ceiling-gazing. "Who it now, Leef's agent?"

Seidelman looked at his boss, chuckling and shaking his head in amazement. "You wouldn't?"

Tonnini spun around, leaning forward and placing his elbows on the desk. "Why not? *Redmayne West*, a movie being made to float a currency deal not win an Oscar, it get a director, the director get work an' his agent get commission." Tonnini held open his hands.

Seidelman stroked his chin, thinking out loud. "And, in return, that agent is able to make available to us another of his clients, namely one Robert Eden, maybe at our budget figure?"

Tonnini rubbed his hands. "Everybody happy, no? Now, find out what the Englishman up to."

Scene 7 . Take 2 .

Seidelman couldn't understand it. Be it Tokyo, Timbuktu or Tipperary, wherever Cooper was, always he had been meticulous in maintaining contact, even when in the depths of the rain forest, so that both baffling and out-of-character was the recent silence. His secretary entered, placing on his desk some papers. Seidelman nodded and spoke, without raising his head. "Dorothy, when did you last call Cooper's hotel?"

"Actually, about five minutes ago." He glanced at her. "Mr. Don, I've called that hotel every hour since lunch and always I get the same answer. They say his key isn't there and neither does his room answer."

Seidelman placed his hands into a cat's cradle against his lips, staring into space. "Not Cooper's m.o." He looked-up at Dorothy. "Call again and demand somebody to go up to his room and thump on his door. Otherwise, tell them we don't pay his bill."

Nodding, Dorothy left.

Seidelman picked-up the 'trades,' reading out loud as he scanned the headlines. *"Japs say no Hollywood pull out . . . New Bochco show biffo ratings . . . Cimino denies 'movie out of control' . . . C.A.A. grabs new client list . . . Carolco pens five movies deal."* He shook his head. "So what's new?"

Cooper awoke to a cacophony of noise. The bedside phone was ringing constantly while there was a continual knocking on the door. He switched-on the bedside lamp, surprised that he was still in his street clothes. The phone continued its ringing while the knocking got louder. "Okay, okay, I'm coming!" He opened the door, to be confronted by a porter.

"*Sênhor*, your telephone? It ring."

"*Si*." Cooper gave the man a tip and raced to the phone, catching sight of his travel clock. "Twenty-three-hundred?" He picked up the instrument.

"Cooper! What's with you?"

Cooper decided against telling Seidelman about the plane incident and the subsequent arrest, figuring he didn't want to incite Seidelman paranoia. "I guess it was something I ate. I took to my bed."

Seidelman was impatient. "So? Can it be done down there, in Imperio? I mean, the locations, logistics, all that crapola?"

"Yes."

"Cost?"

"I haven't finished the budget yet."

"Ball park figure?"

"Don, I've played in your ball park before and I know whatever figure I come up with will be noted and used as future evidence against me."

"James, you're a cynic."

"No, just too used to you. Y'know, experience, intuition . . . humiliation?"

Seidelman spoke into the phone quietly. "Well, *entre nous*. With no come backs."

"My below-the-line guesstimate?" asked Cooper. "And Don, that's guesstimate with a capital 'G,' get it?"

"Just the below-the-line, buddy. I'll look after the above."

"Okay." Cooper inhaled. "Ball park? Twenty-one million, U.S."

"Too much."

"Oh? You've been down here and done your own scout, yes?"

"Cooper, don't get cute with me."

Cooper's voice had an edge. "I'm not getting cute with anybody but if the script remains at one hundred and twenty-seven pages, I'm just telling you Don, that's what it'll cost to put the printed word up on the silver screen."

"James, you guys? You pad a little here, a little there, your cushion, your just-in-case scenario." Seidelman became conciliatory. "I'm the one who knows what's available in the pot, so this isn't your Chasen's budget, okay, it's your K-Mart one, understand?"

"I only have ears for you."

"Then listen up. Below-the-line, including indirect costs, you know legal, contingency, audit, the whole kit and caboodle, cannot exceed fourteen, tops."

Cooper was distracted. By an attempt to push under the door an envelope. He wondered why the porter didn't simply knock, especially when the envelope became wedged.

"James! You with me?"

"Eh, yes. Sorry, you were saying?"

"You on *anything*?" asked a suspicious Seidelman.

"Only my bed."

Seidelman spoke pedantically. "What I said was. Fourteen. Tops."

Cooper knew there wasn't any point nor nothing to be gained by arguing. "You got it. Fourteen. Tops. Is there a T.I.P. overhead?"

"No. So we understand each other?"

"Only too well." Cooper stared at the wedged envelope. "Don, as we've finalized the budget in what, eh, ten seconds flat, what d'you want me to do now?"

Seidelman gave the question some thought. "Get yourself an office, but cheap rent mind, with a phone *and*, a fax."

"Don, I have all of that here in the hotel."

"Not sufficiently secure. Rooms and phones in hotels can be bugged."

"Eh, a secretary?"

The line went dead.

A further attempt was being made to deliver the envelope under the door. Looking at the package, Cooper realized that unless he was Superman, staring at it intently would not open it. Needing an ingestion of the nectar of Bacchus, he shuffled over to the mini-bar, removing the two miniatures of Smirnoff Blue Label. He was unable to recall when he ate last. Was it the peanuts or those pappy pretzels in the Bar Piccadilly? He took a Milky Way bar, thinking that the excuse to Seidelman about stomach trouble perhaps would not be such a big *porky* after all?

At the door, Cooper bent to retrieve it. It wouldn't budge. That's when he realized the envelope was too bulky. Rising up to a crouching position, he opened the door. The packet lay on the floor but as Cooper stretched for it he was prevented from doing so as a foot, petite, shapely and suntanned in a black sling-back shoe, stamped on the envelope. Cooper stood, to encounter a very pretty dark-haired young lady. "And you are?"

She picked-up the envelope. "Your courier. Fed-UPS."

Cooper took the package, looking. No company markings, no name, no address. "How d'you know this is for me?"

"I know lots of things." She moved forward. "Maybe I teach you, yes?"

Cooper barred entry. "What, to suck eggs?"

"I give you good time."

"Thanks, but I've just had a good time. In the Bar Piccadilly."

"Eh . . . you gay?"

"I've been known to be happier. Where do I sign?"

Proffering a magic marker, she lowered her tee-shirt, to reveal the large contour of a tanned breast. "Here."

Cooper did as bid. "Thanks . . ." He returned the pen. "For the mammary."

Stripping-off, he placed the envelope on the desk and crashed into bed. He knew nothing more until around nine the following morning.

The envelope. Cooper regarded it suspiciously, as if it was a booby-trap. He shook it. It didn't rattle. Pressed it gingerly between his hands. Seemed okay. Even smelled it. He opened it, and holding it aloft was astonished to see falling out numerous ten-by-eight Kodacolor prints, *his* prints, and, in cellophane wrap, his 35mm neg strips. He looked at them, astonished. And spoke to himself, "You press the button, and Kodak does the rest . . ."

Situated conveniently in the downtown area but in a quiet residential street lined with mango trees, Cooper had secured offices in what had been originally a private boarding school run by an Order of French nuns. One room had been cleaned thoroughly and given a decent coat of white paint so that Cooper had a fairly presentable base in which to meet people, albeit furnished sparsely, a desk, a couple of chairs, an air-conditioning unit and a small safe.

Surrounded by the kaleidoscope of colored cardboard strips, he knew he should have been concentrating on assembling the production board, but he found his focus being interrupted by the Kodacolor material. Cooper spoke to the prints, as if in so doing they would disclose an answer.

"Thanks to Twit-Miller, we now know we landed in Colombia. And when I came to, all of the exposed film had gone a.w.o.l. And yet . . . here you are? And from where did the Aphrodite of the big boobs get the envelope, with my films?" Chuckling, Cooper sighed. "Aye there's the rub . . ."

"For in that sleep of death what dreams may come?"

Cooper froze. And turned around slowly, to face an athletic-looking handsome Imperian man, in his late twenties.

"So you, you are the movie man, you are the one looking for crew, locations and the one who will need the permissions?"

"And you, you are well-informed."

Smiling, the man bowed. "And, I know Imperio well, very well, better than anybody. I did years of my compulsory military service in a jungle combat unit. There is not a trail in the rain forest that I do not know and I know also very well the city of Santa Mosqueiro."

"Another jungle, right?" Cooper regarded the man. "And how did you find me?"

He grinned. "Santa Mosqueiro is a small city."

"If it's so small, why would I need you?"

"Because some problems can be big, like . . . like Colonel Mendoza?"

"Did he send you? And who the *hell* are you?"

"I am Carlindo Sintra. Carlo, to my friends."

"So what do I call you? Carlo, or Carlindo?"

"That's up to you."

"And what about Colonel Mendoza?"

"He? He is not my friend. I am here because I'd like to help, I'd like very much to work on a movie and you, you are going to need friends."

"How do I know I can trust you?"

"How do I know *I* can trust you?"

Cooper smiled. "*Touché.*" They shook hands.

"Mr. Cooper, I am honest plus I am very well connected."

"Organized crime?"

"Marriage."

Weighing his options, Cooper continued to look at Carlo. "This movie's not green lit yet."

Carlo inclined his head. "I can wait."

SCENE 8. TAKE 2.

The dealer hovered.

A number of paintings had been unwrapped. Some were on makeshift easels, some propped-up on the coffee table, others on the desk.

Taking his time, Tonnini scrutinized each canvas, examining lovingly the composition, creativity, color-rendering and the craftsmanship that had created these masterpieces, gasping and reacting in degrees various, depending on what impact had upon him this visual feast.

The dealer gestured. "As requested Mr. Tonnini, all have an Italian theme."

Nessa studied a canvas. "But isn't this London?"

"By Canaletto," replied Tonnini, without looking up. "An' this, this Italy, by an Englishman."

The dealer whispered in Nessa's ear. "Turner."

Tonnini stood back, in awe of the painting. "A master of color. Imagine how a movie look if there was a D.P. with this eye?"

"He would be nominated." Heads turned. Seidelman had entered.

Tonnini continued gazing at a painting. "He agree?"

Seidelman moved to Tonnini. "With conditions." He said, quietly.

Standing, Tonnini still was concentrating on the canvas. "Which are?"

Sidling beside Tonnini, Seidelman spoke *sotto voce*. "If we take Leef to direct."

"Don, we no in church. No need to whisper."

Seidelman cleared his throat. "If we take Leef, then yes, we can have Robert Eden for *Itatchia*. But. At Eden's normal fee, plus expenses, plus cast approval, director approval and, usual percentage of producer's profits."

"*Sciocchezza!*" All eyes turned to Tonnini.

Exasperated, Seidelman continued. "They're amenable to a deferment."

Immediately, Tonnini calmed. "How much?"

"Half."

"Payable when?"

"From first dollar through the box office."

"Is too early."

Nessa watched, absorbing everything. As always, she was fascinated by the way Tonnini approached problems, in that he never ever considered the possibility of defeat, only ways of winning. Thinking, Tonnini sat. "A deferment has to be farther down the line, much farther, at least after break even, no?"

"Franco, the deferment is half of his *actual* salary. Too far down the line and he's no better off than a net profits participant?"

Tonnini looked up. "Don, profits are no guarantee. A deferment is."

Seidelman shook his head. "I don't think the agent'll buy it."

Concentrating on a painting, Tonnini appeared not to hear. "This Robert Eden? He still golf crazy?"

Nessa suppressed the urge to clap, knowing that the Tonnini curve ball was about to be pitched.

"So far as I know."

Tonnini straightened, looking at Seidelman. "Then try this. As his deferment we mount a golf tournament in his name, *The Robert Eden Pro-Am Tournament*. We let him choose the golf course, the players, other celebrities, y'know like Sean, Clint, an' we pay all expenses."

"Franco! Can you hear yourself?"

"Sure, Don, I hear. An' as I was saying, we pay *all* expenses, an' give Mr. Eden an enhanced per diem. But." Tonnini raised an index finger. "*We* hold copyright of the event. We choose the date, an' we do airline tie-ups, hotel tie-ups, car rental tie-ups, sport equipment tie-ups, sport clothing tie-ups! We sell advertising sites all over the course an' we televise the tournament. To which we hold all rights, an' which we syndicate world-wide, an' to cable in the United States, which we follow with a video release, in NTSC, PAL an' SECAM. We make a nice profit for both ourselves an' Mr. Robert Eden." Tonnini nodded. "As he be giving his services free, we also reduce his tax liability." He turned to Seidelman. "That how we get our star."

Digesting the proposal, Seidelman nodded, slowly. "But what about the agent, what does he get? No deferment, no agent's commission?"

Tonnini thought, but for a second. "We call him the producer of the TV show. He get his money that way, and possibly more, no?"

Smiling inwardly, Nessa shook her head in total admiration.

Seidelman stroked his chin, staring at his boss. "You know Franco, I sometimes think you want to tie up the whole world, all of it?"

Tonnini shrugged. "Why not? Everybody forget we Italians had a great master, who once say, 'ambition should be made of sterner stuff.'" Nodding to himself, Tonnini said quietly. "That always my motto, Don. Ambition. Made of sterner stuff."

The dealer coughed politely, reminding one and all of his presence. "Eh, Mr. Tonnini, I do have other client appointments?"

Tonnini indicated two paintings. "Leave these, the Canaletto and the Caravaggio. I probably take them, but I need to study them more. An' I will want to see a selection of frames."

Raising his hands, the dealer shook his head. "I couldn't possibly leave them here."

"On you way out, speak to my secretary, Mrs.Meyers. You tell her how much we need to increase our insurance cover while they stay here."

Uncertainty clouded the dealer's face. "Well, I don't know . . . ?"

"You want I buy them? You see a pretty girl on the subway. You ask her to marry you right away?" Before there was a chance to answer, Tonnini continued. "No, of course not. You get to know her, her likes, dislikes, her ways, her . . ." In a sweeping movement Tonnini waved an arm. "Moods, her inspiration? Is the same with a painting." He gestured over a shoulder. "Now, you talk with Mrs.Meyers."

Staring at Tonnini, the dealer was speechless, looking back at the Italian as Nessa guided him gently towards the door.

Sighing, Tonnini gazed once more at the Caravaggio canvas.

"Franco, you found a corporation with blocked profits yet?"

The painting was still the object of interest. "Maybe."

Seidelman raised his eyes in exasperation. "Well, have you or haven't you?"

Straightening, Tonnini turned around. "Is an Imperian company. They wan' to open a branch in the U.S., but cannot because they no have hard currency. Until now."

"Discount?"

"We pay them sixty-five cents on the dollar, cash, in New York."

"And what cruzeiro amount will they be making available to us?"

Tonnini studied a thumb nail. "Twenty-one million."

"And, where?"

"Imperio."

Seidelman was visibly irritated. "Which . . . City?"

Tonnini looked-up from his visual manicure. "Oh, Alentejo, the capital."

Nessa glanced at Tonnini. "Franco, it's nearly lunch time, and I don't think you should really eat another pastrami sandwich?"

"You right. We go out."

"Shall I make reservations?"

"No, we just go." Tonini gestured to both Nessa and Seidelman. "We finish this in the car."

The Rolls pulled out on to Century Park East. Tonnini called to the chauffeur. "*Paolo, voglio audare Santa Monica. Drago's.*"

"*Si, signore.*"

Tonnini settled back into his seat. "Now, where were we?"

Nessa answered, quietly. "Twenty-one million."

"Right," said Seidelman, "twenty-one million." He eyed Tonnini. "Cooper figures that could well be the below-the-line cost, but you know how these guys pad their budgets, so as to cover any screw ups in their estimating."

"But Don, that the problem with a movie budget, it can only ever be an estimate, a projection? The true production cost is never known until at least married print?"

"Be that as it may, I said 'no.' Fourteen tops. Which leaves seven million."

Sitting forward, Tonnini turned to Seidelman. "Seven? For *Redmayne West*? Above-the-line? You serious?"

Seidelman pressed a button and the divider slid closed.

Tonnini pointed to the chauffeur. "Paolo no speak English."

"Neither did Caesar." Sitting forward, Seidelman enumerated, using fingers to emphasize his points. "Now, two-point-seven million." He hesitated.

Tonnini nodded towards Nessa. "Is okay. Soon she be a producer."

To Seidelman it came like a bolt from the blue. Clearing his throat and looking at Nessa, he muttered coldly. "Congratulations. Obviously your talent is . . . hidden?" And turned immediately to Tonnini. "Two-point-seven-five, cast and director, one-fifty, script." Tonnini moved to interrupt but was silenced. "I know, I know, paid for, but out of development money which has to be recouped into our overheads, so we recharge it to the movie's budget, right? With interest? That's another twenty five, which adds up to—"

"Four-point-five-zero," said Nessa.

Seidelman paused, irritated beyond words. Then, he mock genuflected to Tonnini. "Producer's fee, one million."

"Associate producer fee." Tonnini indicated Nessa. "Two-hundred-thousand."

Nessa gave to Seidelman *that* smile. "That's five-point-seven-zero." Said Nessa, pointedly.

Seidelman cleared his throat, continuing. "We'll need to float a servicing company down there, which may need Imperian directors, so, an overheads allowance, maybe of some what? Four-hundred-thousand?" Seidelman gestured to himself. "It's CEO. Maybe due a fee, of . . . ?"

"Two hundred an' fifty thousand."

"That's six-point-three million," added Nessa.

Sighing audibly, Seidelman looked out at the passing scene of Olympic Boulevard, seeing himself reflected in the window's tinted glass. "Travel, executive jets, limos, air fares, hotels, per diems, interpreters, secretaries, personal assistants . . ." He turned to Tonnini, and then to Nessa. "What price all that enchilada?"

Nessa hummed. "Eh, Six-point-five. But that's a top of the head guess." She addressed both Tonnini and Seidelman. "And, to be added to that are the fringes. D.G.A., S.A.G., W.G.A. I reckon conservatively that'll take it up to seven million?"

Seidelman looked at Tonnini. "But nevertheless, still cheap at today's prices?"

Tonnini grinned, looking at his two companions. "Then we *all* get a slice of the cake, no?"

Seidelman smiled. "Is that it, eh, the green light?"

"*Si*. But. How much prep time this director need?"

"Well, I guess what we, and for that matter, Cooper, decide to give him?"

Finger nails; the Tonnini rosary beads. "Okay. Fund Cooper an' tell him to get started. Permits, permissions, licenses, an' crew. Whatever technicians he can't find in Imperio, tell him, get Brits. They travel much better an' their fringes cheaper than Americans. But not too many. Hotels, air fares an' per diems, they no show up on the screen."

Having enjoyed a splendid lunch, Nessa and Seidelman waited on the sidewalk. He glanced at her, quickly, twice. "Nessa . . . I eh, I umm . . . I was out of line back there." He lowered his head. "I owe you an apology."

Puzzled, she looked at him. "For what?"

"Back in the car, on the way to lunch? It's just that I'd always figured that when Franco was thinking of another producer, I presumed that person would be me."

"Don. Believe me, *I* never expected what he said."

"Let me finish. Franco *never* said as much, so it was presumptuous of me to think it and I apologize for my rudeness to you when he did say it. That it would be you." He raised his hands.

"Y'know, Don, underneath that sorta, what, equivocal exterior? Maybe you're okay . . ."

Which is when the Rolls rounded the corner, with Tonnini aboard already. Seidelman opened a door for Nessa. "*Grazie*."

Seidelman smiled. "*Prego*."

SCENE 9. TAKE 2.

Everything is relative.

In the average mind, the words Beverly Hills conjure up visions of huge houses, manicured rolling lawns, swimming pools, tennis courts, servants' quarters and garages built to accommodate the largest of large cars, coupes de ville, sedans and customized dune buggies.

But not everything is Bel Air. By the standards of Beverly Hills and Bel Air, there are comparatively more modest residences and thoroughfares such as Laurel Way, where lived actress Susan Chase and her screenwriter husband, Victor Finney.

Auburn-haired, attractive with a soft face, Susan Chase was uncertain as to where she was professionally. She had maintained always that in a screen actor's career, there are five stages—'Who is Susan Chase?' 'Try that Susan Chase.' 'Get Susan Chase!' 'We need a young Susan Chase.' 'Who is Susan Chase?'

Today as every day and with a five pound weight in each pumping hand, Susan had taken her usual morning brisk walk. Laurel, Coldwater, Lexington, Benedict, San Ysidrio, Pickfair, Pine and back to Laurel.

She had showered and was sitting now at the patio breakfast table, engrossed in reading the final stages of a script, her concentration being broken by the arrival of her husband, puffing from the exertion of pushing his walker.

"I'm thinking of writing a script based on a walking frame."

Susan looked at him. "Sounds like a movie for Billy Wilder?"

As he eased himself into a chair, the maid poured him an orange juice. "*Gracias, Maria.*"

"So what's the story line?"

"Well, so far, I've only got the title. *Suddenly Last Zimmer.*"

Susan laughed and returned to her reading as did Finney, to the *Calendar* section of the *Los Angeles Times*. No one spoke, the silence being broken only by the occasional turning of a page. Finishing her reading, Susan put-down the script, gazing off.

"Well?" asked Finney from behind his *Times*.

"I like it."

He lowered the newspaper. "You going to do it?"

"I'm thinking about it seriously, yes."

"Is it well written?"

Susan looked at him, thinking how to frame her answer. "Yes, Victor, it *is* well written but no, Victor, it is *not* as well written as something *you* would have written."

He returned to his newspaper. "Then, it's *not* well written."

Sighing deeply, Susan flipped the pages of the script.

Finney folded the *Times* and took a sip of coffee. "Who's it for?" He pointed to the script. "The movie. Which company?"

"Tonnini International."

Finney scoffed at the mention of the name.

"Tonnini has made a lot of well known movies?"

"Well known as bombs."

Susan slumped. "Can we have *one* conversation without fighting?"

Finney nodded. "Sure, I'll try anything once."

"Victor, everybody knows the studios are making fewer and fewer movies, and we're both getting fewer and fewer offers, you with writing assignments, and me with roles plus I'm fast approaching that age when parts for women are like hen's teeth. Here's a script I like, a decent part, not too demanding, a good story."

"What's the title?"

Susan flipped the cover. "*Redmayne West*."

He studied his wife, speaking quietly, "Susan, that script has been around for donkey's years. Clair Hamilton wrote it back in the sixties, every major passed on it then and every independent has ever since. There's no market today for those big historical action movies."

Susan tilted her head. "Well, I think I should do it. It's a good part and besides, I've never been to South America."

"South America?" Finney shook his head patronizingly. "Now there's a Tonnini master stroke. The story's set in Canada." He frowned. "Why change it?"

Pondering, Susan smiled. "Food." She turned, nodding. "Yes, food. Definitely."

Finney frowned. And then giggled. "*Food*?

"Remember *Scorpio*, a Michael Winner movie? Much of it was set in Paris, only Mr. Winner had a sweet tooth, especially for Sacha Torte."

"You're not going to tell me they shot in Vienna, instead?"

"*Jawohl*. Burt told me."

Finney chuckled. "Well, Sacha Torte would melt down there, so who's directing this one? Knowing Tonnini, it'll be someone cheap, either on the way up or, on the way down."

Midmorning on a weekday and the Polo Lounge of the Beverly Hills Hotel is rarely busy, this Thursday being no exception.

Anthony Augustus Leef. Spelt correctly as 'Leefe', he got so pissed off with people, particularly Americans, pronouncing the name as "Leafy" that he had it changed by deed-poll and thus shortened. Leef was one of those British TV directors who emerged out of the Camelot of BBC2. He had directed a few movies in London which garnered some fair reviews, thus it was inevitable that he would come to the attention of Hollywood, as the L.A. studios always needed directors, scooping them up and spitting them out akin to hamburger meat through a mincer. And, after his first L.A. movie, he stayed.

Mostly the films he was offered were unsuited totally to his style or ability, but the Hollywood 'suits' have never really understood what a director actually does, anyway.

But Leef had two mortgages now, one on his London property and one in L.A. Then there was the Jaguar sedan, a liking for good food, vintage wines, the comfortable life and a penchant for young men, on whom he tended to shower expensive gifts, either in courtship or condolence. If there was anything Leef disliked, it was hard work.

His best known movie was an extremely sensitively handled piece about Robert Browning and Mary Shelly, which turned out to be a surprisingly lucrative box office success, the movie that finally got him out of Hampstead NW3 and into Brentwood 90049. But Browning and Shelley were a long way from Brad and Cindy, the heroic teenage couple of his last movie, the setting of which was Van Nuys so that at this stage of his career, Imperio was of far greater appeal to Leef than was the San Fernando Valley. Plus, there was the per diem . . .

His agent slid into the seat opposite. Irving Resnick was forty-two, clean-cut, a good listener, a good counselor, a good negotiator and, ambitious. Ordering Evian water, Resnick watched Leef refill his glass. Leaning forward to the ice-bucket, Resnick picked up the bottle gingerly, as if it was a live snake. "Oh, *Kristal* . . ." He replaced the bottle and glanced at Leef. "Bit early, isn't it?"

Instinctively Leef checked his watch and then did a double-take.

"We haven't signed yet."

Leef paused. "I thought it was all settled?"

Resnick sipped his water, slowly, eyeballing Leef ."Everybody wants a Midas director."

"Proper order." Leef twirled his Asprey swizzle stick, speaking to the wine glass. "So maybe Mr. Tonnini wants me . . . for me? After all, my last movie—"

"Is best forgotten."

Leef pouted. "Well, there was *Orchard Bay*."

"A nice movie, Anth-ony."

"Irving! How many bloody times do I have to tell you? The 'h' is silent! It's like the 'b' in subtle and the 'p' in bath! Silent! It's *An*-tony, not *Anth*-ony!"

Resnick concealed his loathing. "As I was saying, a nice movie. But the wedding scene? It was so long audiences were embarrassed at not having brought a gift to the theater." He continued to study his client.

Leef yawned. "It had splendid critical reviews."

"Splendid critical reviews don't add-up to box office grosses."

The sulking continued. "Who's in it?"

"They're still talking to people."

"Clients of yours?"

Resnick fidgeted. "Not for this movie, no."

Smiling broadly, Leef leaned back. "So, that's it. A trade off, right?"

Resnick shrugged. "So many people are breaking down my door clamoring for your services?"

"We all hit our out of favor periods."

"Only with some, the periods are longer?" The two men drank in silence. Leaning forward, Resnick put his elbows on the table. "Anth-ony, this is a chance for you. There may not be others?"

"Play or pay?"

"No. Twelve week guarantee only. Oh, and eh, no possessory credit."

"Why not? I always used to?"

Resnick placed a hand on Leef's wrist. "Anth-ony, listen up. This is a

Tonnini picture." The point was emphasized by hand gestures. "Tonnini International Pictures presents a Franco Delli Tonnini production—"

"Of an Anthony Leef film."

Resnick shook his head. "Not this time."

Leef was undeterred. "Approvals? Casting, script, key crew?"

"Dream on."

"What? And my Guild Agreement? The D.G.A. claims territorial rights."

"I don't think Tonnini's South American corporation is a signatory to your guild contract."

"Final cut?"

"No."

Leef sighed, deeply. "Jesus. What about profits?"

"Theatrical only, with double add-on."

Frowning, Leef's mouth dropped. "Double add-on? What the hell's that?"

"For every dollar over budget, they penalize you by two. Personally."

Looking at Resnick, Leef took a long, hard swallow of champagne. "I don't like the sound of this."

"They're business people."

"So was Al Capone, dear."

"Anth-ony, this is a small business. This time, none of that superior pompous British crap. You live in the USA, you work in the USA and you're paid in the USA. So behave like it. And when you're down there scouting, choose the locations for their production value to the movie, not their proximity to a restaurant." Resnick pointed to the champagne. "Lay off the booze and . . ." He looked Leef directly in the eyes. "Lay off the young men."

Leef returned the look. "Better now?"

Resnick stood. "I presume you've read the script?"

"Of course I have!" replied Leef, petulantly.

Resnick pointed at him a stern finger. "How many times?"

"I wasn't counting."

"Then read it again. And again and then again, until you eat, sleep and dream the dialogue and the stage directions."

"Irving, I *have* directed before," said Leef, very snidely.

"Yes. But the real question is, will you direct again?" A reproving stare, and Resnick was gone.

With the departure of his agent, Leef waved above his head the empty champagne bottle. *"Uno màs, por favor."*

Scene 11. Take 3.

"What's bugging you?" Cirla had been watching Rubio for some time, as the boss of the drugs complex stared fixatedly through a window, seeing . . . nothing. Any answer Rubio was about to give was pre-empted by the entry into the office of one of the pilots, who was greeted by the Colombian. "Ah, Mr. Larsen. And, with typical American precision, right on time." Rubio noticed the .38-caliber pistol stuffed into the pilot's belt. "And a gun to match your age." He beamed a smile. "In seven years' time a Colt maybe?"

Larsen said nothing.

"Everything alright?"

"About as right as I usually am at this time."

"Which is?"

"Apprehensive."

"Oh? And about what?"

Lighting a cigarette, the American gestured over a shoulder. "Of making it back." He looked at the two Latinos. "Either you guys fly?"

Rubio shook his head.

"I guess not", laughed Larsen sardonically. "Wouldn't need chumps like me if you did."

"Eh . . ." Rubio tilted his head. "Apprehension?"

Larsen exhaled smoke. "It's always been tight, here to Florida with a full load, pushing the range of the plane to the limit. Then add the changeable weather, especially over the islands, when fuel is low and you have to fly around a hurricane."

"Larsen, hurricanes and islands have always been there." Staring at the pilot, Rubio upturned his spread hands. "So what's the problem?"

"The U.S. Coast Guard."

Rubio laughed, ironically. "Larsen, they've been there almost as long as the hurricanes?"

"Except, not only have they stepped-up their activity with more sophisticated technology, but now they've gotten the assistance of their neighbors, places that before if'n you hit trouble you could put down at like, say, Jamaica, Haiti, The Bahamas . . . Cuba even! But not no more." He indicated both Cirla and Rubio. "And what are your people doing about it? Sweet chicken shit nothing, *nada!*"

Rubio nodded, ruefully. "Rome wasn't built in a day."

Larsen stubbed his cigarette. "It's gotten to the point where the reward's not worth the risk."

Rubio looked out at the Douglas DC3. "Am I about to hear your premium's just gone up?"

"You hear good."

"Larsen, if I recall, the F.A.A. withdrew your pilot's license and you continue to fly on counterfeit papers. Doesn't leave you too many places to find work, eh?"

As Larsen lit another cigarette, Rubio noticed the pilot's hands were shaking. "Rubio, you need me *more* than I need you. I want more, a damned sight more. If not, then don't bother loading my plane."

Smiling, Rubio shook his head. "Oh, I won't, believe me Larsen, I won't be loading your plane, no, no. Not with freight . . . nor with fuel."

Rubio spoke out of the side of his mouth, updating Cirla.

Larsen was the the first to blink. "Okay, but that's it! This is the *last* time. No more trips. Get it?" Larsen looked from one to the other. "*Adios* and screw you. Both!" He exited, slamming the door.

Rubio grinned at Cirla, reverting to Spanish. "That. That is what was bugging me. Larsen. He's seen too many John Wayne movies. Like all *gringos*, he's a flake."

Cirla nodded, understandingly. "So, what's our next move?"

Pondering, Rubio stroked his chin and then looked-up, gladdened. "He said it'll be his last run? Well, we'll make his wish come true."

"How?"

"We load him as per usual, but. Instead of cocaine we load the crates with sand. Of equal weight. We refuel him but, slightly short, so he'll have to ditch." Rubio laughed. "In the Bermuda Triangle!" He calmed. "If he isn't killed, he'll be picked up and handed over to the U.S. Federal authorities." Rubio slapped together his hands.

Cirla digested this. "But what if he *does* make it to Florida?"

"Roberto, it's perfect? *Our* people will find sand instead of cocaine and deal with Mr. Larsen accordingly. Three birds killed with one stone."

Cirla frowned. "*Three*?"

"Sure. One, Larsen. Now history. Two, extortion avoided, and three, the other pilots toe the line." Rubio glanced at the DC3. "Now, go and supervise the, eh . . . refueling?"

"Not top up, but top down?" Both men laughed out loud.

Scene 12. Take 3.

Although Santa Mosqueiro Airport processed about only twenty flights a day and the arrival for which Cooper was waiting was in the slack period, nevertheless he had with him a greet sheet, inscribed 'Wisepart'. The automatic doors slid open, and there she was. A somewhat voluminous figure in both height and width, Golda Wisepart was an English Jewess spinster in her early forties, arriving to become the production co-ordinator on *Redmayne West*. Cooper held aloft the sign, which she spotted immediately.

"You speak English?"

"Yes."

"Right, luggage."

In the hotel they walked to reception, with Cooper carrying her bags. "Golda Wisepart. Tonnini Pictures."

The receptionist gestured. "Passport." It was handed over. Nodding acknowledgment, the receptionist proffered a pen, and the register, which Golda signed. Handing over a key, he smiled. "I'll have a porter bring up your bags."

"Thank you." She turned to Cooper. "Do I tip you or does the company?"

Before he could answer, he was being called-after by the receptionist. "And Mr. Cooper, please check your messages?"

Looking him up-and-down, Golda shook her head. "Bunny warned me about you, your two-faced side." She eyed him further. "Jesus, is *this* going to be a rocky relationship." She headed for the elevator. "Why, at the airport, why couldn't you've at least said *who* you are?"

Cooper shrugged. "Whatever you've been told by my previous co-ordinators is neither here nor there." The rattling elevator arrived. "My gut instinct tells me this movie's going to be a minefield and you and I will be in the thick of it while still trying to get to know one another. So from the off, Golda, it's important we stick *together*."

Her reply was a cold look. "I stick my neck out for nobody."

"Down here in twenty minutes, okay? We've a production meeting."

"Copy that." The rickety elevator ascended, slowly.

Cooper asked himself, should he have said '*Here's looking at you, kid?*'

With Golda beside him taking notes, Cooper watched Leef study the latest shooting schedule, the director handling the pages on an elbow-raised hand between a forefinger and thumb, as if they carried a communicable disease. Finishing his in-depth cursory look, Leef pushed away the document, resting his elbows on the table with hands together, fingers extended fully. "Sixteen weeks?"

Stealing a glance at Golda, Cooper nodded, thinking here we go, complaint number one on every director's moan list. '*It's underscheduled.*'

"Six-day week, a twelve-to-fourteen-hours work day with travel, in these conditions, heat, humidity . . . mosquitoes?" Lowering his elbows, Leef leaned forward. "It's a piece of fiction, worthy of a Mann Booker prize." The two men stared at each other. "I mean, you are serious?"

"Deadly."

Leef pointed to the schedule. "This gives the director, me! No chance to prep the following week's work as the sole rest day is spent overcoming the exertions of the previous week. And, I'll wager I'm expected to spend some of that so-called rest day working with the editor, assembling sequences?"

"Nothing new about that?"

"This . . ." Leef slapped the schedule. Sulking, he looked around the table. "Not even time to wash your smalls?" Nobody smiled.

Cooper felt his hackles rising. "Anthony, I didn't decide the budget, neither did I write the script. The schedule reflects what, in my experience, it'll take to shoot one hundred and twenty-seven pages of script, conditioned by the amount of money available to this production. Okay?"

Banging the schedule on the table, Leef's anger consumed him. "No! It is *not* okay! You call Tonnini now, right now, to discuss the whole matter of this schedule!"

Checking his watch, Cooper looked-up. "It's five A.M. in California." He held out a phone to Leef. "You call him." Fuming, the director turned his back on Cooper.

The co-producer spoke to Leef's back. "Besides, this forum's not the place for such a discussion. My office is." Cooper looked to construction co-ordinator, Syd Walton. "Syd, how're we doing on set building?"

Walton displayed discomfort. In front of Leef he didn't want to add to Cooper's woes, but Cooper would never forgive him if he lied. "I need more men, guv. Especially chippies."

Hector Belem, the 'local' unit production manager from Rio, shook his head. "There are no more carpenters suitable for us, not here in Imperio."

Another Englishman, the production designer Ray Roberts, spoke. "Can't we bring some up from Rio, or Sao Paulo?"

Grinning at the naïvity of the question, Belem smiled. "Imperio gives work permits to specialized workers like me and. . ." He pointed to the Brasilian art director. "Marcos, but carpenters? No way." Belem eyed Cooper. "Besides, Brasilians more expensive in every way."

Turning around, Leef addressed everybody at the table, but particularly Cooper. In a patronizing tone he asked a question. "Which is the more expensive? To have a complete movie crew twiddling their thumbs standing around waiting for sets to be built or fly in some Brasilian carpenters? To me, the answer stands out like a pork chop in a synagogue?"

Knowing Leef was basically correct, Belem answered obliquely. "No more visas for Brasilians."

Leef sighed. "So, I'll say it again. Change it. Change—The—Bloody—Schedule!"

Sitting back, Cooper spoke to no one and everyone. "Anthony, you're the one who insists on raging water for the San Martins location, which means shooting there *before* the end of the rainy season, which is why the schedule is the way it is."

A look of hurt innocence creased the Leef brow. "You mean, *we're* not controlling the water?"

Cooper shrugged. "I don't have the Thames Barrier in the budget."

"Oh." Leef smiled. "Then what are the accommodations like at the away locations?" He grinned at Belem.

"San Gabriel is very small. We take over the one hotel, plus any private houses we can. At San Martins we're still negotiating, while at Borges we live in huts provided by the mining company." Hurriedly, Belem added. "They are air-conditioned."

Leef raised his eyes. "Sounds charming." Again he addressed Belem. "And the restaurants?"

Cooper burst out laughing. "Anthony, this is San Gabriel we're talking about, not Santa Monica."

From director of photography Billy Richards came the next question, the one question Cooper had been dreading, but knew was inevitable.

"When can we expect the rest of the camera equipment to clear customs?"

Cooper removed the pin from the metaphorical grenade and tossed it. "Hector?"

Belem cleared his throat. "Oh, *si*, just a couple of small items to clear, no problem." He gave a faint smile.

Looking at the table, Richards smiled also, to himself. "Small? No problem?" He addressed both Cooper and Leef. "Half the lenses haven't cleared, neither has the geared head, no dollies, no track."

Leef frowned deeply. "This is unbelievable! Only *some* lenses and we can't even move the camera?"

"Anthony, we have *got* the Steadicam," answered a defensive Cooper.

"James," Richards was staring at Belem. "The Steadicam operator's from L.A. and hasn't even been issued a visa yet, so he's still stuck in California."

Throwing-up his hands, Leef stood and began pacing. "Of all the Mickey Mouse movie outfits, this one has to be the dumbest!" He turned to Cooper. "You *have* worked on a foreign location before?"

"Probably more times than you've had hot breakfasts."

The director and co-producer looked at each other with mutual contempt. Leef was the first to speak, quietly. "Then why is the equipment still there, in customs?"

A gentle knock. Carlo entered the room, moving straight to Cooper and whispering in an ear. Cooper stood. "I have to leave." And glancing at Belem. "You carry on, and Golda, take notes, please."

Leef was outraged. "What can possibly be more important than this meeting?"

Pausing at the door, Cooper turned to Leef. "You'll never guess, Anthony. Customs." He followed Carlo out into the corridor.

Where was standing a uniformed official, carrying a large bag such as those used by hockey players.

"He from customs, federal customs."

Cooper knew this wasn't a courtesy call. "Sir, can I help you?"

Carlo gestured to the officer, who held open the bag for inspection. "James, take a look. Put your hand in."

Frowning, Cooper glanced at Carlo. "This like *Roman Holiday?*" Tentatively, Cooper extended an arm. And felt something ice cold. Withdrawing his hand, he found he was looking at a foil-wrapped packet labeled 'Gelson's gourmet beef stroganoff frozen dinner'. He nodded to Carlo. "Shurely shome mishtake?"

Carlo smiled. "See if you can hit the jackpot?"

Looking at the officer, Cooper rummaged deeper, in one hand pulling out a bottle and in the other holding a jar. "Hmmm, Jameson's Irish Whiskey and . . . Taster's Choice decaffeinated coffee." Cooper looked at the customs officer, who was shaking his head, ruefully, and then Cooper to Carlo. "I don't get it?"

Carlo indicated the officer. "He's found four large thermal packs of frozen food, twenty-four bottles of whiskey and twelve jars of coffee. A shipping waybill, yes, to Tonnini Pictures, but no manifest, nothing. So, nothing declared, so all illegal."

Looking at the goods, Cooper shook his head. "This has to be some sort of mix-up." He nodded to the customs officer. "Tell him, sorry, but I don't think it's anything to do with us."

This was all relayed to the officer, who replied both vociferously and animatedly, all the time gesticulating frenziedly to the goods and speaking rapidly.

"He says all this stuff was consigned to Tonnini Pictures but not declared, no carnet, no manifest, no nothing, therefore . . . illegal. He says it will be confiscated and all equipment released so far must be returned to bond, to be re-checked for all and any contraband."

Cooper was ashen, exhaling loudly. "I don't fucking believe it."

"What dear, what don't you believe?" Leef had stepped into the corridor.

Cooper turned, still holding the bottle and the jar.

"Oh goody! It's arrived!" exclaimed Leef. He moved forward, snatching from Cooper the two items. "And *what* are you doing with this?" Which is when he spotted in Carlo's hand the aluminium foil package, which he grabbed also, hugging the loot to his chest. "What the hell is going on here? This *my* property!" He looked around him. "*Mine!*" And pushed through the group.

The customs officer didn't hesitate. "*Sênhor?*" Leef carried on. The customs officer raised his voice. "*Sên. . . hor!*"

Shoulders heaving, Leef turned around slowly just as the officer placed a hand on the holster of his gun. Leef's lips quivered. "He serious?"

"There's only one way to find out?" Cooper was praying Leef would try.

The officer unsnapped his holster.

Noting this, Leef walked forward, whispering almost. "P'raps I'll have

Gaelic coffee another evening." Carefully, he replaced his treasures into the hold-all. Standing erect, he gestured to the bag. "I know exactly what should be in there, *everything*. Anything missing, I make a claim and, I call the Guild."

Cooper nodded. "Anthony, call who you like, but when Mr. Tonnini hears about this, I wouldn't want to be in your shoes for all the coffee in Brazil, decaffeinated or not. Because of your dumb, selfish stupidity," he pointed at the officer. "He wants all equipment returned, to be rechecked for contraband. Thanks to you!"

Leef turned, not saying a word.

Watching Leef's disappearing back and observed by the two men, Cooper slumped against a wall. Addressing Carlo, Cooper indicated the officer. "Does he really want it all back, *everything*?"

Carlo nodded. "*Todos*."

Cooper looked at Carlo, despairingly. "James, there is nothing I can do now, but tomorrow, I'll speak to Boscoli, head of customs."

Cooper ran fingers through his hair. "Carlo, tomorrow's Saturday. What the hell can be done around here on a Saturday?"

Carlo's response was positive. "There are ways."

Cooper only wished he could believe him. They helped repack the contraband.

SCENE 13. TAKE 4.

The Santa Mosqueiro media, both press and TV, covered well the Saturday arrival of cast member Susan Chase.

"My, my, isn't it a rewarding feeling," said Cooper, as he and Hector Belem waved off the limo from the airport kerbside. "To see actors arriving, knowing the painstaking attention to detail is paying off, one more piece fitting neatly into the jigsaw, the giant mosaic of pre-production on its way to completion and soon, soon the written word will become finite and forged indelibly on to the silver screen."

Belem nodded. "Absolutely. A shame we've got no lenses, no lights and no actual film to make a movie with?"

The two men looked at each other and burst out laughing, laughing until Belem's guffaws became racking, raucous coughing, mixed with choking. With tears streaming down his face, he doubled over. Cooper supported him, until the spasm passed. "Jesus, Hector, does this happen often?"

Panting, Belem straightened, wiping his eyes and nose. "Is the Amazon. I find it difficult to breathe around here."

"You do?" Cooper looked dead-pan at his associate. "But Hector, you sniff enough up your nose to clear constipation?"

Belem glanced at the co-producer. "James, at least I shave when greeting my leading lady."

Cooper rubbed his chin. "Whoops . . ."

Belem linked an arm with Cooper. "Come on, forget your troubles, and let's go to the warehouse and hear the latest moans of your jolly English crew. Then I buy you a nice lunch."

A twenty-minute drive across town took them to the warehouse, where were located the camera store, sound store, electrical store, grip and props stores, plus the construction shop.

Driving into the compound, there was not an empty space to be seen, the whole area being crammed full with trucks, an army of peons unloading boxes and crates from the vehicles, under the guidance of the departmental heads.

Cooper exited the car as if in a daze, not daring to believe that all of the equipment had been released from customs, but to his practised eye this was it, *todos*. His awe was interrupted by the strident tones of the propertymaster, Barry Gillette.

"You'd a thought that in the twenty odd years we've worked off-and-on, by now I'd 'ave got used to you pullin' strokes, but this. . ." Gillette made a sweeping gesture towards the trucks and frenzied activity. "This, James, *this* is pure fucking Cooper genius!"

Gillette was the focus of a Cooper poker-face. "Morning Barry, everything okay?"

"No! Why did all the soddin' trucks 'ave to arrive together, for us to be told they gotta be off loaded a.s.a.p.!"

Belem intervened. "Barry, it is my fault. I had little time to round up as many trucks and peons as possible."

Gillette re-addressed Cooper. "Yeah, well, okay, but it's a diabolical liberty, lunchtime. Of a Saturday. And no time to eat!"

Cooper shrugged. "Then charge a no lunch break."

"Can't, can I? You've got us all on an all-in deal. No bleedin' overtime!"

Cooper stood transfixed by the vehicles and the activity around. Still regarding the scene, he motioned to Belem. "Hector?"

"No, James, I don't know how this happened, but maybe we both attend Vigil Mass this evening?"

The stopping of the car prompted Cooper awake, opening his eyes to see a very high brick wall topped with razor-wire and shards of glass embedded in concrete. Sitting-up, Cooper looked around him. "What the heck's this place?"

"*El Yacht Clube do Santa Mosqueiro.*"

Cooper's eyes widened. "Christ, I'd hate to see the local jail."

"And there are two yacht clubs. The other one's for the patricians."

"And this one?"

Belem smiled. "You'll see."

They were being watched intently by an implacable armed guard in a pseudo-military uniform. As Belem drove forward, the guard's gaze never wavered. Drawing level, Belem offered a closed palm to the guard, who took from it a U.S. five-dollar bill. Without the gaze wavering, the barrier was lifted. Belem chuckled. "The green card. Never leave home without it."

Cooper had never seen anything quite like it, nor heard.

They strolled by the olympic-sized pool, while all the time non-stop pop music blared from numerous strategically-sited loudspeakers.

Belem nudged Cooper. "Impressive, no?"

Cooper shook his head, in bewilderment. "Impressive, yes."

Belem pointed, discreetly. "A cross section of Santa Mosqueiro high society, of the aspiring, acquiring, ambitious kind. But, over there, that gossiping group are the nannies." He indicated a smaller pool, full of splashing children of all ages. "Who manage to yap and to watch their charges all at the same time. Now, over there, you'll see better quality sunbeds and loungers." Belem removed his shades, squinting heavily. "In fact, the women are better quality too, but they are the mothers of the brats, and the pampered wives of . . ." Belem pointed. "Them."

Cooper looked. Under the welcome shade of a huge palm tree was situated a bar in the style of a south seas island hut, and beneath the adjoining straw-roofed area sat groups of men.

"The elite," said Belem somewhat bitingly. "The movers and shakers of Santa Mosqueiro, its *nouveaux riches*."

Cooper studied the men cautiously, as they smoked, drank, gambled, wheeling or dealing, but away from their ladies, as if an invisible barrier delineated their respective tracts. And beyond, Cooper noted, moored on the wide river was a number of very expensive-looking vessels, yachts, cruisers and powerboats. To Cooper the whole area stank of money, and although he was getting used to the divide in Imperio of the 'haves' and the 'have nots,' *El Yacht Clube do Santa Mosqueiro* was in stark contrast to the poverty that is most of the city. To Cooper it was the second major surprise of the morning.

"James, if you wish to join our yacht club, you could at least shave."

Before either could respond, Carlo had put an arm around a shoulder of each man. "You must meet some of my friends." He led them to a very large mahogany table, situated in the coolest shade available and placed in such a way that it commanded the best view of both the river and, the club. Everything and everyone could be seen from here, especially by the one man sitting at the head of the table, who was flanked on either side by six other men.

Cooper whispered to Belem, "Easter's early?"

The Brasilian sniggered.

Carlo stood beside the man at the head, indicating Cooper to join him. Speaking quietly, Carlo gestured discreetly to the table. "None of these people speak English." But, thought Cooper, *might they understand it*?

Carlo cleared his throat and whispered into an ear of the man at the head of the table.

"James, this is Mauricio Para. Pronounced *Par-rah*." Para stood, his height of six-two giving him a couple of inches on Cooper. Bowing slightly, Cooper shook hands, looking into a pair of dark brown, cold eyes, bovine-like in their lifelessness. Extremely well-preserved and dressed immaculately for the day, Cooper reckoned he was aged about fifty. In fact, Para was sixty-two years of age.

Speaking in Portuguese, Para nudged Carlo. "Introduce him *only* to the important ones. So that he gets the message." Para sat, nodding imperceptibly to Cooper. The Englishman was dismissed.

Guiding Cooper by an elbow, Carlo indicated the men at the table, speaking their names as he did so. As they were introduced, the men acknowledged Cooper courteously, but briefly, having taken their cue from Para. "His Excellency Ricardo Macedo, Governor, State of Boa Vista . . . General Coelho, Commander Federal Army, State of Boa Vista . . . Captain Presares, Federal Police, State of Boa Vista and—"

"*Mister* Cooper!" Rising, Colonel Mendoza stood and faced the Englishman. He studied Cooper's chin. "Eh, casting yourself in the movie as a villain?" Mendoza smiled, reminding Cooper of a *dago*-like Conrad Veidt.

"Oh," said Carlo. "I forgot. You two know each other?"

"Yes, Mr. Cooper once paid me a . . . *flying* visit." Returning to his seat, Mendoza muttered over his shoulder. "Have a nice day."

Carlo continued the introductions. "Sênhor Altamiro Boscoli, Captain of Customs, Santa Mosqueiro region." While looking at the man, Carlo flicked his eyes Cooper-wards; acknowledgment came via a surreptitious nod. "His Worship the Mayor of Santa Mosqueiro and, Commissioner Enriquez, Chief of the City Municipal Police." The presentation over, Cooper was steered back to where stood Belem. He glanced back at the table.

"Is that a social or a convention?"

"Mauricio Para is the father of my fiancée."

"Congratulations."

"He owns this yacht club, a two-channels TV station, two radio stations and the three leading newspapers of this state."

Cooper watched Para. "Is that all he owns?"

Carlo laughed, not grasping Cooper's *double entendre*. "Isn't it enough?"

"Some men never have enough."

Carlo slapped Cooper on the back. "Well, now you have enough? All your equipment, everything, yes?"

Cooper considered Carlo, to him a different Carlo, a new Carlo. "At what cost?"

Carlo pursed his lips. "Maybe a little, shall we say a little . . . handling fee?"

A deckhand appeared behind Carlo, whispering in an ear. Carlo turned. Para stood by the gangway of his very expensive cabin-cruiser *La Isabella,* ushering aboard his guests while signaling to Carlo. Waving recognition to Para, Carlo spoke. "James, you are like a nomad. You come, you film, you go." He turned, facing Cooper fully. "And just because you pump a lot of money into the local economy, it does not buy you the city." Carlo nodded towards the yacht. "The city is *theirs* and you, you are the visiting team but it is the home side which makes the rules, because it is *their* game. Understand? *Ciao.*" Carlo sprinted away, jumping deftly the widening gap as the cruiser eased away from the dock.

Cooper watched the vessel glide into mid-stream. He spoke to Belem. "Hector, what d'you make of that?"

Exhaling from a freshly lit cigarette, Belem was grim-faced. "It's a warning. Carlo's been told what to say."

Cooper frowned. "A warning? About what? I've done nothing to piss-off the twelve apostles?"

"James, this is a small town."

"Hector, for Christ's sake, don't you bloody well start that as well!"

"But, James, *that* is the point! It *is* small and they, *they,* are big, very big, and they can fuck us in any one of a hundred ways, whenever they choose."

"But what is it they're warning me about?"

Belem shrugged. "Who knows? Maybe just behave yourself, keep your distance?" He put an arm around Cooper's shoulder. "I promised you lunch. The seafood here is great."

As they headed for the club dining room, a preoccupied Cooper bumped into someone. It was Pitt-Miller.

"Well, Mr. Cooper, we do move in high circles?" Pitt-Miller indicated Para and his party. "I've never been invited to the top table."

"Don't worry. The moment you have something Para needs, you will be."

SCENE 14. TAKE 2.

"Christ! I should have listened to you!" Rubio stood in the warehouse, staring at the stacks of crated cocaine.

Cirla pulled a face. "Antonio, believe me. It's no fun being right."

Rubio continued to gaze at the crates, all the time messaging his chin with two fingers and a thumb. "Well, at least we know Larssen didn't talk." He nodded to Cirla. "But you were right. It has back-fired." Rubio continued looking at the crates, and the burlap-wrapped cocaine that awaited crating. "Just look at it, all that pure product and not a single damned plane to fly it in. Talk about frozen assets."

Cirla chuckled. "Mankind always sets itself only such problems as it can solve."

Rubio frowned, regarding his associate in a new light. "Roberto, a bit scholarly for you, eh?"

Cirla shrugged. "Credit where credit's due. Karl Marx. It was a riddle in a piñata. What's it mean?"

"It means I should make some calls."

As usual, Para had enjoyed the ritual Saturday company of his associates, and they, his lavish hospitality on board *La Isabella*; the sumptuous buffet lunch, the incomparable French wines, and then, the cooling cruise on the river.

As the Mercedes stretch limousine headed to Tele Visao Boa Vista, the car phone warbled its shrill cry. Before picking-up, Para ensured the glass partition was closed. *"Hola?"* Nodding occasionally, Para listened dutifully, and carefully. Eventually he responded, in his native Portuguese. "That will be fine. Nobody knows you here but come on a commercial flight. My office, nineteen-thirty. There's a show taping then. *Ciao.*" With the phone, Para pressed a memory button. "Possi? Mauricio. There's a program that needs to be discussed. Might the Colonel and yourself be free this evening, say nineteen-thirty, my office at the station? It shouldn't take long. We'll dine afterwards."

The limo drew up at the administration block of TV-BV. The commissionaire opened the rear door, saluting as he did so. Before exiting, Para spoke to the chauffeur. "Pedro, take Sênhora Para to the bridge club this evening and stay with her. I'll catch a cab home." Nodding to the commissionaire, he entered the building.

It had been some time since Rubio had set foot in Santa Mosqueiro and the Colombian was unprepared totally for the activity at *El Gran Hotel do Amazonas*. The lobby was full, the bar was full. There were even people eating in the restaurant! People? Well, gringos. And these gringos, they were everywhere, but hardly any women. Rubio thought it might be a convention or a tour except for the fact many of the gringos wore work clothes or carried briefcases also, hardly the attire of delegates or tourists?

The Chivas he drank slowly and with relish. Para had taught him to appreciate good whisky and to savor it properly, like the Brits, warmed glass without adulteration, no soda, no water and certainly no ice. Just neat pure peat-laden whisky, full of flavor and taste, so relaxing. Rubio scanned the backs of the people at the bar. One swiveled on his stool. With the glass halfway to his lips, Rubio froze. Jesus, he said to himself, *the gringo who landed at the hacienda.* Over his glass, Rubio watched Cooper. Controlling himself, he decided valor was the better part of prudence. He strolled over to confront Cooper. "We meet again!"

Cooper looked puzzled. Rubio presented the perfect image of a financially successful South American businessman. "You don't remember?"

Cooper shook his head, a feeble smile on his face. "I'm sorry, *Sênhor*, you have the advantage over me?"

"But surely you do? Vargas, Antonio Vargas."

Cooper reddened. "*Sênhor* Vargas, you must forgive me."

"Don't be silly. You must have so much on your mind but it's good to see you!" They shook hands.

Cooper smiled apologetically. "I'll remember in future, Mr.—sorry— *Sênhor* Vargas."

"*Antonio*, please, but I must fly." Rubio signaled the barman. "Give my friend James Cooper the same again, on my tab." And he was gone.

Stopping in the lobby by the newsstand, Rubio checked the bar. To a question from Cooper, the barman was shrugging and nodding his head. Wonderful, thought Rubio, he doesn't remember a thing, *nada* . . .

Surrounded by a number of monitor screens and stills of various stars and celebrities who had at times appeared on TV-BV, Colonel Mendoza and Captain Possi wore civilian clothes, sitting on a sofa while Para sat at his desk, with Rubio standing before them speaking in their native Portuguese.

"So, that's it. All the gringo pilots have quit and all the time we're losing markets, markets that we've fought hard for and have cost us as much if not more, to retain." Rubio looked at his associates. "In short, we have a severe transportation problem." A knock at the door. Rubio paused, looking at Para.

"Come in."

A secretary entered. "A fax just in." Leaving it on Para's desk, she exited as silently as she'd entered.

Mendoza pointed. "See, there's the answer, that's what we need, a narco fax! Something that transmits not just words but powder over thousands of kilometers, in seconds!" Mendoza grinned at Para. "Feed in two kilos of stuff into the narco fax machine at the hacienda and *voila*! Three seconds later and out it pours in Florida, or Detroit or Amsterdam!" They all laughed.

Para pointed to the ceiling. "How about NASA-narco? Send the stuff by satellite and beam it into millions of American homes all at the same time and instead of having pay per view meters, their TV sets will have pay per *snort* meters!"

They were laughing still when there was another, heavier, knock.

"Come", said Para.

Carlo entered, carrying a bulky package. "Oh, pardon me, you're busy."

"Just talking over old times. You know everybody here, Colonel Mendoza, Captain Possi and . . ."

"Vargas," said Rubio. "Antonio Vargas."

Carlo nodded to the company. "I didn't mean to interrupt, just to remind you Mauricio, our tennis game in the morning?"

Para smiled. "I haven't forgotten." He indicated the package. "Shopping early for Christmas?"

Carlo laughed. "No, it's material from the movie."

"The movie? What sort of material?" Para looked at his guests. "Maybe I can pirate a program here?" Everybody laughed.

"I don't think so, Mauricio. It's only camera tests."

Para nodded. "So what are you doing with it?"

"Taking it to the airport. The negative? You know, for processing? It goes to Los Angeles."

A pin could have been heard to drop.

Rubio broke the silence. "Just this once?"

"Oh, no," said Carlo confidently. "Once they start filming proper they'll be sending material five or six times a week."

"Five or *six* times a *week*?" Rubio's eyes were piercing Carlo.

The confidence faltered. "Well, I guess . . . Yes, something like that."

Rubio folded his arms, as if an attorney addressing the jury but for the attention of the whole court. "So, each day's completed filming is sent to Los Angeles for processing, and this goes on for how long?"

Carlo was now on more familiar ground. "Well, the shooting schedule is sixteen weeks so . . . sixteen weeks, I guess?"

"And do you take it there?" Mendoza indicated the package.

Carlo broke into a broad grin. "I wish. No, it goes air freight. The production office does all the necessary paper work and off it goes."

Noting the time, Carlo made for the door. "I'd better scoot! *Ciao!*"

For several minutes, nobody said a word. Mendoza was the first to break the silence. "I'm sure we're all thinking the same thing?"

Grinning as he did so, Rubio shook his head; in disbelief. "Who said the sun shines only on the righteous? A *daily* shipment, *five* or *six* times a week?"

"But to Los Angeles", reminded a thoughtful Para. "Not Miami."

Rubio calmed him. "Mauricio, the main thing is to get the stuff into the U.S.A. Once there, we've the means to get it exactly to where we want it?"

Mendoza leaned forward. "How do we set this up, to take advantage of this God-given opportunity?"

Pacing, Rubio deliberated. "Well, basically we have to get the cocaine here to the film, and then we have to marry a parcel, a *parcel*, not a crate! Of cocaine to a parcel of film." He looked at his associates. "A parcel of cocaine out of here every day for thirty days is much better than a crate every month, and very much more cheaper?"

While sipping whisky, Para looked over his glass at Rubio. "Antonio, the theory sounds fine but what about it in practise? How do we actually get the film consignment into *our* hands, eh?"

Rubio nodded towards the door. "What about him?"

"Carlo?" Para tilted his head. "A reliable pair of ears, but . . ." He spread his palms. "Which, Antonio, brings us back to my original question. How?" Para chuckled. "After all, we can hardly take the stuff to the movie people and say 'Sirs, please put this cocaine in with your film and make sure it gets to our people in Los Angeles', now can we?"

"I think we can."

All eyes turned to the hitherto-silent Possi.

"Colonel, you remember that police co-operation program run by the Organization of American States, and I was sent up to Mexico City to participate? Well, while there I learned many things, like lots of American movies are made in Mexico for a number of reasons, usually cost. There is a Mexican federal government agency which oversees all movie-making within the State. This is Concine. Once a script has been submitted to Concine and approved, how can Mexico and Mexicans be sure they are not portrayed as monsters, or idiots or the country shown in a bad light, how?"

"I don't know, Possi." Mendoza spoke quietly. "Tell us. How?"

Possi shifted to the edge of the sofa. "They have a censor. He is appointed by Concine, the state controller of movies, so an employee therefore of the federal government. All day, he sits on the—"

"The point, Possi," implored Mendoza. "Get to the damned point!"

"The movie set. At at the end of each day, when the film has been packed for shipment, it and the paperwork are handed over to . . . the censor." Possi had a rapt audience. "*He* seals it all, with an official government stamp, a stamp that tells the Mexican export authorities the film is officially cleared to leave the country, a stamp telling the U.S. customs likewise for importation and thus rarely are such regular shipments into the U.S.A. interfered with. And, the parcel is labeled 'Exposed Film Negative. Do not X-ray!' So it sails through all controls, all of them." Sitting back, Possi took a long, slow, drink.

Mendoza turned to his aide. "So what you're suggesting is *we* appoint . . . a censor?"

Possi nodded, affirmatively, looking around the room. "Perhaps a state law has been passed recently, a law requiring any movie filming in the State of Boa Vista must be supervised by a state appointed censor?" Possi looked to Para, to Rubio and finally to Mendoza. "*Our* man. We get the cocaine to him and together with the film he packages it, does it all up with the movie shipment, stamps it with the official seal, adjusts the paperwork, and off it all goes to Los Angeles."

Standing to face his confidantes, Mendoza came to attention. "Has the State of Boa Vista just decided on a censor for movie companies filming here?"

Para stood and raised his glass. "Public morality must be protected."

Rubio looked around him. "But where is our tame censor?"

Mendoza glanced at Possi. "Leave that to us." Possi nodded.

Para rose from his desk. "How about dinner? Uncensored."

SCENE 15. TAKE 1.

To build the set, a large clearing had been hacked out of the jungle.

Leef and his immediate crew were making an inspection of pre-shooting familiarity and orientation of what the script stage directions described as, '44. Ext. Fort Stockade. Day.'

The director struggled with his script. Despite the exhortations of his agent, obviously this was the first time Leef had actually read this part. "What's the first scene number here?" Asked irritably.

Without needing to check, first assistant director David Langley answered immediately. "Scene forty-four. Top of page twenty-three."

Leef read and then looked up to the set, studying the buildings and their layout. Frowning, he re-checked the script; and then, he re-checked the set. "Isn't this the first time they've been here?" He looked around the assembled group, gesturing to the set. "Then how come it's complete? The fort they're *about* to build?" With his trademark pout, Leef turned to the production designer. "*Mis-ter* Roberts, pray, tell me?"

Frowning, Roberts looked at Leef. "Anthony, this is a wind up, right?"

Leef gestured to the set. "More like a cock up!"

Roberts was puzzled. "I, eh, I don't understand?"

"As I can't find it in the script, does Redmayne carry on his person a packet of Instant Fort, y'know, just add water and caramba! It's all built?"

Shaking his head ruefully, Roberts continued. "It's basic construction operation. Start with a full set, dismantle it as shooting is completed on each sequence until is reached the beginning." Roberts looked around him. "Page one?"

Cooper had joined the group. "Added to which, it is more economical, with full set-dressing and tubular scaffolding on rental for shorter periods of time." He grinned at Leef. "Not even page one?"

Leef was fuming, pointing repeatedly at the set. "Are you telling me I'm supposed to shoot this arse about face?"

"A position surely not unfamiliar to you, Anthony?" Cooper and Leef squared up to each other with mutual loathing.

"We'll see about this." The director stormed-off, to be given the bird by Cooper.

Roberts joined his fellow Englishman. "Do we strike the set?"

"Of course we bloody well don't!"

"James, this isn't any way to head into shooting, with the director and co-producer at loggerheads."

"And, with Tonnini and Seidelman constantly snapping at my heels."

"James, d'you think it's all an act, a jockeying for position? After all, he's gay, and sees you as the enemy, a hetero produ—" Roberts squinted at Cooper. "You are hetero, aren't you?"

Cooper leaned towards Roberts. "Give us a kiss and I'll tell you."

They strolled from the set. "Where'd they *find* these so-called directors, anyway?" mused Roberts.

Cooper uttered an ironic grunt. "Not from the movie industry, that's for sure."

"Well, he's too old to have come from film school."

"But not too old to go back?" Countered Cooper, malevolently.

The two men laughed. "What's he done previously?"

"Not much. In fact, his last movie was so bad audiences walked out of it in droves. At forty-thousand feet. On PanAm."

Laughing, Roberts looked at his friend. And then asked, inquisitively. "You ever fancied directing?"

Cooper took a couple of seconds before answering. "I'd give my back teeth to direct."

"So what's stopping you?"

Grabbing a blade of grass, Cooper chewed on it. "Well, the industry loves to pigeon hole, and with the possible exception of Alan Pakula, the perceived wisdom is that production people are simply number-crunchers, singularly uncreative." He glanced at his friend. "*I'm* pigeon holed."

"James, that's a cop out, and you know it."

Cooper stared at the ground, saying nothing. Roberts nudged him. "Cheer up. It's the pre-production party tonight. Who knows, even you might get laid."

"With my luck?" Cooper looked up. "I couldn't get laid even if I was a carpet."

Enlivened by alcohol-loosened inhibitions, the party was in full swing. A cold beer in hand and eaning with his back to the bar, Cooper watched the revelry.

A phone rang. "*Hola . . . hola*?" Edmondo the barman was lost. Eyeing Cooper, he handed over the phone. "*Sênhor James*?"

"Hello?"

On the patio of the house that was home to he and his wife sat Victor Finney. On the table in front of him was a word-processor, paper, pencils, a framed photograph of Susan Chase and, a phone. "*Fala Inglês*? Do? You? Speak? English?"

"Yes."

"Susan Chase?"

"Call the production office in the morning."

"This is her husband!"

Cooper nodded. "She'll be right with you." He looked around, to see Susan chatting with production designer Raymond Roberts. Cooper held-up the phone, pointing the instrument at her.

Moving to the bar, a quizzizcal look on her face, Susan took from Cooper the phone. "Yes?"

On hearing her voice, evaporated all of the restraint Finney had promised himself. "Why haven't you called?"

As soon as she heard Finney's voice, Susan was filled with dread. She didn't want to listen to him, thinking only that at that very moment she was free, over thousands of miles away from the vocal barbs, the silent meals, the empty days, the vacuum of love . . .

"Susan, can you hear me?!"

"Who is this? It's a terrible line?" She moved the receiver rest up-and-down, slowly and silently. "I can hardly hear you?"

A frantic Finney screamed into the phone. "Susan! Don't do this!"

Putting her hand discreetly on the rest, Susan cut off the call, while giving to all and sundry the impression of a pleasant conversation with an old friend. She continued speaking as Cooper joined Roberts, who never took his eyes off Susan, nodding in her direction. "Whaddya think?"

Cooper smiled. "Out of your league, Ray. Stick to art department girl assistants." The smile disappeared more quickly than it had formed. Carlo had entered the room, with Altamiro Boscoli in full dress uniform looking more akin to a character from a Gilbert and Sullivan operetta than the captain of customs that he was.

Having finished her call, Susan rejoined them. "You never told me the *Love Boat* docked here?"

"An error of navigation." Nodding 'excuse me' to Susan and Roberts, Cooper strolled over to join Carlo and Boscoli; he greeted the latter formally, while speaking to Carlo. "What brings him here?"

Carlo nodded to various acquaintances, talking as he did so. "Without him you would have no equipment." He eyed Cooper. "*You* owe him."

Cooper glanced quickly at Boscoli. "So it's pay-off time, right?"

"Could be."

"What's the price?"

Carlo turned to Cooper. "He would like to have a nice dinner."

Cooper nodded. "At my company's expense?"

"Yes."

"Fine."

"With a guest."

"A guest?" Cooper drank.

"Susan Chase."

Lager splattered all over his shirt. "No chance," choked Cooper, wiping off the spilt beer.

"James, customs is like a woman. They can always change their mind? He is your savior, no?"

Looking at Boscoli, who simultaneously bowed and clicked his heels, Cooper would loved to have nailed him to a cross but instead smiled, weakly. "I'll do my best. But no promises, mind."

Carlo relayed this to the increasingly smiling Boscoli. "I tell him an Englishman's word is his bond."

Cooper rejoined Roberts and Susan. "You should've told me it was fancy dress. I do a very good Zsa Zsa impersonation."

But Cooper was watching Boscoli. "Susan, you don't by any chance speak Portuguese, do you?"

"What sort of a question is that?"

With the band having taken a break, extemporization replaced it. Most of the sweating British crew were shirtless, and much the worse for drink. Gillette had taken over the piano and accompanied by a chorus of his fellow nationals in states various of inebriation and undress, was belting out a rendition of *'Maybe it's Because I'm a Londoner'*, which is when Gillette spotted Cooper. "Come on, James, a little tinkling of the ivorys, eh?"

Cooper feigned hearing.

Roberts turned to Susan. "Do American crews behave like this?"

She grinned. "They lack your British finesse."

As the carousing got louder, Gillette shouted. "Come on, James, duty bloody calls, y'know, the old *joanna*?"

Sighing, Cooper excused himself. "Needs must."

Sitting at the piano, Cooper adjusted the stool, racking his musical memory as to what he should play, while thinking, *tomorrow is the first day of shooting, I've got to get these buggers to bed so, something nocturnal.* An accomplished pianist, Cooper eschewed Ravel for Beethoven. The Piano Sonata no.14 in C-minor, opus 27. As the chords unfolded the room lapsed into total, frozen, silence. He played only the first half and as he finished, the room erupted into rapturous applause, led by Susan Chase. She stared at him, saying very quietly, "obviously a man of hidden talents?"

Dawn.

The closed drapes subdued the rays of the rising sun. Ignoring the man beside her, Susan lay in the half-light staring at the ceiling. Even without make-up, she was a stunning-looking lady. The bedside phone rang. Susan groped for it. "Hello? Oh, *bom dia. Si. Obrigado.*"

Cooper rolled over, sitting up. Taking a couple of seconds to gain his bearings, bleary-eyed he glanced at Susan. "Good morning."

She rubbed her face. "God, how I hate the first day of a movie. Every time it's like starting all over, like the very first day of school, like that horrible moment when your mother withdraws her hand from yours, you watch in horror as she disappears, knowing you're suddenly all alone."

Cooper shook his head. "Nobody likes the first day."

Her back to Cooper, she swung-out her legs. "I must shower." Walking to the bathroom, Susan paused at the door, using it to shield her nakedness. "Oh, by the way. The make-up woman?"

"What about her?"

Susan faced Cooper. "She smells. Body odor."

"I'll speak to her."

"Just replace her." Susan thought for a moment. "Or better yet, get somebody solely for me. That *is* what I am used to. In this natural light I need little make-up. Get an English-speaking non-smelly local beautician"

Deliberating, Cooper nodded slowly. "Remember *Love Boat*, the guy at the party?"

Susan nodded. "Who could forget him?"

"He wants to have a dinner. With you. I, we, the company, we owe him."

"So?"

"A trade." Cooper held out a hand. "A beautician, in return for a dinner?"

Susan sighed deeply. "Oh, man. How I loathe producers."

"Loathe? What about last night?"

"What about it? Last night was a piano player." She closed the bathroom door, entered, locking it.

"Our leading man like his lodgings?"

Golda looked up from her desk. "He loves the villa." A phone rang. Picking it up, Golda listened briefly and passed it to Cooper.

"Hello?"

"James? Is Franco. I call to wish you good luck with the shooting, and to hope all go well with you and *Redmayne West*. You put together the movie very well. Congratulations."

Cooper felt desperately embarrassed. "Thank you, Franco. Thank you."

"You welcome." The tone changed. "Eh, James, one more thing. There a drug problem down there?"

"Here? On the movie? No, only the usual sniffing and snorting you get on any show these days."

"No, no, not the movie but gangs. Dealing, trafficking, all that shit?"

Cooper wondered if Tonnini could hear the thumping of his heart. "Not here, Franco. Maybe over the border, Colombia, but no, not here."

"You sure? You sure you no bullshit a bullshitter?"

"I'm sure."

"I hope you right. Give Mr. Leef my best wishes but take no crap from him. Keep him on schedule, okay? I rely on you James, just as you can always rely on me, *capis*? *Ciao*."

Cooper replaced the phone, momentarily lost in thought. He looked at Golda. "Any first day dramas?"

"*Oy vey!*" Her eyes rolled. "*Dos*."

"*Dos*?" Cooper grimaced. "Major?"

"*Uno, mucho* major." Rising, she crossed to a pile of canvas chairbacks, holding one aloft. On it was stencilled 'Tony Leef.'

"Oh . . . God."

"Yes, oh, God." Golda dropped the piece. "All had to be changed rapidly to blanks. I've ordered correctly addressed replacements."

"Well done. And *numero dos*?"

"The censor. Carlo keeps calling in."

"The censor?" Cooper's face contorted. "*What* bloody censor?"

Golda frowned at him. "I presumed you knew?"

Cooper shook his head. "Golda, I haven't the faintest idea what you're talking about. Or who? Where's Carlo?"

"At the location."

"Then so am I."

Do I miss being on set? Cooper watched the organized chaos and knew immediately. *No, I don't miss it.* With a styrofoam cup of coffee in his hand, he strolled over to where stood Carlo, and a young man of about twenty-eight, a face new to Cooper.

"*Bom dia*, James."

"Morning." While sipping coffee, Cooper studied the young man, then turned to Carlo. "Carlo, you know we put out a call sheet in both Portuguese and English, so that everyone's aware of the day's program and I'd swear, on today's, there's a note about visitors to the set?" Cooper gestured to the young man. "We don't have any. Nobody comes to the set unless authorized by me personally. So. Who is this gentleman?"

The young man answered for himself. "I am Francesco Ramalho. I am the appointed state censor." They shook hands.

Cooper stood with one hand on a hip. "Appointed by whom?"

"The State of Boa Vista."

Cooper nodded, slowly. "How come Imperiocine has never said anything to me about this?"

"Imperiocine is a federal agency. This is a state requirement."

Cooper turned to Carlo. "Is it normal for a movie to have to carry a censor?"

"James, how the hell would I know?" Carlo shrugged. "I've never worked on a movie before."

Cooper turned again to Ramalho. "I still don't understand why I wasn't told. Who do I speak to about this?"

"My superior."

"And who is that?"

"Colonel Mendoza."

As Cooper stiffened, Carlo stifled a giggle.

Ramalho continued. "The State Police are charged with safeguarding public morality and that includes foreigners."

Cooper gestured to the set. "This isn't *Deep Throat*.

"Also, we are concerned about how the Indians are depicted in your film. Imperio, and particularly Boa Vista, have had very bad press in your hemisphere about the so called mistreatment of our indigenous peoples, who are the pre-colonial fabric of our great nation, and that criticism is totally undeserved and made without any foundation. In Imperio, the noble Indian is protected, his heritage guarded, his health and well-being monitored, but if one believes all that is written about us one could be forgiven in thinking it is still the dark ages down here." Lighting a cigarette, he never took his eyes off Cooper. "In Boa Vista, we care about our primordial people and we care what is said about their welfare. We do not want to be portrayed in a negative way, nor our people, nor our traditions, our way of life. That's why I am here. No misrepresentations, no insults, then there will no interference from me."

Inclining his head, Cooper inhaled deeply. "Well, that's all very crystal clear. Obviously someone in Boa Vista must have been to Mexico?"

"You have filmed in Mexico?"

"Twice. Durango, Durango, in 1970, and then Mexico City, 1982."

"Then you are familiar with the procedure, including the handling of the film. It is exactly the same here."

"To qualify as a censor, are you required to have any movie-making knowledge?"

"I attended U.C.L.A. Film School." Ramalho nodded, and walked off.

Watching the receding figure of the censor, Cooper thought out aloud. "Carlo, you'd better introduce our friend to Leef, to the script clerk, the assistant directors, the camera assistants, the sound guys and the transportation captain. And tell them to treat him with kid gloves." Arching his eyebrows, he headed towards his car, asking himself, *why, why wasn't I told about this requirement*?

Under a parasol, Susan Chase sat in the shade of her trailer, learning her dialogue, a ritual she did on the location in any free period and always last thing at night, familiarizing herself also with the lines of the other players with whom she interacted, to understand fully the characterizations and their motivations. Pausing, she looked up to see some sixty yards away June Sykes, plying her craft, dabbing make-up on one of the local bit-part players. In her thoughts Susan sympathized with the day player until realizing she was a local, able to counter equally the body odor of the make-up lady.

Cooper strolled into her line of vision. "Well, well, the Rubenstein of *Redmayne West*."

"Hi." Cooper walked over to her. "So I'm a pianist again?"

"Cooper, you've so many faces, so many sides, I don't think anybody would recognize who you really are, least of all yourself?"

"Then maybe I'll survive Armageddon?"

A Susan nod indicated June Sykes. "Got your little speech ready?" She smiled at him. "Remember that old joke?"

"Which one?"

Susan leaned forward. "After Archimedes had made his displacement discovery, so ecstatic was he that he ran through the streets naked, yelling, '*Eureka, eureka!*' to which a passer-by replied, '*You no smella so good yourself!*' "

Rolling his eyes, Cooper walked over to where June was working. Distance prevented Susan from hearing what was being said. What she did see was much Sykes hands-on-hips and finger wagging, an implacable Cooper with outstretched arms and then Sykes storming off.

Cooper turned in the direction of Susan. She mimed applause. At the very same moment June Sykes happened to look back.

"So, what exactly, did Cooper say?" Helen Beverly was at the sink in the hairdressing trailer, rinsing-out the tools of her trade before combing some period wigs on a head stand.

"Oh, something about it not being a reflection on my work."

"Huh! I should think not." Helen spoke over her shoulder. "Considering at the time we'd only been shooting for about four hours."

June shrugged, moving her arms in a weak gesture of withdrawal. "Anyway, he said a problem had arisen, one he wasn't at liberty to discuss, that it would only get worse and he was a great believer of nipping things in the bud."

Speaking over her shoulder, Helen dried her hands. "And?"

June let out a loud sigh. "And, therefore, he wants me off the picture. Immediately. He said it can be down to any excuse I choose, malaria, something like that, but he wants me on tomorrow's flight to Sao Paulo. Said he'd give me five weeks' money in lieu and send me back first class."

Helen grunted. "Conscience." She faced her friend. "So what's your next move?"

June smiled. "Convert the ticket to economy and pocket the difference!"

They strolled among the trailers and support vehicles.

June was shaking her head. "I still can't believe my luck, if it can be called that. This would have been my first decent stretch of work in a year. After the accident, I was in and out of hospital with only the odd commercial to keep the wolf from the door, and now this?" They continued their wandering, June looking ahead of her. "That Yankee cow?" She turned to Helen. "She's something to do with this, I know she is."

Helen looked at her friend sharply. "You think she's fucking Cooper?"

"Afternoon, ladies." The greeting of the American animals wrangler Joe Tors pre-empted a reply.

"Hi, Joe." Helen looked at the various cages, containing the assortment of animals required for use in the movie. "How's Noah's Ark? Or should I say, Joe's Ark?"

"All coming along fine, just fine."

Helen pointed, excitedly. "Ohhh, it's beautiful!"

"Shhh . . ." Joe put a finger to his lips. "We're not supposed to have it." He carried over the animal. "It's a jaguar kitten, protected."

"It is *gorgeous*." Helen's fondling of the animal was interrupted by a mild shriek.

Hands raised in alarm, June was staring into a cage, immobile. Joe rushed over. "It's okay, they're harmless." He reached in and scooped-up a small snake, about twelve inches long.

Involuntarily, June stepped-back, her eyes always on the snake. "Do they really have cold, slimey skins?"

Joe laughed. "Feel." She hesitated. "Go on."

June touched the snake tentatively, watched over a shoulder by Helen. "You know, June, you should call the union."

June continued watching the snake. "Cooper's got us all on a non union all-in deal, remember?"

"That *himbo*." Helen shook her head. "He doesn't miss a trick."

June continued studying the reptile. "Is it poisonous?"

"Nope, but it'll give you a nasty nip if you give it cause."

June looked at the wrangler. "Joe, I was once told that if you have a fear of something, you should always look it in the face. I'm terrified of snakes. If I promise to bring it back, may I borrow it? To help my phobia?"

Golda entered the darkened office, and turned on a light. To reveal a dozing Cooper. "Been playing with yourself again?"

He remained slumped over his desk. "Charming."

"There's someone to see you."

Golda opened the door wider to reveal the six-foot-three, fair-haired figure of the leading man. Although at forty-four a little past his box office prime, Kurt Greene was in demand still, for the superb range and depth of his acting craft, and, for his well-preserved looks. Everybody loved Kurt, his fellow actors, crews, critics, audiences and, the camera. In the limelight now for some twenty-plus years, he kept a low profile privately, earning himself high respect publicly and his ever-cheerful disposition earned him the industry moniker, 'The Smiling Man's Steven Segal.'

Cooper rose from his chair. Wordlessly, the two men embraced tightly. Breaking apart and smiling, they looked at each other.

"How've you been, Kurt?"

"Good, buddy. And now, all the better for seeing you."

"Likewise, likewise." They grinned at each other.

"I got the stuff."

"All of it?"

Kurt nodded. "Slight cost overrun at Chalet Gourmet, ditto Gelson's, but yes, everything." He passed to Cooper some receipts. Kurt frowned. "You got Moctezuma's Revenge or something?"

"Not yet. Any problem at customs?"

"Nothing a few autographs couldn't solve."

"Golda?"

A genuflecting Golda appeared at the door. "You rubbed the lamp, master?"

Her reward was one of Cooper's looks. "They're some things in Mr. Greene's car. Have them put in the freezer and get word to Mr. Leef he can stop sulking and come off his Lenten hunger strike."

Bowing continually, Golda shuffled out, backwards. "Yes, master."

Smiling at her act, Kurt addressed Cooper. "What's he like?"

Cooper shook a limp wrist.

Kurt regarded Cooper through squinting eyes. "Jimmer, don't tell me this is one of those gigs 'I-fucked-everybody-to-get-on-this-movie-who-do-I-have-to-fuck-to-get-off-it'?"

Cooper shrugged. "You be the judge."

"And knowing you, the return half of my airline ticket's already in a safe deposit?" Kurt smiled through a sigh. "When do I start?"

"Day after tomorrow. This evening you've a working dinner with Leef and Susan Chase." Cooper smiled at the actor. "It's good to have you here, Kurt."

"And it's good to be here, buddy." They hugged again. "So far . . ." As the actor passed her, Golda curtsied.

"James, is it really all right to give the rushes to this Ramalho?"

Cooper frowned. "Golda, what are you talking about? And who is Ramalho?"

"The *censor!*"

Cooper was surprised by the question. "Why ever not?"

"He makes me uneasy." She fiddled with a pencil. "Like you, I've done a movie in Mexico. There, at the end of each day's shooting, the censor would come into the office, and then the clapper-loader, who'd handover both film and sheets. The censor would go straight to work there and then and I saw all that was done and when finished he handed it all over to the courier, Airport Harry, who took it straight off to customs."

"So, what's the problem?"

"This Ramalho? He's too secretive."

"So what d'you want me to do?"

Golda breathed deeply. "Better than most, I know when something's not Kosher."

Cooper pondered. "Tell you what, call our lab contact man in L.A. ask if our dailies are arriving there okay? He'll still be there."

Golda nodded in the affirmative. "Copy that."

SCENE 17. TAKE 2.

In her night clothes, Susan was sitting on the bed leaning against the headboard, the script resting on her hunched-up thighs, she marking indelibly on her memory all of tomorrow's scenes.

Finally, she closed the text, pondering what Cooper might have said to the make-up woman. She put it out of her mind as she checked the bedside clock, put a match to the mosquito coil and once it was smoking, extinguished the light and slid beneath the cover.

And froze.

Something. Something was there.

Petrified, Susan did not dare move for fear of provoking whatever *it* was. But the sense of self-preservation told her she had to do something. Finding some comfort in so doing, she spoke aloud. "Now, Susan, you can't . . ." She remembered *it*. So as not to disturb *it*, she whispered. "You can't stay here forever, supine and rigid, until daylight." She swallowed hard. "Think, girl, think straight." She fought the impulse to jerk-away her foot, as *it* brushed against her. "Oh, God," she whimpered. "I know I should have taken Victor's call, I know that now, but, please, please help me, *please!*"

Ever so gently, Susan slid up the bed, outstretching an arm warily. Her hand found the base of the lamp and raised fingers, slowly. To snap on the light switch. As light appeared, with her other hand she flung-back the bedclothes, revealing a snake about twelve inches long, slithering towards her.

Susan screamed, and screamed, uncontrollably and unashamedly.

Above the noise of the rickety elevator Roberts heard the screams. He ran along the corridor and found the room from where emanated the howls. He lunged against the door, on the second attempt the plywood giving way.

Frozen with fear, Susan was on the bed, unable to take her eyes off the reptile. Seeing the parasol, Roberts grabbed it and smashed it down on the head of the snake.

An under-manager appeared in the open doorway. Roberts scooped up the snake and handed all to the man. "God for Harry, England, and Saint George."

With a bemused and hesitant look, the man took the parasol, the snake, and departed.

Roberts sat on the bed, putting around her a comforting arm, remaining thus until the sobbing subsided. He gave her a handkerchief. "D'you want me to get you another room, until this one's been checked?"

After a long hard blow, she spoke. "I don't want to be on my own, not now. Where are you?"

Roberts look puzzled.

"Your room number?"

"Oh, eh, two three seven."

Susan picked up the bedside phone. "Hi. This is Susan Chase. The usual six A.M. call please, but to room two three seven, got that? Yes, Two. Three. Seven. *Obrigado*."

SCENE 18. TAKE 1.

Twenty-two-thirty Santa Mosqueiro time, seventeen-thirty Los Angeles time. The offices were deserted, except for a vacuum cleaner-wielding janitor. And Cooper.

And rain. Incessant, teeming, pounding rain. It hit the roof like bullets.

It dripped from the ceiling, it streamed down the windows, both inside and out while lightning flickered across the tropical night sky.

With the remains of a cold hamburger in front of him, Cooper made the daily schedule report to Seidelman. "It just keeps coming down. We've shot nothing since lunchtime." Cooper paused, listening. "Do? Sit it out, what else *can* we do?" Another pause. "We've used up the weather cover." Cooper listened some more. "Don, Don, I know all that, and yes, I know we're six days behind but no, I don't know any way of swinging it as an insurance claim. I wish I did." Cooper nodded. "Right. Bye." He put down the phone and swiveled his chair, to look out at the unabating rain, the unremitting rain, while nibbling on a lump of hamburger. He looked at 'dinner.' He thought it resembled pumice and figured it tasted about the same. His reverie was interrupted.

"James, James, you 'ere!?"

Cooper heard the heavy footfall and unmistakable voice of his construction coordinator. "Syd? In here."

As best he could, Walton rushed into the office and collapsed into a chair. He raised a restraining hand while regaining his breath.

"What's up?"

"The fort set!" Walton gestured to the window. "This bloody storm? Lightning! Sodding tree right across the set." Walton rammed a fist into the palm of his hand. "Wallop!"

Daybreak.

Revealing a mass of tangled and twisted steel scaffolding, smashed scenic flats and broken, splintered wood, under the weight of a huge mahogany tree. The glum trio of Cooper, Roberts and Walton surveyed the devastation. Cooper looked to Walton. "Syd, how long?"

Walton exhaled loudly. "With overtime, it's taken nine six-day weeks to build."

"How. Long?"

Walton looked Cooper directly in the eye. "James, it's gotta be cleared first." He gestured to the debris. "I'd 'ave to 'ave more men!"

"Done."

Both Roberts and Walton were flabbergasted. "From where?" asked Roberts. "And how come we couldn't have these men the other day?"

"Because the other day is just that, and today, is today, and now . . ." An index finger tapped Cooper's nose. "Now, it's become an insurance claim which gives me some elbow room. So Syd, I repeat. How long?"

"Well, clear the damage first but with extra men." He looked at Roberts. "Seven weeks?" Roberts nodded the affirmative.

Cooper spoke to Roberts. "Before this disaster is cleared, you need to take numerous polaroids of it from *all* angles, a.s.a.p. I'll need them to back-up the claim."

"Sure."

Cooper paced, clenched hand stroking mouth. "And I'm going to have to change the schedule, which'll mean switching around locations."

"Any idea which?"

Looking at Roberts, Cooper halted. "Well, an obvious one to bring forward is the sequence where Redmayne and Ruth are trekking. No build, just pampas?"

"I haven't even thought about that one yet."

"Then I suggest you do, and quickly. And, *find* it even more quickly!"

Observed by the three men, a chauffeur-driven car arrived, out of which stepped Susan Chase. Roberts couldn't take his eyes off her. He ran over to Susan. They embraced, and then kissed.

Walton was shaking his head. "He ought to keep his bleeding mind on the job."

Cooper smiled. "I'd say he is, Syd. Definitely."

Production accountant Con Griffith was like all of the many such people with whom Cooper had worked. Industrious, focused, usually loyal but lacking the light and humorous touch. Griffith shook his head at the plethora of colored cardboard strips spread over Cooper's desk.

"James my son, you need to get up to date, you should be computerized."

"Does it hurt?" Cooper juggled the strips in rescheduling, watched by a fascinated Griffith as he slotted them into the production board.

"James, the six days we're over?"

"What about them?"

"How do I cost them?"

"You don't. I'll include them with the insurance claim. A few . . ." Cooper leaned back, rotating a hand. "Revised production reports and no one will ever be any the wiser, especially the insurers."

Frowning, Griffith studied his associate. "I almost think you're serious?"

Griffith was the recipient of one of those bland looks of Cooper. "Has Roberts been given a float?"

"Sure. I gave him dollars U.S. Okay?"

Cooper was back at the board. "Fine." Golda placed some papers on his desk. "How's Roberts getting to the mountains?" asked Cooper. "And when?"

Folding her arms, Golda recited the itinerary. "Depart zero-seven hundred, light plane, insurers made aware, everything covered."

"Good. But call the charter company. Tell them to make sure their pilot remembers to stay *this* bloody side of the border."

"Copy that." She raised a finger to Cooper. "Oh and James, *you* remember. Susan Chase goes into hiatus tomorrow. For three weeks."

He looked up. "Right. Then do a memo to Con here, re: her per diem, hotel suite and insurance, okay?" Golda nodded. "I presume she's going home?"

"She's on tonight's L.A. flight, via Sao Paulo. Insurers informed."

SCENE 19. TAKE 5.

The next morning. Cooper's office.

"No show!" An unshaven Carlo, with bloodshot eyes. "She was a *no-show*. I wait until the flight close. I watch the aircraft take off." He shook his head in dismay. "But no Susan Chase, no sign of her."

Golda stood behind the seated Cooper. "And you?" she asked slowly.

"You never left the airport?"

"No, never. I moved inside and out, always checking, but never left."

"You've called the hotel?" Asked Cooper.

"Of course. But they say she checked out last night."

Cooper rubbed his face with dry hands. "Christ, I hope she paid all of her incidentals, her personal bill."

"James!" Golda scowled. "Keep a bloody sense of proportion here!" She turned to Carlo. "What about her driver?"

"I called Luis. After he dropped her from the location, she said she would not want him any more that evening."

Cooper looked distraught. "You checked the other airlines?"

"Every one." Carlo shook his head. "*Nada.*"

Locked in thought, Cooper combed fingers slowly through his hair. "Did Roberts get away this morning?"

"Presumably."

Cooper swiveled through one-hundred-and-eighty degrees, to face her directly and speaking quietly. "Golda, Don't presume? Check!" She moved quickly, with Cooper shouting after her. "And see if anyone else was with him."

She turned back. "Like who?"

"Like Susan Chase!"

SCENE 20. TAKE 5.

Above the rain forest. The pampas of the foothills of the Sierra.

Roberts was taking a series of panning stills when suddenly his pan stopped. Lowering the camera, he raised binoculars, letting them drop on to his chest, and then squinting, knowing that through the camera's viewfinder something had caught his eye. "What the . . . ?" Adjusting the eyepiece, with the 400mm lens mounted and using the uni-pod for steadiness, he repeated his pan. And there it was. A building, from which could be discerned rising smoke, the fullness of the building being hidden by the foliage. "Wonders never cease." He finished shooting his stills and made his way back to the jeep.

"I heard talking. Was it you?" asked Susan, sitting in the front passenger seat.

"Bang in the middle of a great set up, a building of some sort, probably some herdsman's hut." He held her hand. "But nothing that can't be treed out, so's Abel will never know it's there."

Susan frowned. "Abel?"

"Our esteemed director?"

"Why *Abel*?"

"Abel Gance was a French director, a 1920s cinematic visionary."

"So?"

"So, you must see the connection of creativity?"

A beat. Then Susan burst out laughing.

"What d'you think of our illustrious director?"

Susan looked over her sunglasses. "I make it policy never to talk about a director I'm working with," said very seriously. "Although I know one thing's for sure."

"What's that?"

"Leef will never get hemorrhoids."

"What?" Robert's turn to frown. "Why ever not?"

"Because he's a perfect asshole."

Protected by anti-snake serum in the lush foliage, the observers were well-hidden, watching every move. Of Roberts and Susan.

Picking-up a map, Roberts spread it on the hood of the jeep. "Now . . . where are we?"

Susan looked into the distance. "I know where I'm supposed to be." Leaving the seat, she turned to him, as he circled a spot on the map. "Have you called her?"

Roberts spoke to the map. "She's lonely."

Susan shrugged, looking at him through darkened shades. "Mother Theresa once said the greatest of all poverty is loneliness. I was alone, terrifyingly alone." Removing the Ray-Bans, she looked him directly in the eye. "Until you *snaked* your way into my life."

The observers continued to watch, each through their own binoculars.

She asked him, point blank. "D'you love me?"

Looking up from the map, he returned her direct gaze. "Susan, it's early days?"

"So where does that leave us?"

He continued holding her look. "When at home, surrounded by wife, kids, dogs, it's a sort of claustrophobia, stifling. I crave release. The phone rings. It's a location movie. Liberation! You grab it and for what, another prison? A small room in an anonymous hotel in some far flung foreign outpost and all that you can call your own fitting into a suitcase." He turned to her. "If it's any consolation, any at all, I love being with you."

With her shoe, she stirred the dirt. "That neither answers my question nor is it the answer I'd hoped for." She continued scuffing the soil.

Noiselessly, silent hands let the foliage fall back into place.

"How many times you been married?"

Susan sighed. "Just the once." As her eyes moistened, she wished she still had on the Ray-Bans. Her voice was a little croaky. "No need to hurt more than one partner."

"Does it hurt him?"

"I'm sure it does."

"But you've never actually told him?"

"I don't have to. He knows."

Roberts moved around the jeep, and embraced her.

The observers made their move. All holding automatic weapons, Cirla, Topete, plus two other men, were almost on the couple when Roberts sensed something. He turned. The presence of the quartet took them totally by surprise. Roberts fumbled for what little Portuguese he spoke. "Eh, eh . . . *Boa* . . . *Boa tarde.*"

Pointing silently at the camera, Cirla gestured with fingers-to-palm for the Nikon. Roberts made not a move. Cirla spoke to Topete, who stepped forward and bludgeoned Roberts with the butt of his Magnum .357. Roberts fell. The camera dropped from his open hand into that of Topete, it being passed to Cirla, who was rifling through the contents of Roberts' bag. Gesturing Topete to collect the map and the bag, finally Cirla acknowledged Susan, grabbing an arm and almost dragging her alongside him. To the two parked vehicles, a Range Rover and a Toyota Land Cruiser.

In the front seat with Cirla behind her, Susan tried to comprehend it all. Who are they? Rebels, insurgents? But if so, what is this favored chariot of Beverly Hills doing in the middle of the rain forest?

With the Range Rover leading, they drove into the compound, parking by the hacienda. Nobody took any notice of the visitors.

Arriving at a small building, Susan was ushered in by Topete, with the two other men dumping a still comatose Roberts on to a cot-type bed. They left, locking the door. Although still daylight, the room was dark, the sole illumination being a grating set high in a wall, which was the sole source of oxygen. It took Susan a couple of minutes for the eyes to adjust. The room was clean, and besides the bed, contained a small chair and a table, with on it a bowl, a pitcher, towel and soap.

She sank into the chair, putting her head in her hands. Fear had taken her beyond the relief of sobbing, and she sat motionless, staring at the stone floor, whispering. "What, dear God, what is it this time, *this* punishment?"

Slowly, Roberts came-to. Susan crouched beside the bed, facing him. "You okay?"

He shook his head, blinking. "Nothing a treble scotch wouldn't fix." He looked around the room, and then at Susan. "Other than that . . . just scared, plain shit scared."

It didn't take long to ascertain that Roberts had departed Santa Mosqueiro accompanied by Susan Chase, her luggage being found in Roberts' room. What was taking longer to discover was their actual whereabouts.

All Cooper could do was wait. And alert everybody. "Don, the moment I hear anything, *anything*, you'll be the first to know. *Ciao*." Cooper replaced the phone. "That's everybody."

"Except one, probably the most important one."

Cooper glanced at Golda. "Like who?"

"The insurers?"

The trademark Cooper fingers combing through hair, while shaking his head. "I can't . . ."

Golda was incredulous. "What! Why *ever* not?"

Cooper held her gaze, speaking *sotto voce*. "Golda, nobody authorized her to be in that plane. She was *not* covered."

Golda closed her eyes. "Oh sweet Jesus."

"So how do I deal with that?"

Before a thought could be made manifest, the door burst open to reveal a breathless Carlo, dragging behind him a shortish Imperian man in his early forties, dressed in a smart quasi-military uniform.

Cooper looked at the man, then to Carlo. "Who's he?"

"The pilot. He fly them."

Like a human cannon ball, Cooper sprang from his desk, to a large-scale wall-map. "*Onde*? Show me! Where'd he drop them?"

Having been questioned by Carlo, the man pointed to a small town. "*Aqui.*"

Cooper leaned against his desk, staring at the map. "Right on the Colombian border. And there were definitely two of them, a man *and* a woman?"

Carlo replied. "Yes, and Roberts says to him, Miguel." He pointed to the pilot. "To pick them up, same place, sixteen-hundred hours tomorrow. Oh, and he says they rent a jeep."

Cooper meditated, and then became his positive self, nodding at the pilot. "Ask him if there's a charter standby rate?"

Carlo did as asked. "He says fifty-five percent of normal daily rate."

"Right, we keep Miguel here on standby full-time, in case anything breaks." Cooper studied the map again, while addressing Carlo. "We need more help, like maybe your future father-in-law."

"I thought you don't like Mauricio. Or, his friends?"

"We *have* to find them! And yes, Carlo, I'm sure this time the cost will be much more than just a dinner?"

Carlo grinned. "Much more."

"Now, first light tomorrow, you fly up there with . . ." Cooper indicated the pilot. "Miguel. Golda will give you photos of Susan to pass around and when you track them down, you call me, *pronto!*"

Carlo glanced at the map. "You know, James, it *is* bandit country?"

"Then it's just like Santa Mosqueiro, right? So no problem for you? Added to which, your jungle combat training will be invaluable?"

"James, I am serious. This is where they grow the coca. It is not small time farmers but Cartel. International, Mafioso. Totally organized, huge operation. Believe me, I know." He pointed to the map. "I know that area better than anyone, even the Xingu."

"Then you shouldn't have much trouble finding them?"

In the already dimly-lit operations room, the light level fluctuated constantly. Both Susan and Roberts found it tiring on the eyes.

Dressed as usual *à la* Rodeo Drive casual, Rubio sat at a large desk, with Cirla beside him. The two men gave their sole attention to the belongings of Susan, and Roberts. Finally, Rubio turned around, to where sat Susan and Roberts, and held high her passport. "*Americano?*"

Susan replied, barely above a whisper. "*Si.*" She indicated Roberts. "*Inglês.*"

Rubio stared at Roberts, and then chuckled. "Maybe he meet his Waterloo?"

At hearing English, both Susan and Roberts expressed surprise.

"Why are you here and what are you looking for?"

Roberts stuttered a reply. "I . . . we . . . we're looking for locations, for a film, a movie—"

"We're lost", said Susan. "It's that plain and simple. We are lost."

Rubio flicked the pages of the passport. "And you, who are you?"

Susan looked at him directly. "I am actress, a movie actress."

"You are famous?"

Actor ego usurped feminine fear. "Certainly I am well known."

Rubio studied the passport. "Susan Finney?" He shrugged.

Roberts spoke. "That's not her real name."

Rubio rounded on Roberts. "Then is it a *false* name?" He shook the passport above his head. "And this? This is a *false* passport?"

"No, no!" Palpable was Susan's agitation. "You don't understand. The passport's genuine but it's in my *married* name. My acting name is Susan Chase, my name *before* I was married?"

Roberts pointed to the passport. "Many actors change their name. Like John Wayne?"

"Oh, I can't wait." Rubio pointed to Cirla. "Especially as he was Roberto's hero!"

"Marion Mitchell Morrison", said Roberts, slowly. "Wayne's real name."

Added Susan. "Marilyn Monroe? Norma Jeane Mortenson."

Slowly, Rubio regarded the two of them, frowning. "As such mines of information then tell me this." He looked at Susan. "You have a passport." And then to Roberts. "But he doesn't. Why?"

"We didn't plan on leaving Imperio."

A radio crackled into life. Rubio was distracted by a Spanish-speaking voice, asking when could be expected the next shipment. Moving to the set, Cirla reduced the volume, but not before Susan had understood the message. Watched by Rubio.

"*Usted habla Espanol?*"

Susan nodded. "Can't get domestic help in California without it." Realizing her blunder, the strain proved too much. Susan broke-down, talking between deep sobs. "We really are lost, you know, just plain lost . . ." She looked at Rubio. "And hungry."

Rubio smiled. "Of course. And we must make arrangements for your return."

Rubio waited until they had left before speakimg to Cirla. "These movie people! They think they're modern day conquistadors, free to roam at will. Well, they aren't, and they can't! They put this whole operation at risk. Brainless gringos!" He looked long at Cirla. "Burn their clothes and then have Pepe do the rest. He knows what to do and how to handle it."

A key turned in the lock. They expected food, but the guard carried not a tray but a Luger PO5 automatic. It was pointed directly at Roberts. "*Pantalones.*"

Roberts hesitated.

"He wants your pants . . . trousers." Irritably, he waved the gun. "If I were you . . ." Roberts removed his khaki drill pants, to have them snatched by the guard.

"Zapatas."

"Shoes." Taken off, and handed-over.

"*Camisa.*" Handing over his shirt, Roberts was clothed solely in his underpants.

The guard looked at Susan. "*Tambien.*"

She hesitated. She gestured to the guard to turn his back. Only when he'd done so did she undress. Raising her feet, she slipped-off each shoe. She removed her slacks, placing them on the guard's shoulder and likewise her blouse, on his other shoulder. As he turned, instinctively Susan folded arms across her breasts, looking at him defiantly. She was dressed now only in a bra, and pants.

The guard left. Bolting the door.

They looked at each other in total silence, not knowing what to say. Which is when they heard the drone of engines, the unmistakable sound of aircraft engines.

Hurriedly pushing the table against the wall and under the grating, Roberts leapt up.

"Anything?"

"It's difficult to see against the brightness of the landing lights but . . . it's an old DC-3."

"Any markings?"

"Wait. Damn!" Roberts stepped off the table. "The lights were killed before I could tell." He held her close to him.

She spoke into his chest. "Dear God. Will we ever get out of this?"

Roberts did his best to be reassuring. "Of course we will."

She pulled away. "Then where's the goddam cavalry?"

"Susan. Someone, somewhere, is looking for us."

Finding a tissue, she blew her nose. "Raymond, at times there's about you a disturbing naivety." She leaned against the table. "Think on this. If they intend to return us, why not now, when it's dark, and when we can't recognize anywhere or any thing?"

Roberts shrugged. "No night-time flying facilities?"

"Jesus, Ray! You've just seen a plane land. In the dark! To guide it down, were there dozens of peons holding flaming torches?"

He frowned. "They'd hardly use the DC-3 for us."

"They don't have to!" She spoke rapidly, almost a whisper. "When we arrived you were still out of it, but *I* saw a light plane. So, if they really mean to return us, why not use that? Now!"

Roberts looked blank. "Return? Maybe. But I wonder. In what state?"

SCENE 21. TAKE 3.

El Gran Hotel do Amazonas. In what had become known at that precise moment as 'The Seidelman Suite' was taking place a crisis meeting.

Hands behind him, Tonnini stood looking out at the big river, his back to the audience. "How much more she have to shoot?"

"We're just about under halfway through her schedule," replied Cooper.

Tonnini nodded. "Design work?"

"Completed."

"So he no loss?"

Even Seidelman was outraged. "Franco!"

Tonnini continued gazing out of the window. "I mean no offense." Turning, he shrugged. " I just try to be realistic."

A phone rang, to be grabbed by Golda. "Carlo? Any news?"

Cooper gestured impatiently for the phone to be passed to him. "What?"

"Nothing. The only person who saw them is the guy who rent them the jeep. Oh, and I check with both the *Federales* and the *Rurales*. No accidents reported."

Everybody was looking intently at Cooper. Tonnini, Seidelman, Golda, Belem, and, Mauricio Para.

"Carlo, check the whole area, search!"

"Search? James, you've flown over the jungle. All you see is the canopy of trees, nothing underneath. All I've got is a fixed wing. I need a helicopter!"

"Okay, you're the Santa Mosqueiro man. Where do I find a bloody chopper?"

"Ask Hector?"

Sighing deeply, Cooper looked at his U.P.M. "Where can we get a helicopter, immediately? Money no object—"

"Now hold on, Cooper!" interrupted Seidelman.

"Don, he right!"

Belem looked at Cooper. "None based here." Belem shrugged. "I don't know?"

Cooper hung his head in his hands.

Tonnini gestured to Mauricio Para. "Is that not why he here?"

"Carlo, hang on a minute."

Digesting what was being asked of him by Belem and nodding occasionally, Para looked at Tonnini, and then at Seidelman and rose, taking the phone from Cooper. In Portuguese. "Carlo? Mauricio. Listen, listen carefully . . ." Para paused, inclined his head and eyed Tonnini, while gesturing to Belem with a forefinger over his shoulder. "*Hector. Aqui*" Putting the phone to his chest, Para whispered into the ear of the production manager.

Nodding understanding, Belem addressed the group. "Senor Para . . . Mauricio? He say to help the movie you give him a screen credit, like, you know, *the producers wish to thank Mauricio Para*?" With a pleading gaze, Hector scanned the group.

Of the stunned assembly, Tonnini was the first to react. "He get the credit. But," he nodded to Para, "only if they found alive."

Bowing slightly to Tonnini, Para resumed the call in Portuguese. "Carlo, call the station, give your number to my secretary. This is not the time nor the place for me to speak. I will call you, but wait. It may be in thirty minutes or five hours. But wait, understand?" He handed back the phone to Cooper, speaking to Belem. "Tell them I have to leave. To see what I can do." Para bowed and then departed.

Cooper was crestfallen. He turned to Belem. "Hector?"

"He'll do whatever he can to get them found."

Cooper felt totally deflated. He eyed Golda. "Her husband?"

"Lied through my teeth. Said we needed to hold her a couple of more days for rushes clearance."

"Good girl."

Seidelman shot Cooper a very meaningful glance. "You sure the insurance people will buy our story, *your* story?"

Cooper swallowed hard. Golda came to his rescue. "I told them she'd be flying to L.A., for which we needed additional cover, and in the same call I put Roberts on cover for his trip, also covering Carlo and allowing for an A.N. Other, in case James went along." Golda looked around her. "Susan Chase could be that A.N.Other?"

The ever-skeptical Seidelman. "How do we explain the leading actress being on a location scout?"

Cooper was on the defensive. "Don, the main point is Golda requested additional cover. Susan became that cover. The reason is secondary?"

"Christ', said Seidelman. "My guts feel like Eddie Robinson's stomach in *Double Indemnity.*"

Tonnini poured himself some mineral water, indicating to Seidelman the meeting was over. As the gathered dispersed, Tonnini spoke. "James, you stay."

Left was Tonnini, Seidelman and Cooper.

Examine finger-nails time. "Why you lie to me?" Tonnini looked up, from cuticles to Cooper.

Cooper was surprised. "Me? Lie to *you*? When?"

"When I ask you about drugs gangs? You say *none*, remember?"

Cooper held elbows close to his outstretched arms. "Franco, at the time I wasn't aware—"

"You were! Your location scout? That landing strip? You knew! So why you no tell me then, eh? Why I have to find out *my* way?"

Cooper was stunned. Sheepishly, he looked at Tonnini. "I felt a loyalty to the movie. I didn't want to see it canceled."

"James," Seidelmn interjected. "All of us, us three, our loyalty is always to the movie, but with loyalty there must be mutual trust? No lies?" Seidelman pointed at Tonnini. "Your first loyalty's to him, to Franco."

Both Tonnni and Seidelman stared at him. Trust? Looking from one to the other, Cooper reckoned he might just as well be looking at Benito Mussolini and Moshe Dayan. "I'm sorry, very sorry. It won't happen again."

Tonnini smiled. "You right, it won't." He looked again at Cooper. "The genius director? He still behind schedule?"

Cooper nodded. "There are dailies this evening."

"See you there, James."

As Cooper left the room, Seidelman turned to Tonnini. "Fire him?"

"An' that find us Susan Chase?"

Cooper slunk into his office. To be greeted by Golda with an outstretched hand clasping a glass of whisky. "Figured you might just need this. Glass warmed, just the way you like it."

"Golda, you're a gem." Cooper swallowed the Scotch. "Come on, I'll buy you lunch."

"To have it deducted from my per diem?"

"No, no way. This one's on me. My treat. You deserve it."

Para spoke to his chauffeur. "Pedro, just drive anywhere, anywhere around the city. I need some thinking time."

"*Si, sênhor.*" The divider was closed once more.

Para fumbled for a piece of paper. Reading from it, he dialed. "Carlo? Mauricio. You speak Spanish?"

"*Si.*"

"I want you to make one call. Get plenty of change as it's a foreign number. Once through, the message is simple. All you say, in Spanish, is . . . call the car."

"Call the car. In Spanish."

"That's it. Here's the number." Para spoke it.

Carlo repeated it. "Consider it done."

"Oh, and Carlo. Destroy the number after the message. *Ciao.*"

Pedro drove alongside the river, knowing of Para's love for it. Which is when the phone rang.

"I am calling the car." It was Rubio.

"Two people have gone missing from the movie, the leading lady and some important technician. Is it possible they could be in your area?"

"Anything's possible."

Para sat forward. "Surprise me."

"They're safe. And sound."

Para nodded. "There?"

"Here."

"How come?"

"Uninvited."

"And back in Santa Mosqueiro, when?"

"Whenever."

"When?"

Rubio snorted. "Mauricio, we don't need the censor or the movie, anymore."

"Oh?"

"We've recruited new pilots, and, their aircraft."

"Antonio, we can't suddenly withdraw the censor. It would arouse too much suspicion. So I ask again. *When*?"

"Certain arrangements have to be made."

"Like, what?" Asked with an edge to the Para voice.

"Mauricio, these people must be taught a lesson once and for all. Twice they have blundered into our plant, twice they've put at risk the whole operation. Twice! And twice is two times *too* many. Jesus, next thing we know, they'll be running bus tours up here!"

His reply, Para chose carefully. "Antonio, if I hear you correctly, I think you are making a mistake, and a big one at that. A point can be made forcefully without resorting to extremes, and I think your emotions may be clouding your better judgment." Para lit a cigarette. "Remember, she is an American citizen, and if something drastic should befall her, the U.S. administration, any, will act. I'm sure it wouldn't take too long for their Special Services to find you, especially if they brought to bear some pressure on Larsen, our one-time pilot, now in U.S. custody. And another reminder. The man? He's a Brit."

Rubio chuckled. "So?"

Ash was knocked into a limo ashtray. "So, nowadays the lion's roar may have been muted and there are many knots in its tail, but Leo has been noted to snap of late."

"Like when?"

"The Malvinas?"

Rubio laughed. "Their last hurrah! Besides, Thatcher's in trouble."

"But they still have the S.A.S." Para stubbed out his cigarette. "And, their   pride." Para paused, to let register his point. "Antonio, one impulsive move by you could jeopardize everything, *everything* we've worked so hard to create." He resorted to gentle, reasoned persuasion. "Return the two gringos in one piece and everybody will be so ecstatic they won't be the least interested, nor care, where the couple has been. Plus, you have the means of ensuring they don't remember anything anyway, right? *Ciao*." Para hit the 'end' key, and then re-dialed. The Seidelman Suite. "Hector?

"*Si*. Mauricio?"

"Tell your people things . . . things have advanced. I expect more definite news by tomorrow, latest." Replacing the phone, Para spoke on the intercom. "Pedro, the Yacht Club. I need some good company and a long drink."

SCENE 22. TAKE 1.

In the make-shift viewing theatre the house lights illuminated. Present were six people. Tonnini, Seidelman, Leef, Cooper, continuity girl Elaine Buck, the editor Ian Marshall, and his assistant, Pat Corcoran.

Tonnini stood and addressed Leef, directly. "Anthony, when I suggest you as director of *Redmayne West*, my right arm," He pointed at Seidelman. "Don, he say you could no direct traffic up a one way street." Tonnini gestured to the screen. "An' you know what? He right! It crap, pure crap! You should be ashamed to take the money, *my* money!"

Leef was calm personified. "Franco, you're a businessman. Me? I'm a voyeur, a creator. Film is like a Lego set. The director leaves room for other elements to fall precision-like into place." He continued, somewhat pedantically. "It's a process known as . . . editing."

Without knocking, Belem burst into the room. "James, everybody, quick! In here!" Belem rushed out, followed by Cooper, Seidelman and Tonnini. They were confronted by two large wooden crates, marked 'Tartar Con Cuidado'. Studying the crates, and noticing small vents for air, Cooper shouted at Belem. "Hector, open them. Quickly!"

Belem nodded to the peon beside him. Placing a chisel under a lid, the peon hit hard. After three hammer blows, the lid was prised loose and lifted away. To reveal a comatose Raymond Roberts, clad only in his underpants, with sweat running off him in rivulets. Cooper grabbed the peon's tools and attacked frenziedly the other crate, shouting as he did so. "Hector! A doctor and an ambulance, *rapido!*" He had the crate open in seconds. Cooper flung off the lid to have confirmed his worst fears. Inside, and like Roberts, dressed only in underwear and perspiring profusely, crouched Susan Chase. Kneeling, Cooper felt her pulse.

"She alive?" Tonnini asked, solicitously.

"She's breathing." Cooper cradled his hands to support Susan's head.

Slowly, ever so slowly, her eyes opened, she turning her head left-to-right, eyes flickering constantly in the unaccustomed light. With some difficulty she focused and re-focused, a recognizable image of Cooper registering in her gaze. Susan smiled, a pained smile. "Rubenstein." She whispered, hoarsely. "We really must discuss the travel clause in my contract?" Which is when she lost consciousness.

Belem introduced their visitor. "This is Dr.Soares. He studied at U.S.C. Medical School."

Tonnini nodded. "You examine *Signorina Chase*, Susan, thoroughly?"

"Thoroughly."

Tonnini held open a hand. "How I put this . . . she, eh, she no been . . . molested?"

Soares shook his head. "Physically? No."

Gesticulating, Tonnini looked to Seidelman, who came to his rescue "Doctor, what Mr. Tonnini means is. Has she been molested *sexually*?"

"No." He looked directly at Tonnini. "No. But. She is in a state of catatonic shock. As soon as he is fit to travel, the man should be sent home immediately, to begin withdrawal treatment, and I suggest for each of them, an air ambulance. In time, he will recover."

"Dottore. Signorina Chase?"

Soares turned to Tonnini, briefly. "She is exhausted. Physically, emotionally and mentally. She needs rest." He turned his gaze to everybody, in turn. "She needs rest. Complete and total . . . rest."

"How much rest?" Tonnini questioned, quietly but emphatically.

"However much it takes."

Cooper looked up. "Then her recuperation is sort of . . . open-ended, indefinable?"

"Precisely."

Seidelman shifted in his chair. "Then in your professional opinion doctor, when might she be able to resume work?"

With eyebrows raised, Dr.Soares tilted his head. "Work?" Said as if the mere mention of the word would invoke the wrath of some unseen power. Again he eyed everybody, his gaze coming to rest on Seidelman. "Work? In *my* opinion, sir? Maybe never. Another doctor may say different, but for your movie? You can forget Miss Chase."

Tonnini stood, bowing slightly. *"Grazie, Dottore. Ciao."* They shook hands and escorted by Golda, the doctor left.

Seidelman leaned all of his weight on an arm of his chair, staring at Cooper, with his other arm the accuser. "How many times did Franco ask you about drugs people in this area?" Cooper said nothing, with his own gaze holding Seidelman's stare. "How many goddam times?"

Tonnini spoke matter-of-factly. "Don, is no the time for recrimination, argument." Tonnini turned to the group. "Is the time to decide, to decide what we do, and is only one question. Do we abort, or we carry on?" He sat down.

Silently, each one thought their thoughts. Leef was the first to speak.

"Carry on? Carry on? Sounds like one of those dreadful Pinewood movies of the sixties. So what's this to be? *Carry On Redmayne?*" He looked around him, as if condescending to a bunch of congenital idiots. "You've all just seen the dailies, the Susan Chase character is well and truly established, but now, now we're told we've lost Susan Chase, possibly for *ever!*" He looked at Tonnini. "Carry on? How?"

Tonnini appeared to evaluate all that had been said by Leef. He spoke quietly. "How?" He shrugged. "Recast? Reshoot? Re-Edit? Rewrite? Retitle?" He looked at Leef, his voice rising. "Re-anything!" Studying his nails, Tonnini spoke without looking up. "Let I.L.M. rotoscope her out." He looked over to an increasingly heated Leef. "Is only film."

"Franco, I signed on to direct Susan Chase, Su-San Chase, in *Redmayne West!*"

"And you did direct Susan Chase in *Redmayne West.*" Seidelman nodded. "Until now."

Leef looked daggers at Seidelman. "I don't recall there being a stop-date on her services?"

Tonnini felt it was time for arbitration, reconciliation. "Anthony, we—"

"No!" Leef stamped a foot. "My contract is crystal clear, specifying—" He raised a pointed finger. "Specifying the actors I direct in the roles of Redmayne and Ruth." He eyed Seidelman. "Kurt Greene and, Susan Chase. *Su-san Chase!*"

While continued this war of words, Elaine and the two editors wished the ground would open up and swallow them. Cooper was enjoying it.

Seidelman's reply was measured and unemotional. "Read further into your contract Anthony, and you'll find a *force majeure* clause, equally crystal clear."

"And I bet I know what I won't find!" By now, Leef was trembling. "I won't find a codicil stating a Jane Doe will play the part of Ruth, eh?"

"So?" Seidelman sat with folded arms. "They said the Third Reich would last a thousand years."

"What the hell's that mean?"

Tonnini stared at Leef. "It mean, Anthony, that situations? They a change."

He looked around the room. Tonnini, Seidelman, Cooper, all staring at him, the rest studying intently the floor. "Really?" He collected his belongings and on reaching the door, turned around. "Then they can bloody well change without me!" He stormed out.

Tonnini looked askance at the open door and then turned to Seidelman. "What a codicil? A small fish?"

Golda re-entered, nodding towards the open doorway. "Was it something I said? Or did Anthony just . . . *Leef*?" It broke the ice, with everyone laughing, including Seidelman and Tonnini, the latter pouring himself some more mineral water.

"Is my fault Susan Chase half dead?" He took a long drink. "With most actors you never notice the difference?" He pointed to Marshall. "You the editor, yes?" Marshall nodded. "What you think?"

Before Marshall could answer, Seidelman spoke. "Queen's don't abdicate. He'll be back."

"Don, Leef ? He fire himself." Tonnini gestured to the group. "In front of witnesses? As far as I concerned, Leef is deader than the Susan Chase character." He turned again to Marshall. "So? How the stuff look, overall?"

"Overall? Eh. *Leef* green."

More group laughter. Tonnini exploded. "How many more these fucking Leef jokes I have to hear?" He eyed them all in turn. "Now, let us get off our chest any more Leef jokes, *capis*?"

Asked by a serious Cooper. "So, Franco, we turnover a new *Leef*?"

An equally po-faced Seidelman. "James, you heard Franco. *Leef* the jokes out!"

Tonnini was not amused. "I try to make a plan here. No jokes!" Once again he spoke to Marshall. "Can anything be salvaged?"

Marshall nodded, vigorously. "In trying to make his own life easier, Leef has done you a favor by shooting everything in script order."

"Which," Cooper interjected, "Accounts for at least four of our six overage days." He looked at the editor. "Ian, and all from roughly the first quarter of the script, the first forty odd pages?'" Marshall nodded.

Tonnini looked directly at Seidelman. "Is a mistake to lose the Susan Chase footage." An impish smile crossed his face. "Beside, her recent ordeal? The trauma? We could use it as a great marketing tool?"

Hands clasped behind his neck, Cooper was looking at nothing while thinking out loud. "Maybe we'd only need to write one new sequence?" Sitting upright, he addressed nobody and everybody. "The Ruth character is killed by whatever means we feel dramatically appropropriate . . . introduce a new woman companion, perhaps an indigenous Indian?" He looked around him. "No big deal? And maybe cast a Brasilian. Cheaper?"

Tonnini looked at Cooper with renewed interest.

Seidelman was his usual cautious self. "A plan James, yes, but. And it's a big *but*. How long to find this phantom actress plus what's the likelihood of her measurements, wardrobe wise, being *exactly* the same as Susan Chase's, so wardrobe time and costs have to be factored in?"

"And," chipped in accountant Con Griffith. "Insurance doesn't cover our director walking, plus the time to find a replacement and do a deal? And we all know D.G.A. policy is against a guild member replacing another member on an existing shoot?"

Tonnini grinned. "But we *do* have insurance. His fee? We pay the agent Resnick *his* full commission, but penalize Leef personally. An' with *his* full commission, the agent no deal the play-or-pay card?"

"Plus," added Cooper, "we can legitimately charge him, Leef, for the costs to the production of his contraband."

Golda spoke. "May I add something, to the fallen *Leef*?" More laughter, even from Tonnini. "When I joined this production . . ." She pointed to Cooper. "James told me that as crew and cast arrive, they surrender their return air ticket in exchange for their work permit, which they've been told must be kept on them at all times."

Seideleman frowned. "Golda, so?"

"So, Mr. Leef's return air ticket is in the hotel safe. It's a long walk from here to Los Angeles." She looked around. "And that's presuming he can jump the Panama Canal?"

Everybody laughed. Tonnini stood. Nodding to Seidelman, he indicated the bathroom. "Don?" Tonnini addressed the group. "*Scusi*. But wait here."

In the cavernous bathroom, Tonnini squatted on the toilet. Closing the door, Seidelman leaned against it. "What's on your mind?"

Tonnini stared at the mosaic floor. "Don, who you think know the script best, the most complete?"

"Well, the editor I guess? He's the one working on the footage."

"But who work on the script, the longest? Who break it down?"

"Cooper."

"*Si*. Cooper."

Quitting the door, Seidelman sat on the bidet. "You thinking what I think you're thinking?"

"Why not? Total familiar with the script, with the cast, the crew, the locations, an' the budget? Done quite a bit of directing plus he an' Kurt Greene also do a movie together before, an' Kurt has director approval?" Tonnini flicked at Seidelman *that* look. "You think he can do it?"

Dabbing a piece of toilet paper to his perspiring brow, Seidelman nodded. "I've always thought of human beings as being like sponges, and if you've been around movies as long as Cooper has, you must've soaked up a lot, an awful lot. I don't like him, but yes. He can do it."

Wriggling out of their respective nests, the two men stood. "It settled?" Seidelman nodded. "*Si*."

"Okay, we tell the others. But no *The Reporter* or *Daily Variety*, right?"

"Right."

They re-entered the suite

Scene 23. Take 1.

"We think . . ." Seidelman glanced at Tonnini and then back at the group. "We hope. We hope we've solved the problem, so we need to talk to James here," pointing at Cooper. "Alone."

The group left. Golda addressed Seidelman. "Do you need me?"

"Not right now. But in a few minutes. I'll shout."

Golda nodded. "Copy that." And quietly closed the door behind her.

Both Tonnini and Seidelman stared at Cooper. "Now what? What's the new charge?"

"No charge." Tonnini gestured to Seidelman. "A suggestion."

"I'm listening."

"How about you taking over the directing of *Redmayne West*?"

Cooper was lost for words. Trying to absorb it all, Cooper looked at both men. "You're serious, I mean, you *mean* it?"

Tonnini nodded. "Serious? *Si*." He stared at Cooper. "An' you?"

Fingers combed through the hair. "Jesus . . . But what about a line producer? I can't do both?"

"James, you know as well as Franco and me, this far in? There's no *way* a fresh line producer could get to grips with this production some six weeks into shooting, and how long would it take to find such a guy, and get visas, injections, work permits, you know, that whole enchilada?"

Cooper looked from one-to-the-other. "Can I think about it?"

Tonnini spoke. "You 'ave fifteen minutes."

Cooper laughed, heartily. "In that case. Yes! But we talk turkey first?"

Crossing to the door, Seidelman opened it. "Golda! Pad and pencil, pronto."

Golda entered. Seidelman gestured her to sit. "You're Jewish, right?" With a quizzical look, she nodded. "Everything that is about to be said here stays within the four walls of this room, *farshteyn*?"

"*Ia*."

"Right, covering everything agreed and finalized here, you will open a file marked 'Santa Mosqueiro slash T.I.P. Accord'. Once typed-up, you send it to me in L.A. under sealed envelope via courier express, *farshteyn*?"

"I understand. Do I keep a copy here?"

Seidelman nodded to Cooper. "He gets a copy." And then addressing Cooper. "What's the safest place to secure a document here?"

"Mauricio Para's office."

Tonnini interjected. "James, be serious."

"Sorry." Cooper thought a brief moment. "I guess it would have to be our bank, where the overnights end up?"

Seidelman looked to Tonnini, who nodded. "Agreed." He eyed Golda. "Ready?"

"Poised."

Seidelman leaned towards Cooper. "Here's the deal."

"D.G.A. minimum," said an emphatic Cooper.

Seidelman grinned, his arms gesturing widely. "But James, you're not *even* a member of the D.G.A.?"

It was Cooper's turn to smile. "Thereby saving T.I.P. a considerable amount of money concerning guild fringes, eh?"

Tonnini intervened. "Pay him the minimum, but no gran'father him in to DGA until a week before answer print. As James say, it reduce our fringes exposure."

"Okay, DGA minimum, payable from this day forward, until answer print."

"No. Until completion of marketing, promotion and interviews."

Seidelman glanced at Tonnini, who frowned. "Agreed."

Cooper nodded to Tonnini. "Thank you." Then back to Seidelman. "Possessory credit?"

Before Seidelman could answer, Tonnini again entered the fray. "No, James. You know as well as Don an' me, this has to go to arbitration, DGA arbitration? So nothing settled until it settled mutual, *si*?"

"Franco's right. In a case where two directors are on one project, what determines who gets the director's possessory credit will be the total amount of each director's screen time input counted within the final cut. And we all know Leef will lodge an objection to the guild."

"Then what about paid advertising?"

"Again," said Seidelman. "Dependent on a DGA arbitration decision." Cooper looked crestfallen. "James, those decisions are out of our hands?"

Sighing, Cooper nodded. "I know, I know." In turn he looked at both Tonnini and Seidelman. "Post? Done where?"

"L.A.," replied Seidelman.

"Then, once there I'd like a self-drive rental, nothing fancy as long as it has A/C, hotel of *my* choice, plus an enhanced per diem and obviously all first class entitlements."

"Okay, but subject to mutual agreement?" Seidelman looked to

Tonnini. "That cover it?" Tonnini nodded. Seidelman turned to Golda. "Type it up a.s.a.p., and let me see a copy straight away, yes?"

"Don, if post's in L.A., do we take our London-based editor there, *and* his entire crew?"

Tonnini looked directly at Cooper. "What on your mind?"

"Well, Marshall is assembling sequences here and as we proceed, obviously I'll contribute to a rough cut but once finished here in Santa Mosqueiro, the cutting copy, all of the exposed footage, trims, out-takes, both picture and sound, will be shipped to L.A., so why waste money there on an English editing crew? H.1. visas, accommodation, per diems, transport, none of which shows up on the screen? I'll edit it, and you guys get the the necessary back-up crew, picture, sound, Foley, music, ADR? All I'll need in L.A. from here is the U.K. first assistant editor."

"You're on. But how much?"

"I'll still receive my producing fee?"

"Sure," replied Seidelman. "That's contractual."

Cooper nodded. "Okay, then no charge for me editing, and Marshall can have the credit." As they started to leave, Cooper continued, "Oh, by the way, my directing fee. Payable in what currency?"

Seidelman stood in front of him. "What do we pay you in now?"

"Sterling."

"Can't." Seidelman shook his head. "As the director you're not a loan-out but are being employed directly by a U.S. corporation, so, you'll be paid accordingly in dollars American. And taxed accordingly. In dollars American, plus, Social Security contributions in dollars American." He smiled. " *Ciao.*"

They left Cooper sitting alone, pondering his fate. He called out to his production coordinator. "Golda, bring me in a legal pad, please."

A distant voice answered. "I can do better than that."

Cooper frowned at what that meant. When entered Golda with legal pad and a large V and T, with ice and slice. Handing it to him, she asked "What would you do without me?"

He smiled at her. "I'd be lost, totally lost." He raised the glass. "Cheers." He savored the cocktail. "You and I need to talk."

She looked at his glass. "Top up?"

"Why not? And get yourself one."

Decided and agreed in the conversation was that Golda would be elevated to production supervisor, with a remit to find immediately a replacement production co-ordinator. And as then it was a non-shooting rest day, Cooper would bury himself in his junior suite, re-reading the script, drawing-up shot lists.

A knock at Cooper's door. "*Entrada*."

Golda entered. "James, I apologize for the intrusion, but the promotion?"

"You're not going to chicken out on me?"

"No, no." Unusually, she appeared embarrassed. "Eh, my much appreciated elevation?" She lowered her head. "Um, more *shekels*?"

Cooper smiled. "Of course."

"And the screen credit. Production supervisor?"

"A definite yes! And Golda, don't worry. I'll square it all away with Seidelman."

She looked at him earnestly. "Our wishes come true? You, directing, me, production management?" Golda backed over to the door. "Thanks". And blew him a kiss. "Maybe Bunny was wrong about you? *Ciao*." And left.

Cooper decided there-and-then, If Seidelman wouldn't agree to a salary increase, he'd pay it himself. But. Seidelman knew her value, and, they're both Jewish.

Having written a list of his priorities, he lifted the phone and dialed. "Kurt, you busy? I wondered if you could spare me a few minutes? Great. See you shortly". Gathering together his bits-and-pieces, Cooper headed out to the villa rented for Kurt Greene.

"The usual?"

"Thanks Kurt, but easy on the ice."

As he fixed the drinks, Kurt smiled. "What's with you Limeys and ice?"

Turning around, he handed to Cooper the requisite V and T. "And, if I remember rightly Jimmer, *you* take whisky in a *warm* glass?"

"Kurt, if God had meant ice to be put in whisky, he'd have called it vodka, and besides, ever since the *Titanic* us Brits have had a problem with ice."

Kurt laughed aloud, and raised his glass. "Bottoms up!"

Responding, Cooper pondered momentarily. "Kurt, I presume you've heard?"

"Heard what? Been shacked up here all day, relaxing."

Cooper took a light sip, and swallowed hard. "Susan? Such is the effect of her ordeal, she's no longer able to continue working on the movie. Mr. Leef finds that totally unacceptable and suggests we go into hiatus. That, of course, is unacceptable equally to both Franco Tonnini *and* the insurers, especially as it's an unknown as to when Susan might be suitably fit, if . . . ever." He sighed. "Plus." He sighed, resignedly. "Leef has walked."

"Jeez, Jimmer, and I thought this was just a social call?" Kurt gulped down his drink and fixed another. "What about replacements?"

"Tonnini and Seidelman plan to recast in L.A., a.s.a.p."

"Director?"

"They . . . they've asked me to take over. But you have director approval."

"Jimmer, you don't have to ask, you've got it!" Refilling Cooper's glass, Kurt raised his. "To us!"

"To us!"

SCENE 24. TAKE 2.

Sitting atop a step-ladder, Cooper was engrossed in his notes.

Carefully, Barry Gillette sited a director's chair, the back of which was inscribed *James Cooper*.

Gillette stood-by, quietly putting tobacco into a cigarette paper, rolling it, then putting it in his mouth. The favored Zippo was ignited. The click of its closing alerted Cooper.

Smiling, Cooper looked down from his perch. "Morning, Barry."

Gillette nodded to the set. "Just like old times, eh, when you was a first A.D. and I was an assistant propman? We was always the first on the set, you and me."

Cooper smiled. "And wasn't that also the time you'd brew a great cuppa, accompanied with a nice thick slice of dripping toast?"

Gillette laughed. "Jesus, don't you forget nothin'?" He pointed to the chair. "Got this though. In the nick of bleedin' time."

Cooper spoke as he climbed down the ladder. "How come?"

"Never 'eard till late that Nero was no longer the director but you was." Gillette pointed to the perfect signwriting. "I was up all night."

"Barry." Cooper was touched, deeply. "It's perfect. And it means a lot, it really does." He turned to Gillette. "Thank you."

Gillette was abashed. "Getaway! We're old mates you and me, we go back further than Abbott and Costello, and mates look after each other, right?" He gestured to the set. "Besides, nobody deserves this more than you do."

Which is when could be heard arriving the vanguard of each day's movie-making. The trucks. Camera, grip, electrical, sound, standby, and to what Cooper referred to facetiously as the 'Armchair Army', wardrobe, hairdressing and make-up. Then the cars, carrying all the location technicians from hotel to location, an activity abhorred by producers, but as Cooper's late mother used to say, *'To make money, you have to spend money.'*

Striding towards Cooper purposefully was David Langley, the first assistant director.

Anticipating Langley's quest, Cooper called-out. "Back there, wide, on the twenty-eight."

Langley stopped dead in his tracks. "Blimey! First set-up. And before mid-day! I'll get the stand ins."

"David?"

Langley stopped in his tracks and looked at Cooper. "Guv?"

"David, no line-ups on stand ins, not before a walk thru rehearsal with the principals. But. With the stand ins watching. Once the principals and I have agreed, that's when you bring on the stand ins for lighting, moves, etcetera. Okay?"

Langley was agog. "Eh, yes, guv." He took the bull-horn slung over a shoulder. "Right, back here on the twenty-eight, that's a wide shot, so if in doubt, get yourself, your vehicle and you're stuff . . . out!" Lowering the bull-horn, he called on his radio. "Gerry, gimme the first team for a line up and walk thru, with the second eleven to watch all the moves."

Cooper handed to him a sheet of paper. "Today's shot list."

Langley handled it reverently. "Man! I haven't seen one of these since the *Magna Carta* was written. Leef thought a shot list was something used on westerns."

SCENE 25. TAKE 1.

"*Pedro! Cuidado!*"

As his beloved Mercedes 560 hit yet another pot-hole, Para wondered if it was worthwhile being a financial benefactor to the City of Santa Mosqueiro, knowing that instead of having filled lunar-sized pot holes, the councillors would be siphoning-off his munificence to fill their own pockets. With the car rocking constantly, and with some fumbling difficulty, Para managed to pick-up the phone. He tapped 'memory'.

"*Hola?*"

"The car is calling you. To say I think you did well, very well. They're in one piece, although traumitized, which is fine, no memory, no recall. And little likelihood of any more blundering by our movie friends."

Rubio sounded curious. "Mauricio, have they actually started filming again yet?"

"On a limited scale, but they never really stopped, not until they ran out of scenes to film without the American woman." He fumbled for a cigarette. "Why? Why d'you ask?"

"Do we still have Ramalho, the censor, positioned?"

"Sure." Para lit his cigarette. "Why?"

"Los Angeles. We continue shipping there."

"You told me you have new pilots? And planes?"

"We have, but why not export to both Florida *and* L.A.?"

Para thought out loud. "Bigger markets, bigger profits?"

Rubio chuckled. "Exactly. You on?"

"Was I ever off?"

"Great! Tell Ramalho to check tomorrow's bus from Valdivia. I'll alert Los Angeles. *Ciao.*"

Leaning forward to replace the phone, the car hit yet another pot hole with such force it threw out of Para's grasp the handset, which thudded to the floor. Para looked at the instrument. "Let sleeping dogs lie." An admonishing finger was pointed at it. "And don't you dare ring!"

SCENE 26. TAKE 2.

As they headed to the catering truck, Cooper spotted his director of photography Billy Richards, and camera operator Godfrey Fox.

"Gents, good morning." They turned, greeting him. "Firstly, as producer I must apologize for the turmoil surrounding this show, something which I hope to overcome. Secondly, because of that turmoil, we haven't had a chance to talk as to how I see the movie." He looked at the two men. "This isn't my first directing assignment, but it is my biggest. Billy, Godfrey, I have my own style, to which I stick rigidly, and I ask both of you to help me in that, even though it might be at odds with Leef's style."

"James," said a po-faced Billy Richards. "Leef didn't have any style, cinematic or otherwise." All three men laughed.

"Well, me? On a day-to-day shooting day? The zoom should be used only to heighten some wanted emphasis."

"James," said Fox. "A zoom can save lots of set up time, like instead of tracking?"

"Godfrey, the zoom brings the object to the audience. A tracking shot takes the audience to the object, like an arrow to a target. Cinematic?"

Richards looked at his operator. "Fair point" Fox nodded. "Any other dislikes?"

"High key lighting. I want everything shot low key, high contrast, *à la films noir*, but obviously in color. Think *Ipcress*, *The Parallax View*, *The Godfather* . . . *The Terminal Man*? Think Russell Metty, think Robert Krasker, Richard Kline, Otto Heller, Henri Decae, Alex Thomson, Gordon Willis, to name but a few."

Rubbing together his hands vigorously, Richards looked at both men. "I think I'm going to enjoy this!"

Cooper turned to Fox. "And Godfrey, I want no framing where foreheads or chins are sliced. That's TV style, and in our aspect ratio of one to two-three-five, we *aren't* a TV movie. Fully-framed, okay?"

Fox nodded, but looked at his D.P. before answering. He got the nod. "Understood."

Richards extended his hand. "James, this could be the beginning of a beautiful friendship." They shook hands, as did Cooper with Fox.

"One more thing. I don't use a Tewe. Have we an Arri 2C body on board? I prefer to use that as a viewfinder to line up with."

Irresistible. Irresistible was the aroma drifting from the catering truck. Of a fry-up. Cooper trudged over to the vehicle.

Kurt was standing in line. He opened his arms. "Hey, Frankenheimer!" They hugged.

Cooper glanced at Kurt and his third place in the queue. "Kurt, amongst other things, your stand-in is supposed to get your food for you. The leading man?"

"Jimmer, you know me? I don't go with all that British class crap."

"Mr. Greene, what can I get you?" asked the caterer.

"Wally, eh, a soft bacon roll with a filling of some small mushrooms. And the same for my buddy here, James."

"Coming up."

Kurt turned to Cooper. "Ready?"

Cooper nodded. "As ready as I'll ever be."

Kurt placed an arm on Cooper's shoulder. "Break a leg?"

Cooper grinned. "Break a leg."

Wally handed over two paper plates-full of their breakfasts, plus napkins, plastic knives and forks. Kurt looked at Cooper's plate. "How come you get baked beans ? *I'm* the frigging star!"

"But I'm the one who's worked with Wally before, and, *I'm* the reason he's here." They walked on, eating as they did so. "Kurt, I'll put in a good word for you with Wally. It'll probably cost you a still, with him and *you* in the picture." Cooper shoveled a forkful of baked beans down his gullet.

"Oh, oh." Kurt was pointing. To the chair, the back of which was inscribed, 'James Cooper', in which was sitting a uniformed man. "James, who he, a Leef agent, DGA *Stasi*?"

Hearing the approach of Kurt and Cooper, the man arose, and turned to the two men. They faced Altamiro Boscoli, Captain of Customs, Santa Mosqueiro. Unsmilingly, Boscoli offered his hand.

"*Bom dia.*"

Unsurely, Cooper returned the compliment, all the time looking at Boscoli. "*Bom dia.*" Cooper shouted. "Carlo!" Both Kurt and Boscoli flinched at Cooper's vocal volume. Cooper looked at his leading man. "Eh, Kurt . . . wardrobe?"

Kurt grinned broadly. "On my way. But. Breakfast tomorrow? Beans!"

Cooper nodded. "*Beans meanz Heinz*", as arrived a breathless Carlo. Cooper gestured to Boscoli. "You ask him here?"

While shaking his head forcefully and speaking at the same time, Carlo exchanged courtesies with Boscoli. "No, James, no!"

"Ask him. Has he not heard about what happened to Susan Chase?"

As directed, Carlo translated, in so doing putting Boscoli fully in the picture. Boscoli answered, with a questioning look. "He says, why wasn't he told? The dinner was not important. He would have sent Sênhora Chase flowers."

Cooper was touched. He bowed to Boscoli, and turned to Carlo. "Tell him, Miss Chase would have been truly moved." He looked again at Boscoli, but while talking to Carlo. "Tell Sênhor Boscoli, thanks to his personal help, we had a deal. Now, ask him how would he like to bring his wife and kids to visit the set, meet Kurt Greene and watch some filming. And then, dinner for his family at a restaurant of his choosing, with a chauffeur-driven limo at his disposal, all day, courtesy of me. All I ask of him is he must let Golda know which date suits him."

While Carlo was translating Cooper's peace offering, the director rechecked his notes. The next thing he knew he was being kissed. By Boscoli.

"*Brigade!*" He shook vigorously Cooper's hand. "*Obrigado!*" Carlo led him away. At the exact moment that could be heard the commanding tone of first A.D. David Langley.

"Showtime!"

Cooper checked his watch. Bang on eight o'clock. He felt as ever he would, ready for the challenge.

Late afternoon.

Langley again. "Check the gate! If it's okay, that's a wrap!"

Gesturing for the bull-horn, Cooper spoke to the crew. "Ladies, Gents, *Sênhoras y Sênhors . . . Obrigado*, thank you. A great start."

Kurt strolled over. "Well, somehow you managed to fumble your way through?" Hugging Cooper, he then pulled away, looking at the director. "A journeyman movie -maker. Ain't too many of those around these days? See you in the morning. *With* baked beans?"

"As we speak, being flown in specially from Pittsburgh."

"*Ciao.*" A wave, and Kurt was into his limo.

Langley approached, holding forth a walkie-talkie. "James? Golda."

Cooper took the radio. "Yo?"

"Something's come up. I need to talk to you. Alone. Can I come to your suite, about seven-thirty? I wouldn't ask if it wasn't important?"

Cooper nodded. "No problem. But over dinner. I'm famished, so why not join me?" No response. "Golda, on me!"

"Great!" was the answer. "Because I'm saving as much of my per diem as I can to buy your end-of-production present. The boxed set of *Sound of Music* videos."

"Oh, I can't bloody well wait. Call room service for seven-thirty. Order me a light salad starter and any fish for my main, and for you, order whatever you fancy. Plus a bottle of Chardonnay. Copy?"

"Salad, fish, vino. Copy that."

As Cooper headed to his car, he encountered script clerk Elaine Buck. "How'd we do? Screen time?"

"Did you have a target?"

"Well, a possibly unattainable three minutes."

Elaine smiled at him. "Two thirty-eight."

"Wow!" He gestured, speechless.

Elaine nodded. "James, not bad? Only twenty-two seconds off your goal. Better than when you and I were on that blue screen unit at Pinewood, eh?"

Cooper grinned. "You betcha! Thanks, Elaine."

The ride back to the hotel was super-comfortable, especially as Barry Gillette had put into the Town Car a bottle of Cooper's favorite Scotch. The euphoria wasn't to last long . . .

SCENE 27. TAKE 3.

A knock. "*Entrada.*"

Golda's head appeared around the door. Entering, she studied the room, frowning at Cooper. "*This* is a junior suite?" Her frown became a smile. "Hi, Junior!"

"Okay, so it isn't Buckingham Palace."

"And you're not the Queen?" She giggled. "*He's* history, right?"

"Golda, it's fine for my needs, okay? Bedroom, en-suite bathroom, outer room for meetings, whatever and . . . eh, dinner?"

Cooper crossed to the drinks trolley and held aloft a glass. "Yes?"

"Please. V and T with ice 'n slice."

He poured them both a drink; four ice cubes for Golda, one for him. "Now, what's so important?"

Golda sipped her drink and looked at the glass, held between her knees. "This morning, Guido called."

"Guido?" Cooper frowned. "Guido Tasso? From Twickenham?"

She nodded vigorously. "The very same. *And*, he didn't make it collect."

Cooper smiled. "But what about?"

"Post. Specifically, the reservation of cutting rooms. He wants it confirmed a.s.a.p. or he'll charge us a cancellation fee."

"Confirmed?" Cooper paced and sipped wine. "I haven't spoken to him in ages." He eyed Golda.

"No, guv, not me."

"Then who?" He sat, ruminating while Golda stared at him. He looked up at her. "See if you can find Ian, the editor, and ask him to come up."

Moving to the house phone, Golda dialed. "Ah, Ian. Golda. You busy? Good. Would you come up to James' suite, a.s.a.p.? Thanks." She indicated the bedroom. "Want me to wait in there?"

"No way. You stay right here. As production supervisor, I want you to be privy to as much of this sort of thing as is justifiably possible."

Without knocking and as bold as brass, Marshall walked in. "What's up?"

Cooper rose. "Drink?"

Marshall nodded. "Any beer?"

Cooper held up a bottle. "Only local. Okay?"

"Fine. Don't bother with a glass." As Cooper handed Marshall his drink, the editor looked from one to the other. "So?"

"This morning," Cooper indicated Golda. "Guido called from Twickenham, asking for the cutting rooms reservation to be confirmed. Any idea who might have made the reservations?"

"Sure." He raised the bottle, and drank. "I did."

"You did?" Cooper stood before his editor. "Ian, you and I haven't even discussed post, especially as until the other day I didn't know where post is even going to be based!" He looked scathingly at Marshall.

"And where is that? Added to which James, on our previous outings you've *always* passed to me the booking of post facilities."

"That's when we were with home-based companies in the U.K. Tonnini is American, and post, all elements of it, will be done in L.A." Pausing, he shook his head. "Ian, why the hell didn't you check with me first before charging off on your own! Guido's threatening us with a cancellation fee!"

As all three eyed each other in turn, the silence was brittle. Eventually Marshall put down his bottle very gently and addressed both Cooper and Golda. "Tell you what, James, you've never spoken to me like that before." He pointed at Golda. "Especially in front of someone like her." He stared down Cooper. "When you were Cooper the producer, I liked you." He moved a step forward. "But Cooper the director? You can *stick* the movie up your arse and cut your own bloody film!" Exit editor, camera right, door slamming hard behind him.

Then . . . a gentle knock at that same door. Golda and Cooper each looked at each other with a knowing smile.

"*Servicio de quarto!*"

The smiles vanished rapidly. Golda crossed to the door, admitting a smiling waiter pushing a food trolley. "*Boa noite.*"

Cooper sniffed. "Mmmm!"

"I . . . I splurged. Green salad, lobster thermidor. Eh, Atlantic lobster."

"Golda, perfect. Just what the doctor ordered." As Golda pushed the trolley out of the suite and into the hallway, Cooper checked his watch. Golda re-entered. "Sit." Into her glass was poured some Chardonnay. Putting down the wine he sat back in his chair and eyed her.

"Okay, by now I know that look well. What is it?"

Cooper sighed. "The editor? I know I can't function on all directing cylinders until I resolve the issue."

Golda studied him for a few seconds, picked up the phone once again and dialed. "Pat? Golda. Eh, sorry to call so late but could you come up right away to James' room? It's two five one." A pause. "Great. Thanks." Putting down the phone, she glanced at Cooper. "The ball's in your court?"

Immediately, Cooper caught her drift.

A knock. Golda answered. "Come on in, Pat."

Whether in Arctic Norway or Equatorial Imperio, the appearance of first assistant editor Pat Corcoran never changed. Disheveled sandy-colored hair, v-neck mohair navy blue sweater, pink denim shirt, outsize baggy denim jeans. Cooper wondered if he had a wardrobe containing nothing but the same sweaters and the same shirts.

Corcoran looked from one to the other. "What's up?"

"Pat," Golda stood. "A drink?"

"Scotch, thanks. Neat, no ice."

Cooper interjected. "Better make it a large one."

Corcoran raised an eyebrow. "That sounds ominous."

Cooper gestured. "Pat, sit down." Golda handed him his drink. Large. Very large. Cooper saw no point in beating-about-the bush. "Ian? He's walked."

With furrowed brow, Corcoran leaned forward, looking from one to the other. "Why?" Then he took a large swallow of his drink.

"This morning . . ." Golda sat on the edge of her chair, facing Corcoran. "I had a call from Guido Tasso. He wanted to know when we would be confirming our cutting room reservations."

Cooper comtinued. "I haven't contacted Guido at all lately, no reason to but obviously somebody has. I asked Ian if he could shed any light on it, which is when he said he'd reserved the rooms. I won't bore you with the rest but I gave him a bollocking as a result of which he told me to stuff my movie up my arse and left. In every sense of the word."

Corcoran digested this, sipping his drink occasionally. "You must've had a reason for not contacting Guido?"

"Of course I did. Post will be done in L.A."

Corcoran looked from Golda and across to Cooper. "Something tells me you want me to take over?"

Cooper nodded. "That's about the size of it."

Finishing his drink, Corcoran stood. "I'd like to think about it, okay? G'night." He headed for the door, which he closed quietly.

"You, you Golda, Golda Wisepart?"

Golda looked-up, to be confronted by a very elegantly-dressed lady in her mid- thirties. "Eh, yes, I am. And you are?"

"Annoyed! I was told there'd be a car to meet me."

A puzzled frown crossed Golda's brow. "To meet . . . You?

"You *do* have a fax machine down here?"

"Of course."

"Then you should have received from Tonnini L.A. a fax advising of my flight arrival, with a car to take me to the hotel, driver to then stand-by and work to instructions."

Golda shrugged. "I, I um, I don't understand, ma'am."

"And don't *ma'am* me! You're old enough to be my *grandmother*."

Golda's eyelids formed into slits. "I'll remember that."

"You should. Now, show me the fax machine."

They walked into the adjoining stationery room. The lady inspected the machine. "Shouldn't this be turned on twenty-four seven?"

Golda frowned. "It is. Always.

"Do Santa Mosqueiro fax machines have a siesta? Or like me, it's blown a fuse. The 'on' light isn't on? Get it fixed, pronto."

They returned to the production office. "Now, get me a car and call ahead to the hotel. I want their best suite."

"And for whom shall I say?"

"Preiss. That's P-R-E-I-S-S, Nessa. I'm the new associate producer.

Refreshed, in every sense of the word. Showered and breakfasted and feeling like a new woman, Nessa approached reception. The lady clerk looked up. "Miss Preiss?"

"The movie company. Might you know where they're working?"

"Yes. Every evening we receive a call sheet detailing the next day's work."

Nessa thought for a moment, during which time the clerk fumbled under the desk, and produced that day's call sheet. It was held-out to

Nessa. "Ma'am?" Nessa disregarded the address, knowing that nowhere in this whole wide world does one piss off anybody manning hotel concierge or reception.

Discreetly, to the clerk Nessa slid across the counter a one-hundred dollar bill. "Would you get me a taxi, please?" She pointed to the call sheet. "To take me here?"

The clerk smiled. "Of course." The clerk took the money. "And thank you."

From a secluded spot, for some fifteen minutes Nessa watched the activity on the set, although with regard to a movie set, 'activity' is more in the nature of an oxymoron. 'Inertia' is more befitting. Such are the mechanics of the movie-making process that whenever Nessa watched the on-set proceedings it reminded her always of the coelacanth—'more living than a fossil.' Just. Although all seemed to be under control, no histrionics, just plodding on. She tapped the driver. "Hotel."

Back in her suite, Nessa spoke directly to the mirror on the dressing table. "Nessa, you've always been a black-and-white person. An answer, be it right or wrong, is always better than a non-answer, yes? Cooper. Big problem. Always able to see the other side of the argument, *their* point. Leads to procrastination, delay. So how do we tackle the current problem, Cooper? Play the 'hell-hath-no-fury shrew' for his emotional indifference or keep it all on a business level, the business of Tonnini?" The moment she had uttered the Italian's name, she knew the answer. *And, why not? The disguise??*

The contact lenses she inserted delicately, as instructed by the Beverly Hills optometrist, and then donned the non-prescription spectacles. Pale lipstick, a gesture to femininity while not diverting from her position as associate producer. The mirror confirmed her 'look.' A no-nonsense executive. Satisfied, she put on the jacket of her tailored suit. Charcoal grey. Just short of all-out black severe.

She stood before his suite. One quick check in her hand-mirror, and then she knocked.

Cooper was seated in an armchair, studying the script. "It's open."

Nessa entered. Cooper stood. "Tonnini?"

"Yes." He indicated a chair, and Nessa sat, skirt placed discreetly but teasingly, crossing her nylon-clad legs noisily, a sound not lost on Cooper. "May I offer you a drink?"

"Can you manage a vodka negroni?"

"Somewhat. I'll join you." Mixing the vodka, Campari, vermouth, orange juice and ice, he passed to her a glass, raising his. "*Salut.*"

"*Salut.*"

Having resumed his seat he looked at her. "Just passing through or here for the duration?"

"Very much the latter." Opening her briefcase, Nessa took-out a sheaf of papers, which were blank although Cooper was not able to see that. Nessa shuffled them. "Ye . . . es." She looked up at him. "Mr. Cooper?"

"James. Call me James."

"James. We've already lost a director, and a leading lady. This afternoon I figured I should see some footage, so I wandered into the editing room to view material on the flatbed. No editor. Now, why not? What happened, and *why* weren't we told?"

In sync, Cooper both fidgeted and sighed. And found the courage to talk to her directly "In my wisdom, lacking as it is, I thought Tonnini had had enough bad news from down here without hearing also that the editor had walked."

"Walked?"

"O-U-T. Out."

Cooper explained to her the circumstances of the editor's departure, and his complete confidence in upgrading to the role of editor Pat Corcoran.

"You ever see the movie *Hellzapoppin*?"

Cooper frowned. "Many years ago. Why?"

"Because I suggest it was better run than *RedmayneWest*?"

"It may appear that way to an outsider."

"I'm no outsider!" Hissed Nessa. "I am an employee of Tonnini International and have had a direct interest in this movie ever since the day the project was green lit. Understand?"

"Perfectly." Cooper wondered there and then, was this another war on a different front?. "Well, given your personal involvement, when can I expect the replacement for Susan Chase? We run out of work around her tomorrow."

"Which is when she'll be here. Tomorrow's flight from Sao Paulo."

It took a few moments for the bombshell to sink in. "To work? When?"

"The next day."

"What about rehearsal time?"

"What about it?"

"It's standard industry practise for a director to spend rehearsal time with the principals."

"Tell that to the insurers, the fund."

Biting his tongue, he glanced at her. "What did you say your name was?"

"I didn't. But it's Nessa."

Cooper gave a doubletake. "She'll arrive dead tired from the L.A. journey, so she'll need to recover. I have to spend *some* time with her! Can't you buy me time, any time, even if only a morning, breakfast to lunch?" He looked at her, pleadingly. "This isn't for me you know, it *is* for the movie?"

"I presume we have a local unit doctor?"

Cooper nodded. "Of course."

"Bribable?"

Cooper giggled. "Nessa, everybody in Imperio is bribable."

"I'll get you a sick note. For the insurers. Give you a chance to work with Claudia."

"That's her name?"

Nessa nodded. "Claudia Klein. Brasilian mother, Israeli father, fluent in both English and Portuguese." She shrugged. "And possibly Yiddish?"

Cooper tapped the script. "This Claudia, Claudia Klein. Was there any footage shot of her, any of the usual artiste tests for unknowns?"

"Negative. No pun intended. But if there was, I'd of known."

"So it all boils down to a Franco slash Seidelman decision?"

Nessa sighed. "Naturally". She looked at him directly. "But isn't a function of directing to extract a performance from the most inexperienced or unresponsive of talent?"

"A number of very good directors worked with Charlton Heston. Can you remember in which one of his movies he gave a *decent* performance?"

Nessa shrugged. "Not offhand. You?"

"The War Lord."

She frowned. "Didn't see it."

"Roger Moore?"

"Who?"

"Quite." He looked at her again. "But please, buy me some time?"

"I'll try."

Later.

The bedside phone rang and before Cooper answered, he knew it would be Los Angeles. Where else in the whole wide-world was anywhere so ignorant of time zones, such as 20.00. PST is 01.00. Imperio time? Yawning, he picked-up the instrument. *"Si?"*

"James? Franco. There a problem, a big problem. For me. Personally."

Christ, thought Cooper. Now what? "Such as?"

"I ever tell you I one of six children, all boys?"

Simultaneously, Cooper both blinked, and winced. "Eh, no, Franco, I don't believe you did."

"I the only one who no go into the family business."

A plethora of Italian professions flashed through the Cooper mind, from pasta growers to Popes, motor engineers to Mafia hit-men.

"But now that change."

"You giving up movies?"

Tonnini scoffed. "James, me, movies? No, never! But, why not another string to my bow? The brothers? They all have these *classico* gourmet delis, Firenze, Roma, Milano, Munich, London, New York. I plan the same for Beverly Hills, but. They use up all the names. I have no *name*!"

Cooper was tempted to say 'You are Franco Delli Tonnini', but decided prudence was the better part of valor. "How can *I* help?"

"You creative? So . . . create!"

"For *Redmayne West*?"

"Fuck *Redmayne West*! Create a name for my deli! I try Seidelman. He no more able to create a fart after a pot of baked beans! You? You a director! Direct me a name!"

Realizing the only way he was going to get any sleep was to come up with a suggestion, a plausible epithet, and quickly. "D'you want it to include *your* name?"

"*Si*! Of course! Charisma!"

Cooper trod carefully. He figured it pointless to even suggest 'Trader Tonnini,' 'Trader Franco's' or 'Bologni Tonnini.' "Franco, how about 'Deli . . . Tonnini'?"

The silence was deafening. Tonnini pondered if it was another of those Anglo Leef-type jokes. "I think about it. Nessa there?"

"Franco, it's gone one in the morning here."

"Transfer me."

"I'll get you back to the switchboard." Cooper switched the call, and climbed back into bed. Exhausted.

Nessa's suite.

The phong rang. Groping for the instrument, Nessa found the light and took the call. "Jesus, James, now what?"

"'*James*' . . . ? Is how you greet your fiancé?"

"Oh, Franco. How was I supposed to know it would be you?"

"He in over his head?"

For what reason she didn't know, but Nessa thought the question intrusive. "Who, Cooper? No!" And surprised herself by her defensive response. She calmed. "He plays things well. As Claudia Klein arrives tomorrow, he's made it a no-penalty rest day, so we lose neither time nor money, and he'll be able to rehearse with the girl." She felt cheerful. "Franco. You made a good decision with Cooper."

"Nessa, he *your* suggestion," said meaningfully. "You the one who remember him?"

"Franco, I meant *director*." For some reason Nessa felt she had to give Cooper good 'press'. "He's always prepared, everybody says not only does he know what he wants but also he knows how to get it, the crew loves him, so does Kurt, and I guess once a production man, forever a production man, so he's always wearing his line producer hat as well."

"That fine, but the line producer hat, it cramp him? Is Cooper selfish enough to be a director, that focused, that, that . . . almost manic?"

Nessa considered her reply. "Well, he's averaging almost three minutes a day with plenty of cover shots, so, sure, he's focused. I don't think he'll let you down."

"An' *almost* three minutes? Tell him I wan' a daily *minimum* of three minutes. *Capis?*"

"I'll tell him."

"Do that. An' behave yourself. *Ciao.*"

Removing the instrument from her ear, Nessa gazed at the phone with a quizzical look. "*Ciao* . . . Franco." The receiver she didn't replace back on the phone rest. She put it on the bedside table.

Seven A.M.

Cooper knocked. Eventually, the door was opened, slowly. Nessa was still in her night clothes. "Oh, it's you." She opened the door wider, gesturing him to follow. "Breakfast?"

"Fruit, toast, confiture and lotsa coffee."

"I'll order while readying myself."

Nessa disappeared, to reappear shortly, fully dressed. She sat opposite him.

He squinted at her.

"Something wrong?"

"The glasses. Yesterday you wore glasses."

"And today I'm not. Contacts." She grinned facetiously. "You any other observations?"

"This Claudia Klein. What accent does she have? I mean Portuguese, American . . . Yiddish?"

"You'll know shortly, won't you?"

Cooper paused, and then spoke. "She arrives this morning. Both you and I should meet her. Then I'll go to the set and do some shooting, then come back here and spend the afternoon with her. I'd like you to take the camera crew and shoot some scenic transition shots and tomorrow . . ." He looked at Nessa. "Tomorrow we throw her in at the deep end."

Digesting all of this, Nessa nodded. "Let's hope she can swim?"

The Arrivals Hall, Santa Mosqueiro International Airport.

"Claudia?"

The attractive young lady nodded, together with a radiant smile.

"I'm Nessa Preiss."

At the mention of the surname, Cooper felt like a bull when cattle-pronged.

"I'm the associate producer and this is James Cooper, your director."

In her suite, Claudia thanked them for the flowers, the fruit basket and the bottled water. Looking at Nessa, Cooper inhaled deeply. "Claudia, how d'you feel after that long journey? I mean . . . tired?"

"No."

"Feel like working this afternoon, here, in your suite. You'll be on call tomorrow and I think we should spend some time together, prepping?"

"Sure. What time?"

"Two-thirty?"

"Fine. I'll be ready." She ushered them out, politely.

In the corridor, Nessa looked meaningfully at Cooper. "Well?"

Cooper mused. "Well, at least she doesn't sound like Golda Meir." He sighed, looking at Nessa. "But. I think, a toughie. Fingers crossed?"

Nessa raised a hand with two crossed fingers.

He smiled at her. "How about a Negroni on the terrace bar? And then you can tell me all about *Nessa Preiss*?" Before she could answer, Cooper continued. "And how about a working dinner. You, Claudia, Kurt and me?"

"All sounds good."

"Earlyish. She'll need some shut eye"

"We all will." She nudged him. "And by the way, James, that was a *different* Nessa Preiss . . . *very* different. So different *you* didn't even remember?" She eyed him. "You scumbag."

He looked everywhere except at Nessa. "I'm sorry."

"Too late."

The day had gone well. The read-through with Claudia was encouraging, the dinner was affable and Pat Corcoran had instaled in Cooper's room a Moviola editing machine, the after-dinner plan being to check the first cut of a particular sequence.

Nessa opened the door. To reveal a dishevelled man carrying a couple of film cans.

"Hi. Pat Corcoran. Editor. Pro tem."

Cooper raised his voice. "Come in, Pat."

Nessa led the way. Corcoran admired the sway of her hips, the shape of her *derrière*. She turned to him. "I'm Nessa Preiss, your associate producer. A drink?" She moved to the drinks trolley.

"Thanks. Scotch, no ice." Removing film from the cans, Corcoran started to lace up the Moviola. "Directing certainly agrees with you, James." Corcoran gestured around the suite. "Got yourself a decent squat at long last and a good-looking woman to go with it."

"The new suite's mine. The lady is Tonnini's."

"Well, the movie was Leef's. Until a couple of weeks ago."

Nessa returned, handing Corcoran a large Scotch.

"Cheers."

All three raised a glass. "This the first cut of the bathing sequence?" asked Cooper.

"Yup." Corcoran checked the sync, as Cooper sat himself at the Moviola, with Nessa sitting beside him. Adjusting the viewer, he ran the scene. And some two minutes later, it was over.

Corcoran was anxious to know the verdict. "Wotcha think?"

"It's okay. And you've used everything, *everything* Leef shot?"

"Not a sprocket hole left lying on the cutting room floor." Corcoran effected his best Mississipi drawl. "I mean, not even a cat."

"And you're not Sam Wood, this isn't Sparta and you're certainly not Hal Ashby". He winked. "Yet." Cooper re-ran the scene, shaking his head.

Nessa eyed him. "What is it, what's wrong?"

"We need at least two more shots."

"Of what?" asked Nessa.

"One on Susan, one on the alligator.'

Corcoran pointed to the film. "The alligator shot's there, the one of it swimming towards camera. The second unit did it."

"But what's needed is a shot to intercut with that, give it some tension."

Nessa and Corcoran spoke almost in unison. "Such as?"

Cooper paused, visualizing the shot in his mind's eye. "It's a water-level shot, moving smoothly, silently, towards Susan's bare back, a sort of aquatic Steadicam. It's the alligator's P.O.V."

Corcoran looked at Nessa, and then at Cooper. "And where'd we shoot this?"

Cooper gave Corcoran a withering look. "Here, wanker, here!"

The editor put a finger to his mouth. "James, read my lips. Susan Chase? She no here, no more."

Rolling his eyes, and sighing at the same time, he pointed at Corcoran. "Call yourself an editor, pro tem notwithstanding? It's on her back, wanker. We use a double!"

"Second unit?" asked Nessa.

"Yes, and I'd like you to supervise the shoot, with Pat here directing."

Cooper ran the scene yet again, shaking his head constantly. "That arsehole Leef, he couldn't direct you to the nearest toilet."

Nessa chuckled. "Now what's he done?"

"It's what he *hasn't* done." Combing hair with fingers, Cooper sighed deeply. "We need to tie Susan and the alligator together in the one frame. Leef should have done a wide establishing shot with her in the foreground, she bends down out of frame to bathe, and reveals the gator swimming towards her."

Corcoran nodded. "Heightening the tension, by letting the audience see the gator before she even knows it's there." Pausing, he looked at both Nessa and Cooper. "That's *three* shots."

"Precisely." Cooper shrugged. "But. Too late now."

Nessa looked at him. "Is it? If Universal can build a mechanical shark, all articulated, an alligator is much smaller and only needs to head towards Susan, not leap out of the water, right?"

Cooper nodded. "Yeah." He glanced at her. "So?"

"Then tomorrow, I'll call L.A., explain the problem and ask if we can have a mechanical gator built, subject to cost, naturally."

Cooper studied her. "As good an idea as that is, to me it would be plan B." He raised a finger. "Plan A should be film libraries, of which there's a ton in L.A., and there must be footage somewhere of a gator shot to suit our sequence? So, Nessa yes, call L.A. tomorrow but stress we need only library footage, which'll be much cheaper than a mechanical gator, and, if we're lucky and is found such footage, remember it has to be in our aspect ratio, two three five to one. Is there anyone at Tonnini who can handle this?"

"Sure. We have an in-house post guy, Kerry. He'd be fine."

"Bu,t" asked a skeptical Corcoran. "How do we get a 'Susan' in the foreground?"

"That's for me to worry about." Cooper checked his watch. "A nightcap, then bed."

Scene 30. Take 5.

Cooper was called to the off-set area. "What's the problem?"

"The name is wrong!" Claudia Klein was pointing to the chair-back. "That is *not* my professional name!"

"Then Claudia, what is?"

"*Martins!* My mother's maiden name. Martins! I refuse to sit in it until the name is correct!"

There and then Cooper felt like giving her a knuckle sandwich right between the eyes. But before he realized what he was doing, he'd grabbed her by an elbow and frog-marched her to behind the honeywagon, where he spun her round to face him. "How many shows have you *acted* in?"

"How many shows have *you* directed?"

The mutual anger was tangible. Without taking his gaze off her, Cooper calmed. Somewhat. "Claudia, I've been in the movie industry for the best part of thirty years during which time I've learned it's a small industry and word gets around quickly . . . *very* quickly."

"So?"

"So what d'you want to be known as? A one-day wonder or a career actress? Either way, your attitude, your persona, your behavior, it'll all be traveling the Hollywood bush telegraph within milli-seconds." They stared at each other. "Your choice." Cooper shrugged. "And, this movie can make you . . ." He bowed with open arms. "Or break you." He smiled. "Me? I can always go back to producing."

Lowering her head, Claudia looked from side-to-side, thinking long and hard. "I was told . . ." She sighed, and looked up at Cooper. "I was told you have to mark out a space, a position, assert who you are?"

"You were told wrong."

Each dared the other to blink. Finally, Claudia faltered. "I want to be an actress." She nodded, more to herself than Cooper. "Yes. I want to be an actress and, I want to be taken seriously."

"Then behave seriously. Act not only the part but aso as an adult." Taking a step back, Cooper gestured to the shooting area. "Like now." His eyes never left hers. "Ready?"

She nodded. "Yes." Claudia started to walk and then halted, looking at Cooper. "I . . . I'm sorry."

"I think we both are."

As they neared the set, Kurt Greene was watching their every move. Eye-balling Cooper, he lowered his chin and looked lower, to a surreptitiously raised, questioning . . . thumb.

Cooper nodded. Kurt smiled.

The director turned to his First A.D. "Okay, let's have a canter over the course."

Langley relaxed visibly. "Okay folks, rehearsal time." Via his walkie-talkie, Langley summoned all of the required team and the only histrionics then were in *front* of the camera.

But with that little drama resolved, Cooper knew bedding-in Miss Claudia Martins *née* Klein had proved more difficult than he had ever anticipated and while appreciative of Kurt Greene's patience, Cooper knew that in future she had to be handled with gloves. Steel gloves.

By the time Cooper returned to his suite, he was exhausted. He decided that after studying tomorrow's schedule, he'd skip dinner and have an early night. Two large vodkas and tonic had *the* desired effect of a) satisfying taste, and b) inducing drowsiness. Cooper rechecked his notes, closed the script and walked into the bedroom. Undressed and in pyjama pants, he undertook the necessary personal ablutions, returned to the bedroom and opened the bedside table, removing a large bottle of Cutty Sark. He poured an amount into a shot glass, returning the treasure to storage. Raising the glass, Cooper spoke aloud. "To tomorrow. Let's hope it never comes." He downed the scotch, and checking his travel-clock display of twenty-two hundred, he climbed into bed. Within a few minutes, he was fast asleep.

Which is when it rang. The phone. Awakened, Cooper froze. And made a decision. An arm reached out, removed the phone from the receiver and placed it gently on the bedside table. Whereupon he turned-over and regained sleep. Only minutes later to be reawakened by a banging on the suite's front door, accompanied by Nessa's shouting. "James! James!"

Not bothering with his robe, Cooper slouched Groucho-like to the door. "You rang?"

Also in her nightwear, diaphanous, Nessa was ushered in.

"Is the bloody hotel bloody-well on fire?"

"Seidelman." Nessa pointed to the phone. "You'd better talk to him."

It rang. "There goes the early night." Cooper picked-up the instrument. "Cooper." His eyes were on the diaphanous nightwear.

"What's with you?"

"Tired, Don, just tired."

"And I'm tired of your shenanigans, so wake up! Now, what's this cockamayme crap about a mechanical alligator? This isn't *Jaws*!"

For Nessa to be privy to the conversation, he gestured her to come closer to the phone. "Don, that's Plan B."

"I don't care if it's Plan *Zee*! First, the creation of such an action prop doesn't happen overnight, right? A crew has to be assembled, drawings made, quotations put out, a shop found capable of building it and then tests, etcetera, etcetera, etcetera! Which means this crazy idea has to be implemented immediately?" His voice rose to a crescendo. "And it may never be used! So what do we do then? Donate it to an aquarium!"

Nessa's eyes rolled. Cooper drooped, as if falling. "Don, I wish I had an answer"

"Well, *I* have."

Cooper glanced at Nessa. The closeness of her was beginning to affect him, albeit a pleasant distraction. "And what's that, Don?"

"Simple. *Your* idea? *You* pay!"

"For what?"

"For everything. The whole gator project from A to Z, including shipping. *You* pay!"

Cooper deliberated. "Tell you what. I'll drop the alligator sequence altogether."

"You don't have final cut. We *retain* the sequence."

"What if I go back to my original role, that of line producer, and you guys find another director?"

"You'd never work this side of the Atlantic again."

"That a threat?"

"No. A fact."

"Does Franco agree with this?"

"I'm business affairs. And this? *This*, is business!"

Cooper and Nessa exchanged looks. She got disconcertingly closer to the phone, and, to Cooper. He tried desperately not to look through her virtually transparent nightclothes. And tried . . . "Don, you have an advantage over me. Time. Yesterday, apart from a day of work and a working dinner, I then worked late, laboring over a scene with the pro tem editor."

"Ah! Something else you never told us about! Y'know Cooper, you're more secretive than the KGB! What else you hiding?" At which point Seidelman disconnected.

Shrugging, Cooper replaced his phone, and turned to Nessa. "You hear all that?"

"Unfortunately." Nessa studied him. "James, what *are* you going to do?"

"I have a choice?"

"It's only a movie?"

"Nessa, it's never *only* a movie. Every one of them is a confrontation, a test, a challenge, to be risen to, to be overcome, to be bested."

"Christ, James, you make it sound like life or death."

"Well, isn't that Hollywood? Life or death?"

Nessa stood. "How about some coffee?" Cooper nodded, while she prodded. Room Service. Having ordered, she sat by Cooper. "You know what you really need?"

His thoughts surrounded her. He put them aside. "A large whisky?"

"An agent."

He stared at her, cogitating. "An agent . . . an agent?" A thought. "What time's it in L.A.?"

"Around six P.M."

Grabbing the phone, he dialed. "Britt? Is Edgar there? It's James Cooper."

"Hi, James. How are you? And yeah, he's still here. I'll put you through."

Edgar came on the line. "Hi, stranger. You in town?"

"I'm in Imperio."

"Imperio? A movie?"

"*Si*. For Tonnini International."

Edgar chuckled. "You keep nice company."

"Which is why I'm calling. I need an agent, quickly. I won't bore you with the details, but I've ended up as the director and basically, Ed, I'm being screwed."

"Director? Listen kid, I'll find you an agent. Gimme your number down there." Cooper gave both phone and fax numbers. "I'll have somebody speak to you before the day's end, without fail. It won't be C.A.A., but it'll be somebody good, very good."

Cooper felt reassured. "Thanks Ed, thanks a lot."

The coffee arrived. Nessa handed to Cooper a cup. "Who's Edgar?"

"Edgar Grossman. A business manager and a straight shooter."

"James, remember the opening of *Casablanca*? And wait and wait."

"Yeah, I know. And wait," chimed-in Cooper. He raised his cup. "Here's looking at you, kid."

The phone rang. They looked at each other. Nessa grabbed the instrument. "Hello?"

"Who's this?"

"Nessa Preiss. Who's this?"

"John Hess, calling for James Cooper?"

Covering the speaker, Nessa held out the phone. "You're in good hands. John Hess, Amalgamated Creative Talent."

Cooper took the phone. "This is James Cooper."

"James? John Hess, A.C.T. Leave this with me. I'll enjoy locking horns with Mr. Seidelman, but I know it's late down there so I'll let you get some shut eye and we'll leave the details until later, but yes, we'll be happy to take you on as a client."

"Without a meeting?"

"Sure. Edgar gave me your C.V. The industry needs directors and you and yours are the last generation to have emerged from the studio system. The modern *wunderkind*? Film School? Teaches them what? The studio system was the best and the *only* film school. Now, how about I call you tomorrow evening, around nine P.M. your time?"

"Perfect. And as is said here, *obrigado*. For everything."

"You're very welcome."

Cooper looked at Nessa. "Thanks to you, I now have an agent."

Nessa giggled. "This, is going to be interesting." She eyed Cooper. "Now, KGB man, where's that secret bottle that's really no secret?"

"In the bedside table. Behind the microfilm and beside the Novichok nerve agent poison."

Nessa found the bottle of Cutty Sark. "Oh, no condoms?"

"Gave it up for Lent."

"How gracious of you." Nessa poured two tumblers-full of the nectar of the Scottish Highlands. Handing one to Cooper, she sat facing him. "To *Redmayne West*."

"And to George Kaplan. Whoever you are." Downing his drink, Cooper studied Nessa. "Am I still a scum bag?"

She inclined her head. "The road to retribution is a long highway."

He returned her look. "You really going to marry Tonnini?"

Nessa rubbed the glass between her palms and countered his look. "James, I think the question is inappropriate, impertinent and frankly, none of your goddam business! Okay?" Finishing her drink, she stood. Moving closer, she kissed Cooper. Very gently. On the lips.

"Then what's that for?"

"Old time's sake." She pointed at him. "Old times. *Verstanden*? The end of a chapter." Leaving, Nessa muttered over her shoulder. "*Guten nacht*." And was gone.

Leaving in her wake a very confused Cooper. Finishing the whisky, he fell asleep. In his chair.

Was it the cold or the stiffness that awoke him? Or feeling like Ray Milland in *The Lost Weekend*, the crashing hangover? Cooper knew he had some somewhere, but where, where is the Underberg? Groping here-there-and-everywhere, it was found. As foul-tasting as it is, he swallowed the contents of two of the mini-bottles. He relaxed, waiting for the root medicine to take its effect. Which it did. "*Danke*," he said loudly. And surprised himself by eating a hearty breakfast of papaya, followed by a ham omelette, confiture and gallons of coffee.

He rose to the challenge of the day's shooting, so that by wrap and to the extent of Elaine Buck's timing, he'd shot three minutes five seconds of cut screen time. He felt good, and painful as it was, vowed to stay off the booze for the evening, do his usual script check and wait for the call. *The* call.

As suggested, it came through at 21.00.local time, and Cooper was ready.

"Here's the deal." It was John Hess. "Directing, six hundred-fifty thousand dollars, through shoot and post. No possessory credit, no final cut, but more importantly, no double add-on. Full screen credit as director, so long as you direct more than half the movie, which we know you will, separate card as director, separate card as co-producer, paid advertising both as director and as co-producer, where and whenever appears the name of Tonnini as producer. Any sequel, you get first offer to direct, you have contractual right to supervise both television and video versions. You'll get twelve percent of producer's gross. If there's a novelization, you'll get a percentage of the royalties and if there's any TV spin-off, you'll be part of that, plus the option to direct all or any episodes of such series. All of this, of course, subject to the usual industry exemptions, and exclusions. Oh, and you won't be paying for the reptile. See you later, alligator?"

Cooper chuckled. But while the scope and structure of the deal was all too familiar to him, what wasn't familiar was that *he* was the subject of such a deal. It took moments to sink in.

"James, you there?"

"Yes, I'm still here. Giddy. Trying to take it all in. How'd you do it?"

"Like you. Trained in the trenches. We happy?"

"Ecstatic."

"Good. I'll fax you a deal memo which you should check, and if in agreement, I'll have a contract drawn up which will be couriered down to you, together with the standard Client/Agency contract."

Ever the pragmatist, Cooper parted the clouds of delight. "John, exactly what am I paying agency commission on?"

"Your directing fees plus any and all residuals or spin offs arising therefrom."

"And my producing fee?"

"All yours. Done deal. Before we were your representative."

Cooper felt that somebody else was in *his* corner. For once. "John, what can I say? I'm lost for words."

"Don't worry. And, when and if you need me, just call. Anytime."

The line was disconnected. For the phone to ring again, immediately.

"This is James."

"And this is Pat. I think I've cracked it. Can I come up?"

Cooper called Nessa. "If you're not busy, come on over. Pat, our pro tem editor is excited. But I'm not sure what about. And wear a robe."

Two film cans and the same wardrobe. Nessa handed Pat a large whisky. As he laced up the Moviola, he looked between both of them. "I found these close ups. So I cut them in to the 'gator sequence. Now, for the 'gator's move I've inserted '*scene missing*,' but see what you think?"

The Moviola clacked into action. Cooper, Nessa and Corcoran watched intently. After the scene had run through, Cooper was silent.

"Well?", asked Nessa.

Cooper smiled broadly. "Pat, well done. I think you've saved the sequence."

"And," added Nessa "A major headache?"

Cooper turned to the editor. "Pat, what about a first assistant for you?"

"Well, we've these two ladies from Sao Paulo, and while neither's a Verna Fields or an Anne Coates, they know the basics, they're keen to learn, they work hard and they're cheerful. Maybe a few bob more? " Corcoran looked from Cooper to Nessa. "For each of them?"

Cooper smiled. "Like Sergio Leone said, Pat, for a few bob more. Yes." Cooper gestured to the Moviola. "And the gator scene? Thanks for saving my bacon."

Corcoran shrugged. "James, where directors are concerned, isn't that what editors always do?" He drained his glass. "G'night."

Scene 31. Take 1.

"When you come back?"

"Franco," said Nessa, "As soon as I've finished down here."

Tonnini frowned. "To finish what?"

"Eh, Con, Con Griffith, the accountant? He's asked me to provide input."

"Input to *what*?"

"The insurance claim, the corporate creative—"

"Nessa, to present the claim they have a whole accounts department down there." Tonnini was becoming more and more irritated. "An' a whole production department an' . . . Cooper! Me? I promoting this James Eden golf thing at Pebble Beach, an' you should be there. With me!"

Normally Nessa enjoyed enormously such occasions. The glamor, the hype, exposure, excitement. "When is that?"

"In two weeks."

"I'll be there."

Tonnini checked the cuticles of his left hand. "An' where you in the meantime?"

"Here. The Susan Chase substitute, Claudia Klein? She's never been on a foreign location before. There's too many sex-starved crew here. She's attractive, vulnerable and needs a chaperone. That's me, okay?"

"No other reason?"

"Such as?"

"You tell me."

"There's nothing to tell."

"Fine. But be back here by the twentieth, *si*?"

"I'll fly direct to San Francisco. *Ciao.*"

From his New York hotel, Francesco Delli Tonnini was calling the world, using his Lazio charm to beguile personalities into giving of their time and their popularity, by participating in the *James Eden Pro-Am Golf Tournament*, to be held at at Pebble Beach, Monterey, California.

He had brought to the hotel Stella Offenheim, his secretary from the N.Y.C. office of Tonnini International. Her henna-laden head appeared around the interconnecting doorway. "Mr. Seidelman. Line two."

Tonnini pressed a key. "*Pronto.*"

"I've just had a call from A.E.C., asking if we have distribution yet on *Redmayne*."

Tonnini was admiring the artwork promoting the golf tournament. "Don, you know we don't."

"But I didn't *know* if you wanted them to know that so I stalled. Then I called around. Word is, they're thinking of re-releasing *Webster's Kingdom*, the Kurt Greene starrer of a few years ago?"

"Re-release?" Tonnini chuckled. "Don, nobody re-release theatrically these days. It now called video."

"What about *Lawrence, El Cid*?"

"They roadshow movies, restored for the *big* screen."

"Whatever. My sources say it's re-release. And those same sources say they'll need another Kurt Greene vehicle, you know, a new movie, to release just ahead of the re-issue."

Tonnini smelled a deal. "You think they look for a negative pick up?"

"For sure."

"Stay on it. But Don, what with the insurance claim? When it settled?"

"Griffith, the accountant? He's been in touch with the loss adjustor, so hopefully in a matter of days."

"*Va bene*." Tonnini ran an eye over the tournament guest list. "If the claim accepted, then we pay this Claudia Klein out of the Susan Chase settlement."

Seidelman could not believe his ears. "Franco, if Chase's agent knows we've been compensated, he'll expect that money for *his* client, or at least a proportion of it."

"So who going tell him? An' Don, you seem to forget, who, of all in Tonnini International Pictures, who tell Susan Chase to climb into that plane with the art director, eh, who? You? Me? Cooper?"

Chastened, Seidelman replied. "No. No one."

"An' this alligator thing. Why you no like Cooper?"

"Who said I don't like him?"

Tonnini sniggered. "Don, don't kid a kidder."

"It's that pompous, patronizing European—"

"You forget!" The voice was subdued, but steely. "*I,* a European!"

"I meant, eh, the *English*. They talk to you as if by condescension."

"Don, every nationality has its little . . . how I put it . . . eccentricities? I suggest you leave Cooper alone. He directing and the dailies I see are ten times better than that Leef crap. So leave him be. Maybe you take a vacation, clear your mind?"

"I don't need a vacation and I'll track the re-issue thing. Okay?"

"Okay. *Ciao*."

The henna-laden head reappeared. "Line one. Your call to Spain."

Tonnini bubbled with affability and charm. "Sean! How are you, is good to hear you . . . No, no, I no call about a movie, I call Mike about that but I call you about golf, yes, golf . . . Eh, no, no I don't play. But this might interest you. *The James Eden Pro Am* event, Pebble Beach . . . Yes, Pebble Beach. When? A couple of weeks' time. You free to join us? Of course, of course First Class. We fly you to San Francisco, then private jet to Monterey, limo to the Lodge . . . Insured? Of course! Expenses? We pay, everything, every possible thing. Who else? Eh, Bob Hope, Kevin Costner, *si*, your old sparring partner, um . . . Paul Newman, Chevvy Chase, Johnny Carson, James Sikking, yeah, the guy you do that movie with at Pinewood, eh, Dan Quayle, Bruce Willis, Gerald McRainey, Arnold Sh— . . . Palmer? No, eh, Schwarzenegger. Palmer, he a golfer? Then we get him! Two Arnolds worth one in the bush . . . That Bush? He play golf? I'll try. An' I nearly forget. James Eden. Other players? Eh, let me think . . ." He covered the mouthpiece. "Stella! Quick, the list, of the players!" It was thrust into his hand. "Sean? Yes, eh, John Daly, Nick Faldo, Phil Woosnam, Sandy Lyle, oh! An ally? An' Severino Ballesteros, Lee Trevino, Greg Norman, Bernhard Lange . . . that all we have, so far. Pardon? My office make *all* arrangements, and then will call you. And Sean? *Grazie. Ciao.*" Tonnini looked at the list of players. "Stella!"

"Yes, Mr. Franco?"

"How many times I ask?" He slapped the piece of paper. "Always have on my desk the list of players."

"That's the fourth copy I've put there today."

"Oh."

SCENE 32. TAKE 6.

Censor Francesco Ramalho was in a hurry. As the film processing laboratory in Los Angeles didn't process exposed film on Saturday or Sunday nights, this shipment of celluloid and cocaine would be the last for the next two days, when he'd report-in sick. From Rio de Janeiro. The former Imperiavia cabin steward had managed to obtain a staff discount air fare and was desperate now to catch the twenty-thirty hours flight, and although he didn't have to bother with the pre-flight check-in, he knew it was going to be a very close-run thing. He thought. The jerk Cooper, of all the nights to film late, why tonight of all nights? Isn't a twilight setting sun the same on any night?

In his rush, Ramalho's system of packing had gone awry, from the moment he tripped, dropping the rolls of exposed film and the metal cans.

"Shit!" he cried. He looked around, alarmed, And, he thought. Just my luck. No empty cans for the matching shipment of cocaine. "Shit!" He searched everywhere but without success. A lack of time prevented him from going back to the camera truck, to obtain more cans, hence necessity became the mother of invention.

Switching-off the light, Ramalho opened two four-hundred foot cans, removing the exposed film in its black paper bags and after groping for a thousand foot can to put into it the two smaller rolls. Replacing the lid and switching on the light he taped-up the can, frantically did the paperwork, affixing the necessary seals and stamps, and was ready then to pack the individual cans into the fiber transit cases.

One final check.

And one small sachet of cocaine.

Which he'd overlooked.

Ramalho was tempted to leave it there until the Monday shipment. He stared at it. "Francesco, Rio will still be there next week but if I mess with Mendoza, I might not."

He looked at the eight, separate, one-thousand foot cans. Three were untaped and unlabeled. "Shit!" he exploded again. "Which the fuck is *which?*" He opened a can, unwrapped the black bag. The film was a three-hundred-fifty foot roll. Which is when he realized the light was still on. Abruptly, Ramalho hugged the exposed film to his body, extinguishing the light by nudging the switch with his shoulder.

Finding the can of cocaine, he replaced the film, thinking to himself how lucky he was that it was Eastmancolor, with its slower emulsion speed and lesser reaction to light than monochrome film. Ramalho taped the cans, separating those containing film from the specially-marked ones with cocaine. Only then did he turn on the light. He packed all of the consignment, together with its accompanying paperwork, seals and authorizations.

He left for the freight area of the airport. And from there, Rio!

Assistant director Langley groaned. "Uh, uh."

"What's up David?"

Pat Corcoran was heading towards them.

"Editor on the set at o-seven-thirty? Can only mean trouble."

Cooper intercepted Corcoran. "Pat, instinct tells me this isn't a social call?"

"I wish it was, guv. Bad news, I'm afraid."

He looked at the editor. "Shoot."

"Bad lab report. Fogging."

"Of, or on what?"

"The magic hour stuff, the sunset you shot the other evening. Plus some of the footage shot earlier in the day. It's all n.g."

Cooper sagged, visibly. "Oh, dear God. No." He looked at Corcoran. "Is any of it useable, I mean, have you seen the footage, any of it?"

"James, slow down. Time difference? The cassette's on its way but won't be here for some time so no, I've seen sweet fuck nothing. I called the lab at the end of the bath, and they'll fax through the report. But as I understand it, none of the magic hour footage is useable, hardly surprising, as it was shot on the faster stock."

With furrowed brow and fingering his lips, Cooper pondered the problem. "Then it's either a camera fault, or most likely a magazine?"

"James, going by the camera sheets, the same mags were used earlier in the day, and that stuff's fine. Except for one roll."

"Same mag, or mags, as used for the magic hour shots?"

Corcoran shrugged. "No. That's the inconsistency. Different."

With a thousand thoughts racing through his mind, Cooper looked at the editor. "Did they say what sort of fogging?"

"Edge fogging, but some leaking into the frame area."

"Then it *has* to be the magazines!" Cooper put his hands to his head. "And, dear Jesus, we've been using those same magazines ever since, so for all we know there's another two days' work up the swanee?" Cooper was becoming frantic, as Langley interrupted.

"James, we need to start lining-up."

Cooper raised finger cautioned. "David, we have a problem. Find me Billy Richards. And quickly."

"Christ!" said Richards. "We're jinxed!" Holding aloft two magazines, he addressed the two assistant cameramen, focus, and loader. He eyed the latter. "Jack, you load the mags. Where'd you do these two?"

"In the changing bag."

"Why not the darkroom in the truck?"

"Here's quicker."

"How many changing bags do we have?"

"Three. Two on our unit, one for the second team."

"Let me see them." Richards turned to Anscombe, the first A.C. "Derek, why doesn't Jack use the darkroom?"

Anscombe sighed. "Mainly because of the censor."

Richards frowned. 'What's the censor got to do with it?"

Cooper interjected. "At the end of the day, all the exposed footage is handed over to him."

"And," added Anscombe. "The guy's always champing at the bit, complaining he'll never get the stuff ready in time for the flight, so Jack mainly unloads and does the sheets and labeling at the location."

Jack Cottrell returned, carrying two changing bags.

Putting one over a shoulder, Richards held-up the other to the sky, backlighting it while moving it slowly through his hands, examining it thoroughly

Cooper watched his every movement. "What are you looking for?"

"A tear, a rent, a hole, anything that could let in light." Turning the bag inside out, Richards checked the stitching beside the zip, the tension of the elastic at the cuffs. "Nothing wrong with this one." The second bag was subjected to the same meticulous search. He looked at Cooper. "Both are lightproof." Richards steered away Cooper from the group, and then faced him. "You realize we can't possibly shoot today?"

Cooper paled. "Billy, what are you saying?"

A paternal-like hand was placed on a Cooper shoulder. "James, what I'm saying is, we don't *know* what it is. *Ergo*, we simply can't risk it?"

Cooper wrung his hands, and paced, eventually confronting his D.P. "No, I can't, I won't! Especially as we don't see the n.g. stuff for at least another thirty hours."

Richards stared at the director. "But James. It's an insurance claim?"

"Not until we can pinpoint the source, and *then* point the finger of blame." He looked again at Richards. "And for all we know, it could have been a crazily-driven delivery truck with cans bouncing all over the place or, even the lab. Fogged when unloading into the bath?"

"James, you know as well as I do, no lab ever admits liability, plus their terms of business deem all risks to be assumed by the customer. Their first blame will be on the camera, which means it'll have to be sent back to L.A. for testing, while we wait for a replacement, or, they'll blame it on faulty film stock."

"Then that's all the more reason why we must keep shooting. How about at the time of each printed take, we change to a fresh mag. It'll keep Jack busy, and I'd need to tell the actors, but it could be a saver? Or, two cameras, side by side?"

Williams smiled. "In which case, I'd hate to think what would happen if you want a tracking shot?" Williams put an arm around Cooper's shoulder. "Once more into the breach, dear James, once more." They rejoined the group and the day's work started.

"Mornin' guv."

Cooper looked up from his script. "Morning, Golda. We need to fax the relevant people about our latest set-back, the negative problem."

"Well, don't say I didn't warn you."

Cooper studied her. "What are you talking about?"

Esther glanced over to where sat the censor, reading a book. "Him. *That* wanker, the double-dealing dago ditz."

Leaning back expansively, Cooper studied his u.p.m. "Why Esther, you're a racist."

"A racist, me? Impossible. I'm a Jew."

Continuing to look at her, Cooper humphed. "Yeah, well, the whole world knows they're the worst, Israel, you know, learned all its tricks and policies from the Nazis?"

She turned on him, furious. "*You're* the bloody racist! I bet you read '*Mein Kampf*' every bloody night instead of saying your *goy* prayers!"

"Golda, calm down. I'm neither a racist nor a Nazi. I'm just a wind-up merchant."

"Well, okay, but there's a limit to everything."

Nodding Ramalho-wards, Cooper spoke. "And you should be more tolerant of our Imperian cousins."

Golda stared at the censor. Leaning forward, Esther narrowed her eyes to slits. "I wouldn't trust that dago sleeze ball any further than I could throw him."

Said in a tone of mock reproval. "Now, is that any way to talk about a guy who's been off sick for a couple of days?"

"Sick? Bollocks!"

"What happened to tolerance?"

"Since we've been one short on the editing crew, I collect the dailies cassette from the airport." She turned to Cooper, speaking confidentially. "Monday? While collecting the cassette, guess who I see getting off a flight from Rio?" She tossed her head in the direction of Ramalho. "The dago ditz. Was I seeing things? No. Was he just meeting someone and him with an overnight bag? No. Was Jesus Christ in Rio healing the sick? No." She nodded emphatically. "Or, did the ditz lie, and wasn't ill at all?" Esther leaned back. "Which is what my money's on." While gazing again at Ramalho, she continued. "I've never trusted the bastard." Golda turned back to Cooper. "Didn't I say that to you on his very first day?"

Cooper nodded.

Golda grunted. "I wouldn't be a bit bloody surprised if he's the one who fogged the film, trying to cut off some from the end of a roll to stick in his Instamatic for a porno memoir of his Rio weekend of debauchery and depravity. I hope he gets a dose of the clap for his sins." Once more she eyed Ramalho, prodding Cooper as she did so. "The more I think about it, the more I know it was *him*, Ramalho. There's something very dodgy about him."

The hectoring voice of Langley was calling for a rehearsal. Cooper stood.

"I don't know about him fogging the neg, but I do know this. If he was well enough to travel to Rio, then he was well enough to be here doing his job." Moving away, Cooper stopped, and turned. "This should be sorted out. Have Hector ask for a meeting with Colonel Mendoza, Ramalho's boss, and also have him find out exactly *when* was enacted by the State government the decree about having a censor attached to any movie shooting in Imperio." Glancing at Ramalho, he addressed Esther. "You've got me going now. And all because of your racial intolerance."

Golda shook her head. "It's not racial intolerance, James. It's feminine intuition. He's a fraud."

SCENE 33. TAKE 4.

A phone call. To Tele Visao Boa Vista.

"*Sênhor Para*? It is Possi, Captain Possi."

"*Bom dia*, Possi. What can I do for you?"

"They want a meeting."

"They? Who's they?"

"The movie people."

"What about?"

Para spoke conspiratorially. "It appears our tame censor has been abusing his position."

"Oh. How?"

"He didn't report in to the movie for two days. Said he was sick. Except he wasn't sick. He was in Rio de Janeiro."

"Besides us, who knows this?"

Possi was heard to inhale deeply. "He was spotted at the airport. One of the movie people saw him come off a Rio flight."

Para ruminated. "You don't think you're over reacting here? So Ramalho fucks himself silly in Rio for a couple of days, so what? We tell him he's been a bad boy, smack his hands and tell him not to do it again." Adding, laughingly. "And deduct a week's salary, to teach him a lesson."

"Sênhor Para." Possi spoke very deliberately. "The Colonel's view is this could be . . . threatening."

Para digested all that had been said. "Where is the Colonel now?"

"At a meeting. He'll be back within the hour."

"Then yes, *we* should have a meeting."

"We'll come over as soon as he's—"

"No, no, not here! Have Ramalho brought to Headquarters. I'll meet the Colonel there." Para replaced the phone and rested his elbows on the desk, extending all the digits of each hand and tapping them rhythmically for some three minutes. He opened a drawer, withdrawing a pocket-sized cell phone, a gift from an Japanese affiliate TV station.

"Hola?"

Spanish confused Para. He spoke in his native Portuguese. "Mendoza thinks we might have a problem."

"Mauricio, not those movie assholes again?"

Para chuckled. "Cooper, your 'blind man'? He's requested a meeting this evening. It's to do with the censor, and for me, that's a little too close for comfort." He paused. "I think you should be there."

Rubio tittered. "In *what* capacity?"

"A good question." To which Para gave some thought. "Eh, 'The State of Boa Vista, Office for Indian Affairs'."

"Should I wear beads and feathers?"

"Antonio, if I didn't think it serious I wouldn't suggest you coming all this way. So you should take it seriously, too."

Rubio chuckled. "Mauricio, believe me, I do. Any move by these film idiots I take very seriously."

"You'll be there?"

"In war paint."

"Nineteen-thirty taping."

"I'm on my way."

"No Possi?" Para looked around the office, his gaze resting finally on Colonel Mendoza.

"Three's a crowd." Mendoza stroked his mustache. "Four's a gossip column."

"And Ramalho. Where's he?"

As if on cue, the door was opened and Possi ushered-in the censor. Mendoza indicated one of the three empty chairs. "Have a seat."

Possi left, closing the door silently.

Mendoza paced behind the chair, while Para stood, looking out of a window, his back to the room, hands clasped behind him.

"All is going well on the movie?" asked Mendoza, pleasantly.

Ramalho stuttered a nervous reply. "As far as I can tell, Colonel, yes."

"So no problems, no interference?"

Ramalho shook his head. "No, sir. None."

"Then as far as you're concerned, all is going smoothly?"

Ramalho gained confidence. "Yes. The gullible gringos—"

"You know who is Hector Belem?" The Mendoza tone was less pleasant.

"He's the production manager."

"He called me this morning. About you."

Silent, Ramalho felt uncomfortable. He shifted in his seat. "Me?"

"You." Mendoza studied the censor. "And Ramalho, don't play cute with me." He smiled. "I was about to say . . . you'll live to regret it, but let's be more accurate." He put his lips close to a Ramalho ear. "You *will* regret it." Mendoza straightened. "Now, where was I?"

"Hector Belem", replied Para, still gazing out of the window.

"Ah, yes. Thank you." Immediately was jabbed an index finger hard into the back of Ramalho's neck, Mendoza pivoting on the digit as he paced. "You missed two days' work?"

Ramalho attempted to look at Mendoza, but the finger bored harder. He hunched his shoulders. "I was ill. Malaria."

In a split second the finger became a fist, smashing into Ramalho's left temple with the full-force of the standing Mendoza. Ramalho and the chair crashed to the floor, the noise being absorbed to some extent by Para, coughing heavily.

The ear was ringing, the head spinning, the eyes glazed. Such was the suddenness and ferocity of the punch, Ramalho didn't know where he was.

Picking up a metal ruler, Mendoza placed it in Ramalho's left armpit, sharp side up. "Stand. Or you'll hurt even more."

Slowly, very slowly, Ramalho stood, as Mendoza righted the chair with a foot. Then, the ruler was placed on a shoulder and pressed downwards. Hard. Ramalho sat.

As if using his foot as a metal detector, Mendoza swept an instep over the linoleum. "Be careful. These floors are highly polished, and slippery, very slippery."

The metal ruler found the bone at the base of Ramalho's neck. He tried turning his head but the pain was too great.

"I must speak to the cleaners. About the amount of polish." With his left hand, Mendoza shook free a cigarette, lit it, and inhaled, deeply. "Now, this malaria?"

"I . . . I went to Rio."

"You." There was a sharp jab of the ruler.

Ramalho gasped.

"Went." Another jab. Another gasp. "To." An even harder jab.

Ramalho stifled a gasp.

"Rio." A harder jab, accompanied by a twist of the ruler.

Ramalho slumped, his hands gripping the seat of the chair.

"With who's permission?"

Ramalho was silent.

Withdrawing the ruler, immediately it was thrust deeper into Ramalho's neck. "With who's permission?" snarled Mendoza.

"Permission?" came the throttled reply.

Mendoza removed the ruler, allowing Ramalho to rub the back of his neck. Which is when he received another crashing blow. The fist found accurately the first wound. Whimpering, Ramalho lay on the floor, gasping for breath.

Para was still looking out of the window. "Where's this leading to?"

"A lesson." Once he had Ramalho standing, Mendoza repeated the routine with the ruler, pressing on a shoulder.

Ramalho sat, only to crash to the floor, striking his head on the forward edge of the chair, the chair Mendoza had *not* placed directly behind him.

Ramalho passed out.

As Mendoza sat on the chair, smoking, Para turned from the window. "You know I'm on the committee of M.A.T.V., Mothers Against Television Violence?"

"It's all right, Mauricio. You secret's safe with me." Mendoza inhaled hard and stubbed out his cigarette. On the back of a Ramalho hand. The censor jerked into consciousness, too pained to cry out. "Like some coffee?" asked Mendoza, solicitously.

"Ye . . . yes . . . Please."

"So would I. But first, a couple more questions." Mendoza made no attempt to help Ramalho, who remained on the floor, too dazed and too pained to move. Mendoza leaned forward, hands on knees. "Belem also said they'd some problem with the film itself. Light had got on to the negative, ruining it." Mendoza slid off the chair and crouched beside the hapless Ramalho. "Have you ever opened any of the movie's cans, enough for light to get in and fog the film?"

Too terrified to speak, too physically pained, Ramalho motionless.

"Take your time," said Mendoza, soothingly. And abruptly grabbed Ramalho's lengthy hair, snapping his head backwards.

Para winced, as he felt the force with which Ramalho's head crashed into the seat edge behind him. A comatose Ramalho crumpled.

Mendoza lit another cigarette, picking off his tongue a tiny speck of tobacco.

Para turned. "His screams set my teeth on edge."

"I could gag him?"

"Hasn't he had *enough*?" Para returned to gazing at the city rooftops.

Finally, Ramalho stirred. He propped himself up, on one arm.

Mendoza crouched closer, speaking softly into a Ramalho ear. "Should I repeat the question?"

With much difficulty and labored breathing, Ramalho sat-up. "I got confused."

"Confused? You weren't confused . . . you were cock happy! Thinking of Rio instead of which can was which, film or product?" Mendoza hauled Ramalho up into the chair, studying his victim. "You will return to your censor job and this evening you will do everything as normal, *everything*, getting the shipment ready in the usual way. But," Mendoza raised a finger, "with one exception. You know where the TV-SM studios are?" As Ramalho nodded, Mendoza glanced at Para, who had turned around. "Now, once all done, do not, I repeat, do not marry the two consignments. Pack them separately and bring them to TV-SM." Mendoza yawned. "And wait. In reception."

Ramalho felt more was expected of him. "Then what do I do?"

"I just told you. Wait!" Crossing to his desk, Mendoza pressed a buzzer and instantly the door opened, revealing a police officer. Mendoza indicated Ramalho. "This man has slipped. Bring him an aspirin and some coffee. Oh, and speak to the cleaners." He pointed to the floor. "Too highly polished."

Bowing slightly, the officer left.

Mendoza held Ramalho's injured hand. "How did this happen?"

Ramalho didn't know how to reply. "You burned it on the barbecue, didn't you?" said Mendoza, sympathetically.

"Yes," was the barely audible reply.

"Yes. The barbecue." With a forefinger and thumb holding Ramalho's chin, Mendoza tilted the head of the censor, eyeing the rapidly discoloring area of the left temple. "Oh, you seem to have hit your head. How?"

Ramalho was fearful that whatever answer he gave, it would be the wrong one. "I, eh, I can't remember."

Mendoza smiled, benignly. "Yes, you can. Didn't one of the movie electricians bump into you with that big lamp he was carrying?"

"Oh. Yes."

Mendoza nodded. "You should complain. You could sue them for that." A knock at the door. "Come!" The officer returned with a tray. "When Sênhor Ramalho has had his coffee, take him to the men's room to freshen up, and then drive him to the movie location."

Neither of them spoke, until they were in the soundproof confine of the elevator.

Mendoza wiped a handkerchief across the back of his neck. "I suppose a policeman should be used to the foibles of human behavior, but . . ." He shook his head in resignation. "Some people simply never know when they're well off. He had it made."

"What happens to him now?" asked Para off-handedly.

"Who knows?" Mendoza glanced at Para. "Who cares?"

"Rubio will be here for this evening's meeting."

"In what capacity?"

"Representing the Office of Indian Affairs, State of Boa Vista."

The two men smiled broadly at each other. Reaching the lobby, Mendoza checked his smile. Para exited. "I'll see you then," called Mendoza, as he was obscured by the elevator's closing doors.

SCENE 34. TAKE 4.

Cooper walked into the reception area of TV-SM, to find there already production accountant Con Griffith. "We the first?"

Griffith nodded to the revolving door. "Here's Hector, and Carlo."

Putting down his location bag, Cooper addressed Belem. "Where's Golda, and Ramalho?"

Carlo answered. "James. She said she would not be coming."

Cooper asked himself. *'Why? Why is it other directors can issue orders which are then carried out while I, personally, seem impotent in this area?'*

"I specifically told her to be here." He looked at Belem. "And the censor, Ramalho, where's he?" He eyed the group. "How many people do I have to tell?"

"Boss . . ." A visibly uncomfortable Carlo spoke. "Ramalho came into the office to collect the film. She, Golda. She refused to give it to him."

Cooper closed his eyes. "There a phone around here?" Belem headed for the reception desk. "Hector. Private?"

The two men were directed to an office. Cooper dialed.

"This is Golda."

"This is James."

"I *don't* trust him!"

Cooper forced himself to be civil. "Golda, we've been through this a dozen times already!"

"Are you the one who hit him?" she asked cheerfully.

"What are you prattling on about now?"

"Somebody's given Ramalho a huge shiner. I want to know who to thank." Golda giggled. "Made my day."

"Just give him the bloody dailies!"

No response.

"Golda!"

"You'll regret it", she said in a reprimanding tone.

Cooper felt his hackles rising. "Golda? Chiefs and Indians?"

She sighed deeply. "Geronimo."

"That's better. Give him the cans, but. Tell him to come here first."

"Copy that."

Replacing the phone, Cooper gestured to Belem. "What did you find out?"

"The state censor stuff?" Cooper nodded. "Very strange." Belem held open his arms. "No record. I could not find any reference, none at all, so I went back through the minutes of the state legislature." Shrugging, Belem's eyes widened. "*Nada*, nothing." He relayed to Cooper all of the other sources he'd tried, in his quest to find out anything and everything he could concerning censor legislation.

Cooper was bemused. "What about Imperiocine?"

Belem smiled. "They didn't even know what I was talking about."

Cooper returned the smile. "Thanks, Hector. Thanks a lot."

Accompanied by two State Police officers, Colonel Mendoza descended the stairs. Greeting Cooper, he bowed slightly. "Mr. Cooper, always a pleasure to see a benefactor of our city."

The two men shook hands. "Benefactor?"

"Why, yes." Mendoza smiled. "The money your movie is injecting into the local economy, the jobs, shops, the purchases, hotels, bars, restaurants?" He gestured. "Shall we?"

Cooper followed Mendoza up the staircase.

"James?"

Pausing, Cooper turned. To see his associates huddled at the foot of the stairs, their path barred by Mendoza's two men. "Colonel?"

Mendoza stopped in his tracks.

"Your officers. Would you speak to them?"

Mendoza turned, ever so slowly. "About what?"

"About letting my colleagues pass. I want them in the meeting with me."

Staring at Cooper, Mendoza descended leisurely, finishing one step above the director. "Mr. Cooper, when you hear what I have to say you won't want *anybody* around, believe me."

Cooper nodded. "Colonel, that's interesting, because once you've heard what I have to say *you* won't anybody around, either." He gestured over his shoulder. "Plus I need a translator. I neither speak nor understand Portuguese."

"Fortunately for you, I do." Mendoza nodded towards the group. "They can stay here. My men will protect them."

"From what, the *The Tele Tubbies*?" But already Mendoza was way past the first landing.

Cooper was led into the palatial office of Mauricio Para, and was amused by what he recognized now as the obligatory television set, reminding him of the terrace bar at the hotel, although in this case there was a number of monitors positioned either on tables or suspended on shelves cantilevered out from the walls. All were showing the same TV-SM programme, albeit mute.

Unsmiling, Para rose from behind his desk and shook hands.

Rubio stood. "Remember me?"

Cooper clicked fingers and thumb. "Eh, don't tell me . . . Antonio Vargas." As they shook hands, Cooper added, "I never forget a face."

And the smile never left Rubio's lips, retained there by the knowledge that Cooper's power of recall was not as strong as the director himself would believe.

"Colonel, does this meeting concern these gentlemen?"

Mendoza fussed around. "Sit down, Mr. Cooper. No need to stand. And let me take that." Relieving him of his location bag, Mendoza steered

Cooper to a sofa. "Now, you were asking why are these gentlemen here?" Para handed to Mendoza a tumbler of whisky, on the rocks.

"May I have one of those please? No ice."

"Forgive me! Mauricio, a whisky for our guest." Mendoza looked heavenwards. "No ice." His attention returned to Cooper. "Why are these gentlemen here? Well, it was your office that requested this meeting." He passed a large whisky to Cooper. "Chivas. *Salut*." All savored the drink. "And, as Sênhor Para's television programmes are subject to the same scrutiny from the censor's office as is your movie, I thought it might be useful? Calm your fears, if you will."

"And Sênhor Vargas?"

Ice-free whisky tumbler in hand, Vargas stood. "I've been appointed recently to represent the Office for Indian Affairs, State of Boa Vista. We work very closely with the censor's office." Glancing at Mendoza, the two men nodded.

"Nice try."

A faltering smile creased Rubio's face. "Pardon me?"

Cooper picked up a telephone directory. "I bet if I looked in here, I wouldn't find 'Boa Vista, State of, Office for Indian Affairs,' now would I?"

Smiling, Mendoza answered, quietly. "Of course not. You said yourself, you neither speak nor understand Portuguese? Nor can you read it?"

Cooper watched Para, sitting in front of a monitor, a mute monitor, his lack of English precluding him from the conversation. Cooper turned to Mendoza. "Colonel, let's stop picking the fly shit out of the pepper, eh?"

Mendoza laughed. "Mr. Cooper, you have a masterful grasp of your mother tongue, but what does it mean?"

For the sake of effect, Cooper downed some whisky. "It means, Colonel, there's no such legislation here requiring movie companies to have a censor on set."

Mendoza decided to remain silent. Let the gringo have his moment.

"No. Such. Legislation." Cooper looked around the room. "At either state or federal level, nothing. The Imperiocine people hadn't a clue as to what we were talking about and the past two years' minutes of the state legislature neither record nor reveal any such thing. We checked with our lawyers, they said, 'no, never heard of it.' We even asked *Diario do Boa Vista*, the main newspaper of this state." Cooper pointed to their host. "A *Para* newspaper, and even they said 'no, no such law exists here'." Cooper stared at Mendoza. "So, what gives?"

Para looked at Rubio. "Is he accusing me?"

"No Mauricio, he's just talking about one of your newspapers."

"I thought he couldn't read or understand Portuguese?"

Rubio heaved a sigh. "Mauricio, forget it."

Mendoza drank, slowly. "Mr. Cooper." He studied the liquid remaining in the glass. "If you had not called this meeting, I would have done so myself." He continued, in a quieter, more confidential tone. "You are absolutely correct. There is no censor requirement, never has been, and no state office dealing with Indian affairs. That's all handled at federal level." Studying Cooper, Mendoza finished his whisky.

Shaking his head, Cooper was smiling. "Then Colonel, as you've confirmed what I know already, you can call off your so-called censor and thus I see no point in continuing this meeting?"

"Mr. Cooper. I don't see you as one to walk out of the theater before the movie ends?"

"Colonel, *what* are you talking about?"

Mendoza smiled. "A surprise ending."

They climbed the stairs. Mendoza waited until they'd rounded the landing and were out of sight of Cooper's colleagues. He turned, standing one step above Ramalho, causing the censor to crane up to the police chief in an uncomfortable way, exacerbated by the weight of the dailies parcel he was carrying. Mendoza studied Ramalho, causing the censor to feel intimated, totally. Which was the idea. "You understand the seriousness of your position?"

Ramalho's eyes flickered, blankly.

"Drugs trafficking?"

Ramalho's gaze was trance-like.

"And that I can have you taken care of?"

Ramalho blanched. His gaze faltered.

"Taken care of in one of two ways. Either you cooperate, in which case the slate will be wiped clean." He raised his hands in a gesture of caution. "Or, the other option . . . and look at me! Do I have to paint a picture?"

"No, Colonel."

"*No, Colonel*' is right." Taking out two cigarettes, he lit both, putting one between Ramalho's lips. "When we get upstairs I'll be asking you some questions." Mendoza leaned forward. "You will confine your answers related directly to the question being asked, understand?"

Ramalho nodded. "Yes, Colonel. Related directly to the question."

"No qualifying, no embroidery, rather as if you are under cross examination in court, which to all intents and purposes you will be, with me as the judge *and*, the jury." Each inhaled, deeply. "Have I made myself clear?"

"Yes, Colonel."

"Right, cigarettes out." Relieving Ramalho of his cancer stick, Mendoza stubbed-out both butt ends. Which is when Ramalho's hair was grabbed by Mendoza, his head being yanked sideways, causing his eyes to smart. Looking at the bruising on his left temple, Mendoza chortled. "You really should watch where you're going." The policeman pushed on the censor's chin, forcing back his neck, to great discomfort. "Just yes or no. Remember, *you* are the sole author of your future." Mendoza gestured to the parcels. "You know which is film and which is not?"

"Yes, Colonel."

"You sure?"

Ramalho nodded emphatically. "Sure."

"Good. I'd hate for you to have fogged the product."

The surprise showed on Cooper's face. "Did you tell *him* to be here?"

Mendoza prodded Ramalho into the centre of the room. "Mr. Cooper, I'm the policeman. *I* ask the questions." Nudging Ramalho, Mendoza pointed to the floor. "Put the parcels in front of you."

Surprised to see the dailies transit cases, Cooper stared at them. "And, Colonel, if the spectral Mr. Vargas is employed by the phantom office for phantom Indian phantom affairs, why's he here?"

"He's a federal agent," was the curt reply.

Cooper turned to Rubio. "Sênhor Vargas, refresh my memory. Where was it we met? I mean, besides the hotel?"

Mendoza stood in front of the director. "Mr. Cooper, we're not here to discuss the social rovings of Sênhor Vargas. No, we are here . . ." He made a grand gesture, towards Ramalho. "To question the suspect."

Cooper did a double-take. "The suspect? Suspected of what?"

"It is an interesting story." Mendoza gave Ramalho a disdainful look, and then turned to Cooper, smiling. "But perhaps one you won't like?"

Why, he couldn't determine, but suddenly Cooper felt distinctly uncomfortable.

"We speak in English, understood?" Hands held behind his back, Mendoza paced. "Name, full name?"

"Francesco Clovis Mello Ramalho."

"For crying out loud, Colonel, we all know his bloody name!"

"Formality. Simply formality." Circling Ramalho, Mendoza stopped, looking the man up and down. He peered closer at the left temple. "That looks nasty." He glanced at Ramalho. "How did you get such bruising?"

Ramalho stared ahead. "On the movie."

"On the movie?" Mendoza frowned at Cooper. "How?"

Ramalho continued to stare ahead. "An electrician bumped into me."

Mendoza resumed his pacing. "He must have been Godzilla for you to get a bruise like that?"

"He was carrying a big lamp on his shoulder. He turned. It hit me on the side of my head." Ramalho indicated the wound. "Right here."

Mendoza eyed Cooper. "He could sue you, you know?" He circled Ramalho once more, studying the wound. "While our federal government is shall we say . . ." With pursed lips, Mendoza inclined his head. "A trifle to the right of center, paradoxically, our Workmen's Compensation Decree does tend to favor the worker."

"Colonel, a few minutes ago you commended me for mastery of my mother tongue, so where did you learn *your* excellent English?"

"Self taught."

"Colonel, I do have other things to do?"

Mendoza raised a hand. "Not long, now." He faced Ramalho. "Francesco Ramalho. What is your current employment?"

"I'm a movie censor."

Cooper scanned the ceiling. "And I'm the bloody man in the moon!"

Mendoza ignored the outburst. "And what was your job before that?"

"Airline steward."

Mendoza strolled to the drinks cabinet, refilling his glass as he spoke. "With which airline?"

"VARIG."

Mendoza sauntered back, to face Ramalho. "A Brasilian airline. Why did you leave?"

Ramalho looked at the floor "I lost my job."

"Why?" No response. Mendoza was coaxing. "Redundancy? Or was the national airline of Brasil playing the ethnic card, not liking employees from Imperio?"

Ramalho looked at the floor. "I was fired."

"Oh dear. Fired." Mendoza gave a fair impression of being surprised. "Why?"

"Misconduct."

"Misconduct?" Regarding his audience, Mendoza smiled. "Not reading to passengers the safety card, groping the lady cabin crew, pilfering booze from the galley?"

"Smuggling."

"Smuggling? And what? From where, to where?"

"From Rio. To Los Angeles." He looked at the floor. "Drugs."

Cooper sat forward, his heartbeat quickening. Rising, he crossed to replenish his tumbler.

"The VARIG job didn't pay well enough?"

Ramalho barely whispered. "I needed extra money."

"Speak up!" Looking across to the cabinet where stood Cooper, mesmerized. "I don't think your movie's director can hear you."

Ramalho raised his head, speaking normally. "I needed extra money."

"A family bereavement? A new car, computer? Or maybe done to feed your own . . . addiction?"

"Yes."

"Which?"

Ramalho looked Mendoza directly in the eye. "Addiction."

"Well, well, our favorite recreational past time!" Mendoza held out an empty glass. Rubio took it over to the cabinet, whereupon Cooper moved back to the sofa, transfixed by the ongoing revelations.

"But I'm clean now. I kicked the habit."

"Good for you, Ramalho, good for you. The United States D.E.A. would be very proud of you. But after VARIG, what did you do?"

"The same. Airline steward. With Imperiavia."

Mendoza strolled the room. "The national airline of our fatherland." He stood in front of Cooper, his back to Ramalho. "Good job?"

"Yes."

Mendoza turned, to look at Ramalho. "Were you there long?"

Hesitation. "No."

"Another redundancy, or maybe . . . the same old problem?"

"Yes."

Giving Cooper a glance of 'what did I tell you,' Mendoza ambled over to Ramalho. "Now, we all know your general duties as censor on Mr. Cooper's movie, but let's hear some specifics." He spoke over his shoulder. "Not long now, Mr. Cooper." He returned his gaze to Ramalho. "Have you sent film, just film and nothing but film, to Los Angeles?"

Cooper was paralyzed.

Ramalho quivered, dumbfounded. And resumed his straight ahead stare.

"Should I repeat the question?"

"No."

Mendoza frowned. "No? No what?"

"No, not just film."

The police chief feigned surprise. "Oh? Then what? Mangos? Pinga . . . Porno?"

Ramalho answered, hesitatingly, whispering. "Drugs."

Not a Cooper muscle moved.

Rubio handed to Mendoza a fresh tumbler of whisky. "Drugs. What drugs, specifically?"

"Cocaine."

Cooper wanted to wake up out of this nightmare, but he knew it was all too real. He took a sip of calming whisky. It was no panacea.

"Cocaine." Mendoza paced again. "Sent in what form?"

"Refined powder."

"Can you show us how it was sent?"

Ramalho wavered. He looked at the police chief. Mendoza's eyes lowered to the packages. Kneeling, Ramalho opened a transit case, removing a circular metal can. A film can. He stood.

As did Cooper, slowly, his eyes focused fixedly on the film can.

Mendoza nodded to the can. "I said, show us."

For the very first time that evening, Ramalho looked over to Cooper, a look that conveyed . . . contrition, sorrow, regret?

"Show us."

As he was bid, Ramalho started peeling off the adhesive camera tape.

In a flash, Cooper rushed from the sofa, clamping his hands on Ramalho's wrists. "We've had enough fogged film!"

Mendoza flicked a nod at Rubio, who dragged away the director.

In Cooper's face, Mendoza wagged a remonstrating finger. "Never," he said quietly. "Never *ever* prejudge circumstantial evidence. You should read more Agatha Christie." He nodded to Ramalho. "Open it."

Cooper struggled so violently that Para had to assist Rubio in restraining the director.

Ramalho peeled off the tape.

Cooper wrestled even more strongly.

Ramalho removed the lid.

Cooper threshed like a mad man, kicking both Rubio and Para, knowing that more of his precious movie was about to be ruined, horrified as he watched Ramalho remove the lightproof black paper bag, to let in light, to fog the negative, to reveal . . . white powder, in small plastic bags.

Taking one, Mendoza swung it pendulum-like in front of Cooper's eyes. The director ceased his struggling, with Rubio and Para cautiously releasing their grip.

Turning away, Mendoza repeated the same action in front of Ramalho. "A leopard never changes his spots? So, yours, yes?"

Ramalho seemed hypnotized, staring, in sync with the pendulum. "Yes."

"And so you smuggled drugs, using the movie as your mule?" Holding it in the palm of a hand, Mendoza studied the bag. "Would I be correct in thinking the destination was Los Angeles, California, U.S.A.?"

Ramalho nodded, wearily. "Yes."

Inconspicuously, Mendoza pocketed the bag of cocaine. "In this, eh, enterprise, you were the sole . . . entrepreneur? You acted alone?"

A mumbled "Yes."

Mendoza indicated the door. "Wait outside." As Ramalho passed, Mendoza whispered to him in Portuguese. "In which box is the film?"

And was answered in Portuguese. "The one on the right." Ramalho exited.

Mendoza rubbed-together his hands, excitedly. "Sit down, Mr. Cooper." The Englishman remained standing. Sitting made him feel vulnerable. "At our first meeting, did I not make you aware of your precarious position, and did not your Mr. Pitt Miller . . . ?" Mendoza's tone changed. "Did you know he plays polo? A good chap." He studied his glass, and spoke to it. "Mr. Cooper." He turned to the Englishman. "You are in serious trouble. Drugs running, drugs dealing, drugs trafficking?" He lit a cigarette. "Any act to do with the dissemination of drugs in any manner, shape or form, is a federal crime under the Imperian Penal Code, for which the penalty is either execution, by garrotting or a long, very long, imprisonment." He smiled, brightly. "The former is actually preferred, as it's less of a drain on the federal exchequer." He inhaled deeply on his cigarette.

Suddenly, Cooper felt cold, very cold, very alone and, very frightened. He sat down, slowly.

Mendoza continued his pacing. "When you finish filming down here, what's the next step in the process?"

"Post."

Mendoza frowned. "Post?"

"It's short for post-production. Where is brought together all of the elements of the movie's making, for it to become what you see eventually up on the screen."

"And where will this 'post' be undertaken?"

"Los Angeles."

Mendoza was on the move again. "Ah, yes, L.A., the movie-makers' mecca." Continuing his perambulation, he was shaking his head. "And you, not an American?"

Cooper frowned. "So I'm not American. So what?"

"Well, while the Americans generally welcome immigrants, they're not too disposed to felons, and as for alien felons? No go, no access to the U.S. of A., and a felon convicted of a drug offense? Bye bye visa, bye bye L.A., bye bye U.S.A."

Cooper looked at the three men, one to the other. All of whom were watching him. And then the bubble burst. "Jesus, what a birdbrain I've been." He laughed, crazily, confounding his three opponents, while in turn pointing at each of them. "It's *you*, *you* lot, Ramalho's just the boy. It's *your* drugs operation, you and whoever else, *you* pull the strings!"

Giggling, Mendoza looked at Rubio, and then Para. And back to Cooper. "Ah, the ever fertile imagination of the movie-maker."

Taking his time, Cooper stood. "You lot can go fuck yourselves. Sure, the U.S. authorities will know, because I'm working for an American company, and if you don't think Mr. Tonnini doesn't have connections in high places, then you're more stupid than even I've come to realize." Cooper headed for the door.

"Mr. Cooper?"

The director took no notice, turning the handle, and opening the door.

"I think you had better look."

Cooper halted, his back to Mendoza.

"And possibly kick yourself for eternity, for not taking just a little, tiny, tiny peek?"

Cooper turned, rather as one indulging a tiresome child. To see . . .

Mendoza sitting on a corner of Para's capacious desk, in one hand a film can, held under the bright bulb of a desk lamp. He started to peel away the tape, v-e-r-y slowly . . . "Surely you don't want to remain in Imperio a second longer than you have to? I mean, wouldn't it be awful if more film was fogged, you had to film those scenes all over again, and explain yourself to Mr. Tonnini, and, to the insurance people?"

Glancing at onlookers Rubio and Para, Cooper looked then at Mendoza. "You're bluffing?"

"Aha," cackled Mendoza. "A poker player?" He peeled away the last inch of tape, letting it drop to the floor, like a discarded snake. Mendoza gestured to the can. "Open, sesame?"

Closing the door, Cooper leaned against it. "How do I know that's not a can of cocaine?"

"My dear Mr. Cooper, it's your *Dirty Harry* moment. Is it, or, isn't it? Only one way to find out?" Mendoza pressed the can to his stomach. He began to pry off the lid.

Cooper moved back into the room. "Okay, Colonel, you've made your point. And I presume there is a point to all this?"

Bending down, Mendoza retrieved the tape, winding it securely around the can. "I apologize for the sideshow, preventing your film making tonight's flight. Put it down to Imperian incompetence." Moving a hand to chin, Mendoza brightened. "And yes, there is a point." He looked directly at Cooper. "The point being, *you*. You do nothing. The film is shipped out in the usual way, you allow Ramalho to continue his function on the movie exactly as previously, and, as an expression of your satisfaction with the arrangement, the movie will pay his salary." Mendoza lit yet another cigarette. "And, the movie pays his Social Security. You wouldn't want to deprive him of that?" Mendoza exhaled in Cooper's face. "*You'll* be reminded of the extra curricular payments, and how they should be paid. Understood?"

All Cooper understood was his panic to get away from these people in one piece, and, alive. "Understood, Colonel."

"Oh, and more thing." Mendoza reached into an inside pocket and pulled-out a passport. "Yours, I believe? But it may have no further use?"

He wasn't quite 'Norma Desmond,' but Cooper descended the stairs as if in a vegetative state. He feigned the close-up.

"Blimey, James. You alright?" Asked Con Griffith.

Cooper sighed the sigh of sighs. "I'll live. Hopefully."

"D'you want to talk?"

Cooper shook his head.

"Back to the hotel?"

Cooper nodded. "Please."

"Hotel it is then." Followed by Belem and Carlo, they headed for the exit.

Once into the car Griffith couldn't contain himself. "Well, did you sort out the business of the censor?"

Cooper looked out of the window. "In a manner of speaking."

As the car moved off, Rubio was running alongside the vehicle. "*Sênhor Cooper*, Mr. Cooper!"

Cooper looked out. "What the hell's he want? Better stop the car."

Griffith signaled the driver.

Rubio opened the front door. "You may not forget a face, but you forgot this!" He held high Cooper's location bag, and placed it on the front seat.

"*Obrigado*, Sênhor Vargas."

"You're more than welcome." Rubio waved away the car.

"Seems a nice chap?"

Cooper grunted. "I think he's the one Goebbels child that avoided being poisoned."

Griffith frowned at his boss. "That's an odd thing to say?"

"It's been an odd day. Life's never what you expect it to be."

"James, very profound. But the meeting? What went on, and what happened?"

"Nothing. There's really nothing to tell." Cooper slumped into silence.

"Before I forget. Tomorrow night, eight o'clock, conference call with Henry Spencer, the loss adjustor? He says the claim is so obvious that he feels there's no need for him to fly down here."

Cooper refocused his attention. "This the Susan Chase claim?"

"Primarily the Fort Set."

"Is Hooray Henry smelling victory or am I simply jaundiced?"

"Only time will tell?"

They arrived at the hotel. Cooper gestured to Griffith. "Thanks, Con."

"For what? I didn't get to do anything?"

"Yes you did. You stayed."

The teenage porter took Cooper's location bag. With both hands. Griffith watched him wrestle it. "Modern youth. Wimps, no back bone."

Cooper smiled. "All it has in it is a script, a breakdown, a schedule and yesterday's *Herald Tribune*."

Out of the side of his mouth, Griffith spoke *sotto voce*. "The bigger the struggle, the greater the tip?"

Into the lobby they followed the struggling porter. To be confronted by Nessa, holding aloft Cooper's room key. Frowning, she tilted her head. "Jesus, James, you look like death!"

A faint smile. "That's how I feel."

Nessa tipped the porter. It revived his energy. "Suite one ten." The porter took the bag into the elevator.

"What happened?"

"Let's get to my room. I'll try to tell you there."

Nessa found the Cutty Sark. Having warmed a tumbler, she poured a large measure and handed it to him. He put aside the glass, a move not un-noticed by Nessa. "James, I've never seen you like this before?"

"I've never felt like this before."

"The best place for you is bed." Nessa bent down and removed his jungle boots, fanning her nostrils as she did so. "You know, the hotel *does* have a laundry service and they actually launder socks. You might care to try it some time."

"They're my snake repellents."

She gestured. "Move."

He staggered into the bedroom. Pushing him backwards on to the bed, Nessa undid his belt, pulled-off his pants, followed by his shirt. He was left only in his underpants. She retrieved the whisky and placed the glass on his bedside table. She looked at him. He was asleep. Somehow maneuvering the sheets, she managed to position him under the covers. Nessa studied him, wondering, is it all really worth it? Looking at him for a few moments longer, she kissed him gently. "Good night, sweet prince."

Cooper awoke early, pondering how it was he was in bed in only his underpants. He looked at the whisky on the bedside table, but knew this wasn't the time. Donning a robe, he wandered into the main room. Cooper felt like a character in a Kurt Vonnegut novel. There was this feeling of disconnect. But it was all there. The Moviola, the desk with the lap-top and printer, the television, the VCR, the coffee table, his mini-stereo plus CDs, and . . . his location bag. Sitting, he pulled it towards him. It seemed heavier. Unzipping it, he was surprised to see it was filled with a number of large manila envelopes. "Mendoza's submitting a spec. script?" he said aloud. "*Confessions of a Dago Cop*. No, *Confessions of a <u>bent</u> Dago Cop*. Nah, too long a title." Cooper noticed that there were some dozen filled envelopes. "Trust Mendoza, a bleeding mini series." He shook his head. "No chance then of Raul Julia for the lead." He removed an envelope, slitting it open and peering inside, gingerly. *"What!"* he cried, dropping both the envelope and the letter opener. Horrified, Cooper just stared at the envelope for several minutes. Without taking his eyes off the bag, he grabbed the phone, and dialed.

A very drowsy Nessa answered. "Yes?"

"It's James. Come in here, quickly. Call Golda, and get her up here too, plus some coffee for all of us."

"James, it's around four A.M."

"Nessa, get in here. Please!"

While Golda poured the coffee, Cooper handed to Nessa the envelope. Both ladies wore robes over their night-clothes.

Holding it upside-down, Nessa shook the envelope. From which poured many bundles of U.S. dollar bills. Puzzled, Nessa looked at the dead-pan Cooper. She opened more envelopes. More U.S. dollar bills.

Which is when Golda put down two cups of coffee. "Oh! James, you're finally increasing our piss-poor per diem!"

Without looking up from the money, Cooper replied. "Golda, this isn't the time for frivolity. It's a time for clear minds and to know what the hell we do?"

Nessa opened the last envelope. No money, but a letter, which she passed to Cooper. Unfolding it, he read aloud. *"Dear Sir.* Period. *Some of your goods have been damaged through negligence.* Period. *This company's responsibility is both acknowledged herewith and accepted,* comma, *hence we have pleasure in forwarding the enclosed,* comma, *in full and final settlement,* comma, *without prejudice.* Period. *Yours faithfully, for and on behalf of Assurannza Amazonas.* Period." He looked at the two ladies. "No signature. Nothing." He turned to Nessa, indicating the bills. "Any idea how much is here? Ballpark?"

"Ballpark?" Nessa studied the money, looking at the various piles. She looked up at Cooper. "I'd guess close to two-fifty grand."

"What the hell do we do with it?" He hugged his knees, rocking back-and-forth. "How'd we explain it?"

"Try. How'd you come by it?" An accusing look. "What've you been up to?"

Puzzled, both Nessa and Golda looked at Cooper.

"It's a long story. Me, the movie itself, have received threats, serious threats. It's best, and safer, that you don't know, either of you, believe me." He gestured to the money. "But we must get rid of it. We *have* to."

From studying Cooper, Nessa turned her gaze to the money. "Santa Mosqueiro's a typical south American city. You're either stinking rich, like Para, or you're grovel poor. So in this city there's plenty of charities. Why not give it to them?"

"That's fine. But how?"

"I'll do it."

"Nessa, you're too high profile. Every one in Santa Mosqueiro knows you're associated with the movie." He eyed the two ladies. "Any of us here Catholic?"

"Don't look at me," chimed Golda.

"Nor me. Lutheran. Anyway, what's Catholic to do with it?"

"A priest. Sworn to secrecy. He'd know the charities. We distribute the money through him and he gets us a receipt."

Golda giggled. "James, a *receipt?*"

"I'm taking no chances. How do we know this won't blow up in our faces?"

"But", added Golda. "We still don't have a carrier?"

"No, but I'll sleep on it." Cooper eyed the two ladies. "I know I can trust you two not to say a *dicky bird* to anybody about this, right?"

Golda answered. "My lips are sealed."

"That's a first." He looked at them again. "Listen, guys, I'm most grateful for you coming in, but suddenly I feel tired, very tired."

Watching him disappear into the bedroom, the two ladies moved to the door. Nessa opened it and Golda walked through, expecting Nessa to follow. Which she didn't.

"You staying?"

"It's not what you think, Golda, no way. But I don't think he should be left alone. I'll sleep on the sofa."

Golda nodded. "*Ciao.*"

"Golda?"

The production supervisor turned.

"Thanks. For helping tonight. Or should I say, this morning?"

"We've moved on from our first encounter?"

"For sure."

Golda moved closer to Nessa. "James? You've known him before, right?"

Nessa smiled. "In another life."

"What about the next life?"

"Golda, I'm engaged to Franco Tonnini." Nessa gestured over her shoulder. "D'you like him?"

Bursting out laughing, Nessa shushed Golda. "What's so funny?"

"Yes, I like him, but way too high maintenance for me. Besides, he likes bacon sandwiches, which for me are *verboten*."

"But you're good for him, Golda. You hold the center. For which you have my grateful thanks."

"Then we're on the same side?"

"You bet. Get some sleep."

Cooper eyed the bedside clock. Both hands were perpendicular. "Janey, six A.M."

He wandered into the main room and for a number of minutes he stared at the loot. Then the pangs of hunger hit him. He dived into the shower and dressed into his work clothes. Picking up his location bag, loot included, he headed for the door, which is when he noticed Nessa on the sofa. "Couldn't find your way back to your own suite? Still, *mi casa es tu casa*. And I know you can't hear me, but I'm going down to see if I can get an early breakfast'. He was tempted to kiss her forehead but didn't want to wake her. He closed the door.

El Yacht Club do Santa Mosqueiro.

Another early breakfast, *al fresco*. Mauricio Para, Colonel Mendoza, Antonio Rubio.

Mendoza turned to Para. "He must've found it by now?" He looked at Rubio. "The money?"

Rubio burst out laughing, his mirth taking some time to subside.

Given was a Mendoza grave look. "What's so funny?"

"I'm sorry." Rubio produced a handkerchief, dabbing his eyes. "I was just thinking of something." He blew his nose. "When we were at the embassy in Buenos Aires . . ." He gestured to the other two men. "My father was the ambassador. Anyway, he had this book, English, a pictorial review of the years between 1919 and 1939, and I always remember one photo in particular, which showed this little German girl. The Reichsmark had collapsed, the currency was useless and it cost about a million marks to buy a loaf of bread. Anyway, in the picture this kid has bundles and bundles of bank notes, which she'd built up into an arch like toy building bricks, as there were so many of them, hundreds and hundreds of banknotes, all worthless." He looked at his colleagues. "Just like Cooper's got!"

Para played with his eggs benedict. "And what will Cooper build?"

"If he's wise, a coffin." Mendoza stirred his coffee. "Mr. Cooper is a Brit, and these days they don't have too much imagination. They always have to play it straight, be the good chap." Mendoza grinned. "He'll find his biggest problem is trying to figure out how he'll put that money through the movie company's books?" He opened his hands, nodding to Para and Rubio. "Obviously Ramalho's screw-up will have caused them problems, problems they'd resolve normally by insurance, and as we've shown him, *he* can't go that route, but being the good chap, he'll still want the movie reimbursed, so, he's wondering how the hell he's going to do it, y'know, reimburse the movie, without any questions being asked?"

Para gestured. "Any other problems he might face?"

A waitress poured more coffee.

"One." Said Mendoza. "Just one."

"Which is?" Covering his coffee cup, Para spoke to the waitress. "A Chivas. No ice."

With both hands, Mendoza held the cup in front of his lips. "If he has any money left over, then trying to decide what to do with the rest of it?"

Rubio nodded. "And haven't we helped him there?"

Both Para and Mendoza looked at him. "How?" Said, simultaneously.

Rubio addressed both of them. "Don't Europeans with hot money always head for Rio?" He looked again at his two collaborators. "Look what we've saved him on the air fare?"

The three men laughed heartily. "Especially . . ." Mendoza dabbed his eyes, "especially as it's all counterfeit anyway, so everyone saves!"

More hearty laughter.

The whole breakfast area was empty. He looked into the Patio Bar. Likewise. Apart from the concierge, everywhere was deserted, even the lounge, into which he wandered. Sitting in an armchair, he looked around the room, asking himself . . . *Who designs and decorates these rooms, trying to make an hotel lounge in sweltering Santa Mosqueiro resemble an English drawing room in chilly Chichester?* Cooper espied the piano. Picking up the location bag, he walked over to it. He tinkled the keys, and then sat down, asking himself, *when did I last play? Oh, yes. The night of the party.* Both hands were on the keys. Involuntarily, the tinkling became a tune, the tune had a vocalist. Cooper. "*The summer wind came blowing in, from across the sea, it lingered there, it touched your hair and walked with me, all summer long and sang a song, and then we strolled that golden sand, two sweethearts and, the summer wind . . .*" He stopped. He couldn't remember the rest of the lyric.

But someone else did. And sang. "*I lost you, I lost you to the summer wind.*" Nessa moved to, and stood behind Cooper, placing her hands on his shoulders. "Play, James, play *The Summer Wind*."

He found the tune. Nessa sang. Cooper joined in the singing. *"The autumn wind and the summer wind, they have come and gone, still those days, those lonely days, they go on and on, and guess who sighs these lullabies through the night that never ends, my fickle friend, the summer wind . . ."*

Which was followed by clapping. Surprised, Nessa and Cooper turned, to be faced by Alfredo, the concierge. "Can we sign you up?"

"I've a movie to finish, but if it's no good, I'll consider your offer." Cooper nodded to Nessa. "Yes? But how about some breakfast? Papaya, mango juice, toast, confiture and coffee? For two?"

"Of course. On the terrace?"

"Please." Cooper checked his watch. "And Alfredo. *Rapido*?"

Breakfast, on the terrace, in the cool of the morning.

Nessa eyed Cooper. "You look distant?"

"Yesterday was a very strange day."

"Tell me when you have a normal one."

"I look forward to that day."

Nessa gestured to the lounge. "What were you doing down here at six-thirty, playing the piano?"

"A sort of relaxing. Besides, I don't know how to play the violin."

Drinking some coffee, Nessa rested her cup. "You can do better than that."

"Okay. I don't know how to play the cello."

"I thought you wanted this directing gig to work?"

"Of course I do. But not in the way it's panning out."

Nessa gestured to the lounge, and the piano. "Somehow, this all strikes me as irresponsible, a sort of abdicating?"

"I'm rehearsing for *Pretty Woman Two*."

Nessa shook her head. "James, has it *never* occurred to you when Franco and I talk, we inevitably discuss this movie, everything about it, including you?"

"Okay, so you spy on me and then report back to *Il Duce*."

As he never saw it coming, it hurt more than one way, as Nessa slapped him with all of her might. "How dare you!", she said coldly. "Who the hell d'you think got you this show?" They glared at each other. "Why do men always presume their reputations precede them? In anything. And everything?"

To soothe the stinging feeling, Cooper put a handkerchied to his cheek.

Nessa calmed. "Franco never remembers names. Unless it's someone who's crossed him." She buttered her toast. "For this gig Franco wanted a European. Your name popped out before I could stop it. James, you're here . . ." Her knife she pointed at him repeatedly. "Because of me, and me *only*."

"Should I give you ten percent?"

"Christ, Cooper! Can't you *ever* be human, like, like . . . normal?"

Cooper looked contrite. "In which case . . ." He turned his head and pointed to his right cheek. "I deserve another slap, right here."

Nessa smiled. "No you don't." Placing fingers to her lips, she kissed them and put them on Cooper's tingling cheek. "I'm sorry."

"So am I, I'm sorry for what I said, and I'm . . ." He couldn't find the words. Looking at Nessa, he continued, softly. "Sorry. We still friends?"

"Just about."

Breakfast finished, they wandered back into the lounge. Cooper couldn't resist sitting at the piano. Motioning him to one side of the stool, Nessa sat, her back to the piano.

Cooper looked at her. "This a love seat?"

Resting her hands on her thighs, she studied them. "You know I was nuts about you?"

He tapped out the opening bars of *Colonel Bogey*.

"What's the significance of that?"

"I'm lost for words."

"Another first." She glanced at him. "But you know, time, and Franco, are great healers." She nudged him. "And I remember those moods, some black." She swiveled to sit next to him. "How are they today?"

Before Cooper could answer, they were interrupted.

"Boss?" It was Rafael, Cooper's driver. "It late?"

He grabbed the location bag, and Nessa. "Ride with me."

"How do I get back?"

"Rafael will drive you back. Now, come on!"

Relaxing were the smoothness of the Town Car and its air-conditioning. Nessa scrutinized Cooper.

"What?"

She nudged him, playfully. "That mind, that devious mind? Might you be a man with a plan?"

He nodded. "I might well be such a man. With a possible plan."

"Then, my man, what is that plan?"

He turned to face her. "Apart from the conundrum of what to do with the loot, how do we know it's legit and that it's not counterfeit?"

"You still haven't told me how you came by it?"

"I can't. Which is why we must get rid of it."

Nessa looked at the location bag with its loot, and then at Cooper. "To whom, to where, and how?"

"No more questions. But we return it." He raised the car's glazed partition, preventing Rafael from hearing any of their conversation. "To Police Headquarters, addressed personally to Colonel Mendoza, via U.P.S. or FedEx, which he, or some other cop, will have to sign for."

Nessa nodded, contemplatively. "I get it. And I like it, I like it a lot. The biter bit, right? Let's do it. Okay for me to put Golda on it?"

"Copy that." Retrieving his script, he closed the bag. "Guard this with your life. Put the parcel together in your room, not in the office. And make it look as official as possible."

The car stopped at the location site. Cooper alighted, telling Rafael to return Miss Preiss to the hotel.

"James . . ." Cooper returned to the car, the opened window, and Nessa. "Lean in." He did. To receive a delightful on the lips kiss. "To help you get the first set-up, a.s.a.p." They smiled at each other. He returned the kiss. "What's that for?"

"You figure it out." And he walked off towards the camera, script in hand.

Evening. Cooper's suite. In attendance, Cooper, Nessa and Griffith.

Once again it was being combed with fingers. His hair. "I don't understand it. *Not* coming down?" Cooper gestured to Griffith. "You ever heard of such a thing on a major claim?" He looked longer at Griffith, and then at Nessa. "The loss adjustor not visiting the scene of the accident?"

"Maybe he's twigged your four days' claim?" Suggested Griffith.

"That's as maybe," nodded Cooper. "But he can't dispute the Fort Set claim. That's irrefutable."

Nessa looked at him. "That's a big word."

Cooper spread his arms. "The bigger the claim." His arms he opened wider. ". . . The bigger the words." Nessa smiled. "But Con, have you? Ever known any loss adjustor not to visit the location, to see the circumstances and get as much background info as possible, to get the facts for himself?"

Griffith shook his head, slowly. "No. It is odd, very unusual."

"Unusual?" In turn, Cooper looked at his two colleagues. "It's downright bloody worrying!"

Nessa glanced at Cooper. "Why?"

Cooper turned to Griffith. "What documentation has he had?"

"Everything." The accountant spread his arms. "Every bloody thing! Production reports, shooting schedules, call sheets, weekly E.F.C.s—"

"Eh, guys, chaps?" She eyed the two of them. "Me, Nessa the neophyte. What's an E.F.C.?"

"Estimated Final Cost," replied Griffith. He gestured to Cooper. "It's a weekly exercise by the producer and the production accountant, a projection based on each week's cumulative expenditure, averaged out to give an idea of the final cost, and sent to the studio." He returned his attention to Cooper. "To reiterate. Hooray Henry has had every single piece of paper relevant to the claim."

Cooper twiddled his thumbs. "Which is why it's worrying."

Nessa looked at the two men. "But why, *why* is it worrying?"

"Because, Nessa the neophyte, if Hooray Henry has all the paperwork and doesn't see the necessity of coming down here . . ." Pausing, Cooper looked at Griffith, and then to Nessa. "Either he's seen something we haven't, or, we've forgotten to include something and he's spotted it?" He looked at his two colleagues. "There's something rotten in the state of Denmark, or, should I say in the state of Boa Vista?"

Golda's head appeared around the door. "Hooray Henry, line one."

"Golda?" The head reappeared. "Get in here quickly with a pad and pencil. You need to be privy to all this." Both hesitatingly, and relunctantly, Cooper picked-up the phone. "Hello?"

"James? Henry Spencer."

Cooper covered the mouthpiece. "Golda, get down as much of this as you can."

"James?"

"Henry, one second, I'm putting you on the speaker." Cooper placed the receiver on the instrument. "Can you hear?"

"Loud and clear. A sort of 'Broadsword calling Danny Boy.'"

"Fine. Henry, privy to this call are Con Griffith, who you know, Golda Wisepart, who you know, and, Miss Nessa Preiss, who you don't." He winked at her. "Miss Preiss, eh, that's P-R-E-I-S-S, is the Tonnini International representative. The associate producer. And as an aside, she's also engaged to Francesco Tonnini." Cooper put his ear closer to the speaker. "Was that a gulp, Henry?" Nessa giggled. "Henry, to me, this all seems unusual. I mean, your not coming down here and doing all of this negotiation and settlement by phone?" Glancing at the others, he raised his eyebrows. "May I ask why?"

"Of course. I owe you that much."

Covering the mouthpiece, Cooper eyed his three colleagues. "I don't like the sound of this." He resumed the conversation. "Henry, you've lost me?"

"The Fort Set? Information in my possession indicates this claim is a total fabrication, pure and simple."

"Henry, are you suggesting I'm mendacious?"

"Egregious. In the past James, you and I have crossed swords many times, but in all our previous jousting never, ever, have you presented such a baseless claim. You now into Ponzi schemes?"

As Cooper's anger was increasing, Nessa grabbed the speaker "Mr.

Spencer, Nessa Preiss. As we're all privy to this conversation, how can you make such an assertion when you've not even been down here to survey the damage, the damage that was documented on Polaroids, all of which were sent to you in support of the claim?"

"Miss Preiss, as I'm sure we all want to wrap this up as quickly as possible, I will counter your claim. Eh, no pun intended." He paused. "Now, I have all of the production's supporting documentation on the destruction of the Fort Set, the production's total of this claim being one hundred and ninety-seven thousand dollars, a not inconsiderable amount of money. Then we have the impacted days, shooting days claimed because of the Fort knock-on effect, at one-hundred-twelve-thousand-dollars per day, totalling four-hundred-and-forty-eight-thousand-dollars U.S. An awful lot of money. Probably more than Imperio's G.N.P. for a whole year? But, Miss Preiss, I also have something else." Spencer paused once more.

Giving Cooper the chance to eyeball his crew. All looked bewildered.

Spencer's patronizing attitude was beginning to grate on Cooper. He indicated to Nessa to pass the speaker. "Henry, what *is* the 'something else' you have?"

"What I have, James, is a memo, a copy of a memo on *Redmayne West* stationery, a memo which states categorically—"

"Who's it to?"

"You, dear boy. You."

Looking at his colleagues, Cooper shrugged. "And who's it from?"

"Anthony Leef."

"Anthony Leef!" Cooper squinted at the speaker, as if it had transmitted false information. "Henry, are you sure? Anthony *Leef*?"

"James," said Spencer, with more than a hint of irritation in his voice. "It's to *you*, dear boy. With a copy to Con."

Cooper looked at his accountant, who indicated ignorance. "Henry, neither of us knows what the heck you're talking about."

"Well, James, in this instance, you'll see ignorance is not *bliss*. Thanks to this memo, it proves irrevocably that the claim's invalid, a con." A pause. "Eh, Con, no insult intended."

Nessa spoke. "Mr. Spencer, you *must* give us the chance to see this memo? After all, you produce it at the eleventh hour like some latter day Perry Mason and we're all supposed to roll over? Every year, Tonnini International produces a number of movies. Maybe we should change our insurer?"

"Miss Preiss, I don't like your attitude."

"And me neither yours! Now, either get your ass down here pronto to assess the damage, or, let us see the memo, a.s.a.p. via fax. You have the number!"

"Of course," replied Spencer, haughtily.

Cooper signaled Golda to the fax machine.

"And James, while the faxed memo spans the airwaves, let us talk about the Susan Chase claim. Eh, was that a gulp, a swallow?"

Cooper gave the Agincourt salute to the speaker phone.

"And, James, I have just one question for you."

With dread written all over his visage, Cooper looked at both Nessa and Griffith. "Which is?"

"Did anyone, any *one* of the Tonnini organization or on the *Redmayne* production itself with the authority to do so, did *anyone* tell Miss Chase she could accompany the production designer fellow on his location recce?"

Cooper's answer was immediate. "No."

"I thought as much."

"Hold on Henry." Golda had returned. "I've just been handed the fax. Tell you what, give me five minutes, and we'll call you right back." Golda killed the connection.

Holding the paper under a desk lamp. "This is a memo from our late lamented friend, Anthony Leef." In turn, Cooper glanced at Griffith, Nessa and Golda. "It says, and I quote, *I confirm our location conversation of today, with regard to the Fort Set, namely, that I will not shoot it in its existing complete form, and therefore it must be dismantled to be re-erected in stages, to accord with the action needs of the script, whereby each scene will be shot sequentially, in script continuity order, with the relative amount of plausible building having taken place between the shooting of each sequence.* Paragraph. *Obviously this will entail a number of visits to this location set, so with that in mind, the shooting of it has to be rescheduled. Anthony Leef, Director.* End quote." Cooper scanned the paper further. "Oh, and this is to 'file,' copies to Raymond Roberts, Syd Walton, Con Griffith." Cooper waved the piece of paper at Griffith. "You ever seen this before?"

Griffith shook his head. "No, never." Pointing to the fax, he asked "Who typed it, who's initials are on the memo?"

Cooper checked. "None." Raising his hands as if celebrating Communion, he asked. "Should there be?"

"Yes. Golda's drummed it into every secretary to always put on any correspondence the initials of the person sending it, and, the person typing it." He indicated her. "Right, Golda?" She nodded.

Watched by the others, Cooper studied the fax yet again at some length, as slowly he grinned and grinned again, until a huge smile lit-up his whole face.

"I know that look," said Golda.

"So do I," added Nessa.

"*Moi aussi,*" whispered Griffith.

Cooper waved the fax. "Not worth the bloody paper it's written on! Henry's in for a big disappointment. Golda, get me the day file and the production reports file, please."

"Copy that."

Griffith removed his spectacles. "We allowed in on the secret?"

Cooper held aloft a restraining hand. "Must check my facts first." The files were placed in front of him. "Thanks, Golda, but hang about, we may well need to send a return fax to Hooray Henry." Cooper thumbed through a file, and removed a report. With the second file, he repeated the process. And smiled even more broadly.

While studying Cooper, Golda nudged Nessa. "Been like this ever since early childhood." She turned to Nessa. "He never had a train set. Did you know that?"

As Nessa's giggles increased, both ladies were subjected to a Cooper look, one akin to that given by Sikorski to Hitler. "Con, come 'ere." Griffith leaned over a Cooper shoulder, who pointed to the first report. "Look, look here. The date?"

Griffith nodded. "Uh . . . uh."

Cooper proffered the second report. "And here . . . ?"

Griffith stood erect, shaking his head in disbelief. "That old queen. Talk about 'hell hath no fury'?"

Cooper handed to Golda the two extracted reports. "Fax these up straightaway, please." Cooper dialed the phone. "Henry, it's on its way up to you by fax."

"What is, dear boy?"

"Documentation supporting both the credibility *and* the validity of our claim."

"James, done some quick improvising and alterations, have we?"

"Henry, just *what* are you suggesting?" When could be heard from the other end the rustling of paper.

"James, don't be tiresome. I've seen this already."

"Yes, Leef's memo. But what date's on it?"

"Eh . . . March, March twenty-nine."

"Right. Now look at the other sheets faxed up to you. One is a production report. Go to that one's 'remarks' heading at the bottom, and you'll see it quotes the destruction of the Fort Set. The *destruction*?"

"Yee . . . sss."

"And what's the date of that?"

"Eh . . . February ten."

"Yes, tenth of February." Cooper winked at his team. "Exactly six and-a-half weeks before Leef's memo was even written? That memo says, and I quote, '*I confirm our location scout of today.*' Today?" Cooper suppressed his glee. "He wasn't even on the movie then, he'd walked! Added to which, you must have on file a copy of a fax from me to Robey in London, advising of the damage and that a claim would be forthcoming, and if you look at the other sheet, you'll see it's a pre-production report, of the actual day we *did* do the tech scout to the Fort. Note the date. The seventh of January. Leef's *today*, his twenty-ninth of March." Cooper leaned into the speaker phone. "I rest my case."

"I need to study these."

Cooper looked at his attentive and eager audience. "Henry, take all the time in the world, but eventually you'll arrive at the one, irrefutable conclusion. So just get your bloody cheque book out!"

Spencer's voice was ice cold. "James, don't fall into the trap of counting your chickens."

"Henry, never, but. May I ask how the Leef memo came into your possession?"

"It's no secret. Mr. Leef called me, said he'd heard about the claim and asked if he could help in any way, to the extent of offering me his notes, notes he'd made during the course of location scouts and, production."

"Albeit some six weeks after he absented himself from said production."

"He maintains he was fired."

"Fired or walked, what's the difference? The dates, Henry, the *dates* confirm it's a stitch up? He walked, Henry, he walked because of the Susan Chase situation." Cooper relaxed somewhat. "And talking about that Henry, what about the cost of doctors and the air ambulances to repatriate Miss Chase to the U.S. and and the production designer to the U.K.?"

"The couple were found in Colombia. Their injuries were sustained in Colombia. The insurance, placed by your Miss Wisepart, stipulated the designer would be scouting in Imperio. Nothing about Colombia. Need I say more?"

"I guess not." Looking at Golda, Cooper gestured a drinking hand to mouth.

"Copy that." Golda departed, to return with a bottle of Cutty Sark, and four glasses. She poured for the ensemble.

Cooper sank his in one. His held-out glass was refilled immediately. "Okay, Henry, I'll yield that one, Susan Chase. But. We're discussing my *Fort* claim. You want more time to look at those documents and their dates, fine. But I have a movie to direct, so Miss Preiss will be handling the claim henceforth." He smiled at Nessa. "And she's a much tougher nut to crack, believe you me. She will expect your answer, your positive answer, within two working days. Oh, and we'll expect payment in dollars U.S., not cruzeiros Imperian. *Boa tarde.*"

His three associates clapped.

Mock-bowing, Cooper looked at all three. "But did you get that?"

Griffith was shaking his head. "We all fade, as a leaf . . ."

"Not Leef, you schmuck, Hooray Henry! He's lumped together the four days with the Fort. He's bought it as one claim!"

"Then we've a winning chance?" Asked Nessa.

Ever the cautious, Griffith spoke. "But will he accept what we're saying?" He pointed to the speaker phone. "You heard him. '*Done some improvising, James*'?"

Wordlessly, Cooper opened a drawer and removed a Filofax. Scanning it with an index finger, he found the entry he sought. He glanced at Griffith, at Nessa and at Golda. "You ain't heard nothing yet." He dialed. "Anthony? Is good I catch you. *Si*, is me, Franco Tonnini."

Putting a hand to her mouth, Nessa gasped. Shaking his head, Griffith covered his ears. Golda surpressed giggles.

"Anthony, tell me, you a write or contact the fund loss adjustor? Yes or no? Anthony! You wanna to work again this town? Then call the guy an' tell him the truth. *Pronto! Ciao.*" Replacing the receiver, Cooper smiled at the group. "He put in a thumb, pulled out a plum and said, what a good boy am I!"

Griffith turned to the two ladies. "I heard nothing. Golda, did you? Or Nessa?"

"Every word", replied Golda. "Loved every syllable." She turned to Nessa, to see her kissing Cooper on the lips, very gently and . . . very tenderly.

An action which even took him by surprise, totally. "What's that for?"

"From Franco." It was Nessa's turn to wink. "For the impersonation."

Griffith collected together his things. "I'm for dinner. Anyone care to join me?"

"Yes, I will," said Golda. "The hotel does a great *gefilte* fish and chips."

Griffith studied Cooper. "You enjoy going right to the edge, don't you?"

"No," said Cooper candidly. "But any movie I work on has to be protected from amoral incompetents like Leef. The cover may not be in the Insurer's portfolio, but in my book, it is."

"That's a fine line, James, a very fine line." Griffith nodded to Nessa as he held open the door for Golda. "Goodnight."

Cooper came around the rear of the grip truck, bumping into Francesco Ramalho, literally. The censor winced, putting a hand to the dressing over his left temple.

Cooper mumbled. "Sorry . . ."

As obviously Ramalho was dazed, Cooper held-out a steadying hand. "Francesco, you okay?" The censor continued to hold his head. Cooper gestured to the wound. "Mendoza did that, right?"

Ramalho nodded.

"How of a hold does he have over you?"

"I am trapped. Like this." Ramalho closed the fingers of an upturned palm, slowly.

"Isn't there anyone you can turn to? For help?"

"I wish there was. Mr. James, Imperio is a small country. Mendoza is part of something big. He's a police chief, I'm a reformed junkie, but with a record, so who, who would ever believe me?" The man shrugged. "I no longer have a life of my own. I am *owned* by him, by Mendoza." Ramalho laughed. "My Svengali."

With a foot, Cooper toyed with a pebble. "You know . . ." He looked-up at Ramalho. "There's always a light at the end of the tunnel?"

Ramalho smiled faintly. "Sure. Probably Mendoza's flashlight?"

"Look, Francesco, Mendoza's a bully, and history tells us that bullies always get their comeuppance." Cooper gestured. "Mussollini, Hitler, Galtieri, Noriega . . . Richard Nixon?"

"I hear you, but how many have to suffer before that day comes?"

Ramalho turned and walked away. As Cooper watched the receding figure of the man, he remembered he had a date, a lunch date.

Expecting to see Nessa surrounded by the Boscoli family, Cooper was surprised to encounter only the Captain of Customs, and a flaming redhead. Standing, Boscoli gave to Cooper the traditional South American male's bear hug greeting. The director offered to Nessa a look of total bewilderment. As they took their seats under the sun canopy, Cooper nudged Nessa. "Where's the *Trouble* and the *Saucepans*?"

"The . . ." A frowning Nessa stared at Cooper. "What?"

Cooper unfolded a napkin. "And I thought you guys spoke English." As the wine-laden meal was served, Cooper turned to the redhead. "And you are?"

The reply was in a soft Irish brogue. "Bridgit Coelho."

She and Cooper shook hands, greeting her. "*Cead mille failte.*"

She curtsied. *"Go raibh mille maith agat."*

"Rural Irish?"

"Sea. Ros Comàin. Four Mile House."

"Ah, yes, four Irish miles to six English miles. But Bridgit, the invitation was to the whole Boscoli family." He shrugged. "Where are they?"

Before answering, she sipped her wine. "Elida, Sênhora Boscoli, she had a headache and also wasn't prepared to take her children out of school."

Kurt Greene arrived. "Hope I'm not too late?" Shaking hands with Cooper, he kissed Nessa lightly on the cheek.

"Kurt, may I introduce Senor Boscoli, the Captain of Customs." Another bear hug. "And Bridgit Coelho."

Kurt kissed her hand. "Charmed." He winked at Nessa.

Cooper proposed a toast. "To Santa Mosqueiro."

With hand on heart, Boscoli stood, and countered. "Imperio!"

All glasses were raised to "Imperio!" Then Kurt was busied with signing multiple autographs in the many books presented to him by Boscoli.

Cooper addressed the colleen. "Bridgit, tell me, what exactly *is* your relationship to, or with, Sênhor Boscoli?"

"I'm, eh, his official interpreter."

"Is there much call for English in Santa Mosqueiro?"

She answered sternly. "You'd be surprised."

"But you didn't learn Portuguese in County Roscommon?"

"Of course not. My husband is an Imperian. He taught me."

Nessa whispered to Cooper. "Back off."

Cooper continued. "Bridgit, tell me . . ." He gestured to the Chief of Customs, busily plying Kurt Greene with even more autograph books.

"How does Sênhor Boscoli view Colonel Mendoza?"

"Mendoza? I can tell you without asking Altamiro. He loathes him."

"Any particular reason?"

"Altamiro thinks Mendoza is not true to his calling."

The lunch continued, while Cooper mused over Bridgit Coelho's final remark. "When you're through, and you're both welcome to stay here as long as you like, how about you and Altamiro joining Nessa and me for dinner this evening?"

"I'm sure Altamiro would be flattered." Winding her napkin around a finger, she smiled at Cooper. "May we keep the limo?"

"Be my guest."

Kurt Greene glanced at his watch. "Jimmer, shouldn't you be back on set? I'll do the honors here" And said pointedly. "On my *non* on-call day?"

"Kurt, ever the gentleman." He turned to Bridgit and Boscoli. "Duty calls. Excuse me."

Nessa squinted at him. "Cooper, something in that nefarious mind of yours?"

"Like the summer wind, walk with me."

Leaving the group, they strolled towards the filming area as peons collected discarded styrofoam cups and plates from around the catering truck. "We provide garbage bins, but why is it nobody can be bothered to use them?"

Nessa sighed. "James Cooper, the David Attenborough of movie enviromentalism." She took his hand. "Now, what's really in that odious mind of yours?"

"Nessa, what d'you think would arouse less suspicion?"

"Of what? And what are you talking about?"

"Santa Mosqueiro Police H.Q." He cupped her chin. "A parcel carried by a U.P.S. or a FedEx driver, or, a parcel delivered by a uniformed captain of customs, in an official car?" He removed his hands from her chin.

She studied him. "Jesus, James. How do you come up with this stuff?"

"Call Golda. Tell her to keep the parcel, and on no account to deliver it. If she's called any courier company, tell her to cancel them, but she *must* keep the parcel."

She looked at him with approval. "See you at dinner."

"Call Golda."

"Copy that."

Laughing, they each walked in opposite directions.

"Mr. Cooper?" It was Bridgit Coelho. "Altamiro? He asks a favor?"

Cooper pondered what he was letting himself in for. "Which is?"

"Well, when watching the filming?" She seemed to be lost for words. "He wondered, if, umm, if he could sit . . . in *your* chair?"

Cooper laughed. More out of relief than humor. "Sure. And you can tell him when to say, in English, 'action' and 'cut,' but on *my* cue."

As Bridget Coelho digested the commands of movie-making, Cooper heard that distinctive and infectious laugh. He turned around.

Nessa was wearing Boscoli's Customs Officer hat, tilted askew, her left arm around his shoulder, his right arm around her waist. Which is when Cooper heard it.

Crack!

"What's that?" Asked Bridgit Coelho. "That bang?"

Crack!!

"There it is again, that bang?"

"That's no bang. They're shots!"

Nessa and Boscoli were clowning around so much they heard nothing above their laughter.

Crack!!!

Then Cooper saw her. A small dark woman, holding a handgun, a snub-nosed twenty-two. In the manner of the best television cop series, the woman took aim, legs apart, both hands on the weapon. Crack!!!!

As the bullet struck the ground, dust kicked up around Nessa, the still giggling Nessa.

Now the woman was running, screaming expletives as she did so. And as abruptly, stopped. To take aim, very careful aim.

Cooper yelled. "Nessa, Nessa! Get the hell away. Run . . . !"

Confused by the sudden commotion, Nessa looked all around her, stupefied.

Instantaneously, Cooper found himself running and in a rugby tackle, caught Nessa behind the knees and rolled with her out of harm's way.

Crack!!!

Cooper looked up, to a scene redolent of an assassination attempt, of crew and others running helter-skelter in all directions, with Boscoli being chased by the gun-toting woman, who in turn was being pursued by Barry Gillette. The woman was firing wildly with the nine-chamber gun as Gillette apprehended her, none-too delicately chopping her wrist with one hand and grabbing the gun with the other.

The woman turned on him like a cornered tigress, arms flailing, kicking, screaming, pouring forth Portuguese invective, while all the time Gillette held her head at arm's length.

"Now, now, darlin', calm down, lady like you shouldn't be firing a gun. You know that's the armorer's job, 'im over there, from Bapty's."

Nessa was shaking.

"You alright?"

Nessa looked at Cooper. "What the *hell* is going on?"

Cooper pointed over to where lay the downed woman. "Her. She tried to kill you."

"What? Me! Why?"

"Let's find out." They walked slowly, to join the group. "Barry . . ." Gillette looked up at Cooper. "One of your location romances gone sour?"

"Leave it out, guv," said an indignant Gillette. "I ain't never seen 'er before. Besides, if she was a bird of mine she'd 'ave shot straight."

Boscoli and Bridgit joined the group. Boscoli knelt beside the woman, while speaking to Bridgit.

"What's he saying?"

"He's asking for help, for a car."

"David!" The first A.D. appeared instantly. "Get a car for Annie Oakley here and put her in it." Langley ran off, shouting for the transportation captain.

"Why, why was she shooting at me?" Asked a still shaking Nessa.

Bridgit answered. "A case of mistaken identity, I'm afraid. Elida thought you were me."

"Who the hell's Elida?" Asked Cooper.

"She's Altamiro's wife. Sênhora Boscoli. I told you, at lunch?"

"So," said Cooper, "She puts two and two together and gets five?"

A car arrived and Elida was placed into it. Boscoli spoke to the driver and the car moved away, slowly.

Langley reappeared. "David, let's get back to work."

"Folks, break it up, let's go. Showtime!"

"Mr. Cooper."

He looked at Bridgit. "Call me James, or *Sean*, if you prefer?"

"*Sean* is John."

"Then what's James?"

"*Seamus*."

Nessa giggled. "A cheap detective. And if the cap fits . . . ?"

"Anyway, James, the events of this afternoon and the effect on Miss Preiss? I think maybe we should cancel dinner?"

He nodded. "Probably a good idea."

Nessa glanced at Cooper, and then at Bridgit. "Um, then how about breakfast? Say seven A.M., James's suite?" She looked to Cooper. "Okay? And they can keep the limo until then?"

A resigned Cooper sighed. "Why not?" He turned to Ms. Coelho. "But Bridgit, tell Altamiro, no more bear hugs. He almost broke my rib cage."

"I'll tell him." She walked over to a contrite Boscoli, whispering into an ear. Boscoli saluted Cooper, who beamed a smile back, and a wave.

Bridgit waved. "*Slàn*."

Cooper waved in return. "*Sin a bhuill*."

"*What*? Is that?"

"Gaelic, Nessa. *Oirish*, if you will."

Nessa sighed. "I know I should've taken that Esperanto course . . ."

Exiting the car, Cooper walked into the hotel, as if drugged.

He was watched by the concierge. "Sênhor James, you look knackered?"

Cooper turned slowly to him. "Now, Alfredo, wherever did you learn such a phrase as that?"

"I worked hotels in London."

Smiling, Cooper nodded. "Good for you, sunbeam."

He dragged himself to the elevator and had just about enough strength left to press the button. As he reached his floor and the gates opened, he was confronted by the censor, Ramalho.

"Changed your job?"

"No, Sênhor James, I've come to my senses."

Cooper nodded, earnestly. "You've found someone to help you?"

"Yes." Ramalho smiled. "Me."

"You?"

"I thought about what you said. And I've figured a way out. I think I know now how to escape Mendoza, away from his Svengali reach, where he won't ever be able to hurt me again. Ever." Ramalho walked to the elevator. As he pressed a button, he eyed Cooper. "Nor you. *Ciao.*"

After three attempts, Cooper managed to get the key into the lock of his suite, entered, staggered to his chamber and collapsed on the bed. Fully dressed, boots an' all.

Which is how she found him the next morning. At six A.M. Nessa shook him, violently. "Wake up", and shouting louder. "For God's sake Cooper, wake up! Breakfast! Boscoli?"

He sat up. "Christ!" He focused on Nessa. "Blimey, where'd I be without you?"

"Get in the bathroom and clean yourself up. Now, git!"

Without modesty, he stripped and moved to the bathroom. To emerge twenty-minutes later as the quintessential English gentleman.

"James, you actually look human."

He eyed Nessa. "How'd you feel? Not exactly your every day?"

"That's for sure. My first time as a target, as in 'target practise'?"

The door buzzer sounded. Crossing the room, Nessa opened the front door, to reveal Boscoli, and Bridgit. "*Bom dia.*"

In turn, each kissed Nessa in polite greeting, and as Cooper joined them, Boscoli greeted him with outstretched arms.

"No, Altamiro. No!"

Scared stiff by Bridgit's order, Boscoli froze. Whereupon Cooper took the outstretched hand, and grabbed Boscoli in a bear-hug. Smiling, while rubbing his ribs, Boscoli bowed. *"Touché."*

Well-breakfasted, Cooper prepared for the rigors of the day.

"Mr. Cooper . . . Seamus?" Bridgit gestured to Altamiro. "Given the events of the past twenty-four hours, Altamiro feels he owes you a big favor. He asks how can he repay you, both?"

Nessa and Cooper glanced at each other other. Gesturing towards Boscoli, Nessa answered. "Does he have an official car?"

"Of course."

"With an official driver? Uniformed?"

Bridgit nodded. "From the motor pool."

"Bridgit, this is very important to both James and me." She squeezed a Cooper hand. "Would Altamiro be prepared to deliver a package for us, a very special package, to Colonel Mendoza at State Police H.Q.? With Altamiro in uniform and in his official car?"

"I'll ask." A quick conversation in Portuguese, and an emphatic nodding of his head, by Boscoli.

"I'm sure you've gathered, the answer is 'yes.' But he asks another favor."

Cooper's heart sank. Dear God, not a night with Nessa?

"Yesterday. He got all of the autographs, but not yours nor that of Mr. Cooper". She put forward an autograph book. "Please?"

Each signed the proffered autograph book.

"Nessa, you're in charge of 'Operation Return.' Me? I have to go and direct a movie. For your fiancé?" He kissed her on the cheek and said his goodbyes. He waved to the remaining group.

"A very interesting man." Bridgit turned to Nessa. "Your lover?"

Nessa laughed. "Strictly business. Plus I'm engaged to his boss. Now, 'Operation Mendoza'?"

An interruption from Boscoli. "Altamiro asks . . ." Giggling. "He asks, d'you want a receipt?"

"You betcha!"

"From Mendoza, *personally*?"

"Just something signed, and stamped. Excuse me" Nessa crossed to the phone. "Golda, are all systems go?" A pause. "Great. We'll be down in about a half-hour." She looked at her two guests. "Bridgit, I presume Altamiro's personal car is at his workplace?"

She nodded.

"Okay. How's this? Altamiro goes and gets his official car, ideally with a driver, then he comes back here and picks up the parcel. Ask him if that'll work?"

More frenzied Portuguese. "Altamiro says 'yes,' but can he bring his camera?"

Nessa frowned. "A camera?"

"He wants a picture of you and me, together."

Nessa was dead pan. "For *Elida* Boscoli?"

Bridgit laughed loudly as she gestured to Boscoli. "We won't be long."

"Bridgit!" Nessa stepped forward. "You can't go, you musn't be seen in his official car."

Pausing, Bridgit nodded, lapsing into Portuguese. "Altamiro, I can't come. You go and get your car and a driver. And then come back here."

"Tell him to wait in the car, and send the driver up here to collect the package."

The instructions were relayed to Boscoli. He kissed Bridgit, saluted Nessa, and left.

"So now begins the worst part, the waiting?"

"No. The worst part will be the waiting once the driver's collected the parcel." She looked at Bridget. "I'll order some coffee. Calm the nerves."

The coffee was long since finished. The quiet could be sliced with a knife.

"Is this what it's like, waiting for the birth of a baby?"

Nessa smiled, wanly. "I wouldn't know. I've never had a baby."

Bridgit looked at her. "Maybe . . . . One day?"

A knock. The two ladies glanced at each other as Nessa crossed to, and opened, the door. To reveal a grinning Boscoli, thumbs up, camera in hand. Nessa turned to Bridgit. "Mission complete?"

The Irishwoman spoke Portuguese to Boscoli. "Yes, mission very much completed." She gestured to her lover. "Just the photograph."

Boscoli marshaled the two ladies into his preferred camera angle, and took several snaps.

After the stills session, Nessa ushered them out. And moved to the telephone. "Golda? Mission accomplished. Would you come over to the hotel? I'll be up in my room, but I need you to do something for me, okay?"

Golda entered the suite. "What's all the mystery?"

Nessa laughed. "No mystery, but tell me Golda, what do you *really* think of Cooper?"

"Easy. Sometimes I could fucking kill him, other times, hug him. You?"

Nessa giggled. "Mostly your first observation."

Golda looked directly at Nessa. "Now, you tell me, woman to woman. What do *you* think of Cooper?"

"Let's not go there Golda, especially as I have somewhere else to go?" Nessa handed to Golda a small, gift-wrapped package. "This is for you. With my thanks for all your help, and your unfailing loyalty."

"Jesus, am I about to be knighted?"

"No, you're about to make some travel arrangements. For me."

Golda produced a pocket notebook and pen. "To?"

"San Francisco."

"First class. Round trip?"

"First class." Nessa sighed. "One way."

Golda looked up, surprised. She relaxed the pen and notebook. "*One* way?"

"One way."

"You're leaving us? Who's to take your place? James can't direct *and* produce this movie, not without you?"

In a gesture of petition, Nessa raised her hands. "Golda, you and James are a formidable team. But also I have other pressures, other . . .

192

obligations, y'know?"

Golda nodded. "I understand." She sighed. "You'll be missed."

"I'll miss you guys, too."

"And James?"

"History."

"That easy?" Golda nodded. Then scanned her notes. "This'll mean a very early start. Car pick up at oh-four hundred."

"I'll be ready."

"Copy that." Golda held high the package. "And thanks for this."

"You're very welcome." With Golda gone, Nessa moved to the desk, took out some notepaper and began writing.

The movie location. Lunch break.

Cooper sat alone, when approached Griffith, a piece of paper in hand.

He was gestured to sit. "This good news?"

Griffith waved the piece of paper. "This fax came today." He passed the note. "From Hooray Henry."

"This my death knell?"

"Read it."

Cooper read aloud. *"To Con Griffith comma copy James Cooper comma Nessa Preiss comma Golda Wisepart stop. Having thoroughly reviewed again all of the supporting documentation concerning the current claim on Redmayne West comma namely the Fort Set and associated days comma the following items* blah, blah, blah, *less deductible of five thousand dollars U.S. comma the full and final settlement of the claim totals six hundred and forty thousand dollars U.S. stop."* Cooper looked at Griffith. "Con, let me read this again." Which he did. And then held-high the fax, sighing. "I just wish we'd managed the Susan Chase claim as well?"

Griffith was incredulous. "James, for crying out loud! Never look a gifthorse in the mouth!"

"Meaning?"

"Meaning, you've got your four days claim, some might even say, four very questionable days?"

Cooper nodded, slowly. "You're right, absolutely right, as usual." Putting an arm around a Griffith shoulder, Cooper smiled. "Con, I'm lucky to have you. You're a treasure."

SCENE 38. TAKE 1.

Rushing to tell Nessa the good news, he was surprised to see a note wedged in the door of his suite. Removing it, he entered, then fixed himself a large vodka and tonic, with ice and slice. Sitting and supping, he remembered the note, which he opened. *'James, I've retired early as I have a five-thirty flight in the morning so please! Please don't disturb me. Good luck with the rest of the shooting. Maybe see you in post? Nessa.'* For the second time that day, he found himself reading something twice. He felt deflated, totally. Holding the note in front of him, he refilled his glass and moved to the stereo. What seems appropriate, he asked himself. A bullet from Elida Boscoli? For me? I should be so lucky. He put on a CD, the Moody Blues. An appropriately-named group, an appropriately sorrowful song.

"*The summer sun is fading as the year grows old, and darker days are very near, the winter winds will be much colder, 'cos you're not here. I watch the birds fly south across the autumn sky, and one by one they disappear, I wish I was flying with them, 'cos you're not here!*" Drinking in both the music and the vodka, he spoke aloud. "Cooper? You blew it!"

SCENE 39 TAKE 2.

Shuffling a wad of papers, Seidelman placed them in front of Tonnini. "You gonna sign these now, or take them with you?"

"Where to?"

Seidelman pointed to the desk calendar. "It's the nineteenth. Shouldn't you be travelling up to Pebble Beach?"

"*Si.*" Tonnini looked through the papers. "But I fly up each day, from

Santa Monica. Private."

Seidelman gestured to his boss. "Won't that be tiring?"

"Not as tiring as sharing an hotel for five days with a bunch of mega egos, actors an' golf players." Toninni pressed the intercom. "Kay, there some signed papers here, when you ready." Placing his elbows on the desk, he leaned forward, checking his nails. "So, where are we?"

"Schedule wise?"

"No!" Tonnini's look was one of extreme irritation. "The corporation. Is all set up, to handle future sports tournaments?"

Seidelman pointed to the pile of papers. "You just co-signed it into existence."

"We get the name I want?"

"Sure . . . T.I.G., Tonnini International Golf."

"*Va bene*! An' I want the same name for the tennis corporation."

Seidelman was unsure if he'd heard correctly. "You . . . you want to name a tennis outfit Tonnini International *Golf*?"

Tonnini's eyes narrowed. "This another Teamster joke?" He continued staring at Seidelman, while pounding his desk. The door opened, to reveal Kay.

"Yes?"

"Not now! I buzz when I want you!" He rounded on Seidelman. "What I want is a link, a common identity. Same logo, same name, all Tonnini." He looked at Seidelman, smugly. "*Eureka*! I got it! Tonnini International Tennis!"

"The T.I.T. acronym spells . . . *tit*."

"Oh." The ensuing silence was broken eventually by Tonnini. "What it they say, in tennis, when they win? What it called?"

Seidelman scowled. "Franco, I'm at Pebble Beach already. Golf is my game." He looked at the Italian. "Game!"

"I hear you the first time." Tonnini pounded his desk once more. "An' it not game!"

The door flew open. "Kay, I tell you, I buzz, okay, Kay?" He waved her away, putting his head in both hands. "It three letters . . ."

Seidelman mumbled under his breath. "Game . . . set . . . and." He looked up. "Set?"

Tonnini clapped."*Si*. Set!" He grinned at Seidelman. "That it, set!"

"Great. And meaning what?"

Tonnini raised an arm, with fist clenched. Up popped an index finger. 'S'. A second finger pointed to the ceiling. 'E'. To be joined by a third. 'T'. That the name for the tennis corporation."

"Franco, you're not listening. Meaning, *what*?"

"A good point." The intercom buzzed. "Well?"

"Mr. Diller, line one."

"I busy. Tell them we call back." Releasing the switch, he looked at Seidelman. 'S,' for what stands 'S'?"

"Star?"

"Star . . . star?" Tonnini debated the word. "What another name for a star?"

"Asshole?"

"Don!" An accusing finger was pointed at Seidelman. "This serious!"

The intercom buzzed.

"What now?"

"Mr. Gordon, line two."

"Which one?"

"Two! I just told you, line two!"

"Which Mr. Gordon!" Screamed Tonnini.

"Hold on," said an exasperated Kay.

"Forget. Tell them we call back. I in conference." Leaning back in his chair, he clasped hands behind his neck. "Where were we?"

"'S', for star."

Tonnini frowned, shaking his head. "No, no. There another word, I know, classier, but it mean the same."

"Thesaurus?"

"Not 'T'! 'S'! It begin with an 'S'!"

Mentally, Seidelman counted to ten.

Tonnini leaned forward. "What the Latin for star?"

"Stellar?"

"Stellar . . . stellar?" He inclined his head. "Stellar. I think that it!"

Stretching, Seidelman picked up a magazine from the coffee table, opening a page to Tonnini. "Here's a company whose product is *Stella*.

And they promote sports events. Conflict." He looked over the outstretched magazine. "Conflict? Equals litigation. Thinking cap back on."

"It no come off!"

Seidelman hoped he both sounded helpful and, interested. "Franco, is *'super'* too ordinary, too quotidian?"

"Quo . . . *what*! But 'S', for super? I like. Now, 'E' . . ." With both men locked in thought, Tonnini flipped the intercom.

"You taking calls, now?"

"No! Bring in a dictionary open at the letter 'E'. Please."

Re-entering, Kay placed in front of Tonnini a large Webster's, opened as commanded. Looking at the two men, she left, quietly.

The Tonnini tracking finger hovered, then raced, paused, darted, hovered. And stopped. He looked happily at Seidelman. "How about this? *'Edentata'!*"

Seidelman winced. "*Eden* . . . what?"

Tonnini was expressionless as if just having uttered the most commonly-used word in the American language. *'Edentata.'* He opened his palms. "S.E.T. *Benissimo*, no? It roll of the tongue wonderful. Listen. 'Super Edentata Tennis.'"

"Sensational. What's that word mean?"

Tonnini consulted the dictionary. "Eh, here, here it is. An order of mammals with no teeth."

"Well, that describes the players. Besides, *where's* your name?"

"Oh."

Seidelman shrugged. "Then T.A.T.?"

"Great! What it mean?"

Seidelman grinned. "Try Again Tonnini."

Tonnini huddled over the dictionary. "*Enthrall? Super Enthrall Tennis*?" He shook his head. "*Epic.*" He stabbed the page. "Epic! It describe the movies, the stars, the play? Toninni Epic Tennis! T.E.T. What you think?"

Seidelman thought *yes, so we can get this over with.* "Great! Now, the deli?"

"I thought we agree, it called 'Deli Tonnini'?"

"That's the corporation name, yes, but don't you want a trading name? You know, like *Franco's?*"

"*Franco's?* No. It too much like Musso an' Frank." He swiveled his chair through one-hundred-eighty degrees. "Deli Tonnini . . . Deli Tonnini. Hey!" The chair quickly completed the circle. "Initials again! It *D.T.*s!"

Seidelman effected a cough. "Eh, Franco, you ever see *The Lost Weekend?*"

"*Si.* Is Ray Milland. He get an Oscar."

"Right. Then you know he played a dipso, an alcoholic?"

"Don, what Ray Milland an' dipsos to do with my deli?"

"In the movie he suffered from *delirium tremens*, hallucinations brought on by excess booze. *Delirium tremens* is known as *D.T.*s."

The Italian seemed deflated. "Then it 'Deli Tonnini'." He pondered. "Beside, I like the *double entendre*."

"Yeah, clever. Your idea?"

"No. Actually, Cooper. His idea."

Seidelman grimaced. "Not so clever."

Tonnini chuckled. "Don, why you so dislike him? What he ever done to you?"

A bemused Seidelman shook his head. "He just grates me, is all." He looked at Tonnini. "I always feel like he's talking down to me."

Tonnini looked over his spectacles. "You sure it not that inferiority complex you Jews carry around?"

"Me? Feel inferior to Cooper? *That'll* be the day."

"Don, you a businessman." Tonnini held out his spectacles, cleaning the lenses with a tissue. "You know as well as me, emotion blurs, it bend the straight lines that one should think in, an' that no good?" He replaced the glasses. "Listen, I tell you before, Cooper is alright. He no make waves, he work hard and he no threat to you?"

"I didn't say he was a threat." He looked off. "I just think he's a prick."

Tonnini laughed, genuinely. "Don, Don, however much I dislike someone, I never let it get up my nose, affect my judgment."

"Well, I see that," said Seidelman, ingratiatingly.

Tonnini studied him. "You do?"

"Sure. Especially when it comes to Cooper."

Tonnini chose his words carefully. "Cooper? Why would Cooper get up my nose?"

Seidelman outspread his arms. "You're able to rise above it, which is great, one of the many things I admire about you."

"Above it?" Tonnini decided to appear not too interested, but he was curious to know exactly where was Seidelman heading. "Above what?"

Seidelman congratulated himself. *Don, old boy. Well maneuvered! You've got the Old Man on the run and one stone will kill two birds.* "Cooper. And Nessa."

Folding his arms, Tonnini sat back. "What about Cooper and Nessa?"

A short knock and Kay entered, placing a sheet of paper in front of her boss. "Kay, take these papers. They all signed." He waited until she had left. "Cooper? And Nessa?" He stared at Seidelman.

Seidelman returned the look. One of forced sympathy. "Well, they lived together."

Tonnini's gaze was unfaltering. "Don, Nessa's life before we came together, it just that, *her* life, not mine? It nothing to do with me. So, it was Cooper." He pointed at Seidelman. "You no think she don' tell me? An' if previous liasons are going to affect later life, then we all end up with noses shaped like serpents?" He glared at Seidelman, and then picking up the paper left by Kay, read it and flicked the intercom. "We arrange pick up for Miss Nessa?"

"Car at SFO. Takes her to The Lodge at Pebble Beach."

Tonnini nodded. 'Kay, she be tired after that long flight. Fly her to Monterey. So, car pick up at SFO, then General Aviation, either SFO or Kaiser at Oakland. Arrange charter, an' a car to meet her at Monterey. Okay?"

"Understood, Mr. Franco."

"*Grazie.*" He switched off the intercom.

Seidelman sneezed. "Excuse me."

"Nose clear now?"

"Clear as a bell." Seidelman stood. "Franco, when do *we* leave?"

"For where?"

"Pebble Beach."

"I leave tomorrow, at ten. I tell you already, private charter from Santa

Monica."

Seidelman felt awkward. "So where do *we* meet? I mean, do I fly up with you or what?"

"*Si*, you fly, but not with me, no. *You.* Fly to Santa Mosquiero."

Seidelman's eyes blazed. "What!"

"Don, this neg-fogging insurance claim. You need to go over it with Cooper. We have no details of it, an' as we can no bring him here, you have to go there. An', what about his post schedule? We have nothing confirmed, nothing? He not D.G.A., so do we have to give him ten weeks director cut? An' what about editing rooms, A.D.R., Foley, music, effects, final mix? And crew? Okay, there Cooper an' his English assistant. But we need more post crew, sound editor, dialogue editor, music editor, their assistants, but we have nothing, no?"

"No." Sedelman sighed loudly. "Nothing."

"Like I say. So get your ass down there a.s.a.p."

Seidelman tried not to sulk. "How long will I be away?"

"That depend on you." And, thought Tonnini, *it also depends on me.* He flicked the intercom. "Kay, tomorrow, travel. Book Mr. Don through from LAX to Santa Mosquiero. First class, open return. An' a car to meet him at the other end, an' fax Golda the intinerary." Switching off the intercom, he looked at Seidelman. "Have fun."

Feet resting on the sill, Seidelman sat looking out of the window, rocking to-and-fro in his desk chair. Abruptly, he kicked the sill and then dropped his feet, sitting forward. *'Damn! Damn!! Damn!!! Damn you Cooper! Instead of Pebble Beach, where will I be? In God damned stinking Santa Mosquiero, wiping the post-production ass of the limey know-all, Mr. High and fucking Mighty Cooper!'* Crossing to a bureau, he removed a glass and a bottle of bourbon. He flicked the intercom. "Kay, honey, bring me in some ice, please."

Minutes later, she appeared. "Kay, what's the difference between us and Imperio, timewise?"

"They're five hours ahead of us. Anything else?"

"No, that's fine, thank you."

From his closet, Seidelman removed his practise golf game, spending the next few hours putting at Pebble Beach, his game fortified by numerous lubrications of bourbon, and all in his office.

"Zero-one-one, five-five-five, two, two-one-eight, seven-seven, six, six."
"El Gran Hotel do Amazonas. Boa noite."
"Suite one-o-one, please."Seidelman checked the time, and smiled to himself. "One A.M."
"Eh, sênhor? No reply."
"He's probably asleep. It's his head office. But please keep it ringing."
"I leave it ringing, sir."
"Obrigado."
Seidelman noticed he was wearing odd socks, recalling how someone had told him once that it meant good luck. He thought to himself, if Santa Mosqueiro instead of Pebble Beach is good luck, then I'd hate to have been wearing two odd socks.

"Hello?" Cooper answered the phone in the hope it was Nessa.
"James? Hi, Don Seidelman"
Cooper glanced at the clock. "Don? Oh, hi."
"Did I wake you? What time is it there?" Said knowing full well.
"A little after one A.M."
"Jeez! Tell you what. I'll stay up until about two A.M. my time, and call you then?"
"Don, I'm awake now so let's get this over and done with, okay?"
"Okay, buddy." He stifled a giggle. "It's just that we don't have the full info on the insurance situations?"
"Don, the Fort claim? They settled. Nessa has the actual figure and she's on her way back to California as we speak."
"Great! But. The film fogging claim, and no info from you about your post schedule or your needs? So I suggested to Franco I should come down there which he thinks is a good idea, and then you and I can go over all of this shit."
"When?"
"Saturday?"
Cooper groaned. "Don, that's our first day off in nine days."

"James, buddy. Who's being paid two fees here?"

Cooper bit his tongue. "Will it take long?"

"James, the ball's in your court?"

"Okay, Saturday morning it is."

"Great! I don't want to spend a minute longer in Santa Mosqueiro than I have to."

"Imperiavia has a Saturday evening flight to L.A."

"Oh, man! Have Golda book me on it. Now, you get some shut eye."

Giggling maniacally, Seidelman replaced the phone. He calculated. A Saturday evening flight from Santa Mosqueiro, with changes, would still get him into LAX on Sunday, making possible Pebble Beach that day, and certainly by Monday. He pressed the intercom. "Kay, you still there?" He glanced at his watch. "I guess not". He loped out to the fax machine to send to Golda details of his Santa Mosqueiro itinerary, and then, all the way through to Monterey, and . . . Pebble Beach!

Cooper found it impossible to regain sleep. His insomniac state he didn't attribute as much to Seidelman as more to . . . Nessa. Opening the bedside drawer, he split in half a sleeping tablet. Downed with a large swallow of Cutty Sark. He looked at the label. *'Drink sensibly.'* "Bollocks," he said aloud.

Sleep came instantly.

SCENE 40. TAKE 5.

Morning.

As Cooper deposited his key, Alfredo the concierge flashed his eyes repeatedly at the two uniformed men waiting close by.

"Alfredo, something in your eye?"

More eye flickering and inclined head. "Sênhor James, they for you."

Cooper turned, smiling at the two men. "*Bom dia.*"

With one each side of him, suddenly he was frog-marched out to a waiting police car, blue light flashing. They bundled him into the back, one man either side of him. The car took off at speed, siren blaring. Cooper felt like Roger O.Thornhill in *North by Northwest*. He looked from one to the other. "*Fala Inglêse?*"

"*Solo Português.*" Answered the man to his left.

Cooper figured that as there were three of them, he'd let himself be taken for a ride. Like happened to Holly Martins in *The Third Man* . . .

Out of Downtown, they had reached the inner suburbs, dominated by residential high rises. The car swerved into a side street and then into the courtyard of an apartment block, with siren blaring and tires squealing. The vehicle sped around the side of the building, where was situated a number of single-storey individual lock-up garages. Cooper pondered, was this an Imperio re-run of the *St.Valentine's Day Massacre*? The car skidded to a halt behind an ambulance, where was standing a knot of people, the ghoulish and the just plain curious. Cooper was ushered out, to be confronted by Golda and Hector Belem.

"Morning guys. Care to tell me what the hell's going on?"

Belem was the first to speak. "James, they said you had to be here."

"They?"Cooper frowned. "Who's *they*? And why?"

Belem pointed to the ambulance. "The coroner's department."

"Hector, you know as well as I do, I've a movie to direct, so why am I here losing valuable shooting time. What *is* this shit?"

Belem spoke placatingly. "He left some letters, and one was addressed to you, which means under Imperio Civil Law, you become some sort of witness."

"To what, for Christ's sake? And *what* are we talking about!"

"James . . ." It was Golda. "It's a death. Suicide."

Cooper paled. "Suicide?" He looked at both of them. "Who?"

Belem answered quietly. "Ramalho, Francesco Ramalho. The censor."

Stunned, Cooper sighed, gazing at the sky. Calming, he looked from one to the other. "When do I get to see this letter he wrote me?"

Belem exhaled. "The autopsy first, which is immediate. Then, the inquest. Which will probably be this time next week."

"Then can we leave now?"

"Let me check." Belem walked over to some officials.

"Well," said Golda. "At least he's made amends for fogging the film."

Cooper glanced at her. "How'd you know he fogged the film?"

"Everyone knows." She returned his gaze. "Except, apparently, you?"

"And how'd he make amends?"

Golda looked ahead. "Forget it. Just me being my usual uncharitable self."

Cooper looked over to where Belem was engaged still with the officials. "You got much on your plate today?"

Golda eyed Cooper, suspiciously. "Just the usual. Why?"

He gestured over a shoulder. "Not exactly an auspicious start?" He nudged her. "Let's just say I'd like to see a familiar and friendly face around the set."

"And that's all?"

"That's all."

"This anything to do with Nessa Preiss leaving?"

"You read too much Barbara Cartland. But I think I need my hand held today, metaphorically speaking."

"Is Kurt Greene on call?"

"He is."

"Then," said Golda. "I'm your man, metaphorically speaking."

Belem rejoined them. "It's okay, we can leave." He turned to Cooper. "Is possible you may be required to appear at the inquest."

"Oh, great. Now, let's go!"

Belem drove like Fittipaldi.

"Hector, the Brasilian Grand Prix was *last* week."

"I thought we were in a hurry?"

"Yes. But to the set, not the bloody morgue."

Belem reduced speed. "They may want you to identify the body."

"Hector, by the way, who were those cops?"

"Municipal police."

Cooper leaned forward. "Nothing to do with Colonel Mendoza?"

"No, nothing. He Boa Vista State Police."

Cooper relaxed back into the seat.

While a lens was placed on the camera's turret, D.P. Billy Richards stood beside Cooper, as the director looked through the viewfinder. "That's it." He turned to David Langley. "Actors?" And looked through the camera once more, to satisfy himself of the final framing.

Richards spoke into his ear. "D'you think it was suicide?"

Cooper turned to face the D.P. "No, Billy. I don't think it was suicide. I *know* it was suicide."

Richards was watching diffusion netting being placed on some reflectors. "How can you be so sure?" He turned to Cooper.

"A locked garage? Blankets wedged under the door to seal it, a rubber hose attached to the exhaust pipe, the other end into the car, windows wound up? Switched-on engine? Carbon monoxide poisoning. Q.E.D."

Richards made a face. "And nobody heard? Nobody smelt?"

"Billy, Santa Mosqueiro? Smelly cars? Every car in this city needs a bloody tune up. They all smell, smelling of exhaust fumes."

Richards shook his head. "Well, it takes all kinds. Some men are strong, others . . . ?" He looked at Cooper. "I guess Ramalho was in the others category?"

Checking his script, Cooper looked up, removing the pen held between his teeth. "Personally, I've always thought of suicide as something almost brave, noble even."

"You do?" asked a surprised Richards.

Lowering the script, Cooper looked off. "Despite its many hurdles, I believe most people love life, its sights, its sounds, its sensuality, and I don't think anyone forsakes that lightly." He turned to Richards. "To consciously, when the pressures become too great or the ability to counter them is exhausted, to consciously abandon the beauties of living? I think that takes guts." Cooper looked at the ground. "I've never had that sort of courage."

"You ever been tempted?"

He was still looking downwards. "Tempted? Once or twice it looked as if it might be the solver of seemingly insoluable problems."

"What stopped you?"

Raising his head, Cooper looked Richards in the eye. "Fear."

"Fear? Of what?"

"The unknown."

"The unknown, you?" Richards laughed. "But you're a freelance producer-director, you're motivated by the unknown?"

Cooper raised the folder in his hand. "But with a script, and always knowing the ending. But I didn't then, nor did I have the guts to find out."

Kurt Greene and Claudia Martins arrived on set for a rehearsal.

"Besides," added Cooper. "Movie freelancing is enough fear for a lifetime."

Richards smiled. "I'll drink to that." He glanced at Cooper. "Showtime?"

Exhausted, Cooper closed the door, leaning against it. He couldn't recall a time when he'd felt so drained. As one who'd always pooh-poohed stress as a failing in the ability to cope, he pondered if this was stress? Would he be able to complete the week by making it across the suite to his bedroom or would the week of Nessa's departure, Mendoza's menacing, Ramalho's suicide and nine days of consecutive work conjoin to petrify him with fatigue, condemning him to spend his rest day leaning against this door. Which is when he remembered. Rest day, what rest day? Tomorrow? Oh God, It's bloody Seidelman Saturday.

The shower refreshed him. He decided bed was the best bet. Plus a soporific. A.k.a. Scotch. A shot, plus half a sleeping tablet. *'Sleep. Sleep that knits up the ravel'd sleave of care.'* On to the bed he crashed.

Scene 41. Take 2.

As Nessa exited S.F.O. Arrivals and into the concourse, she searched for Francesco Tonnini or at least his chauffeur, Paolo. But amongst the forest of greet sheets held high by limo chauffeurs, she saw not a familiar face. She was unsure of her next move.

"Miss Preiss, Miss Nessa Preiss?" A tall middle-aged African-American man was tipping the peak of his chauffeur's hat.

"You from Tonnini Pictures?"

"No, ma'am, Music Express. I'm Leroy. At your service."

"I was expecting Mr. Tonnini, or at least his chauffeur."

"All I can tell you ma'am is I was heading up the one-o-one back to the city, and the dispatcher? He radioed me to turn around and get back to SFO a.s.a.p., to pick you up." He took her bag. "See you kerbside in eight minutes. I'm 'Music Fifteen'."

The stretch limo glided away from the kerb. "Ma'am, there are soft drinks and cocktails in the cabinet beside you, and Miss Preiss, feel free to use the phone, resting on the shelf behind you."

Nessa twisted around to look at the instrument. "Leroy, can I make international calls on this?"

"Yes, ma'am, from Salinas to Singapore. But make it short, mind, as we're only going to General Aviation, just across the airport."

Too much to say, too little time. "Sorry, James," she whispered.

Scene 42. Take 4.

"Raimundo, let me look at you." While his wife checked the knot of his tie, Mendoza raised his chin, to take a surreptitious glance at his watch.

"You've plenty of time for the plane."

"Those early flights? They fill up quickly."

"On a Saturday?" Sênhora Mendoza stepped back, admiring her

management of resources. "Nobody can iron a shirt like me. Turn around."

Obediently, Mendoza did as bid.

She smoothed some pleats. "And why, what's so important you have to fly down to the capital on a Saturday? And, at a moment's notice?"

Mendoza raised his arms. "Monica, my love. Who knows?"

"Could it be a promotion?"

Mendoza contemplated. "Mmm . . . possibly."

"Well, d'you think it is?"

He turned to her. "Maybe. Maybe the airline ticket will provide a clue."

"How?"

"Whether I'm seated in the back of the bus, or in the forward cabin." Holding out arms straight behind him, Monica Mendoza put the jacket on her husband. "This my good luck uniform?"

Chuckling, she shook her head. "Raimundo, you forget, I know you."

"Is it?" he asked sharply.

She smiled. "Of course. The dress uniform you wore when His Holiness visited Imperio, the one you wore when you received the Papal blessing."

Bom dia. In his native Portuguese, he spoke politely at the check-in agent. "There should be a ticket for me here, in the name of Mendoza?"

As the agent tapped on a computer keyboard, Sênhora Mendoza pulled gently on her husband's jacket. "Remember. No creases. Take this off on the plane." Mendoza patted her hand.

The agent looked up from his computer. "I.D.?"

Mendoza passed over his official state police badge.

"Ah, Colonel Mendoza, my apologies. It doesn't-"

"In which section am I seated?"

"*Carnival.*"

Mendoza looked perplexed. "What is that?"

"It's Imperiavia's First Class."

Smiling broadly, Mendoza turned to his beaming wife. Hugging her, in unison they said softly, "Promotion!"

"I thought we'd agreed eight-thirty?" said Seidelman, through a mouthful of food.

"Don, I've just worked nine days on the trot, nine bloody days! This is or was, my first rest day."

"Buddy, you're being paid for two jobs? So, you work twice as hard." Seidelman slurped coffee. "Jesus, they call this coffee? It tastes like mud."

"Well, it was fresh *ground* this morning? And better than that colored water crap that passes for coffee in the U.S." Cooper glanced to the television set, suspended from the trellis of the Terrace Restaurant. Playing was *Sesame Street*. With the sound muted. "I wonder what Big Bird sounds like in Portuguese?"

"About as dumb as it sounds in American." Suddenly, Seidelman shot out his left arm. "Whaddya think?"

Cooper studied the outstretched sleeve. "What am I looking at?"

Seidelman pointed to his wrist. "Jeez, I felt so lousy the other night, waking you up an all, so I bought a second watch. One on L.A. time, the other on Imperio time." He punched a Cooper arm. "No more midnight calls." He belched loudly. "Jesus, I'm thirsty." Seidelman was patting his stomach. "What's made me so thirsty? Damned airline food, first class or not."

Cooper saw his opportunity. From a jug he knew to be filled with the local tap water, he poured the liquid into the American's glass.

Seidelman studied it. "This stuff okay to drink?"

Cooper nodded. "It's spa water, bottled by monks from a natural spring by a monastery near the head waters of the Amazon. It's mountain pure."

Seidelman sipped. "No kidding?" Draining his glass, he belched again.

Cooper refilled it, thinking to himself that a dose of Moctezuma's Revenge was a fair trade for a sleep-interrupting phone call.

Seidelman held the glass, studying the water. "You sure about this stuff?"

"With hand on heart and on my late mother's death bed. Yes!"

Seidelman frowned. "Late?" He held up the glass. "She ever drink it?"

Cooper was expressionless. "If she had, she'd have still been alive today."

"But all those stories about the water in these places?"

"French mineral water companies' propaganda."

Cooper refilled Seidelman's glass. To the brim.

"Right," said Seidelman. "To business. Especially as I want to be outta here tonight." Smiling at the director, on the table he placed a legal pad. "Okay, one." He wrote. "Insurance latest, fogged neg." He looked up at Cooper. "Amount of claim?"

Cooper returned the stare. And then spoke. "No claim."

Seidelman put down his pencil, slowly. "*Claim Meister*, did I hear right?"

"It doesn't exceed the deductible. That's ten-thousand-dollars, which is more than the incurred extra expense."

Studying Cooper for several moments, Seidelman retrieved the pencil and drew a line through the heading 'Insurance Claim', to feel a restraining arm on his wrist.

"Let's not be too hasty."

Seidelman leaned back in his chair. "Why?"

"Don, I don't want to go into the nitty gritty, let's just say I am partly culpable in the fogging claim, and so, *I'll* pay the ten thousand dollar deductible. If that's okay with you?"

Leaning forward, Seidelman glanced through narrowed eyelids. "Paid how?"

"Out of my directing fee?"

"If you admit culpability, it should come out of your producing fee."

"That's paid in sterling."

Seidelman pondered. Briefly. "Okay, you're on. You'll advise your agent, Hess?"

"I'll have Golda draw up the words, which I'll sign, and it'll be faxed. With a copy to you."

Seidelman took another gulp of water. "Let's move on. Post. How long?"

"Off the top of my head, I can't remember what's in the budget."

"I'm not talking about the budget, I'm asking. How long?"

"Well, ten weeks for director's cut."

"You're *not* in the D.G.A. so you don't qualify for the mandatory basic agreement cut."

"Then what the fuck do I qualify for?"

Seidelman smiled. "Tut, tut, James. However would you have managed if Anglo Saxon had never been invented?"

"I'd have been fucked, wouldn't I?"

The pencil was pointed like an AK-47. "Listen, you Limey know all. I haven't flown seven thousand miles to put up with your profanity."

Without warning, Seidelman thumped the table. "I hate flies!" Looking at his hand, the insect was wiped off on the table cloth.

Cooper controlled his pique. "You have a distributor?"

Head snapping-up, he eyed Cooper. "In the pipeline."

Cooper stayed calm and rational. "Don, with a distributor there'll be a contractual running time, and once that's known I'd be able to tell you how long it'll take to edit."

"Between one-eighteen and one-twenty-five-miniutes."

"Including titles?"

"Main and end crawler."

Writing on a napkin, Cooper made some calculations. "Don, I've warned you guys repeatedly about script length." He scribbled some more. "So, I'd say the assembly will come in between two hours thirty, two hours forty-five."

"Way too long! The exhibitors expect to get at least four screenings a day, hopefully five."

Cooper cleared his throat. "I understand all that. But *it's* an assembly! Hence I'll need all of ten weeks." Cooper pointed at the American. "But. What I will give you in that time frame is not only my cut but fine cut. Which'll save you some six weeks on the post schedule."

Leaning across the table, Seidelman retrieved his legal pad. "Ten weeks, from the last day of principal?"

"No."

"Then from when?"

"Ten weeks from the first day of L.A. editing." He raised a cautionary finger. "And, we'll need an H.1. visa for the editor Pat Corcoran and one for me."

Seidelman checked his notes. "Eh, composer. Any thoughts?"

"Bernard Herrman."

Seidelman wrote-down the name. "Who represents him?"

"God."

Mystified, Seidelman frowned, at the same time shaking his head.

"Don, no recent scores?" Cooper called a waiter for a beer. "He's dead, Don, gone to that great scoring stage in the sky."

Seidelman had many doubts about Cooper. To him, one had just been confirmed. "James, composer. Don't take too long. Horner, Barry, Fenton, Zimmer, Williams, Kamen? They're all booked up months in advance, years yet, so let's get real here."

A beer was placed in front of Cooper. "Eduardo Homrich."

"Who?" Seidelman grabbed his stomach, belching loudly. "Je . . . sus." He eyed Cooper. "You sure this water's okay?"

"Never lost anyone yet." Effecting a look of concern, Cooper asked. "D'you want some Pepto Bismol? And you agree to Eduardo Homrich?"

"Yes, yes, Pepto Bismol."

"And the composer?"

"Yes, yes, but please . . . Seidelman was clutching his stomach. "Please, please get me to my room."

Cooper signaled the head waiter. He watched as was carried away the sickly Seidelman, to whom he raised his glass of beer. "Good health, Don, and thanks for Eduardo Homrich."

SCENE 44. TAKE 5.

"Colonel Mendoza?"

The policeman bowed slightly. "At your service."

A hand was extended. "I am Jorge Conde, with the Justice Department." He gestured to two other men. "This is Sênhor Archino and, Sênhor Caito Vinci. They are both with the Ministry of the Interior."

As the group was shaking hands they were joined by another man, more elderly, and distinguished looking.

Mendoza's eyes narrowed. "Forgive me, but, eh, your face? It is very familiar?"

The man was gracious, but unsmiling. "Superior Court Judge Eduardo Mello." He did not offer his hand.

Wearing a sickly smile, Mendoza nodded. "Yes, of course."

On the table in front of him, Conde opened a folder, flattening it by spreading his palms over it repeatedly. "Good flight down?"

Surprised, but Mendoza didn't display such. But then, he felt it was all of the comforting process, leading to the subject of . . . promotion. "Eh, yes, it was fine. And thank you."

"Colonel, how long have you been a policeman?"

Mendoza stroked his mustache, feeling the question was exactly proper, given the matter in hand. Promotion. "Let me see now, eh, approximately twenty-five years. I entered the Police Academy here in Alentejo, I spent time at Hendon Police College in London and also at the L.A.P.D Academy in Los Angeles. At which two latter institutions I learned my *excellent* English."

"No university?"

"I had always wanted to be a policeman. I felt it was a calling, a vocation."

"And your service has not gone unrecognized?"

Mentally, he was clearing his desk already, for the higher position, and the larger office. "No, it has not."

Watched by the other three men, Conde studied the folder. "Various commendations. The Governor's Medal, the State Police Distinguished Service Medal, plus, a Federal commendation." Conde looked-up. "A record like that must make you very proud?"

Mendoza felt it was staring him in the face. Promotion. "If I was guilty of the vice of pride, such pride would stem from my being a policeman." He glanced around the table. "My job, my work, those are rewards enough, but if along the way I get recognition for work I feel privileged to have done", smiling, he opened his palms. "Then, that is the frosting on the cake." He sat back, wondering if promotion would bring a bigger official car.

It came out of left field. "And how long have you known Francesco Ramalho?"

Mendoza felt the blood drain from his face, in its wake washing-away all hope of promotion. He frowned. "*Who*?"

"Francesco Ramalho?" Conde tapped the folder. "Our information is that he worked for you."

"Me?" His look was a mix of amazement and disbelief. "Me?" He looked around the table. "Gentlemen, I like to think I know every one of my officers, but Ramalho? What was his rank, his department?"

"He's dead."

Albeit surprised, Mendoza retained his composure. *So the little asshole o.d'd. But is there anything to link him to me, anything*? "So, he's dead?"

"Then you admit you knew him?"

Mendoza smiled graciously. "I don't recall denying it?"

Removing from the folder two sheets of handwritten notepaper, Conde placed them on the desk, pinning them down with a finger. "This is a letter sent to the judge here, written by Francesco Ramalho shortly before his death, in which he makes some allegations, allegations of a most serious nature. Against you."

Mendoza remained calm, at least outwardly.

Conde pushed the letter in front of Mendoza. "I think you had better read it."

Eyeing the letter uninterestedly, he looked at the eager faces, thinking, *these nerds of civil servants reckon they can take down Raimundo Mendoza*? Pushing away his chair, he crossed his legs. "Sênhor Conde, with respect, I don't need to read it."

"Oh?"

"As you all know, I've been a policeman for a very long time." He pointed to the letter. "I can probably tell you what it says, almost word for word." Mendoza checked the shine of his boots and of his leather gaiters. He resumed his attitude. "Probably some nonsense about me being mixed up in drugs, that I'm part of some cartel operation." He smiled at the group. "Would I be correct?"

The three men looked at each other meaningfully. Conde's gaze never left the policeman. "Colonel, perhaps you'd care to elaborate?"

"First, let me answer the letter's accusation." From a jacket breast pocket, he removed a pack of cigarettes, and a faded Dupont lighter. "May I?"

"Feel free. There's an ashtray behind you."

Which Mendoza retrieved, and then lit-up, inhaling a huge drag, to exhale . . . smoke rings. "Ramalho was right. But only half right." Uncrossing his legs, he leaned forward. "And I presume he mentioned Mauricio Para, saying I'm in cahoots with him?"

Not believing their ears, the three men murmured amongst themselves.

Mendoza drew on his cigarette. "Eh, any chance of some coffee?"

"Of course." Conde pressed an intercom, ordering refreshments.

In turn, Mendoza looked at all four of his inquisitors. "Gentlemen, you could have saved the taxpayers a first class airfare, had you bothered to call me on the phone about this, this . . . fairy tale?"

"Fairy tale?" It was Judge Mello who spoke. "Francesco Ramalho was my nephew, and at times he may have wandered off the path mapped out for him, and may have been into many things, but, for all his faults, he was *not* a liar."

Looking at Mello, Mendoza stubbed his cigarette. "Right, Judge, he was into many things. He was a convicted junkie. You name it, he was into it. Such as debauched weekends of sex in Rio. And, he had so many needle marks his arms looked like a darts board." Mendoza ignited another cigarette, exhaling a large cloud of nicotine-laden smoke.

"I'll not parry words with you, Colonel, but my nephew was *not* a liar."

"Now Judge . . ." Mendoza was pointing a remonstrating finger. "In the course of your illustrious career, you must have presided over cases involving drug addicts, yes?" Mello nodded. "Then you know as well as I do, the very nature of their addiction, with its compounding craving dulling the ability to distinguish between right and wrong, it makes them liars. To them, all lies are the truth. And your nephew? He was no exception."

Mello could hardly hide his distate for Mendoza. The frigid silence was broken by a refreshments-laden trolley being wheeled-in.

Conde spoke. "Perhaps we should take a short break?"

Coffee cup in hand, Mendoza strolled over to the window, gazing out on downtown Alentejo, watching the streets, crowded with shoppers, vendors and vehicle traffic. All the while pondering his strategy. *How to play this, how to exculpate himself and deflect the arrows to other targets*?

"Colonel, shall we continue?"

"May I finish my coffee?" Turning to face Conde, Mendoza figured that if he stayed in front of the window, he'd be a silhouette, and the outside glare would tire the eyes of his inquisitors. Finishing the drink, he placed the cup on the window ledge, remaining there. "Gentlemen, you may recall that a few minutes ago, in relation to the junk—" He stopped himself, instead smiling at Mello. "The Judge's nephew, I said, he was only half right?"

"Yes, Colonel. That's what you said." Conde produced a pocket recorder. "It's all on here. *'But he was only half right.'* "

Mendoza smiled. "Of course I was mixed up in drugs. But undercover. How else could I obtain their confidence, and evidence to convict? So, I donned various disguises and became accepted into their activity. I soon learned that one of the major players is Mauricio Para."

"The Boa Vista media man?" Conde eye-balled his colleagues. "Then why didn't you arrest him?"

"Simple. One, I didn't have enough evidence, but two, and more importantly, I might scare off the leaders, the ones I really wanted to get, to put an end this insidious evil." He lit another cigarette. "But gentlemen, my investigations brought home a very painful truth. This cancer has spread into the ranks of my own, the Boa Vista State Police." Mendoza held open-wide his arms. "What if the public gets to hear of this? Their faith in their police force would be destroyed, maybe for generations?" He shook his head, remorsefully. "And me, like a father to my men." He looked across to the four men. "And the ringleader? A policeman."

"Are you serious?"

"I wish I wasn't."

"Then obviously you know who it is?"

"I said, Sênhor Conde, a painful truth." He strolled across the room, to stand in front of the quorum. "My aide. Captain Vincenze Possi."

Created was the desired effect. All four men looked incredulous. "And *just* him?"

"Isn't one enough? Isn't one *one* too many?"

"But how did such a dreadful thing happen, how?"

"Sênhor Conde, I've asked myself that question a thousand times. But. Somehow, Possi got into this drugs thing with Para." He glanced at the judge. "When Ramalho came out of prison the last time, Possi got him a job on a movie which is currently filming in Santa Mosqueiro, which enabled him, Ramalho, to pass drugs into the United States." He stared at Mello. "Tell me judge, did he put *that* in his letter?"

Conde was eyeing Mendoza, a deep frown furrowing his brow. "Colonel, something bothers me here. With all of this information, why did you not make any arrests or . . ." He gestured to both Archino and Vinci. "Or bring this matter to the attention of the federal authorities?"

Mendoza sighed. "Looking back . . ." And glancing at all four men. "And hindsight is a great vantage point." He held up a hand. "Maybe vanity? Pride? I wanted them all, all in one fell swoop," a swift movement of an arm emphasizing his point. "With the virus having spread into my own department, who else had Possi recruited, who could I trust? I had to go it alone." Walking to the trolley, he poured himself another cup of coffee and while stirring it, he continued talking. To the urn. "But how? How could I discover the organizers, those at the top? So," he turned to face them, "knowing of their involvement, about six days ago I had both Ramalho and Para over to police headquarters. I questioned Ramalho first and he was beginning to break, which is when Para suddenly attacked him, giving him a terrible blow to the head."

"The temple?" Interrupted Judge Mello. "The *left* temple?"

Mendoza hesitated, pondering. "Eh, yes, I think it was, judge, now that you mention it. Yes, the left temple."

Mello turned to the other three men. "It showed up at the autopsy."

Mendoza looked suitably atoning. "Needless to say, I never got the answers I sought." Remaining by the trolley, he sipped his coffee.

Conde was re-reading the latter. "Ramalho mentions a Vargas." He looked over to Mendoza. "Who's he?"

"Vargas?" Placing the cup on the trolley, he strolled over to the table. "Vargas?" And shook his head. "No idea."

Conde tapped the letter. "Ramalho says he was there, this Vargas. And so were *you*."

"Drugs do terrible things to the memory, to recall, to facts?"

Reflected in Conde's tone was a compounding of exasperation, and frustration. "Except, he is very *clear* on this one point."

Eyeing Conde, Mendoza folded his arms. "And what is that?"

"You, Colonel, you. You are the only person Ramalho actually indicts, not Para nor the mysterious Vargas, not your Captain Possi, but you, Colonel Mendoza, just *you!*"

Throwing up his arms in feigned total disbelief, Mendoza effected a loss of words. "You're going to nail me to the cross, when the excellence of my police work, where my cover was so successful that the judge's nephew, in his drug-addled state, actually thought I was one of *them*?" Looking at his audience, his voice rose. "That's *exactly* what he was supposed to think! And this is my thanks?" He crossed to the window, looking out. "But. It is not too late for you to save the situation." He turned, facing them. "That is if you move quickly enough."

Vinci looked at his associates. "By doing what?"

"How many people know about it, Ramalho's letter?"

"What is the relevance of the question?" Asked Conde.

Mendoza moved forward. "Walls have ears. A telephone call to Santa Mosqueiro." He snapped his fingers. "And phffft! We lose them. No puppeteer, no *jefe*." A heave of the shoulders was directed at them. "No Para and no Captain Possi?" He gestured failure. "All across the border, all of them, into Colombia?" In turn, he looked at each man. "Can *we* afford that, can Imperio afford that, with no extradition agreement?" He shook his head. "I don't think so?"

"Exactly what are you driving at?"

"Arrest Mauricio Para and Captain Vincenze Possi. Immediately."

Skeptical looks from the quorum. Conde's gaze was unwavering. "The charge?"

"You want me to spell it out?"

"Certainly I think we should know we're on firm ground here?"

Mendoza smiled. "Drugs dealing. Drugs trafficking, drugs distribution. Money laundering, illegal currency transactions, involuntary manslaughter, possibly even murder. That firm enough for you?"

Conde continued glaring at Mendoza, while Vinci spoke. "Sênhor Conde, how quickly do you want to move on this?"

The staring remained on Mendoza. "You do realize Colonel, this is a very serious move?"

Mendoza nodded. "And one not taken lightly, sir, believe me."

Conde gestured to Vinci. "Use your judgment."

Vinci picked up a phone, and dialed.

Leaning forward, Mendoza spoke very quietly, looking pointedly at Conde, Archino and Mello. "Gentleman, one more thing, one very important thing. We *must* be careful, very, very, careful, to preserve my acceptance by these drugs people. If approached, I will of course deny any involvement in or knowledge of, the arresting of Para and Possi. So I have to maintain their confidence, which will lead me to the *jefe*. So my position must *not* be compromised!"

Vinci put a hand over the phone. "Relax, Colonel. We will be using the Federal Treasury police, which means it'll be impossible to establish a link between them, and you. Your cover is assured." He returned to his call.

SCENE 45. TAKE 1.

"Rafael! Stop! Now!" Cooper's pounding on the partition so shocked his driver that the car screeched to a halt, the squealing of tires being drowned immediately by a chorus of honking horns.

The partition was lowered. "Sênhor James, I can no stop here."

"Then pull on to the sidewalk!"

"Sênhor James, is no—"

"Rafael, just do it, just bloody well do it!"

Ashen-faced, Rafael studied the director. Who is this new Cooper, this screaming Cooper, this now typical gringo?

As the car nudged on to the sidewalk, Cooper was out, running, back to the window of an electrical store. He shouted. "Raffy!"

Opening the passenger door, the driver leaned out, looking at Cooper.

"Raffy, come here! I need your help!"

Rafael obliged. Cooper was pointing through the store window to a number of TV sets, all showing the same scene, of Mauricio Para being led to a car by uniformed men. "What's happening, what are they doing, what are they saying?"

Eyelids screwed, Rafael shrugged. "I do not know, I cannot hear."

"For Christ's sake, find out!" Cooper bundled him into the store.

"Is Mauricio Para."

"I can see that! But what's happening to him? What?" Another scene flashed up on the screens. "Who's that guy?"

"A . . . Captain Possi." Rafael cocked an ear to the sets. "He arrested also."

"With Para?"

"I think."

"But what's actually happened?"

Rafael raised a restraining hand. "Is drugs. They part of drugs." Rafael translated the commentary. "Mauricio Para and Captain Possi arrested. Suspected of drug trafficking . . . Money laundering . . . More arrests are expected."

The picture cut to a newscaster.

"That it?"

"*Si*. They arrested by Treasury Police."

"Was anything said about a Mendoza?" Cooper tried to keep in check his anxiety. "A Colonel Mendoza of the State Police?"

Rafael was studying the TV, for any futher revelations. "No." He turned to Cooper. "No Mendoza. They just talk about these two. But the Possi?

He *State* Police."

Cooper put an arm on a Rafael shoulder. "Let's go. And thanks for the translation."

As they headed for the car, it was in the process of being ticketed by a parking warden. Cooper pulled out a twenty-dollar bill. "Raffy, give him this. Tell him the gringo made you stop here." Cooper got in the car, to see a smiling warden tearing-up the parking ticket.

The sedan arrived at the familiar surroundings of the production base. "Rafael, you go home now. I'll take a cab back to the hotel."

"Sênhor James, you sure?"

"I'm sure. And thanks. *Ciao.*"

SCENE 46. TAKE 1.

Strolling toward the offices, that's when it hit him. "Shit!" He said aloud. He looked up at the sky, thinking, *Cooper, you idiot, you unthinking bloody idiot!* He stopped in his tracks. *You, you berk, he's got you either way. If Mendoza's arrested, he points the finger at you and takes you down with him, and if he isn't and stays out of harm's way, then you're his patsy, his Trilby. You're his way out. Cooper, either way, you're fucked!* But. He decided there and then to put Mendoza out of his mind, and to let fate take its course. *'I am but a small tile in the large mosaic.'*

As he walked through the deserted production offices, Cooper was surprised to encounter Golda. "What are you doing here?"

Pausing, she looked up. "That's a nice way to greet a girl working on her *rest* day."

He leaned against a desk. "Did I ask you to be a martyr?"

"My, my, *we* are in a charming mood."

Cooper sighed. "I've managed to piss off at least three other people today, so why not you?"

"You're about the right age." She studied him. "Male menopause, male

P.M.S."

Cooper laughed. "I've certainly had my share of hot flushes today. In fact, most of today I've been well nigh impossible."

"Oh, and *just* today?" She pointed to a pile of papers. "I need your approval."

"For what?"

"Sub charter."

"We've an undersea location?"

"No." Golda chuckled. "The away locations, Borges and San Gabriel? It's to do with runway lengths or lack of, and suitable planes, or lack of. We need a Seven-Thirty-Seven."

"So get one."

"Nada aqui. Esta in Brasil. VASP."

"What's that? An insect?"

"A Sao Paulo-based airline."

"Fine." Cooper nodded understanding. "Get it."

"It'll cost more. Quite a bit more."

"What's the alternative?"

Golda rolled her eyes. "Amazonair. Two separate trips, each journey."

Cooper sighed. "Typical."

"Well, the biggest plane they have is a BAe 146."

"The Brasilian plane has to be cheaper in the long run. Do the deal." He checked his watch. "Has Seidelman left?"

Golda burst out laughing. "Of course, you wouldn't have heard?"

"Heard what?"

"Mr. Seidelman has locked himself in his room. Says he'll only talk to you." Cooper pointed to a phone, which Golda dialed. "Seidelman *casa, por favor.*"

"What a linguist." The phone was passed to Cooper. "Don? What's up?"

A weak, croaky voice answered. "Hel . . . lo?"

"Don, it's me, James Cooper."

"Buddy, I . . . I'm dy . . . ing." Heavy panting could be heard. "My . . . stomach? It . . . it's like Pearl Harbor, December seventh . . ."

Cooper stifled a laugh. "D'you feel dehydrated?"

"I feel . . . Dead."

Grinning, Cooper put a hand to his forehead. "Don, I told you, water! You need water, and lots of it. Just run the tap, the faucet, and hold your mouth under it. And eat some fruit, but first wash it under the tap, y'know, get rid of all those nasties. Water, that's what you need."

"Wha . . . what I need is a . . . doc . . . doctor."

"Oh, and don't forget the H.1. visas, okay? *Ciao*." He looked at Golda. "What a trooper. He loves it so much down here he's decided to stay on a bit." He thought for a moment. "Golda, see if Barry Gillette's still around and if he is, ask him to come on over."

"Copy that."

Cooper went to his office. Sitting at his desk, he checked his script notes for the next day's shooting. "Golda," he yelled. "Any word from Tonnini?"

A shouted reply. "Like what?"

"Our average screen time?"

"So you're managing three minutes a day. Whaddya want, an Oscar?"

When appeared Barry Gillette, *the* bottle in hand. "Golda? Three glasses, please." He motioned Gillette to be seated. Golda entered, with glasses, and took the bottle from the property master.

"No ice."

"If God had meant—"

"I know, I know, he'd of called it vodka, right!" Golda poured and handed around the glasses, taking the remaining seat. She raised her glass. "To *Redmayne West*." They drank.

Cooper leaned forward. "Barry, a little job to tax your ingenuity. I'd like you to make up a six pack of mineral water, all sealed with proper labels and that plastic packaging stuff. It must look absolutely authentic, but. The water you put in *must* be tap water, understood?"

Gillette nodded. "You up to one of your little tricks?"

"Perhaps. But once filled, you leave it with the concierge at my hotel, telling him it's for Mr. Don Seidelman." Cooper passed to Gillette a ten dollar bill. "Tip the concierge." Smiling like a Cheshire cat, he raised his glass. "To mineral water."

They drank. While looking at Cooper, Golda spoke to Gillette. "Barry, how many movies have you two done together?"

"Let me see now." Silently, he counted off his fingers. "He was a First A.D., then, me an assistant propman. Eh . . . this'll be the ninth."

She looked at the property master. "What wheezes did the devil incarnate here, Mr. Machiavelli, have you get up to on the other eight?"

"Well, 'e's the guvnor, en 'e? We go back a long way."

"To where? Wormword Scrubs, Dartmoor . . . Alcatraz?" Golda raised her glass once again. "To Machiavelli."

SCENE 47. TAKE 2.

It was a surprise, a 'Welcome Home Nessa' brunch. A dozen close friends, friends that Nessa had not seen for some time, friends who's company Nessa relished and although being his usual gallant and caring host, Tonnini relaxed also and enjoyed himself, the eschewing of sparkling mineral water for Chianti, contributing considerably to his all-too-rare mellowness.

Having changed into something less formal, Nessa was in the process of selecting a sun hat, reaching up to the wardrobe shelf, when she became aware of Tonnini's presence. He was sitting on the bed, admiring the shapeliness of her legs, the silence prompting her to turn around.

"Nice view?"

He chuckled. "Is some time since I was able to enjoy it."

"Well, I'm home now."

"Home?" He shrugged. " Then why you sleep in this guest room?"

She stood in front of him, hands on hips. "Franco, last night, when we finally got back here? I'd been traveling for umpteen God-awful hours, from Imperio to SFO. Then I was whisked in another plane, to Monterey, and a limo to Pebble Beach. A peck on the cheek from you, some boring golf and then another flight, to Santa Monica and then finally . . . here. I am pooped, exhausted! So, not wanting any, *any* distractions, I chose to sleep in a guest room."

Tonnini stared at her, equivocally.

"Nothing devious Franco. Just plain old fashioned jet lag."

Tonnini nodded to the wardrobe. "I no see your clothes in there?"

"Franco? You're not listening! I was too darned tired!"

"Gina could have done it. Or any of the other maids?"

"My jet-lagged brain? I just wanted sleep. In an uncomplicated bed."

Tonnini looked at her, intently. "You act strange."

"Me, strange?" She tapped her chest, leaning towards him. "I'm away six weeks, *six* weeks. In all that time, did I ever get a phone call from *you*?"

"We speak, while you down there."

"Excuse me!" Her voice had risen. "You *weren't* calling *me*! You were calling Cooper or Con Griffith, but not *me*!" She didn't give him a chance to answer. "I get back here, you're not at the airport, you don't send your car, not a flower, not even a note. Nothing!" She placed her hands on her hips. "And *you* think *I'm* acting strange?"

"You sleep with anyone down there?"

She froze. "What's with you?" Attending to the wardrobe, her back to him, she replied. "And the answer to your question is . . . *NO!*"

"No one?"

"No one!" She faced him. "What is this, *Jeopardy*? No, Franco, no!" She half-turned and then reversed, to face him. "Tell me, Franco, you sleep with anyone while I was away?"

"That a stupid question."

"No more stupid than your stupid question to me!"

His quieter tone contrasted sharply with hers. "I just ask, okay?"

"Then let me ask a question. Like why do I never hear you say a certain word?"

He looked puzzled. "Word? Which word?"

"Why, Franco, you got the first letter right, with *three* words."

"What?"

"No, Franco, that's not the word but another that starts with a double-u."

Tonnini was frowning. "Why, why all this?"

Nessa's voice volume increased. "And it's not 'why' either!"

"When you—"

"Ah!" She leaned forward. "Franco, you've used many double-u words, except maybe . . . one?" Moving closer and lowering her head, she barely whispered. "The word, Franco, the word that so eludes you is . . . wedding!"

The word seemed alien to him. "Wedding?"

"Jesus!" She looked off. And then at him. "You asked me to marry you, remember? And I accepted, remember?"

"*Si!* Of course!" He nodded. "Sure, we get married."

"When?"

He checked his nails. Both hands. "Eh, is Cannes next month, then there the Venice festival, and '*Itatchia,*' it shoot soon."

"Maybe we could get married one lunch break?"

Tonnini studied her. "This a new Nessa, a different Nessa. We no speak like this before?"

"You're right, we haven't, and maybe that's the problem?" She challenged him visually, combatively.

Tonnini stood. "Perhaps we should take some time to think things out?"

"I think we should."

Nessa dried-off her showered body, put on a robe and wandered into the guest bedroom. She lay back on the bed, and drifted off to sleep.

To be awakened later by a gentle knocking. It was evening, the room almost dark. The knocking continued. "Who is it?"

"Is me. Franco."

"It's open."

Also wearing a robe, Tonnini entered. Nessa moved to switch on the light. "Is okay, leave it off." Sitting on the edge of the bed, he toyed with the cord of her robe. "Nessa, I been thinking, an' you are right about me neglecting you an' I wrong, wrong not to call you, to meet you. I do too many things wrong, an' we should not fight. Is enough fights in business, especially movie business, without you an' me fighting, so I apologize."

Smiling, Nessa nodded. "Apology accepted. *Grazie.*"

"*Prego.*" Tonnini pulled on her cord, gently . . . but firmly.

"Not now Franco."

He stared at her. And shrugged. Sighing loudly, he left.

SCENE 48. TAKE 2.

Driven by a lady, a modest sedan with two occupants traveled the early morning deserted streets of Santa Mosqueiro.

Sênhora Cabral spoke. "It must be important?"

Floriana Cabral turned to his wife. "What makes you say that?"

"When was the last time Mauricio Para called you, personally?"

Cabral nodded. "Sometimes an attorney is needed simply for, you know, formalities?"

Sênhora Cabral concentrated on driving. "Where do we turn?"

"Third left. You'll know when we're there, by the high wall."

"Ugh!" Sênhora Cabral shivered. "I don't envy you, especially if it's like that other time." She glanced at her husband. "Remember? The noise, that blaring pop music, those awful *nouveaux riches*? It was like some Bacchanalian orgy."

"Elisabet. It was *his* birthday party."

"And it'll be worse today, Saturday. That's when they have the weekly *fejoida* buffet."

"There!" Cabral pointed. "Where the guard is."

The car pulled into the entrance. Sênhora Cabral identified herself and her husband. The barrier was raised. The car drove through.

"My, God!" Open-mouthed, Sênhora Cabral looked around, as did her husband. "*Where is* everybody?"

Cabral spoke through his chuckles. "Elisabet, you sure it's Saturday and not Monday?"

"Of course, it's Saturday." She glanced at Cabral. "You're not wearing a suit."

"Well, drop me off here. Maurico must be around somewhere." He kissed her. "I'll call." Cabral exited, watching the car drive away. He looked around, at the immaculate but totally deserted patio and pool.

"Floriano!"

Cabral searched for the source of the voice, Para's voice.

"Here, over here!" Para was standing by the gangplank of his beloved cabin cruiser, *La Isabella*.

As Cabral boarded the vessel, he gestured to the deserted areas. "What happened?"

Para surveyed the scene. "This is *my* club, for me to do with it what I please. *I* built it when those pompous sons of colonial pricks refused me, Mauricio Para, refused me admission to join their club. 'Fuck you!' I said. 'I'll build my own'! And I did." Para gazed at the emptiness. He turned to Cabral. "But this morning, as I need hardly remind you, this morning I was charged under Section Three One Zero Zero Zero One of the Imperio Penal Code, charged . . . *'pending further investigations and enquiries, charged with being involved in drugs trafficking, money laundering, specific charges to be laid at a date subsequent.'* " Para leaned on a rail. "And when I do come here, I don't need every member to be talking about me, pointing me out, raising their hypocritical eyes to heaven, saying, 'There goes the evil drugs czar.' " He lit a cigarette, and stood erect, jabbing a thumb into his chest. "I . . . am Mauricio Para. The owner of three newspapers, a multi channel TV station, an FM radio station and this yacht club. *This* is my club, *not* theirs!"

Cabral nodded gently. "When will they be let back in?"

Para smiled at his attorney. "That depends. On you."

The large cabin cruiser headed out into the main shipping channel. Para had set the vessel to automatic, the on-board computer reading the radar and thus controlling accordingly, the throttle and the steering.

Para offered his guest a cigarette. Cabral shook his head. "No thanks. I've managed to give them up."

Para took one, lighting it. "I wish I could. How'd you do it? Acupuncture, counseling, what?"

"None of that. I just decided it was a mug's game, there being many more negatives than plusses, and I've never smoked again."

"Isabella, my wife, she begs me to quit, but I'm like Mark Twain."

"Mark Twain?"

Para took another drag. "Mark Twain is quoted as saying '*it's easy to give up smoking, I've done it hundreds of times.*'" The two men laughed. As Para flicked overboard his cigarette, he turned to Cabral. "How much time can you give me?"

"Mauricio, you pay by the hour."

Para smiled. "Then there's no hurry?"

Having left the main channel, being navigated now was a smaller waterway, into which poured many tributaries, creating the myriad of islands that are dotted up river. It was just wide enough to accept *La Isabella*. Disconnecting the computer, Para took over, throttling back to 'slow' to prevent any damage being done to the vessel by the overhanging trees or underwater obstructions. He cut the engines. The silence was uncanny. There was no bird chatter nor noises of insects, and as Cabral looked up, the rays of the sun were obscured completely at times by the dense overhead canopy of foliage. The vessel cruised, silently.

Cabral appeared worried. "What happens if we get stuck?"

"We wait for high tide." Para studied Cabral. "You're a drinking man, aren't you?"

Cabral smiled. "Oh, I get it. We drink gallons of booze and then pee into the river to bring up the water level?"

"Floriano, I didn't realize you were a nautical man!" Para lowered the anchor. "We drink, to pass away the time, waiting for high tide. We could call the coastguard, but it's nowhere near as much fun."

"Is it okay to swim in this?"

Para smiled. "You decide." He disappeared below, to reappear with a package. He walked directly to the prow. "Floriano, here. Look."

Cabral walked quickly up the port side but suddenly cried out, lurching precariously by the low rail. Grabbing him, Para dropped the package, it falling to the deck and splitting open, revealing raw steak. Para slid it over the side.

"Now. Watch."

Within a milli-second, the water was a foaming cauldron.

Cabral knelt, clutching the rail. "Pirhana?"

"Yes. Just like the Treasury Police. They wish only to devour. Here, let me help you up." Para aided his attorney to his feet. "You been drinking already?"

"What? No!"

"Then why'd you keel over?"

"I tripped."

"Tripped? On the '*Isabella*'? She's like the wife she's named after. Perfect!"

"Mauricio, I tell you, I tripped." Cabral pointed. "That deck plank there, see? It's warped, it's thrown a screw."

Para examined the spot. "As soon as we get back, I'll have it fixed."

"You know, Mauricio," said Cabral with mock seriousness. "I could sue you? Negligence?"

Para pulled a face. "And what would you have sued the pirhana for?"

"Invasion of privacy."

Laughing, Para pointed to Cabral's feet. "Let's get you some deck shoes, and then a drink?"

"I'll take the drink first."

The two men were seated on the deck above the bridge.

"What was the final amount? For my bail?"

"Ten million cruzeiros."

Para whistled. "Phew . . ."

"Mauricio, it could have been higher."

Para stood, leaning back against the rail. "Floriano, it's still a lot of money, an awful lot of money?"

Looking into his glass, Cabral sipped his Chivas. "And, it had to be paid in dollars U.S."

Para was visibly shocked. "You're kidding?"

"I wish I was, but Mauricio, the judiciary is as assailable to inflation just as much you and I are."

Para turned, staring ahead at the waterway. "How much, in dollars?"

"Fifty-thousand," said Cabral, flatly.

Para groaned. "You've spoken to my accountant?"

Cabral nodded. "Of course."

"There's enough in the dollar account? I hate the thought of having to change cruzeiros for dollars at the official exchange, especially when the black market rate is better by a percentage of one-sixty-two-point-five?"

Cabral nodded. "You'd enough in that account to more than cover it. It's been paid."

From a Waterford crystal decanter, Para refilled their glasses.

Cabral raised his glass. "Did you do it?"

"Do what?"

"What the Treasury Police are accusing you of?"

Para carefully put down the decanter. "Floriano, you and I have known each other a very long time, since I was a cub reporter, and since then, with the help of the Lord and my wonderful wife, I've built a thriving business. D'you think, really think I would jeopardize all that, *family*, businesses?" He pointed to the deck. "This yacht. This life style, for which I've striven all these years? A television station, a radio station, newspapers, a yacht, a *yacht club*? Six cars!"

Cabral remained calm. "Mr. Robert Maxwell owned many newspapers, Mr. John DeLorean many cars."

"Unlike Mr. Maxwell, I'm not robbing Peter to pay Paul, and you won't find me floating by this yacht, dead!" Para smiled. "Not unless I trip on that damned warped plank."

"John DeLorean was arrested in a drugs bust."

"Floriano . . ." Para breathed heavily. "You're not hearing what I'm saying. I'm not trying to save a crumbling communications empire nor retrieve a floundering car factory. And, I abhor drug-dealing. It's evil."

"And Mauricio, you're not hearing what *I'm* saying. You not answering my question costs you money, because I'm not leaving here, warped piece of decking notwithstanding, I'm not leaving here until I hear your answer. Now, did you or did you not do what you're accused of?"

Para looked his attorney directly in the eye. "No, Floriano. I did not."

Cabral relaxed. "Then we've nothing to worry about, have we?"

"Except for one thing."

Cabral frowned. "Which is?"

"Who?" Para lit another cigarette. "Who is making these accusations against me, without foundation, without any foundation at all, but, with sufficient credibility to convince the authorities to take the action they have taken?" He raised his arms. "Who, and why?"

"Anyone have a grudge against you, an old score to settle?"

Para sat, on the edge of a deck chair. "Floriano, you know as well as I do, all is fair in love and war, and business is a war." He shrugged. "It's inevitable, to make enemies in one's professional life." He glanced at Cabral. "And I didn't get to where I am today by turning the other cheek."

"Well, as you say, whoever it is, they've been able to convince somebody of your involvement, and by implication, guilt." Cabral tapped Para's wrist. "And, when the Treasury Police are involved to make an arrest, that's not done on hearsay, believe you me."

"What are their sources?"

Cabral chuckled. "Mauricio, they don't divulge their sources. They glean information from all over, y'know, other agencies, the streets even."

"Such as?"

"Federal government departments, even foreign governments, offshore bank accounts, and various state agencies."

"Like what?"

"Well, a first port of call would be the local state police."

"The Boa Vista State Police?"

Cabral held apart his hands. "Yes, the Boa Vista State Police, any of the other state police in this country for that matter. Municipal police, Rodovaria, the Revenue Service, customs, any agency thought to be helpful to the investigation."

Para drained his glass. "Do you have anyone on the inside?"

"Me?" Giggling, Cabral shook his head. "No."

Para looked at the horizon. "Maybe that's why you're still a small law firm?"

"And maybe it's also why I sleep soundly at night."

Being flipped into the Para mouth were macademias. "What happens next?"

"You'll be arraigned, you'll make a formal statement." Cabral was scratching feverishly the back of an elbow. "There mosquitoes around here?"

"Billions. But you were saying?"

Cabral was checking all over his body for the blood-sucking insects. "Eh, the formal statement, they'll wrap up the investigations, and a trial date will be set."

"Floriano, you mentioned earlier, the State Police would be contacted?"

"Of course. One of the accused is a Captain Possi. Of the State Police."

"Ah, yes. Captain Possi." Para meditated. "He out on bail?"

Cabral laughed. "A Policeman? Mauricio, get real." He shook his head. "Bail was refused, but the local chief, Colonel Mendoza, he offered to provide surety for Possi."

Para smiled. "Honor amongst policemen."

"Mauricio, world-wide, most police forces are comprised of masons. Imperio is no different." Cabral checked his watch. "Is our meeting concluded, officially?"

"You tell me? But I think we've covered all the bases? So, how about a light lunch, followed by a little cruise?"

Cabral checked his watch. "Four billable hours?"

"Money well spent. Caviar?" The two men descended below.

"Chi Chi!" The boatmaster saluted. "There's a loose deck plank on the port side. Fix it, immediately."

"Right away, Sênhor Para."

Cabral checked his watch. "I should call my wife, to pick me up."

"Floriano, I'll run you home." They walked across the vast emptiness of the deserted club. "If I recall, it's on the way?" The chauffeur opened a door. "Give Pedro your address."

As the Mercedes glided away, Cabral checked his watch, yet again. "My wife has a distant cousin staying with us. I said I'd take him to Vigil Mass."

"Are you a regular churchgoer?"

Cabral nodded. "I go as often as I can. Which isn't as often enough as my wife would like."

Para smiled, knowingly. "Ah, yes, the ladies. They love the ritual and mothering the priests."

Cabral glanced at him. "I gather you don't approve?"

Para lit a cigarette. "I used to attend Mass regularly, at Santa Maria de Faro Church." Para studied the cigarette. "I've had a very good life, and I felt the least I could do was to say 'thank you' to somebody, and for me, that somebody is God the Father and Christ the Son." Para inhaled, deeply. "And I contributed. I paid for the instalation in the church of a new speaker system." He glanced at Cabral. "Radio mikes, to save the priests straining their voices. I provided the presbytery with a car, so that the priests could get around the parish more easily, to serve their flock better, and, I paid all the bills." Ash was flicked on to the floor. "Not my companies, not my foundation, but me, personally. Car insurance, gas, oil, tires, servicing, all. *I* paid." Para looked at the passing vista. "When my eldest daughter wished to remarry, she the victim of an adulterer who couldn't keep his hands off his neighbors' wives nor, for that matter, their daughters. When she wanted to remarry, naturally we all wanted a church wedding, in Santa Maria de Faro." He doused the cigarette. "They refused." He turned to Cabral. "My daughter was a divorcée. The wronged party, but they wouldn't even listen. Divorce? A sin, as far as the Church was concerned, a mortal sin. So, I withdrew my patronage. She remarried in the registrar's office." He shifted in his seat, lighting another cigarette. Another huge inhalation. "But Floriano, I know Catholic women in this city who've had children but who also have had their marriages annulled by the Church?" He slapped a knee. "Annulled! On the basis of non consummation!" He laughed. "Kids. But non consummation?" He chuckled some more, turning then to Cabral. "But then, the Immaculate Conception is an elemental basis of our Church's doctrine, eh?"

As departed Cabral, Para waved. "Pedro, take the long way home."

The chauffeur looked in his mirror. *"But the Sênhora said—"*

The divider slid upwards, to be closed. Para picked up the phone, and hit 'memory'.

"Hola?"

"It's the car calling." Para heard Rubio catch his breath.

"Everything okay?"

"No, not okay. This morning? I'm minding my own business, Isabella and I are having our usual breakfast, there's a ring at the door and here I am, having been arrested. And fifty thousand bail dollars lighter!"

"What! Arrested? *You*?" Rubio was not a panicker but certainly he was uncomfortable. "Are they on to us? And where the hell's Mendoza?"

"Lying low. Possi's in jail, so Mendoza is compromised," said Para, keeping to himself his suspicions of the colonel of state police.

"Jesus, Mauricio, how'd this all come about?"

"There's a pattern, and, I think more than just coincidence." Para wasn't sure where to start, so jumbled had everything become. "Do you remember that meeting where I said I didn't trust that excuse for a human being, Ramalho?"

"I remember."

"He cracked. Committed suicide."

"The little shit. Does that have anything to do with your arrest?"

"Antonio, I just said, *more* than pure coincidence."

"When's the inquest?"

"The inquest?"

"Yes, Mauricio, the inquest! On Ramalho? It's a formality. But it may tell us something. He may have left a note or notes, which will be produced and read out. And if he's the one who pointed the finger, your legal people won't have too much difficulty in refuting the written ranting of a known drug addict with a prison record, eh?"

"I hear you. *Ciao*" Para disconnected and redialed. "Carlo? Is Mauricio. You still interested in being a reporter? Carlo, Carlo. The movie won't last forever. What will you do when the circus leaves town? Think ahead. And just because you are betrothed to my daughter Josefina, it doesn't mean you never have to work again, does it? Am I supposed to keep you? No, that's right, '*of course not*'. So, a little assignment . . . well, if they stop you any money, I'll make it up. And, in some way it's to do with the movie, yes, Ramalho, the censor who committed suicide. Find out when is the inquest and cover the proceedings . . . say who you're from? *Diario do Boa Vista*. First thing Monday, call Ellisette, my secretary. She'll get a press card for you. And Carlo, once you've written it up, you show it to me first, understood? Me *first*! *Ciao*."

He'd returned from a day's location shooting.

"Sênhor Cooper . . . Mr. James?"

The director looked around the lobby, as he was approached by an assistant manager. "Your colleague? How long is he staying?"

"Who we talking about?" Asked a bemused Cooper.

"Your friend, Mr. Seidelman?"

Cooper frowned. "He's still *here*?"

"Yes, sir." The young man gestured. "That's the problem. The tourist season is approaching and we need to know when we can offer the room."

"I'll talk to him."

"Now. Please?"

Cooper pondered if Steven Spielberg had to tramp hotel corridors, seeking out abusers of hotel hospitality. He groaned. "Okay, yes. Now."

Five-eight-one. Cooper knocked. And waited. Nothing. Knocking a second time, he did so more firmly. To no response. He tried the handle. It moved. He opened the door, slowly. Then opened it wider, enough to poke his head through. Cooper stage-whispered. "Don?" Nothing. He whispered to himself, quietly. "Have I got the right bloody room?" He groped for a light switch. Fortune found him one. He flicked it.

"Off! Off!", cried an hysterical croaky voice. "Turn it off!!"

Cooper did as he was bid. "Don . . . Don Seidelman?"

"Go away, away, leave me alone. I'm . . . dying . . . dying."

Cooper found another switch, shouting. "I have come back, Miss Havisham, to let in the sunlight!" He peered around. "Miss Havisham?"

"Turn it off. The light. Turn it off!"

"Miss Havisham, I do that then I can't see a bloody thing!"

Seidelman pulled the covers right over himself. Completely.

Cooper sniffed. "Christ, what *is* that awful smell?" Covering his nose, he looked around the room. Every window was closed, every drape pulled, the air conditioning was off and the room had to it a pungent, dank and invasive smell. "Don, you been barbecuing chihauhuas up here?

236

The place smells like Kentucky fried. The State of Kentucky. Fried." Cooper stood at the end of the bed. "Tell me, is hibernation a Tonnini Pictures rest cure?"

Slowly, but slowly, appeared the head of Don Seidelman, looking as if he'd just spent two months in solitary, and blinking at the unaccustomed light.

"Good God. You look like something out of a Tobe Hooper movie."

"And why not?", he croaked. "They've been shooting *The Texas Chain Saw Massacre*. In my stomach."

Cooper couldn't believe his eyes. "Don, when did you last eat?"

"Ugh! Don't even mention food." He dragged his eyes to focus on Cooper. "You ever feel the bottom's fallen out of your world?"

"Frequently, Don. Frequently."

"Well, I feel as if the world's fallen out of my bottom. I've been on the throne longer than Queen Victoria."

"So what, if anything, have you eaten?"

"Nothing! Nothing since this thing started. Just fruit. And like you said, washed under the faucet. I was very particular about that."

Cooper felt a pang of conscience. Just one. "Why didn't you call a doctor?"

Seidelman's jaw was sagging. "I asked you to get a doctor!"

"You did? When?"

"Yesterday!"

Smiling, Cooper crooned. '*All our troubles seemed so far away.*' He eyed Seidelman. "Yesterday was a rest day."

"Not for me it wasn't." A pallid tongue ran over Seidelman cracked lips. "I'm dying."

Cooper was nodding. "Don, you've got that line right." Cooper paced, at the foot of the bed. "I thought at first you were having trouble with it, might need a couple more readings, rehearsals, but no, you've mastered it." He nodded confirmation. "A print. Check the gate!"

Seidelman looked hollow. "I should be at Pebble Beach."

"Building sand castles?"

"The James Eden Pro Am."

"What's that, an airline?"

"A golf tournament!"

"Don, have you called your family, your wife?"

"I'm not married."

"Nobody would have you?"

"What?" Seidelman belched.

"Have you called the doctor?"

Seidelman tried to raise his voice. "I told you already!"

"Don. The *House* doctor?"

Seidelman shook his head. "I don't want some dago quack! I want the company guy, that one who qualified in the States."

"Okay, okay." Cooper opened his palms. "It's too late to do anything tonight, but Golda will get him to you first thing tomorrow. Okay?"

Seidelman managed a weak nod.

"I'll order you some soup. Consomme or chicken broth?" Seidelman uttered a loud retching-like noise. "You don't have to eat it, but try." Cooper patted the bed, and with the wave of a hand, backed away.

"James! Don't leave me!!"

"Don, don't muck around. I've a movie to direct." Cooper pointed to himself. "Remember, the one you don't want to pay me for?"

Seidelman sulked. "You don't know what it's like, stuck in here, nothing to read. Even the *Gideon's* in Portuguese."

"Naughty, naughty! Been peeping at the New Testament have we?"

"And that?" Seidelman pointed to the television. "That's no company. Everything's either in Portuguese or Spanish!"

Cooper felt pang number two. Faintly. "Tell you what, first thing in the morning I'll have you moved into my suite. I'll advise the hotel, but in there I've got a TV and a VCR, and loads of cassettes. You might be bored watching dailies, but there's movies too, all in English. And, you can get CNN. Plus, I'll have the office get you some magazines and newspapers, *Time, Newsweek, The Economist, Diarrhea Digest.*"

"That's not funny." Suddenly, Seidelman grabbed his stomach, rolled out of the bed and headed for the bathroom, his knees together.

Cooper took this as his exit cue.

Mendoza rode the elevator, walked along the corridor and entered the office, the outer office, the empty office. Where worked Possi. Normally.

Mendoza flipped the intercom. "Vera, good morning. I'm in. A new man, if you notice?"

A brief knock and entered Vera, carrying a cup of coffee. She studied her boss. "I like it. It makes you look . . . younger, gentler and, more handsome!"

"My wife maintains a mustache reminds her of Hitler, so it had to go." He looked at her, thinking should *I* do it, or have Vera make the call, the seal of officialdom? "Vera, I want want you to call the capital, the Ministry of the Interior. A Sênhor Vinci. I don't know his first name." He smiled at her. "For all I know, it could be Leonardo?"

Giggling, Vera departed. Two minutes later, the call came through.

"Sênhor Vinci? Good morning, Colonel Mendoza, Boa Vista State Police."

"Good morning, Colonel. What can I do for you?"

"Sênhor Vinci, it's about what you have done already. For me. I call to thank you for the impeccable co-ordination and the swift way you made your moves." Mendoza stroked his non-existent mustache, frowning. "Such was your prescience that I anticipate making a major arrest, almost imminently."

"Colonel, this is great news! Your . . . *El jefe*?"

"Sênhor Vinci, this is not a secure line."

"I understand, Colonel."

Mendoza placed the phone closer to his mouth. "Secrecy. The constant need for such. Confidentiality, the assurance that my operation will not be compromised, in any, any way. You understand?"

"Totally."

Mendoza had to know. "The inquest?"

"What about it?"

"We know Judge Mello received a letter from his deceased nephew, a letter in which the drug-crazed unfortunate directed the finger at *me*."

"Colonel. Your point?"

"My point is that at an inquest, aren't any letters, notes, whatever, don't they all get taken in as evidence?"

"They do."

"Then . . ." Mendoza spoke more quickly. "Then, as my name appears in one of those letters and perhaps *all*, then *I* become a material witness, with my cover blown?"

"Oh, my God!" Vinci regained his telephonic composure. "Colonel, thank the Lord one of us is thinking rationally here."

Mendoza was comforting. "Just part of a policeman's job." He felt he could progress. "Do we know how many letters Ramalho actually sent, and to whom?" He could hear the re-shuffling of papers.

"Eh, we have a record of three. One each. To the Judge, his brother, a priest, and a third, written, but not mailed. It was found in the car."

"Where's that letter now?"

"Sequestered. By the Coroner."

"Was it addressed?"

More papers being shuffled. "Eh, yes. Must be a foreigner? A Mr. James Cooper?"

"Cooper? Of course!" Mendoza was genuinely surprised. "It all fits! I should have made the connection." Mendoza effected a stage sigh. "But you know, sometimes when you're that close sometimes you don't always see the wood for the trees, especially as this isn't the only case I'm working on. Might the Cooper letter have been sent?"

"Quite possibly. But this Cooper? Is he your *El Jefe*?"

"Too early to say. Possibly." Mendoza lit a cigarette. "But tell me Sênhor, can these letters be withheld, not declared at the inquest, because if they *are* introduced they could severely compromise my investigations. Can you do that, ensure they're *not* presented?"

"Of course. I would not wish to be the one who obstructs a police investigation, especially one as far reaching as yours. You have my word Colonel. They'll not be introduced. But, that's presuming they've not been sent already."

"Sênhor Vinci, thank you for both your understanding and your co-operation. I will of course keep you updated on our progress."

"Colonel, I appreciate that. Was there anything else?"

No, thought Mendoza. For the first time in days, he felt comfortable, secure. Except. Except for that other letter, the Cooper letter. "No, thank you. *Ciao.*"

He jogged. Always, every evening, unless had to be attended some official or social occasion. He appreciated the benefit of the exercise but more importantly, the thirty-minute jog allowed Mendoza to clear his mind, think things to the core. Running through the up-market suburban streets of Vila Nova, this evening his thoughts were on the Cooper letter. '*Raimundo, has it been sent and if so, how can I get a look at it?*' Then it occurred to him. Call in a few favors. From the other side of town.

Dropping his location bag, Cooper looked around the unfamiliar room although did the aroma breed . . . contempt? It wasn't as pungent as when was resident here Seidelman, but, it was lingering there, just like *The Summer Wind*. He flopped on to the bed, the mail he'd collected from the concierge still in his hand. He propped himself on an elbow, glancing at the letters. Immediately, his eye went to the official-looking buff envelope, which he opened. Within it was another envelope, that had been opened previously. Removing this, Cooper withdrew the letter, and read aloud. '*Sênhor James. You know I said I figured it out? I have. By the time you read this, and I hope it reaches you, I will be only a memory, but, no tears, please. I do not cry, because there is no one to blame except me. Mendoza? He did not get me on drugs, I did that. That is what got me into trouble, lost me jobs, send me to jail. But Mendoza? I had to get away from him and I knew of no other escape. I am sorry if my stupidity cause you problems, but now I come to my senses, I hope, to help all of us. So please, no tears, just sing, courtesy of your Mr. Lloyd Webber, sing 'Don't cry for me Boa Vista!' Ciao, Francesco Ramalho.*' Cooper stared at the letter, knowing it had been written by a once-live person who was no more. He spoke aloud. "Don't cry for me, Boa Vista . . ."

Feeling desperately sad, Cooper lay on the bed. Whatever thoughts he had were interrupted by the shrill of the telephone. "Hello?"

"Don, Don Seidelman?"

"No, This is Cooper, James Cooper."

"James? Is Franco. I call him an' I get you. Why?"

Cooper smiled. "He's been ill. Moctezuma's Revenge? So, to make life more bearable for him, we swapped rooms."

"Why you no tell the switchboard of your musical chairs?"

"Franco, *I* do have other things on my mind, y'know? Like directing *Redmayne West*, *your* movie? Plus, actually I *did* inform the hotel."

"What time it down there?"

"Eh . . ." Cooper checked his watch. "Nine forty-five P.M"

"He probably asleep by now?"

"Probably." Cooper was dying for a drink. "Is that it, Franco?"

"Eh, Nessa?"

"What about her?" Cooper felt distinctly uncomfortable.

"Anything happen down there, anything that might upset her?"

Cooper's eyes raised to the ceiling. "Like what?"

"You tell me."

"If I had something to tell, I'd tell you."

"She act very strange back here. Not like my Nessa, the Nessa I know an' the Nessa I love."

Rising were the little hairs on the back of Cooper's neck. "Then you must know her moods, her concerns?"

"James? You guys date, Nessa an' you?"

"No, Franco, no. That was a long time ago." Cooper thought about a wind up. "Although we did have breakfast together one morning."

"In her room, her suite?"

"Eh, no, the Terrace Restaurant."

"When?!"

A Cooper mischievous lie. "The morning she arrived from L.A."

"When you last see her?"

"The day before she left. And no, I didn't see her that evening."

"Who see her off?"

"The limo chauffeur."

"An' where were you?"

"On location! Directing *YOUR* movie! Okay?"

242

"Anyone make a pass at her down there?"

"Jesus, Franco! What am I, Kevin Costner to Nessa's Whitney Houston? I'm directing *your* movie down here. I'm not the head of an escort agency, okay?"

"Women . . ." Tonnini chuckled. "It the wedding."

Cooper gripped the phone so firmly it should have shattered. "The wedding?"

"*Si*. You know how silly women get about weddings, especially when it their own?"

"Oh, yes, when it's their own," repeated Cooper, *sotto voce*.

"You do good screen time. Keep it up."

"You want to talk to Seidelman now?"

"Seidelman? What about? *Ciao*."

SCENE 51. TAKE 4.

In what was normally Cooper's suite, Seidelman lay on top of the covers, having neither the energy nor the peace to actually get into bed. Dressed still in pyjamas, he'd lost count of the number of times he had padded from bed to bathroom and as he knew the route so well, no longer did he bother switching on lights, neither in the bedroom nor the bathroom.

Seidelman sat on the toilet, seeking relief, the thousand natural shocks that flesh is heir to . . .

The maid didn't knock. Quietly, she unlocked the door, crept in, unfolded the bed cover, placing on the pillow the two large chocolate fondant mints inscribed in three languages *Sweet dreams, Gran Hotel do Amazonas*. Looking around, she tip-toed to the door, holding it open with a foot. "Psst! Psst!"

Hurrying down the corridor noiselessly, the two men passed into the suite, one placing into the maid's top pocket a ten-thousand cruzeiro note, in the process groping a breast and causing her to muffle a giggle.

Closing the door quietly, she took out the bank note, looking at it lovingly. She thought. More than a week's wages. Just for letting two guys into a suite so they could make a surprise apple-pie bed for somebody.

They donned gloves and ski masks. They worked swiftly and silently. And had been told that most likely the letter would be in an official-looking envelope, a buff envelope from the coroner's office.

One man took the bedroom, the other Cooper's office-cum-seating area.

They opened drawers first, working upwards, saving time in not having to close a drawer before opening another. They pulled out the contents, sifting, sorting, discarding, and anything that might clatter? That was dropped on to the carpeted floor.

The minibar was prised open, the freezer compartment checked. The minisafe, Moviola editing machine, desk, closets, videotapes, audio cassettes, even the TV-set and VCR, all were ripped apart, silently but meticulously.

The bed was stripped, the mattress ripped open. The insides of shoes, under rugs, the pockets of all hanging jackets and pants, anywhere and everywhere that might conceal a letter. Every book, magazine, newspaper, all were scrutinized to see if was secreted between the pages a letter, a letter from Francisco Ramalho to James Cooper.

One man nodded to the bathroom.

They glided over, one taking the handle silently and throwing open the door to the darkened interior. To reveal a startled gringo standing with his pyjama pants around his ankles.

To protect that most private of moments, Seidelman lunged for the door.

One of them pushed him violently with such force that the bath mat slipped on the highly-polished floor, and Seidelman fell backwards into the bath striking his head on the faucet, the one in the shape of a laughing gargoyle, which mocked silently the inert Executive Vice-President Business Affairs, Tonnini International Pictures, he who lay in the empty tub, his pyjama pants nestling on the ankles of his feet, which hung over the side of the bath.

Removing their gloves and masks, they checked the corridor. It was clear. The two men left the suite empty handed, turning the door sign thoughtfully to *Do Not Disturb*.

Replacing the house phone, Con Griffith walked to where stood Golda.
"Well?"
"Nothing. The operator let it ring for a good five minutes. Nothing."
Golda checked the time. "Con, I've got to confirm a charter by tomorrow, so sod sleeping bloody Seidelman beauty."

Griffith pointed to the *Do Not Disturb* sign. "Shouldn't we wait?"
"Shame I can't read." Golda rapped on the door. Nothing. She thumped harder. And for longer. They looked at each other. Resuming her personal wake-up call, Golda pounded on the door with both fists. "I feel like King Kong trying to get to Fay Wray." She paused for breath. And squinted, putting an ear to the door. "Was that a moan?"
"All I can hear is your panting."
From a door opening behind them appeared a maid trailing a vacuum cleaner.
Golda indicated the suite's door. "Eh, Mrs. Mopp, *por favor*?"
The maid looked blank.
Confronting her, Golda grabbed the key chain hanging from the maid's belt and dragged her screaming and struggling across the corridor. The maid's protests fell on deaf ears. "I bet you're great in the limbo dancing contest?" Golda tried keys various. One worked. The door opened. The maid pointed to the sign. Golda flipped it. "There. *Make Up Room.* Satisfied?" Releasing the keys, Golda took out two cruzeiro bills. "Con, you're a witness. Two thousand washers paid to Mrs. Mopp here, with no receipt."
Griffith was ceremoniously solemn. "Duly noted."
They walked into the suite.

"Jesus H. Christ!" Exploded Golda the Jewess. Griffith was speechless. They stood surveying the damage, the devastation. Golda looked at the upturned mattress, the total destruction. "Blimey, that's some guts ache he's got?"

Heard was a moan.

Golda nudged Griffith. "Sounds like the khazi. Man's work." She shoved him towards the bathroom.

Opening the door slowly, he disappeared within. "Golda! A doctor!"

Moved to yet another room, the house doctor had cleaned and dressed the wound to the back of Seidelman's head, and for good measure, administering also an anti-tetanus shot. Once the doctor had left, Golda and Griffith remained in the room.

A tentative Seidelman hand hovered over the back of his head. "Ah. It's still there."

"What is?" Asked Golda. "And Don, what the hell happened?"

Seidelman looked pitiful. "You ever been mugged on the john?"

Golda shook her head. "No, but I've been screwed on the job."

"Well, I was mugged on the john."

Griffith was stern-faced. "Is nowhere sacred anymore?"

"Don, d'you think they were after the toilet paper?"

"Golda! I could have been killed?"

"And all for soft tissue. Alas, poor *Andrex*." She glanced at Griffith. "I knew him, Con."

Griffith coughed. "Given the damage, they must've been after something specific?"

"I hear *Delsey* is very big on the local toilet paper black market?" Golda caught a stare from Griffith. "You learn that look from Cooper?"

"Don, there was a lot of very expensive stuff in that suite, and, this is a very poor country." Griffith shook his head. "And yet they don't seem to have taken anything, not even your credit cards?"

Golda nodded. "Probably maxed out?" Her remark was ignored.

"And", continued Griffith. "You heard nothing?"

Seidelman shook his head. And winced. "Nothing. Not a thing."

"Was the TV on? Or the stereo?"

"Con, the only noise was coming from my stomach." Seidelman rubbed his mid-section. "In which I think an armistice has been signed." He motioned to Golda. "Thanks for the Doc. The guy I asked for, right?"

"Negative. House doctor."

"Golda! I said wanted the company doctor! I don't want *one* of those dago quacks touching me!" The sulking returned. "Not one!"

Golda adopted her school mistress stance. "Don. There *wasn't* time, and besides, he wasn't South American. He bowed when he spoke to me." She read from a business card. "*Doctor Udo Pfaff.*"

"Sounds like a fucking perfume!" His face contorted into a dozen angers. "What sort of a name is that?!"

Golda was innocence personified. "German."

"German!" His head lolled. "German?" Twenty tons of TNT seemed to erupt beneath Seidelman. "Christ, Golda? They! Hate!! Jews!!!" He screamed. "I want on Schindler's Ark. Now, right now!"

Golda slipped into her 'Dr.Ruth' mode. 'Don, he was very nice."

"Blue eyes, blonde hair, sickly smile?" Said shriekingly. "*Just obeying orders*'?" As if drunk, his held rolled from side-to-side. "Either way, I'm dead, fucking . . . dead!" He looked at both of them. "We're in a South American country! He could be Dr.Mengele!"

'Dr.Ruth' again. "Don, I'm a Jew. I wouldn't mind being touched by him."

"That's because you're a woman first and a Jew second!"

She patted the pillows behind him. "Don, calm down. You're doing yourself no favors with these hysterics? Now relax. Dr.Pfaff was so concerned about you, he's coming back after lunch."

"No doubt in an S.S. uniform and with a cyanide pill!" Tired, he laid back on the pillows. "How come you guys found me?" He turned to them. "And thanks."

Griffith spoke. "We need you, for twelve thousand U.S., wanted down here immediately."

Seidelman frowned. "What the hell for?"

"We need cash dollars for an air charter deposit. Now, I could use next week's per diem money to pay both the deposit and the charter fee, but that would run me very close to the edge. Too close."

"Yep." Seidelman shook his bandaged head, very slowly. "Just have the L.A. office wire it down."

Griffith shook his head. "Don, that won't work. Every bank along the line will siphon it off to make interest. It'd take forever to get here."

"Then what's the answer?"

Golda made a suggestion. "Could it be brought down personally?"

"By who?"

Griffith eyed Seidelman. "Our associate producer?"

"Franco, sorry to call you so early, but we have a little problem down here."

"Don? That you?"

"Yes, Franco." He both felt and sounded exhausted. "It's me."

"Where you?"

"You mean, right now?"

"That what I mean!"

"In bed."

"Bed! What time it down there?"

Seidelman glanced at the bedside clock. "Eleven-thirty."

"A.M. or P.M.?"

"A.M."

"What you doing in bed at eleven-thirty A.M.!"

"Franco." Seidelman speculated. What had happened to sympathy? "I am ill. I've had the most terrible stomach. Enteritis."

"I thought you were in Imperio?"

"I am!"

"Then where the fuck this Enteritis?"

"In my God dammed fucking stomach!"

The placating Tonnini. "Don, plenty people go to South America an' get the trots. If everyone behave like you, half the continent would be in bed?"

"Franco, *The Tet Offensive* was being re-enacted. In my stomach!"

"You returning here or planning to take Imperio citizenship?"

Seidelman held his head "It's great to be appreciated."

"Don, I pay you to be Executive Vice President Business Affairs, not to lie in some fucking bed! You an' me, we agreed long ago, long ago! The way to success for a movie company like ours is to restrict overhead, not

248

be top heavy with execs, staff, offices. You remember?"

"Sure I remember, Franco." He picked at a thread of the cover. "It was my idea. *You* remember?"

"An' we stick to that formula, right? We none of us scared to roll up our sleeve an' get our hands dirty, no?"

Seidelman contemplated. When was the last time those perfectly manicured Lazio hands had been anything other than virgin clean? "Right, Franco, right."

"We got *Redmayne* shooting, *Itatchia* in final stage of prep, *Nostromo* out to directors an' the *Guernica* miniseries now in post. An' I remind you, beside you an' me, we have only two creative execs. I have my hands full with this Pebble Beach thing. Full! We all working like crazy while you, you sunning yourself in Imperio!"

"My room was ransacked last night."

"What they steal. Your return airline ticket?"

Seidelman's head was throbbing and aching. "Franco, we need twelve thousand U.S. down here, immediately."

"Twelve thousand dollar? You got more money down there than the whole Imperio treasury!"

"Franco, raging inflation? Lots of businesses won't deal in the local currency, they want hard currency, and we need cash dollars, pronto."

"So, we wire some down."

The shaking of his head increased the pain. "That takes too long. Can't you just have somebody bring it down personally on a flight?"

"Like who, Don? Who?" The Lazio ire was erupting. "Who I send? Randall, Weitz?" Tonnini barked. "Kay? My secretary? Now you wanna take away my secretary from me? An' a flight? It cost. Who pay? Me or the production?"

"Then use my secretary, Dorothy. I'll pay."

"An' trust her with twelve thousand dollar cash? No way!"

"Goddamn it, Franco!" The Seidelman head was about to explode. Or so it felt. "We're paying for an associate producer on this show. Let her bring it down!"

"Don." The ire was abating, but the edge wasn't. "The *her* as you so impolitely refer to my fiancée, *her* just got back from Imperio. *Her* very tired plus, I need *her* with me, at Pebble Beach, not Santa Mosqueiro. So no, Nessa no come down. You send somebody up."

"Like who? Cooper, Griffith? Golda?"

The voice was quieter, almost mocking. "Don, one of your jobs is not to make problems, but to solve them. The Amazon? It make your brain like . . . like . . . amoeba! Use the overnights! Now, when you come back?"

He sighed, wearily. "As soon as I'm fit to travel."

"An' who decide this?"

"Doctor Mengele."

"Then I hope you no come back as a lampshade. *Ciao.*"

SCENE 52. TAKE 3.

"Nothing, Carlo? *Nothing* at all?" Para was seated in his study on the antique desk chair, purchased at an auction in San Francisco. U.S.A.

Carlo rubbed together his hands. "No, nothing. The Coroner made no mention of any letters."

Para sighed impatiently, staring intently at the mock Adam fireplace, always admired but never fired. He looked at his soon-to-be son-in-law.

"What we say to each other is *strictly* confidential. Understood?"

"You never have to doubt me, Mauricio."

"You ever hurt my Josefina and you'll wish you'd never been born."

"I love Josefina. I'd never do anything to either harm her, hurt her, or, harm her family."

"Then we understand each other." Para studied the hearth. "Carlo, there are many people out there who want my hide, the same ones who would say to my face they are my friends, so, I have to be careful, very careful." He turned to his future son-in-law. "How much they pay you, the movie?"

"Fifty thousand cruzeiros. A week. For a seven day week."

Para stroked his chin. "I'll pay you another two hundred-fifty dollars cash, into your hand." He stared at Carlo. "No deductions, none of that shit, and when you want cruzeiros you change cash dollars on the black market." Para leaned forward. "Now you work for me as well." Para placed two hundred and fifty dollars into the hand of Carlo.

Studying the notes, Carlo asked. "What do you want me to do?"

"Visit Captain Possi. In jail. See if he has any clues as to who had us arrested. He must have some idea."

"When?"

"Tomorrow. I'll have it arranged. Use your press card. And let me know a.s.a.p. what he says."

Standing, Carlo indicated the dollar bills. "Thank you."

"Earn it."

SCENE 53. TAKE 1.

Carlo waited in a small ante-room. Into which was led Possi. Gesturing both men to sit opposite each other, the guard spoke. "All hands on the table, all the time. No touching." He stepped back, to lean on a wall. Lighting a cigarette, he split the end of the used match and proceeded to clean-out his nails.

Possi studied his visitor. "Reporter?"

Carlo spoke in a hushed voice. "I am engaged to the youngest daughter of Mauricio Para. He sent me."

"I'd heard he'd been arrested. So where is he? He's not in here."

"He's out on bail."

A wan smile puckered the corners of Possi's mouth. "Ah, yes. Bail."

"Mauricio asks if he can get you anything?"

Possi grunted. "A good attorney. And maybe a suit of armor."

"What?"

Possi stared at Carlo. "They see me as a bent copper. In prison a bent copper's considered fair game, and by some of the guards, also"

"Fair game?" The lack of comprehension showed.

Possi dragged a forefinger across his adam's apple. "There are inmates in here who I helped *put* in here. Now d'you understand?"

Nodding, Carlo lit two cigarettes, handing one to Possi.

Taking a long drag, Possi spoke softly. "Why are you really here? Not for a quiet smoke and to enjoy the scenery?"

Glancing at the guard, Carlo rested his forearms on the table and leaned forward. "Mauricio wants to know . . ." Carlo checked the guard again, who was preoccupied now with oral-manicuring, chewing-off bits of hard skin around the cuticles and spitting out the residue. "Mauricio asks if you have any idea who did this, having you both arrested?"

Possi pointed to the younger man's breast pocket, indicating a pen. Passing it, Possi gestured for him to open his hand. On the palm, Possi wrote 'Mendoza'.

Carlo looked long and hard at his hand, and then to Possi. "But, but he's a policeman, the chief, your boss?"

"So he's my boss. So what? He's also human."

Carlo found it all so difficult to accept. "But why would he arrest you, his aide?"

Possi was making finger patterns in the dust on the table. "To divert attention."

Carlo frowned. "From what? Or who?"

"Keep your voice down." The doodling stopped. "From himself." Possi glanced up at the guard, using now the matchstick as a toothpick. "His actions alone point to him. *He's* the one involved in this drugs thing, he's the culprit." More dust doodles were made. "He must've got wind that the federal authorities were closing in, he wanted to save his own skin and . . . " Possi looked up. "Here I am."

Carlo nodded, absorbing all he'd been told. "How can you be so sure?"

"You ever been arrested?"

Carlo shook his head.

"You're allowed one phone call. I don't have an attorney, never needed one, but suddenly I needed somebody who could help me, so I called Mendoza. His wife answered, saying he wasn't there, that he was in Alentejo at the Ministry of the Interior." He looked at Carlo, pointedly. "On a Saturday? Like Mauricio Para, I was arrested that same Saturday, by the Treasury Police. And which ministry is that force under the jurisdiction of? The Ministry of the Interior." He sat back. "To me, all more than just coincidence. And you can tell that to Sênhor Para."

"Mendoza? He definitely said that? Mendoza?"

"Yes, Mauricio." Carlo nodded.

Para stood looking at the river, his beloved river, and at the yachts, some bobbing at their moorings, in the breeze their sail ropes pinging against aluminum masts while others, the larger and the more stately, rode the waves serenely.

Carlo remained seated, at the only table occupied in a vast patio area of empty tables. The bars were shuttered, the restaurant closed, even the TV monitors were darkened and blank. The whole Yacht Club was deserted. Except for the docking crew of Chi-Chi, and the teenage boy, sitting on a bench by the kitchen and the two overalled workmen, hosing-out and cleaning the now-empty Olympic-sized swimming pool.

"Mendoza, eh? And Possi, he's certain of this?"

"Yes." Carlo studied Para's back. "Mauricio, may I ask you something?"

Para remained looking riverwards. "Go ahead."

"Did you do it?"

"Do what?" He asked vaguely.

"What they arrested you for."

Para turned, slowly, looking directly at his future relative. "No, and Carlo, d'you think I'd be this upset if I was in any way guilty of what they claim?" The unemotional bovine-like eyes stared at Carlo.

"No, I guess not." He frowned. "Then, how come all this has happened?"

"Carlo, you have to understand, there are people who are jealous of me, jealous of my wealth, my position, my power even?" He crossed to the table, and sat. "I control three newspapers, a TV station, a radio station. I try to oversee personally the day-to-day running of these enterprises, but even I haven't found a way of being in three places at once. I try to maintain total editorial control, but . . ." He raised his hands in exasperation. "It is not always possible." A finger was wagged at Carlo. "What *is* possible is that one of my editors, a sub-editor a leader writer, who knows? But it is more than possible that in one of my many media, one of my staff at some time or another may have said or written something innocuous that nevertheless gave offense to Colonel Mendoza. And human nature being what it is, such slight festers, the passage of time compounding the perceived insult rather than erasing it." He sighed, deeply. "Then, an opportunity arises to right the supposed wrong, and here I am, a pillar of society, now an outcast in my own community." He eyed Carlo. "And why? All because some police colonel has been able to fabricate evidence against me and all because of some bitterness, grievance, completely unfounded"

Lighting two cigarettes, Carlo passed one to Para. "Can't you prove the accusation is false, that you're being framed?"

Para inhaled deeply, exhaling slowly. "No. And why not? Because until the formal charge is made, we don't even know exactly what has been laid before the courts." He regarded his prospective son-in-law. "Carlo, I ought to talk to Colonel Mendoza. It is wrong, wrong for me to prejudge this situation, jump to the wrong conclusion." He shrugged. "For all I know, Possi has some grudge against Mendoza, got passed over for promotion or something suchlike. The bit about Mendoza being in Alentejo could all be a pack of lies."

"You want me to make contact?"

Para gestured the affirmative.

"Your house?"

"No Ask him to come here, to the club. We can go out on the *Isabella*, without fear of eavesdroppers, have a bite of supper, even. See if he can be here at six. Oh, and Carlo, tell him. No uniform, no official car." Para winked. "So as to preserve anonymity."

With the closure of the Yacht Club, of the tall standards with their clusters of halogen lights, none was illuminated. There was just the basic security lighting.

The outer barrier was raised.

A car moved forward slowly, as if surveying, its headlights raking the deserted club area. The vehicle came to rest, the engine silenced, the headlights remaining illuminated.

Hearing a door open, the strong glare of the headlights prevented Para from seeing who was standing beside the car. Everywhere was very still, and very quiet, the hush of tropical twilight broken only by the *putt-putting* of the ageing British and Italian outboard engines powering the many small boats plying between the city and the outlying islands.

Para stood where he could be seen. "Raimundo, is that you? I'm up here, on the *Isabella*."

Before extinguishing the headlights, Mendoza placed in the small of his back a snub-nosed thirty-eight caliber police-issue handgun. He'd decided he'd take no chances and, if he was forced to use the gun, he calculated that circumstance and public opinion would be on his side. Mendoza was dressed in blue deck shoes, cream-colored pants and a navy blue casual shirt. He walked silently through the deserted patio areas, to the pontoon.

Para gave a friendly salute. "I thought we'd go for a little cruise."

Normally eager to enjoy Para's cabin cruiser, Mendoza felt prudence was the better part of valor. "I wish I could, but I have a P.T.A. meeting this evening. I'm on the committee."

"In that case, we'll have a quiet drink here, but aboard the boat."

They sat on deck, drinks in hand. "It's reassuring to see you, Raimundo. These are trying times, very trying."

Mendoza looked around. "Where are all the members?"

"They'll be let back in when I feel like company."

Mendoza eyed his host. "We the only guests?"

"Yes."

"Just us? Only us?"

Chuckling, Para pointed. "Somewhere over there, sitting on a bench, is Chi Chi, plus his dumb-assed kid assistant and Pedro, my chauffeur. Then there's the gateman and in the office, a security guard. Comfortable?" He asked ambiguously. Looking Mendoza directly in the eyes, Para raised his glass. "To old times and to old friends."

"To old times."

Peering over the top of his glass, Para studied the police chief.

"Raimundo, why did I have to be the first to make contact?"

Mendoza was gazing at the river. "The only way I can help you, and it goes without saying that I want to help both you and Possi." He turned to Para. "But the only way I can do that Mauricio is by keeping my nose clean."

Mendoza offered cigarettes, lighting them from the faded Dupont. "Which means attending to things I normally deal with." He lowered his voice. "I'm the best bet you have, but your case is being handled by the Treasury Police, a federal agency, and there is simply no valid reason for me to be seen taking a professional interest in it." He nudged Para. "Any interest on my part might trigger suspicion."

Para frowned. "Suspicion?"

The voice was even quieter. "Mauricio, people don't have to delve too far for evidence of our association." He exhaled through his nostrils. "But I'll find him."

"Who? Who we talking about now?"

Mendoza was surprised his remark needing qualifying. "The whistle blower."

A Para eyebrow was raised. "You got anything?"

"Possibly. I'm working on it." He glanced at Para. "Quietly."

Para's eyes never left Mendoza. "Is that why you went to the capital?"

"The capital? Me?" Mendoza chortled. "Mauricio, I haven't been to Alentejo in, oh, two months or more." He returned Para's gaze. "Where'd you get that idea from?"

"You know, so much is going on at the moment, my head's just spinning." He gestured to Para's glass. "Like it? It's a double malt."

Mendoza nodded, holding-out an empty tumbler. "I thought at one time it was Ramalho."

"Ramalho?"

A full ice-laden tumbler was handed to Mendoza. "You know he's dead? Suicide?"

Para pointed to snacks on the table. "The olives are pitted." He drank from his two-thirds full glass. He glanced at Mendoza. "My attorney says Ramalho left some notes, letters?"

"Where'd he hear that?" Mendoza shook his head. "Nothing came out at the inquest."

"You went?"

"We get an inter-agency transcript. It was handled by the Municipal Police, together with the coroner's office." Mendoza frowned. "But there wasn't any mention of letters."

Para leaned on an elbow. "Maybe somebody hushed it up?"

The policeman grinned. "Ramalho was not an interest of national security." An olive was popped into his mouth. "What do you hear from Possi?"

Para appeared unconcerned. "Raimundo, you know full well I am legally prevented from consorting with him. Collusion?"

Mendoza sighed. "But your future son-in-law? He could see him for you. Like he did yesterday."

"Carlo?" Para sipped his whisky. "My Carlo? But he's working on the movie."

"He was seen at the federal jail, and, he saw Possi." He leaned forward. "He even signed in as 'Carlo Sintra', no pretence."

Para was frowning. "He's a very well-meaning boy."

Mendoza saw the chance of a two-pronged attack. "Mauricio, it's times like this the cockroaches climb out of the woodwork." A finger was pointed. "With him married to your daughter and you out of the way, Carlo, that his name? He'd be very well off, wouldn't he?" Mendoza supped some more. "Or, is he simply doing your carrying and fetching?"

"I told you, he works on the movie."

"Which didn't stop him getting your message to me?"

"I could hardly have come or called in person now, could I?"

The two men exchanged looks. "Petty bickering is not going to help you, is it?"

Para shook his head.

"We have to get the charges dropped, and to do that, we have to find the culprit."

"You make it all sound so simple."

Mendoza was looking at the patio area of the club. "Will the old place ever be the same again?"

"This 'culprit'? I know you, Raimundo. Who's in your sights?"

Swiveling around, he proffered an empty tumbler. "Cooper."

Pouring a generous measure, Para almost dropped the glass, his face grimacing. "*Cooper*?"

Mendoza warmed to his subject. "Cooper has everything to fear from me. With his movie being used to ship cocaine into the U.S.A. that makes him an accessory, and he knows as long as I am around, he can know no peace."

"But Raimundo, *he* didn't blow the whistle?"

"Of course not!" Mendoza remained one tweak above patronizing. "Given the circumstances, the fragility of his position, he knew he could never get anything to stick, with me a senior police officer, but, knock down a couple of that copper's associates and hope somebody, to save their own skin, might squeal."

"Are you suggesting I'm a grass?"

"Mauricio! Don't even think like that!"

Para considered all that had been said to him. "But Cooper? He didn't even know Possi?"

"Mauricio, you must defer here to my professional experience." Some more olives were consumed. "Remember, it was *Possi* who recruited Ramalho to be the censor? And when he fucked up, fogging their film, he knew he was a marked man, that I'd be on his back, so he figures 'if I'm going down, why not take a copper with me?' Such as Possi?"

Para stared at the police chief.

"Ramalho didn't have to write or send a letter to Cooper. He saw him every day, on the movie? So Ramalho tells him who we all are. Cooper sees his golden opportunity, and takes it!" Finishing his drink, Mendoza checked his watch. "I must go. It wouldn't do for a committee member of the P.T.A. to roll up drunk." Mendoza eased himself out of the deck chair. "Mauricio, those old *Perry Mason* shows you screen in the late evening? You'd learn quite a lot from them, such as the least likely person is always the one who did it."

Mendoza was seated in his car.

"By the way, Raimundo." Para placed both hands on the sill. "It takes ten years off you."

Mendoza was puzzled.

"The mustache?"

"Oh, that? It was my wife's idea." Waving a languid hand, he drove away.

Para stood, watching the car until it disappeared. Briskly, he walked to the Mercedes. In the darkness he heard running footfalls. "Not now, Pedro. I'll tell you when." Para waited until he saw his chauffeur rejoin Chi Chi. Only then did he enter the car. Picking up the phone, he dialed directory assistance. "Alentejo. Imperiavia, the airline?"

"Imperiavia, good evening. This is Antonia. How may I help you?"

Para made no attempt to disguise his voice. "Ah, yes, my name is Mendoza, Colonel Raimundo Mendoza, chief officer, Boa Vista State Police."

Respect for authority ousted the tone of familiarity. "Yes, Colonel?"

"I made a trip last week from Santa Mosqueiro to Alentejo, round trip, and as stupid as it may sound, for the life of me I cannot remember if I flew down on Friday or Saturday and I have to have it correct, for my report."

"Mendoza is a very common name. Let me check." Para could hear computer keys being tapped. "I have a Colonel Mendoza travelling Santa Mosqueiro to Alentejo Saturday last, the twenty-second."

"Of course. Saturday! My wife gave me hell, *fejoida* day. I was supposed to have taken her out for lunch."

"Do you need the flight numbers for your report?"

"Antonio, you should've been a detective. Thank you."

"You travelled ex-Santa Mosqueiro zero six thirty-hours, IV 761, returning on IV 768, ex-Alentejo eighteen-hundred."

Para was gracious. "That's a great help, thank you." While he had her on the line, he felt he should check further. "Eh, Antonia. I wonder? It's a case I'm working on so I can't divulge too many details, but would you see if there is any record of travel from Santa Mosqueiro to Alentejo within the last ten days of a Mr. James Cooper?" Para waited while the computer sifted through its memory.

"No, Colonel, I have no record of a passenger named Cooper traveling that route. Sorry."

"Oh, no, you've been most helpful, believe me. *Ciao*."

"Thank you for calling Imperiavia."

Para stabbed the memory dial. "I know who shopped me."

Rubio did not answer immediately. "Who's the canary, and do you have proof?"

"Antonio, before owning newspapers, I was a reporter." Para continued pontificating. "And, as a cub I learned very quickly to check sources, verify my information." He lit up, inhaled, exhaling loudly. "You want a catalog, or my word?"

"I'll take your word."

"Mendoza."

"Then we have a problem?"

Para was silent, thinking, hard.

"Mauricio, you there?"

"I'm thinking. You're in a better position to deal with this than I am?"

"Mauricio, don't contact me for a while, *I'll* contact you. And if there's a lull, don't worry. We won't be idle. *Ciao*."

The line went dead. Replacing the phone, Para shouted. "Pedro!"

Rubio put down the small cell-phone, watched by Cirla. "I heard you say 'problem.' The movie?"

"No, not this time. Something else has cropped up." Rubio tapped on the table a staccato rhythm, a distant look in his eye. Then he stood erect. "Roberto, find Topete. We need him in Santa Mosqueiro, tomorrow."

"He'll need a passport."

"All the more reason to find him quickly, photograph him and doctor-up a passport?"

"What name?"

Rubio put on his thinking cap. "Eh . . . yes. Topete Jensen. Colombian mother, American father."

"Cool!" Cirla departed, rapidly.

Topete was thinking. *Even in the evening, in this heat? How the hell does anyone jog in a track suit?* From the shadows he watched his quarry, as the man left his house and began the regular exercise. The Colombian checked his watch. Twenty-one hundred hours, on the dot. His eyes followed the jogger down the street until the corner was turned. Topete re-checked the time, knowing that within thirty minutes exactly, Colonel Raimundo Mendoza would return. He decided on a smoke while he checked the Luger, screwed-on the silencer and put it in his courier's sack. And checked his bicycle, marked '*Messageros Mosqueiro.*'

Before seeing him, he heard him, the rhythmic pounding on the sidewalk combining with the regular but now heavy, breathing, the policeman pacing himself to a methodical beat.

In the shadows of twilight, Topete watched him constantly. The Luger was in the sack slung across from his left shoulder, resting on his right hip. He donned his safety helmet.

Mendoza entered his front yard, the gate closing slowly, until it clicked shut.

Pedaling up the deserted street, the only noises audible were the grunts of the policeman, as exercises were being undertaken. His left leg resting on a small wall, Mendoza was stretching both arms forwards along the limb, trying to touch his toes.

Topete parked the bike, facing it back to the city. And checked once more the still-deserted street, putting into his left hand an official-looking envelope, his right into the sack, where it grasped the Luger. He walked purposefully to the house, as if expecting the gate to be unlocked. He rattled it. Loudly.

Hands clasped behind his head while doing upper body exercises, Mendoza looked round. "Yes?"

Through the safety helmet, Topete's reply was both distorted and muted, aiding his not-so-perfect Portuguese. "Personal delivery."

"What?" Shaking his head, Mendoza walked to the gate. "What did you say?"

"Personal delivery."

"At this hour?"

"They said it couldn't wait."

Sighing, Mendoza extended a hand. "Okay, give it to me."

Topete did, raising the sack and firing twice, both shots into the chest. Mendoza did not cry out. He spun around and knocked back by the force, he collapsed. Topete fired into him once more, where he lay. Adjusting the sack, he walked casually to his bike and rode away silently, a courier returning late to the dispatch office.

Topete checked. The car was in its reserved space, the chauffeur snoring.

Joining the throngs heading for the *Late, Late Show*, Topete patted his pocket, reassured at feeling the gloves.

He entered the lobby, recallling Rubio's instruction. *'When in any unfamiliar place where guards or security personnel can be encountered, be definite, never hesitate, always walk with a purpose, as if you know exactly where you are going, even if you don't. Never hesitate, be definite, unswerving. Falter, hesitate in any way and they'll know immediately you are a stranger, a possible risk, a threat.'*

Topete took an elevator to the second floor.

To ensure they were empty, he checked silently and thoroughly all of the other offices.

And then he was outside *the* door. He put on the gloves, aided speedily by the talcum powder he'd put inside them. Pressing down on the handle, the door was opened . . . slowly. Rubio was correct. The several monitors were all playing, both picture and sound, enough to stifle any strange sounds. The door, Topete closed. And locked.

A whisky tumbler in one hand, Para was leaning on the desk, half turned to his left to a monitor, watching the opening titles roll of the *Late, Late Show*. Enthralled by his own program, the TV-SM answer to Carson, Hall and Letterman, Para neither saw nor was able to hear the Colombian as Topete put together noiselessly the gun and silencer. He came up behind Para. Placing the gun within one millimeter of the right temple, he fired.

The immediate blaring of the TV startled Topete, as spasm-like Para's hand had jerked out, hitting the volume of the remote control and scattering objects everywhere. The tumbler fell and shattered, diluting with the blood that was all over the desk and the other furniture.

Regaining his composure, Topete thought the job had been almost too easy. From door to death. Fifteen seconds. Nudging Para, the large man slid off the chair and crumpled to the floor. Into Para's right hand Topete placed the gun, ensuring that initially it was gripped tightly.

SCENE 55. TAKE 2.

Of the twelve overnight faxes, there was one in particular that Conde read, and re-read. *'Sênhor Jorge Conde, Department of Justice, Alentejo. This is to advise that Colonel Raimundo Mendoza, Chief Officer, State Police of Boa Vista, was found last night shot to death in the grounds of his house in the Santa Mosqueiro suburb of Vila Nova. Shortly thereafter was discovered another body, that of one citizen, Para, M. Ballistics match both killings. Preliminary investigation indicates Para killing Mendoza and then taking his own life. A weapon was found beside the body of citizen Para. As both crimes occurred within city limits the investigation is being conducted by the Municipal Police under my command. I will keep you informed of all and any developments. J. Montforte, Superintendent. Dated April 19.'*

"Look at this." Conde passed over the fax. Reading it, Vinci frowned, glanced at Conde, and then read it again. Slowly he put down the fax, staring at it. "Does this wrap it up?"

"I'd like to think so, but . . ." He raised his hands in frustration. "Had you spoken to Mendoza recently?"

Vinci nodded. "He called to thank me for the speedy way the arrests had been handled."

"That all?" Repeatedly, Conde pressed the retractable top of a pen. "In the light of what's happened, he say anything else of relevance?"

Vinci shrugged. "You remember the letter sent by the deceased nephew to Judge Mello?"

"Sure."

"On no account did Mendoza want that letter disclosed at the inquest, or any other letters, for that matter. He said they would compromise his ongoing investigations."

"Compromise?" Conde chuckled. "More like bury him deeper."

"You really think he was a part of it?"

Conde sighed. "He always made me feel uncomfortable. He was just too pat by far, like a politician on TV. He'd always have an answer ready before he'd even heard the question."

Vinci smiled. "Oh, and he was even more interested in the letter sent to the foreigner."

"Who's the foreigner again?"

"Cooper. One James Cooper."

"Nationality?"

"Not sure. American or British. One or the other."

Looking again at the fax, Conde read it for the umpteenth time. He tapped the paper. "Someone like Para? It's way out of character for a man like him, a successful thriving businessman, a self-made millionaire. Killing a policeman and then kills himself?" Conde paced. "It simply doesn't fit the profile." Returning to his desk, he sat. "Besides, men like Para don't kill. They have people to do it for them." He looked up at Vinci. "Then there's all this drugs stuff from the guy Ramalho. Could he be believed?" He thumped the desk, startling Vinci. "Could *any* of them be believed?" He groaned with frustration. And was lost in reverie. When a thought struck . "Oh . . . "

Vinci was disconcerted. "What?"

Such was his excitement, Conde could just about speak. "Caito, the whole thing has its roots in drugs We have a bilateral agreement which we should honor!" He flicked the intercom. "Sonia! I wish to speak urgently with a Mr. Richard Barton. He's with the U.S. Drug Enforcement Administration in Washington D.C. The number's in the Rolodex."

Scene 56. Take 6.

Being lined-up was the final shot on the Santa Mosqueiro location. Cooper had arranged for some bottles of champagne and much more beer, to be brought to the location for a post-filming day's last drink. *Kristal* and *Beck's*. Drunk out of styrofoam cups.

The director stood beside the camera. D.P. Billy Richards was setting reflectors with one eye, looking through the eyepiece with the other. He gestured to Cooper. "Final check?"

As Cooper examined in camera the framing, Williams spoke quietly into his ear. "We're just getting out in time. You've heard the latest?"

Cooper flipped the eyepiece filter. "Joel Silver's come in on budget?"

"*Two* murders last night, here in Santa Mosqueiro."

"That's *news*?"

"When it's a copper and the local Citizen Kane, yes." Richards looked at his director. "The word is the copper was in bed with some druggies, he got greedy and got his come uppance, instead."

"Are the rights available?"

"James!" Shaking his head, Richards checked the sky with his pan glass, speaking quietly as he did so. "We could be in the middle of a drugs war, Pedro Escobar and his mates?" Dangling the pan glass around his neck, he turned to Cooper. "And they don't exactly have the nicest of table manners."

Cooper frowned. "What's Charles Foster Kane got to do with Pedro Escobar?"

"It was a senior police officer who was killed, and, the local press czar." Richards raised his eyebrows. "I wonder if he wrote his own entry for the obituary column?" Richards looked. "Czar? Funny, it rhymes with his surname."

"Which was?"

"Eh, the czar? Para."

His legs felt like jelly. Cooper had to sit. And, he thought, it had to be. Mendoza and Para. Which means who? Who is next?

"You alright, old chap? You look a bit peeky around the gills?"

Before Cooper could answer, Langley was shouting. "Billy, we ready to shoot?"

"It's all yours."

"Standby." Actors and crew were poised. "And . . . roll it!"

As Cooper rose out of his chair, he glanced at his D.P. "Like you said, Billy. We're just getting out in time." Cooper turned to the scene. "Action!"

Cooper was satisfied. "That's a print." He signalled Elaine Buck. "Print takes two and three."

"Check the gate!"

"Okay gate."

"That's a wrap." Declared first A.D., David Langley. "Folks, we have a few farewell drinks arranged, thanks to . . ." He gestured to Cooper. "Our director, James Cooper."

Cast and crew applauded and although Cooper wanted out a.s.a.p., he knew he had to have at least one drink with his colleagues who had worked so hard for him, and so hard with him. Raising a glass of beer, he looked all around the beaming faces. "*Salut!*" All joined in the celebration.

He felt a presence beside him. It was Golda. "Well, Orson, keep up the three-plus minutes a day and in three weeks we can all be out of Imperio, for ever!" She kissed him lightly. "Well done." And looked at him, frowning. "Are you packed?"

"No Golda, I'm whacked."

The Boeing Seven Thirty Seven taxied to its stand. The engines whined down.

In the cockpit, Captain Huerta turned to the First Officer, Pepe Babenco. "Was that it, *you* buy the champagne?"

"That *was* it," came the laughing reply. "My first solo landing in a Seven Three."

The Senior Cabin Attendant stood in the doorway. "Captain, how long are we here in Santa Mosqueiro?"

"Our take off slot is booked in three hours' time. If loaded, then earlier."

"Enough time to go into town?"

"Fraid not, Alicia." Releasing his harness, he turned to face her. "My, we do look smart in our new regulation blouse and skirt. But take them off."

"What!"

He eyed her directly. "You ever flown a charter planeload of movie technicians before?"

"No."

"Without exception, they are the horniest, randiest people under the sun, and this lot? They've been here for a *very* long, long time."

Alicia was confused. "May I borrow your pants then?"

To be followed by both cockpit crew's laughter. "Alicia," said the captain. "I'm *not* going fly this thing wearing a skirt." He stood, and stretched. "Your overnight bag? You have jeans, pants?"

She nodded.

"The other two girls?"

"Probably the same."

Huerta nodded. "Then tell them to wear pants, jeans, whatever, but no skirts, regulation or not, otherwise you'll all be groped from here to Borges."

Alicia flicked a smile. "Do we get danger money for this?"

Huerta shook his head. "All in the line of duty. And I know it's against both *IATA* and company rules, but dispense with the safety demo unless, as you raise your arms to put on the life vest, you want many groping hands on your breasts."

"Maybe I should have stayed with that job in the bank?"

He smiled. "Just have the passengers read the safety card. Twice. And tell the other girls. Especially about the skirts."

As the movie crew personnel streamed across the tarmac, Babenco watched them. "I was involved in a movie once." He nodded to Captain Heurta. "In a sort of minor role." He continued to view the movie people. "I flew this producer guy all over the Amazon, Imperio *and* Brasil." He addressed Huerta. "We even went up into Guyana one time. He took one look and said, '*Nada.*'" Babenco laughed at the memory. "But I flew him all over Amazonia."

Captain Huerta spoke while writing-up his log. "So that's how you made such a perfect landing." He nodded to Babenco. "You know every crack, ripple, and rut in this runway?"

The F.O. laughed. "I'm not so sure about that but what I am certain of is I'd be a rich man now if I had a cruzeiro for every time I'd landed here."

Huerta gestured to the controls. "But Seven Threes are more of a challenge than a Cessna, or a Piper?"

"I dunno." Babenco shrugged. "Those small planes? They're a lot of fun to fly." He looked again at the motley crew, half-wondering if he would see a familiar face. *What was the guy's name? Cooper? That's it, Cooper. Not a bad gringo for a Malvinas-stealing Brit.* He pondered. *But that was a while back and the Brit must've finished his movie by now?* Looking out of the cockpit to the apron, he figured this was a different lot, a different movie. *But.* He thought. *There's a lot of gringos, an awful lot of them.*

"Pepe, go back there and check the loading. Not the passengers, but that equipment being stowed in the blanked off section of the cabin. Then check the trim and maybe bring us back a couple of coffees?"

"Sure thing, Captain."

From Alentejo, he flew up to Santa Mosqueiro.

In the Federal Building, Conde was in a small conference room, which with the benefit of its twelfth-floor elevation had a panoramic view of the city. He was fascinated by the vastness of the big river, feeling almost humbled by it. His day-dreaming was invaded by the opening of a door.

"Hi, I'm Barton." Craggy-faced, he was just fifty years old, ten years older than Conde, but with the appearance of a considerably younger man. Six-feet-two inches in height, he was dressed in a tan gabardine two-piece suit, blue shirt, yellow woollen tie. He carried an overnight bag.

The two men exchanged greetings.

"Mr. Barton."

"Dick. I'm known as Dick by my friends."

"And I'm Jorge. And also, I am nervous. I have not conversed in English for many, many years."

Barton smiled. "You're doing real good so far, but Jorge, if you get stuck, don't expect a helping word of Portuguese from me."

They laughed.

"What's occurred since we last spoke?"

Conde leaned against the window frame. "Well, although the police investigation is inconclusive, they see a chance to close the file, get a case off their books."

"Because it ties up nice and neat?"

Conde nodded. "But for me? The evidence? It all too good to be true."

Looking out, Barton stood beside Conde. "I'm glad you said that." He turned. "Because like you Jorge, I think it's as phony as a nine dollar bill." He held up the digits of one hand, counting off with the other. "Five, five people were a part of the Ramalho drugs conundrum, and now three of them, *three*, are dead. Which leaves us Possi and this Cooper guy, yes?" Conde nodded. "You have jurisdiction here over the municipal police?"

"The Federal Justice Department has jurisdiction over *all* law enforcement agencies in the country, both civil and military."

Barton digested this. "How long can you hold this Possi, now there's no Mendoza evidence against him?"

"Officially? Not long." Conde pulled a face. "It all depends on how bright the police federation lawyer is." He tilted his head. "But unofficially . . . ?"

Barton grinned. "You think he's heard about the death of Mendoza?"

"For sure."

Barton wiped a hand across the back of his neck. "That's a pain."

"Dick, there no way Possi not know. The whole country knows."

"I was hoping we could pressure him into turning state's evidence, y'know, by using the threat of Mendoza?" He shrugged at Conde. "I guess that's out the window?"

Conde's look was enigmatic. "Possi does not know what has or has not come to light in the investigation." He opened his briefcase, holding aloft a letter. "Like this. A statement about Possi, signed by . . ." He handed the paper to the American. "Colonel R. Mendoza."

Barton read it intensely. "Imperiavia?" He looked at Conde. "Isn't that an airline?"

"Mendoza's code name."

"Maybe I should be known as Pan American?"

Laughing, Conde held high the Imperiavia schedule. "The report is all in code. But it is a telling indictment of Possi."

Such had been the force of the blow that the skin had been broken—split more likely—on the bone below the eye, and the eye itself was bloodied, the immediate area around it being bruised, puffed up and extremely discolored.

Possi inhaled long and deep, looking appreciatively at the cigarette. "*Americano?*"

Eyeing Possi, Barton spoke. "He speak English?"

"*Fala Inglês?*"

Possi shook his head.

Barton was looking at the brutal swelling around the eye. "Who hit him? Rocky Balboa?"

Conde translated, while Possi studied Barton. "He say he walk into something."

"Like what? A railroad locomotive?" Watched by Possi, Barton pointed to the eye. "Must be tough in here, being a cop?" He handed to Possi the pack of cigarettes, and spoke, exaggeratedly. "Ra-Mal-Yo? *Si?*"

"*Ramalho?*" Shaking his head, Possi showed no recognition. "*No.*"

Sighing, Barton stood. "Jorge, we're wasting our time here." Conde gave the American a look of uncertainty. "Leave him to the inmates."

"What's he saying?" asked Possi.

"He's saying, Possi, you're a waste of time."

Possi was truculent. "He, you, both of you, you have nothing on me."

Conde smiled. "I know, like everyone else in this jail, you're innocent, right?"

"Yes. Innocent."

"I'll tell the gringo that." As the dialogue was relayed to Barton, Possi watched.

Barton returned the gaze. "Jorge, repeat to him what I say as we go along." Sitting, Barton leaned forward, elbows on thighs. "We have two letters." By way of emphasis, he held aloft a couple of fingers. "*Two!* And, both state, unequivocally, that you are part of a drugs smuggling operation, a conspirator, a trafficker, who knowingly, *knowingly*, passed illegal drugs into the United States." As were translated the words, Barton studied the prisoner.

Possi sneered a reply. Barton looked at Conde, inquiringly. "He say, the . . . ramblings, yes, the ramblings of a drug-crazed dropout while of unsound mind."

"Jorge, you did good." Barton patted Conde. And turned to Possi. "Well, I see we've got our memory back, suddenly we remember Ramalho, and, of course, we remember Colonel Mendoza?"

Possi mumbled."Jorge, you catch that?"

"He say Mendoza is dead."

Barton retained his dead pan look at Possi. "He ever wonder who did it?"

The question was put to Possi, who directed his answer at Barton.

"He says what he have to do to get out of here?"

Barton continued his study of Possi. "Does he have any idea of who I am?" He glanced at Possi. "I mean, who I'm with?"

Possi replied to Conde's question. "F.B.I."

Staring directly at Possi, Barton shook his head, slowly. "C . . . I . . . A."

Hearing the spoken acronym, Possi became visibly more erect.

"Jorge, remind Captain Possi the agency has a very long memory and an even longer reach." A stick of gum was put into the Barton mouth.

"He understand. He says, what does he have to do?"

Barton leaned back. "The truth. Tell him, it's that simple. And Jorge, does he know *your* credentials?"

"Give me a minute." While Conde addressed Possi, the latter did not take his eyes off Barton. "He know who I am now and he know I the only one who can have him released."

"Good." Barton was smiling, eyeing Possi. "We have an understanding here." Barton folded his arms. "The allegations made by Ramalho. Are they true?"

Possi listened intently while Conde put the question. "He says half true." Conde gave a running translation. "Yes, it was him who recruited Ramalho, but not his idea."

Barton grunted. "Presumably Mendoza's idea?"

"No, not his. James Cooper's."

The facial expressions were unchanged, all round. "There a movie—"

"Tell him we know all about the movie! We're interested in what he knows about this James Cooper?"

"He . . . the movie producer."

Barton stared at the Police Captain. "Jorge, he's playing us for a couple of suckers. If we've not gotten anything within five minutes, we send in the posse to Possi." Barton stood. "Try this one on him. He says the recruiting of Ramalho was Cooper's idea. What I'd like to know is, how'd the idea come about, how does a complete stranger come up with such a plan, and how come two senior police officers decide to along with it?" He raised his arms. "It makes no sense?"

Conde let Possi finish speaking, translating then. "Strategy. Mendoza had arrested Cooper once before."

Frowning, Barton looked quickly at Conde, who was translating more. "Mendoza figured the gringo Brit was in it knee deep, and that he could lead us to more ring members if we appeared to be playing along. His plan was to dupe Cooper, let him think the Colonel was with him and then wham! The Colonel takes them down, all of them."

Barton was shaking his head. "Y'know, you and I could be having a nice cold beer somewhere? Try this one on him. Was the whole Mendoza ploy simply for the entrapment of Cooper?"

A beat. And the policeman nodded, vigorously.

"I still don't get it." Barton was exasperated. "Okay. So, who killed Mendoza?"

"He says Cooper."

Barton scratched his head, exhaling. "What little I know about movie making is it's a highly paid job, requiring something like fourteen hours a day work, twenty-four seven. So why would a foreign movie person get involved in all this shit? Like I just said, it simply doesn't make sense?"

Possi was speaking rapid Portuguese.

"He says, Cooper find out Mendoza straight not crooked, and that he was about to close in."

As if clearing it, Barton shook his head. "Is this guy related to Hans Christian Andersen?" Barton resumed. "Then did Cooper kill them both or does he think somebody else killed Para?"

That this was news to Possi was very apparent.

"Jorge, I think we've surprised him."

Conde picked up his file, passing to Possi a copy of the fax from the Santa Mosqueiro Municipal Police. And as had Conde and Vinci before him, he read and re-read the note. He paled. A shaking hand returned the fax.

Barton stood, directly in front of the policeman, underscoring his words with a pointed finger. "They, he, whoever, they're all getting closer, Possi." He leaned forward, wagging finger and all. "Seems anybody who knows anything about them is a threat?" He straightened, as Conde finished translating. "You're better off in here, safer in jail. A black eye is preferable to a bullet, eh?"

While Conde spoke to Possi, Barton gathered together his things. "Jorge, we're flogging a dead horse here. What's the name of the guy at the British Consulate?"

"He'll be a great loss . . ."

Barton looked at Pitt-Miller. "He will?"

The Englishman shook his head. "The old place won't seem the same without him." He looked from Barton, to Conde. "He was poetry in motion, pure . . . poetry."

Barton narrowed his eyes. "You've lost me. We talking about the same person here?"

"Of course", said Pitt-Miller haughtily. "Colonel Mendoza."

"Oh." Barton smiled, humbly. "It's just that I'm not used to hearing such ornate phrases as 'poetry in motion' used to describe a flatfoot."

"Mr. Barton, I was referring to the Colonel's prowess in a chukker."

Barton frowned. "A chukker?"

Conde came to the rescue. "Colonel Mendoza was a polo player."

"D'you play, Mr. Barton?"

"Only as a teenager. In my High School swimming pool."

Pitt-Miller pondered. *How'd you get polo horses and players into a swimming pool?* "Well, the colonel was a player *par excellence*. When the 'Save the Trees' conference was down here a couple of years back, the colonel gave H.R.H. a run for his money, oh yes, indeed. A right royal roasting, you could say."

Studying the Englishman, Barton wondered. If Putz-Miller was representative of the sons of Brittania, how did the country ever make it, reckoning further that America must have been colonized by all those Brits fleeing to escape Putz-Miller's ancestors.

"As I said, the old place just won't be the same."

"The old place?"

Pitt-Miller reacted as if addressing a child. "The club, my dear chap, the Polo Club."

Barton turned to Conde. "You keeping up with this?"

Conde chuckled, whispering. "Doing my best. By thinking about that cold beer."

Pitt-Miller memories evoked a smile. "The Colonel was a *very* popular member of the club, I can tell you."

"What can you tell me about your countryman, James Cooper?"

"Cooper?" He looked at the two men. "Not much. I only met him the once. Struck me as a little too flippant, too glib, for his own good."

"Glib?"

"Came up with some cock and bull story about he was down here to make a film, he'd been doing a location recce over the jungle, where he crash landed, and was knocked unconscious." He shook his head. "I think he was confusing it with an episode from *The Twilight Zone*." Pitt-Miller looked at the two men, his gaze resting on Barton. "Why? What's he been up to?"

"Making his movie. Here, in Santa Mosqueiro."

Pitt-Miller was incredulous. "Well I never. Nobody mentioned anything, either at the Polo Club, the Cricket Club or the Yacht Club."

"That the yacht club owned by the late Mauricio Para?"

"Good God, No!" Pitt-Miller was offended. "That posturing field of the *nouveaux riches*?"

Barton was impatient to get back on course. "What was the occasion when you first met Cooper?"

Pitt-Miller thought for a moment. Then looked at the two men. "I presume you both know Cooper was arrested by the State Police?"

Both Barton and Conde nodded. "That was the occasion. In deference to Cooper's nationality, Colonel Mendoza called me. He could have thrown the book at Cooper, but he let him off with a warning." He glanced at Barton. "I hope he heeded it?"

Barton cleared his throat. "D'you have any thoughts as to who might have killed Mendoza? Off the record?"

Pitt-Miller eyed them suspiciously. "I didn't realize I was *on* the record?"

"It's a figure of speech. So we're figuratively speaking here. So to speak." Said a smiling Barton.

Pitt-Miller gave the question some thought. "As far as I'm aware, he was popular." He looked at the couple. "Certainly at the club."

"But a policeman makes enemies?"

"Occupational hazard, dear chap. Goes with the job." Placing a peppermint in his mouth, Pitt-Miller shrugged. "Well, obviously not the Para man, otherwise you wouldn't be canvassing my opinion?" He crunched on the candy. "Why not ask Cooper who killed Mendoza?"

"I intend to."

"*Hola!* Anyone one at home?" Looking around the deserted reception area, Barton glanced at Conde. "What sort of a movie company is this?"

"Maybe they at lunch?"

"They are on location."

They both turned. "On. Location?" asked Barton.

"Yes," said the athletic young man in his late twenties. "Up river."

"Where?"

"Who's asking?"

Conde showed his I.D. "Department of Justice. Who are you?"

"Sintra. Carlo Sintra."

Barton gestured. "You work here?"

"Yes."

"How long they away for?"

"About three weeks."

Barton was looking at the paper-laden clipboards hanging on the wall. "And then what?"

Carlo shrugged. "They finish."

Barton flipped some call sheets. "You know James Cooper?"

"Sure."

Barton turned to face Sintra. "And where's he now?"

"I told you."

"No you did not!" Interrupted Conde. "You just say '*up river*'. Where, where up river?"

"Borges. Then they go to San Gabriel."

"Cooper comes back here, then?"

Carlo nodded. "I guess."

"And then where to? London?"

Carlo shook his head. "No. Los Angeles."

Barton was surprised. "Vacation?"

"No. What they call post-production. Where they put together the movie, you know, editing, sound, music, all that stuff."

"So he'll be working there?"

"Yes. Working."

"Art? Dick, Barton. I'm down in Imperio on a case. Your secretary has my numbers. But Art, d'you still have your contact in the I.N.S.? I've a suspected drugs trafficker, name of Cooper, James Cooper. He's a Brit, currently working here on a movie for Tonnini International Pictures and he's shortly coming to the U.S. to finish the picture, which means somewhere there's an H.1. visa application in the works, and as Tonnini International is based in L.A., they must be the sponsors, so start there. Inform the I.N.S. that we, the D.E.A., we want the H.1. denied on the grounds of suspected drugs dealing and or trafficking. His presence in the United States would be undesirable. Get on to it pronto and let me know as soon as you have something. Have a good one." Slamming down the phone, Barton's excitement was apparent. "Jorge, whenever I'm on a case I try to keep an open mind and not jump to conclusions, but God dammit, the way Cooper's name constantly comes up, I think we have our man!"

Conde smiled. "I think you right. But we cannot wait *here* for him to finish his movie?"

Barton nodded. "I've no intention of sitting around this hotel. We go get 'im."

"Borges?"

"No, no, the other place."

"San Gabriel?"

"Yes." Barton was nodding. "We wait there, and make ourselves into the local welcoming committee." Taking two beers from the minibar, he handed one to Conde. "To San Gabriel."

Frowning, Tonnini stared at him, hard. "There . . . there something different." The Italian studied Seidelman, up-and-down. "The suit, it look like it come from Mother Teresa's tailor?"

"I lost eleven pounds."

"*That* suit you. The suit does not."

"It wasn't planned. The gastritis did it."

"Then maybe you use this gastritis more often? It work for you."

"I'll bear that in mind," said a quietly fuming Seidelman.

"You catch up on everything?"

Seidelman nodded. "Yeah, I think so."

"So you know we get a *Redmayne* sale?"

Seidelman was energized. "What!"

Tonnini was beaming. "American International Cinema. They take *Redmayne* on a negative pick up."

Seidelman rubbed together his hands, feverishly. "Great! And I trust we're talking dollars U.S. here, not cruzeiros Imperian?"

Tonnini grinned. "Shhh . . . they may hear you!"

"When's delivery?"

Tonnini eased into his chair. "As soon as. It all being worked out now, but what they do know is they want no more than one a hundred minutes screen time, tops."

Seidelman whistled. "*Oi yoi yoi.*"

"For why the Wailing Wall? It a condition of the sale."

Seidelman cocked his head, accompanied by a hand gesture. "Cooper's always maintained the script was way too long, over length." He looked at the Italian. "He reckons the first assembly will come in around two-thirty, two forty-five."

Tonnini flicked the intercom. "Kay, bring me a glass of seltzer, quick." He looked at Seidelman, dumbfounded. "If, in fine cut, *if* Cooper manage to chop three minutes off each reel, that still only about thirty-six minutes?" He threw up his hands. The conversation was interrupted by Kay arriving with the seltzer. As she left, Tonnini had downed it in one swallow. "That calm me. An' my stomach."

"I know *that* feeling."

"But we now back at roughly two hours? Plus, titles, an' end roller?" Reclining in his chair, he was left with his thoughts. Which prompted him to swivel his chair. "When he start?"

"Who?"

"The editor. Lincoln?"

"Cooper's expecting *his* man Corcoran to be with him in L.A., so what do we do about that?"

"Simple. We have Corcoran supervise the shipping of all the material, all of it, from Imperio and then we fire him."

Seidelman shook his head. "The reason?"

"I no have to have a reason! Now, Lincoln. For the second time. When he start?"

"Two or three weeks, whenever they complete principal. He comes on a week before Cooper gets here, to sort out and set up the editing rooms, receive the material from Imperio, select crews, all that stuff."

Tonnini spoke quietly. "Bring him on now."

Seidelman stared at his boss. "Franco, what's he going to cut? There's nothing here yet, the cutting copy's still in Imperio."

Tonnini pounded his desk in rapid succession. "Don't say John Lincoln have nothing to cut!" He pointed at his Executive Vice-President Business Affairs. "If I want an answer Iike that, I ask the panhandler who squeegee my windshield!"

Seidelman's expression reflected his hurt. "Franco, don't be like that. It's unnecessary."

The pounding resumed. "Why, tell me, why? Why I have dogs but always have to bark myself, eh?" The next three words were underscored by in-sync pounding of his desk. "Why I bother?!" Tonnini looked at Seidelman intensely, his voice dropping to a monotone. "Don, the negative? It *here*, in Los Angeles, at the lab, right?"

Seidelman nodded. "Right. So what?"

Tonnini sighed intensely. "So what? So we, you, *you*. Call Corcoran, Cooper's editor in Santa Mosqueiro, an' tell him to fax us a *complete* list of all printed takes."

"Franco, hold it right there. We already have that list."

"We do?"

"Of course. That info's on the continuity sheets, which we have right here."

"Who, who have them?"

Seidelman indicated the outer office. "Kay. They'll be in the *Redmayne* file together with all of the production reports, call sheets, camera sheets, e.f.c.s, etcetera, etcetera."

Tonnini mused on this news. "So, who here can do the list? It tedious work, no?"

"How about that interns?"

Tonnini was surprised. "We have some?"

"Two."

"Is fine." He flicked the intercom switch. "Kay, the two interns. Put them to work. I want found all, *all* of the printed takes on *Redmayne* an' then these kids list them and type them up. *Grazie.*" His attention was directed at Seidelman. "An' you, you call this Corcoran. What we want from him is a list of *which* takes went into the cutting copy an' he fax it up to me, *personally, capis?*"

"*Si, Franco, me capis.*" He checked his watch. "It's around six P.M in Santa Mosqueiro." He addressed Tonnini. "I'll call him tomorrow."

"Now!"

Rising, Seidelman sidled to the door, saying to himself more than to Tonnini. "Running all the way."

"I not finish yet. Come back!" Seidelman retraced his steps, to stand in front of Tonnini's desk, thinking to himself the accused stands before the judge. "Once we have the cutting copy list, then you tell Lincoln to order up reprints, an' within a few days we have material, material Lincoln can start cutting, from info on the continuity reports?"

"Brilliant."

Tonnini compared one hand with the other. He looked over his plinth-mounted desk. "An' Lincoln, he have a fresh eye, his eye an' mind no polluted by the mania of a director, wanting this shot here, that close up there, this reaction shot here an' hold on that look for twelve seconds, when five will do."

Not wishing to ignite another outburst, Seidelman tried to sound as matter-of-fact as possible. "Cooper has director's cut in his contract." He failed.

"So let him sue me! My negative pick up is more important to me than his director's cut! He calmed down. "An' when we go video on *Redmayne* . . . "

Seidelman appeared shocked.

Tonnini was reassuring. "It alright Don, *we* keep the video rights, only theatrical included in the pick up an' then not *all* territories. But," a smile creased his cheeks. "When we go video, we do like Orion do with *Dances With Wolves*. We produce a Director's Special Edition, the *full* version." The Italian started laughing. "An' this, this will be Cooper's contractual director's cut, subject to *our* final cut to which he have no contractual right, an' this become the pick up version, at a one hundred minutes." He held his arms open wide. "We get the best of all world's an' Cooper get his contractual cut. All legal?"

Seidelman shook his head. "Machiavelli could *only* have been Italian." His chuckling abated. "Corcoran. What if he smells a rat, figures something is wrong?"

"Fuck *him!*" Tonnini waved a dismissive arm. "Tell him we have to strike a low contrast print for a possible TV sale. Now, send the fax, and get Lincoln started!"

"By the way, how'd Pebble Beach go?"

Tonnini clapped. "*Fan . . . tastico!*" He eyed Seidelman. "Why you no come?"

Seidelman summoned his most venomous look.

"Oh, I forget. You sambering in Santa Mosqueiro."

Rubio heard the familiar drone of air-cooled piston engines. A DC-3 was making its final approach, to load up with yet another consignment of cocaine. For Florida. Breaking out of the clouds, the plane made a long, lowering descent, touched down and taxied off the strip to the ramp loading area.

In the office-cum-control room, Rubio gestured to the recently-arrived aircraft. "Who's that?"

"Cobb, one of the Australians. He radioed in, saying some of the runway lights flicker, like they're about to blow."

Rubio smiled. "Was he drunk?"

"How can you tell? He's Australian?"

"Roberto, did you know Australians are the most mentally well-balanced people in the whole world?"

"No." Squinting, he stared at Rubio. "How come?"

"Because they have a chip on *both* shoulders." Both men laughed.

Cirla studied his boss. "Antonio, we've known each other a long time, and I know that look. What's bothering you?"

"Loose ends."

Cirla frowned. "Loose ends? I thought that's what we sent Topete to Santa Mosqueiro for? To tie up loose ends. So what did he miss?"

"He didn't. He did what he was ordered to do, and, he did it well. No complaints. It's my screw up." Rubio walked to the window, observing the loading of the DC-3, and the beautiful tropical cloud patterns, of which he never tired. He turned to Cirla. "We still have that pretty little thing down there?"

It was half way to her mouth, the lipstick, when the door bell chimed. She hesitated, looking in the mirror at her reflection.

She unlatched the deadbolt, but not the chain, allowing the door to open but a little. "Yes?"

A woman's voice replied. "Sênhora Possi? A delivery."

Removing the chain, Regina Possi opened the door to its full width, revealing a very pretty young dark-haired lady with laughing eyes. Pinned to her uniform was a badge, inscribed *Angela*. She smiled. And held aloft a gaily-wrapped box, the red-hued cellophane wrapping of which was tied with a huge red bow. "It is a gift. For Sênhor Possi. Is he home?"

Regina Possi looked at the present. She was unable to think of anyone with such consideration for her husband. "Who's it from?"

Laughing, Angela shook her head. "I don't know. I am with *Carnival Confections*. Somebody came in and said they wanted the best cake available and paid for it, cash. They said it was to cheer up Sênhor Possi." She looked past Sênhora Possi. "Is he ill?"

"Eh, yes." Regina forced a smile. "Migraine."

Angela handed over the gift. "I hope he likes it. Maybe it helps?" she asked, considerately. "Enjoy. *Ciao*."

"Here, wait a moment. For your trouble."

"No, no, please, it's my pleasure," said Angela, thinking to herself *especially as I didn't have to offer my left boob for a signature*e. Back at the van, the plain white panel van, she slammed the door and drove off.

Scene 61. Take 3.

Regina thought . . . *he's aged ten years since he's been in this place. Can I let the children see their father like this*? Lightly, she passed a hand over the wound. "Can't this be stopped?"

Despite the gentleness of her touch, Possi winced. "Most of the guards do their best, but they can't be everywhere."

"And in the meantime what are we to do, let the inmates beat you to death?" Regina asked a question. "What about the CIA man?"

Possi shook his head. "Nothing. Nor from the Justice guy, Conde." He squeezed her hands. "How are the children?"

"It's not easy for them, especially at school." She fiddled with her wedding ring. "Vincenze, ever since this nightmare began, I've never doubted you, but then, neither have I ever asked you?"

"Asked me what?"

"Whether it's all true or not?"

"If you never doubted, why are you asking me now?"

"Because I like to think there have never been any secrets between us, that it hasn't changed?"

Possi smiled. "It hasn't."

"Then did you? Were you involved in this terrible drugs thing?"

For some two agonizing minutes, wrestling with his conscience the whole time, Possi could look only at his wife. The look never faltering. Ever so slowly, he nodded.

"Oh! Vincenze!" She had wanted the truth, but not this.

He was shaking her hands. "Regina, I didn't do it for me, it wasn't for me!" He looked at her, pleadingly. "I wanted my wife and my children to have the best. For years, I tried for promotion but Mendoza always blocked it."

"But, Vincenze." The tears were flowing freely. "How would you feel if it was *our* children who became hooked on drugs, what if it was *their* lives that were ruined, and what would you feel about the people who make the drugs, the traffickers, the dealers?"

"Regina!" His fists were clenched. "You know the answer to that!" He calmed a little. "*I* didn't see it as a plot to destroy others, simply as a way to benefit my family."

In silence, they gazed at each other, while the tears continued their cascade. Regina dabbed a tissue to her eyes.

"I've had plenty of think time lately." He looked about him. "It's about the only luxury in this place." He held her hands. "And as far as not telling anybody anything, there's good reason. There was no way of knowing what Mendoza would have done, got at me in here or worse still, got at you or our children out there. I couldn't risk that, so, I stayed silent, but Conde, and the CIA guy? They knew I was lying."

"But when they saw you, Mendoza was already dead, the threat had gone?"

"No it had not! There are people above Mendoza and Para and *they* are still around!"

In contemplation, she was looking at her husband. "What about the Witness Protection Program?"

Possi managed a smile. "That's why I'm desperate to get hold of the Conde guy." He lit one of Barton's cigarettes. "It would mean moving, possibly even to another country, a new identity."

"But it *would* mean we could both look each other in the eye?"

He nodded. "Yes, it would mean that, and it would also mean we would be free, truly free."

"Will I have to bring it up again?"

He was smiling, broadly. "No. I know the only way out of this torment is to tell the truth."

She half stood, the guard watching her. Keeping both of her hands visible on the table, she leaned across and kissed him on the forehead.

Smiling, the guard relaxed. He picked up a parcel, its red cellophane wrapping vivid in the drabness of the visiting room and placed it on the table.

"*What* is that?"

Regina answered. "It was delivered just as I was leaving. It's from a well-wisher."

He leaned back, spreading his arms in a grand gesture. "A well-wisher, to wish *me* well? How do I know it isn't a bomb?"

"Because we've scanned it already," said the guard, laughing as he did so. He unwrapped the parcel carefully, eventually handing to Possi an envelope.

"A card." Possi read from it aloud. *"To Captain Possi. You still have friends. Enjoy."* He turned over the card. *"Carnival Confections. We let you have your cake and eat it."* He laughed.

Having opened the box, the guard wiped a hand on each pants leg and then took out a fine-looking cake.

"Vincenze, it's covered in almond marzipan." She smiled. "Someone knows your weakness."

Possi scooped off some of the covering, licking a finger. "Possibly people in the office."

"But they haven't signed the card."

Possi shrugged. "Probably best not to be seen giving me support."

Regina sniffed the cake. "Holy Mother! It's drowned in Amaretto." She looked at the two men. "I'm not sure if it's a cake with Amaretto or Amaretto with some cake!"

All three of them were laughing. "Shall I cut it?" asked the guard.

Smiling, Possi gestured.

The guard cut two slices. Regina looked-up. "Are you not joining us?"

He chuckled. "I thought you'd never ask!" The guard cut a third slice. They toasted each other, in Amaretto cake.

Regina and Vincenze Possi, they each had two slices.

SCENE 62. TAKE 3.

Surveying the Borges airstrip, Cooper wondered how long it would be before the charter was loaded and they would be airborne. He watched Kurt Greene using his video camera, documenting locations, photographing cast and crew alike, his visual diary of day-to-day life on *Redmayne West*.

Squinting up at the primitive control tower, Cooper noticed the pilot and first officer were still drinking *cafezinho*, chatting and smoking, suggesting that departure was not imminent.

From the control tower, Captain Enrique Huerta and First Officer Pepe Babenco also watched the activity around their VASP Boeing 737-400, the loading of which was painfully slow, hindered by the total lack of any mechanized equipment at this field, the deficiency being made up by an ant-like army of peons, with ladders and a block and tackle.

Huerta checked his watch. "Thank God we're not taking on catering here, or they'd be carrying on each tray separately."

The controller also was looking at his watch. "Captain, Borges is a daytime field only. If you don't watch it, you'll be stuck here, or at best, have to overnight in San Gabriel."

Huerta nodded. "There'll be hell to pay from these movie people if we don't make it out this evening." He turned to his F.O. "Pepe, go down there and see how they're doing. Call me from the flight deck."

"If I can reach it."

First Officer Pepe Babenco skipped down the stairs two-at-a-time, his shoes clattering on the metal steps.

Hearing the earnestness of the approaching footfalls, Cooper moved to one side, allowing the person to proceed unimpeded. As Pepe passed him, Cooper thought, excellent, we must be getting near to take-off, and about bloody time.

The tiny airfield of San Gabriel looked like JFK on a bad day. Everywhere, there were trucks, minibuses, cars and cabs, awaiting the arrival of the *Redmayne West* charter. Conde drove the little red VW Beetle slowly, seeking desperately a parking space.

"*Ker . . . rist!* Who they expecting. Michael Jackson?"

Conde chuckled.

"Oh, and Jorge, I know you don't smoke, but as we're sharing a room, do you snore?"

"I don't know Dick. I never been awake to find out."

For the Amazonian heat and humidity, both were dressed in the casual style of designer T-shirt, light pants and loafers. Barton and Conde watched the aircraft touch down, the screaming reverse-thrust braking shattering the peace of the surrounding rain forest, prompting thousands of birds to take to the late afternoon sky while the watching local populace jumped up and down, pointing, shouting, and clapping. Barton was intrigued. "What's with these people?"

"Apparently it is the largest plane ever to land here."

Barton pointed. "But it's only a Seven Thirty Seven?"

"Dick, everything is relative?"

Barton turned to his colleague. "You can say that again." He nudged Conde. "Jorge, let's mosey over to the arrivals area, see if we can get a fix on our man."

They scanned faces. "Jorge, quick! You any paper?"

Conde was cautious. "I have a pocket diary."

"Lend it me would you?" Barton held out a hand. The diary was placed in it, and Barton scooted across the area, to confront a tall, good-looking, sturdy man.

Kurt Greene knew always when he'd been recognized. "Hi. How are you today?"

"Hey". Barton gushed. "I never expected to see a famous movie star in a one horse town like this." He offered the diary.

"Who's it to?"

"My daughter, Christine Nancy."

Kurt signed the autograph.

"I eh, I guess you're on a movie, like now, here?"

"We're nearly finished." Kurt returned the diary.

"Famous director?"

"He soon will be." Kurt pointed across the hall. "That's him, over there. James Cooper."

They watched the director, waiting for him to claim his luggage, in turn enabling them to check the color of the labels.

"Green," mused Barton. "I wonder which place is green?"

Golda Wisepart was standing in the centre of the hall, clipboard in hand.

Barton nudged Conde. "Your turn."

Conde walked over to Golda. "Sênhora Redmayne?"

"Bit casually dressed for a driver captain, aren't we, and fala-ing *Inglês* yet?"

"Is my smart clothes. I no have suit. This poor area."

"Poor?" Golda pointed to his outfit. "They look as if they've come from an Austin Reed catalog?"

Conde smiled. "Please, which house is the green label?"

"The hotel, my good man, the one and only hotel in your seething metropolis, the half star *Hotel Albuquerque*, which, I might add, is not for the likes of hoi-poloi *comme moi*. It's for the big guns, like him." Golda indicated Kurt Greene. "And him over there, the new breed of director, Mr. James-eighty-six-the-video-assist-Cooper."

Conde bowed. "Thank you, Sênhora."

"*Da nada*", curtsied Golda. "And wear your *Redmayne* badge in future, so's I can recognize you easily!"

Conde was panting.

"You okay?"

"Dick, I just meet the original Amazon. Of the Amazon. *In* Amazonia." Conde regained his breathing. "Cooper? He staying at our hotel."

Barton smiled. "Then we go back, have a cold beer, and wait."

The sun was very low in the tropical sky.

Looking out of the cockpit, Captain Huerta called the tower. "What's the latest time for take off this evening?"

"Eighteen-fifteen, Captain."

Huerta glanced at his Rolex. "Pepe, we're here for the night."

The F.O. eased himself out of the right-hand seat. "Shall I forget the flight plan and concentrate on rooms instead?"

"Yes. Ideally five rooms, but take what you can get. If we have to double up, we double up."

"Okay." He glanced at Huerta. "Captain, deferring to your seniority, a single for you and I'll double up with one of the girls."

"I'm touched by your consideration." He spoke over his right shoulder. "Hitch a ride in one of the movie cars. We'll all catch up at the hotel."

"Roger that."

The V.I.P. VW Beetle was deemed a 'limo' by the fact that suctioned to the inside of the windshield was a plastic vase holding a plastic flower, the seats covered in a cheap leopard-skin material and there was a notice on the seat backs, '*No fumare.*'

Glancing at Cooper, Kurt gestured to the car. "Jimmer, by no *stretch* of the imagination is this a limo?"

"Maybe not Kurt, but it's better than walking."

Kurt slapped a Cooper thigh. "You must be feeling pretty good right now?"

Looking at the passing scenery, such as it was, Cooper half-smiled. "Kurt, what I feel right now is the need for a bath. Since leaving Santa Mosqueiro a week ago, all I've had are showers, and none of them hot."

"Well, how'd you think the rest of us have been showering?"

"I know, I know, but Kurt, in an earlier life I think I was a hippopotamus, because what I like to do is soak, soak in a bathful of hot, soapy water." Cooper made suitable Flanders and Swann hippo-bathing grunts.

Kurt laughed. "What I actually meant Jimmer was, here we are in San Gabriel, two weeks from finishing, on schedule and I believe, way under on film stock?"

Cooper mock-punched his leading man. "Like I said before, Kurt. Couldn't have done it without a little help from my friends."

The 'limo' had entered San Gabriel.

Scanning out of the window, Kurt frowned. "The place is deserted."

"Must be screening an old Burt Reynolds movie in the Oxfam tent?"

"Vegas this ain't . . ." He turned to Cooper. "Anyway, what happens to all that unused negative stock?"

"It usually gets sold. There's plenty of places in L.A. that'll buy it, but for considerably less than it cost originally."

Kurt was thinking. "I've a better idea." Suddenly he turned to Cooper. "Blue . . . movies!"

Cooper's face expressed . . . bafflement. "Blue . . . movies? What, with a Panavision camera and a full crew?"

"Well, we wouldn't need wardrobe, now would we?" He thought further. "We round up some local chicks—I do the casting—you direct, and, I've got some great titles."

"Kurt, are you serious?"

"Jimmer, you'll love this one." Kurt held up two forefingers. "*Sexcalibur.*"

Cooper smiled.

"And Jimmer, the sequel . . . " Kurt was laughing now. "The sequel is .

. . *Cumalot*. Get it?!"

Now, both men were laughing hysterically. "Kurt, if we're going to call on the classics, how about *A Tale of Two Titties*?"

"A Dickens of a good title! To be followed Jimmer by our masterpiece, *Great Sexpectations*!"

Looking in the rear view mirror, the driver wondered if all gringos were as *loco*.

Still giggling, they walked into the lobby of the small colonial-style hotel.

"There, Kurt, the reception desk beckons." Cooper indicated the elderly clerk. "And waiting to show us to our sumptuous suites is Sênhor Scrotum, the wrinkled retainer."

Kurt burst out laughing.

"Cooper ? Sênhor James Cooper?"

He turned. "Oh, hi. You must be the mayor?"

"My name is Jorge Conde. I am with the Department of Justice." He produced his I.D. "And I wish to speak with you." Inclining his head, Conde gestured to the lounge. " Now?"

Kurt Greene watched. "Jimmer, I did warn you to keep up those maternity support payments?"

Cooper stifled a giggle.

"Sênhor Cooper. Please?"

"Sênhor Conde, I've just arrived from Borges where I've been working for the past week without a break. I'm tired, I'm sweaty, I need a bath and I haven't the foggiest notion of why you would want to talk to me. Whatever it is, I'm sure it can wait."

"No it cannot!" Conde was firm. "I do not travel two thousand kilometers from Alentejo and wait here for two days for you, only to wait some more! No." He stared at the director.

"Jimmer. Dinner?"

Looking all the time at Conde, Cooper replied. "Which night?"

Kurt laughed. "See you later."

Conde gestured to the lounge. "After you."

"I can tell. This isn't going to be about my next movie, is it?"

"Hi." He shook hands with Cooper. "Dick Barton."

Cooper looked around, like a mimic. "Where's *Jock* and *Snowy*?"

"Pardon me?"

"Well, you are a Special Agent?" Cooper glanced at him. "Aren't you?"

Barton showed his badge.

"D.E.A." Cooper gestured. "This a TV series or for real?"

Barton nodded. "The United States Drug Enforcement Administration."

Cooper savored the vodka. It was the first alcohol he'd had in over a week. Taking a final swallow, he put down the glass and turned to the D.E.A. agent. "Mr. Barton-"

"Dick. You can call me Dick."

"Okay, Dick. I'm James. But what are you actually here for?"

Sitting forward, Barton spoke quietly. "If I told you that you're a lead suspect in an international drugs trafficking case, a case that also involves murder . . ." He leaned back. "What would you say?"

"I'd say you're off your rocker." Studying the two men, Cooper contemplated if they could see any activity under his shirt where his heart was thumping like a yo-yo. Cooper fought hard to remain calm. "A lesser known . . ." He cleared his throat. "A lesser known Hitchcock movie was arguably one of his best. Henry Fonda is this bass fiddle player in a New York nightclub. It's New Year's, so on the way home he stops at this liquor store to buy a celebratory bottle. The store's been robbed a number of times, the owner thinks he recognizes Fonda as the robber, and calls the police. Fonda's taken into custody, not unduly worried as he knows it's a case of mistaken identity. But. The robber always wrote his demands, never spoke them. So the police dictate one of the robber's notes for Fonda to copy out. It's something like 'open the drawer', only Fonda spells 'drawer' d-r-a-w, exactly as the robber had. Despite his innocence, he's arrested and convicted on this evidence. It destroys his life and his wife ends up being committed to an asylum. And *that,* my friend, is my point."

Barton shook his head. "But *I* don't get your point. What's the title of the movie?"

"*The Wrong Man*." Cooper paused as a waiter placed in front of him a large vodka and tonic. He thumbed his chest. "I . . . am the *wrong* man."

Once again, Barton sat forward, speaking confidentially. "All the evidence, and we have lots of it, the evidence we have all points to **you**." A finger emphasized his words. "Points to you as a leading participant, perhaps even the initiator of the scheme? Every avenue we pursue, every door we knock on, we end up with the same name." Barton stared at the director. "Cooper. James Cooper."

Cooper returned the look, thinking, *whatever evidence these guys have can only be circumstantial, but many before me have been convicted on less. 'The Wrong Man'? That movie was based on fact, and Manny Ballesteros—Henry Fonda—was innocent?*

Conde interrupted his thoughts. "You not going to touch your drink?"

Cooper figured he should remain *compus mentis*. "It can wait."

"James, I haven't traveled all these miles on a whim, a mere suspicion, unless I'm pretty sure of my facts."

"D'you want to hear my side?"

"That's why we're here." Barton sat back. "Shoot."

Cooper twirled the stem. Of the cocktail glass. Which, for the moment, he felt was best left untouched. "You know all about Francesco Ramalho?"

"We do."

In turn, Cooper looked at each man. "Mendoza, Para and Possi are in bed with some drugs operation. They learn we ship film daily to Los Angeles. It's a perfect set up for them, too good an opportunity to miss. So they dream up the idea of a censor. Ramalho was the pawn. He's forced on to the movie as the censor, something I'd encountered before on a show in Mexico, so a censor was nothing new to me, nor strange." He looked again at each man. He had their full attention. "The censor is responsible for sealing the shot film. Which is when Ramalho added the drugs to another film can, making it all look like one shipment of exposed negative. He then parcels up the whole lot, puts official seals and stamps all over it and off it goes. One of their men receives it at LAX, separates the drugs from the film, which latter goes off to the lab." He looked at the two of them. "Foolproof?" Sighing deeply, Cooper eyed Barton. "We never had any suspicion. Why would we? And it must have fooled U.S. Customs, but my complicity, or that of the company?" He shook his head.

Barton nodded. "And I thought the Irish had the gift of the gab?"

Conde spoke. "Mendoza, who I question at great length, he claim the whole time he was working undercover."

"Sure he was. A drugs dealer. Working undercover . . . as a cop."

"What about your arrest?" Asked Barton. "Weren't drugs found on you?"

Cooper allowed himself a little ease. "I take it you're referring to the episode with Colonel Mendoza, where my location bag was seized and when it was returned, Colonel Mendoza *found* in it a sachet of white powder. Oh gosh! Had he planted it there? Does the Pope wear funny slippers?" He knew he wasn't being positively persuasive. "Look. How do I convince you guys? I've no reason to lie, because I've nothing to hide and have nothing to gain by lying?"

Answering Cooper, Barton glanced at Conde. "What were you doing in Colombia, and I'm not talking movie studios here?"

Cooper mused. Should he? After all, he'd told it dozens of times. But then, maybe they'd not heard. "Same as I told Mendoza and the British Consul, Twit-Miller."

Barton laughed. "I call him *Putz-Miller*. But go on."

"We got lost, off course, running out of fuel, desperately seeking somewhere to land."

"Oh, that old chestnut. The one about landing in one place and waking up in another?"

Cooper bit his tongue. "Dick, I tell it like it is. No reason to lie."

Barton was reading from a pocket notebook. "The pilot. Babenco?"

"Yeah, Pepe Babenco."

"He can corroborate your story?"

"Absolutely." Cooper looked at the two of them. "Why don't you ask him?"

Barton muffled an ironic laugh. "We should be so lucky." He tapped the notebook against the table edge. "You don't really expect us to believe that you landed on a paved strip here, but woke up by a dirt strip there?"

"Dick, I'd be the first to agree it sounds far-fetched . . ." He gestured with open hands. "But truth is often stranger than fiction?" Cooper sat back, glancing at the two men. Then it hit him. Suddenly he held hands to his forehead. He stared, for seconds, then in turn slowly looked at each man. "Jesus!"

Barton and Conde glanced at each other. "You okay?" asked Barton.

Cooper gestured frustration. "I work in a visual medium, but in all this time?" He gesticulated. "Jesus! I didn't see it, I *just* didn't see it!' He continued shaking his head.

"What James, you didn't see *what*?"

"A paved runway!" He screwed up his face, looking at them. "In the rain forest, the jungle, a paved runway in the middle of nowhere? Military?" Cooper was shaking his head. "No! We'd have been buzzed and detained." Cooper was warming to his subject. He sat forward, pointing a forefinger at Barton. "We landed at their drugs factory, distribution center or whatever. So, they knock us out, take us somewhere else, in the meantime having refueled our plane. Oh! And yes, the guy who found us by the dirt strip? He said there'd been two planes, so one crew flies our plane, leaves and flies back with the others to their strip. They call their associate Mendoza to arrest us and scare us off, and Mendoza has Babenco deported, ensuring he won't ever fly over the area again." He studied the two men. "That has to be it!"

Barton and Conde, each looked at the other but said nothing, digesting Cooper's analysis. The American spoke. "But why, why fly you somewhere else?"

"And why not kill you?" asked Conde. "That is their usual M.O."

"Maybe they flew us elsewhere so's we couldn't recall the strip and maybe they didn't kill us because we were foreigners and I was working for an American company?"

"Hypothesis."

"Dick, I may work in fantasyland but this is the truth and nothing but the truth, so help me God." In Barton's eyes Cooper saw the first glimmer of pluasibilty, of . . . belief. "Dick, it's the airstrip!" Cooper jabbed vertically. "All of those satellites you have up there, which from fifty miles high can detect a wart on as cow's arse? Surely they can detect the strip? Eh, a call to NASA?"

Barton thought. "Not necessarily. If *their* operation's as sophisticated as it seems, they'll have taken steps to hide it."

"Then how come *we* found it?"

Conde spoke. "Luck. *It* found you. Your Guardian Angel, he or she, was guiding you."

Cooper noticed the V and T. "Lent's over, isn't it?" He took a long gulp. "Dick, the strip. It's the key! We *know* it's about two hours' flying time from Santa Mosqueiro and, it's in Colombia. That *has* to narrow it down?"

After some moments, Barton spoke. "How long you here for?"

"A scheduled fourteen days. Why?"

A finger tapped the table. "Well, for a start, who'd this Babenco work for?"

"Keep calm." From his location bag, Cooper removed a large diary. He flipped pages. "Here we are. *A.T.A. Air Taxi Amazonas*, based in Santa Mosqueiro."

"You get that, Jorge?" The Imperian nodded. "Okay, that's it." He pointed at Cooper. "For tonight. I want to sleep on it, but you be damned sure I'll have other questions."

Cooper nodded. "Dick, I'm indentured. I have a movie to complete." He stood. "And I'm not going anywhere, except to bed. I haven't even checked in yet, let alone eaten. And I'm ravenous."

"The restaurant? It close at eight thirty."

"And", added Barton, "there's no room service."

Cooper picked up his location bag. "Thanks guys, thanks a lot."

In unison, Barton and Conde replied. "You're welcome."

"Jorge, you awake?"

"*Si*. It too hot to sleep."

"Mind if I put on the light?"

"Go ahead."

The low-wattage bulb brightened and then dimmed, sadly.

Barton sat-up. Under a thin sheet, he was wearing only undershorts, but was covered in rivulets of perspiration. "Man, this heat."

In undershirt and underpants, both of which were streaked with sweat, Conde was lying above the sheet. He rubbed his eyes. "And the humidity . . ."

Barton pointed to the carafe on the bedside table. "This water okay?"

Conde smiled. "I would not trust it."

Barton raised his eyes. "And no twenty-four hour markets here." He pointed to the water. "Jorge, tomorrow, we buy some bottled water."

"For sure."

He turned to his associate. "What d'you think? Y'know, Cooper?"

"Dick, I am sure like me, you conduct many interrogations. In my experience, if over several interviews the story change, even in little details, I know they lie. Cooper? His story does not change. He tells the truth, I know."

"I'm inclined to agree with you." A quick glance to Conde. "But we don't let *him* know that." Barton looked around the room. "There are times I wish I smoked."

"You had cigarettes the other day? You gave them to Possi."

"You know when you want a child to do or say something?"

Conde nodded. "*Si.*"

"You tempt them with candy, right?"

"Right."

"Almost everybody in this country smokes. I figured Possi did. So I bought the cigs as a nicotine temptation." Barton chuckled. "Not that it worked." He smacked a shoulder. "Gotcha, you little blood sucking motherfucker!" He opened the drawers of the bedside table. "There's no snake here, y'know, that thing to burn, to guard against the mosquitoes?" He grinned at Conde. "We need to start a shopping list." He sat back on the bed, stroking his chin. "I'd accept Cooper's story if only we could find the pilot and have him confirm everything."

Conde smiled. "Dick, we know who the pilot is."

"We do?"

"Sure. Cooper told us. He gave us the guy's name and where he'd worked, which means he's on file with the Air Ministry in Alentejo. They will have a photo of him, so in the morning I fax them for his photo." He looked at his partner. "That a start?"

"It sure is. G'night, Jorge."

Conde switched off the light. He lay on his bed, only to see the silhouette of Barton, sitting up still. "You not sleepy?"

"The mind's working overtime." He sighed deeply. "Repeatedly, Possi kept pointing the finger at Cooper, while Cooper maintains he hasn't a clue who Possi is, claims he's never even met the guy." In the darkness he looked towards Conde. "Would it be possible to have Possi brought up here?"

"Sure. He could be flown up under armed guard. Why?"

"One sure way to find out if Cooper's being truthful is to confront your Senor Possi with our Mr. Cooper?"

Conde lay back, hands clasped behind neck, surveying the ceiling. "I make two calls in the morning."

Silencing the alarm on his wristwatch, Barton looked over to Conde, still asleep. Getting out of bed, he grabbed his toilet bag and headed for the shower.

Ten minutes later he felt like a new man. The renaissance didn't last long, the oppressive humidity putting paid to that. Dressing, he noticed an envelope under the door. It was for a '*Sênhor Jorge Conde*'. "Jorge, wake up." Barton shook him.

"Eh?" He squinted. "What time it is?"

"Seven." Barton handed him the envelope. "This came for you."

Yawning loudly and stretching, Conde sat up, opening the envelope half-heartedly. He removed the fax, and read. Immediately holding the paper closer, His face paled. Having read it twice, he handed the note to Barton, without a word.

Taking it, Barton read. And paused. "Jorge, it's all in Portuguese." He returned it.

Conde read aloud. *"J. Conde. Hotel Albuquerque, San Gabriel. This is to advise the department has been informed by the federal prison service of the death of . . . "* He looked gravely at Barton. *"The death of Vincenze Possi."* The American was ashen-faced. *" . . . While in detention, together*

298

with wife Sênhora Possi who was visiting and prison guard Presares. This is an open fax line. All further details will be sent to your personal office. Yours truly, Alejandro Mira, Information Section." The fax dropped out of his hand and on to the bed.

After a long silence, Barton spoke. "They got to him."

Conde nodded. "He posed a threat. And in getting to him and his wife, they make two children orphans." He stared at Barton. "Dick, these people, they just don't care how to get what they want. They will stop at nothing., nothing! Until *they* feel secure."

"So how long before they put two and two together and come up with Cooper?"

"Maybe he not so glib now?"

Barton paced, slowly. "Don't you think that in the back of their minds is that nagging thought, that one day he'll remember in *his* mind and pin-point that runway?" He halted, turning to Conde. "If, on the one hand you had doubt, and on the other no scruples, would you put at risk a multi-million dollar operation?"

"No." Conde shook his head emphatically. "No way."

"I wonder how they did it?"

Conde headed for the shower.

"Jorge, I'm taking the mug file with me."

Barton flipped through the Imperio Department of Justice mug file, the pages full of numerous photos, of known drugs traffickers, dealers, distributors, and all and any person suspected of any activity within the nefarious trade. He looked around the small, crowded, very crowded, dining room. It seemed everybody was breakfasting at the same time. Leaning over the side of his chair to place the file on the floor, Barton came face to face with a pair of navy blue slacks standing behind Conde's chair.

"Bom dia."

Barton straightened. "Oh. Hi."

Pepe pointed to the empty chair. "May I?"

"Sure, help yourself. My friend's making a couple of calls."

As he sat, Pepe called out his order in Portuguese, ensuring the instant attention of a waiter. The coffee arrived.

From the cafetière, Pepe poured a large cupful.

Black.

Five teaspoonsful of sugar.

Accompanied by a cigarette.

Barton was engrossed. "This your normal breakfast?"

Pepe nodded.

"This a diet?"

"The VASP diet."

Captain Huerta appeared, pointing to his watch and gesturing.

"My captain calls." Pepe grabbed the cup of coffee. "*Adios*."

"Nice meeting you."

A spruce Conde arrived.

"You make the calls?"

Having sat, Conde squeezed lime on to a papaya. "Both."

"And?"

He wiped his hand on a napkin. "Possi? Poison. Cyanide. In a cake soaked in amaretto. The alcohol drowned the smell."

"Nifty."

Cooper and Kurt scanned for an empty table.

"Jimmer, that's him" Kurt pointed out Barton. "The one who wanted your autograph?"

"He has it already." Barton beckoned. "Kurt, order me a coffee and toast. I'll be with you in a sec." He walked to where sat Barton and Conde.

"Gentlemen." He glanced at Barton. "Now what?"

"A minute of your valuable time." Barton picked up the mug file, which he handed to Cooper.

"A minute you said. This'll take ages.".

"Try. Just try. See if there's anyone you recognize."

Eyeing Barton, Cooper pointed to the mug file. "I know. You want me to cast the D.E.A. nativity play?"

"Just do it."

Watched by both Conde and Barton, Cooper flipped through pages and pages quickly and then stopped. He flicked back a couple, studying the photo intently. Lifting the file, he studied it at arm's length. Placing it on the table, he spun the file so both men could see. He pointed to a photo. "Him."

Barton peered. "This guy?"

Cooper nodded. "That guy. Antonio Vargas."

Conde also studied the photo. "No, no. This Rubio, Antonio Rubio." He looked at Cooper. "You must be mistaken?"

"Let me have another *butchers*." The file was spun back. Cooper was adamant. "No, no question. Antonio Vargas." He eyed the two men. "A Mendoza associate." He checked the photo yet again. He challenged them. "I never forget a face." And looked up. "The meeting I told you about, in Para's office?" He tapped the mug shot. "*He* was there, this Vargas." Cooper held out his left wrist. "Your time is up. You owe me three minutes twenty-eight seconds. *Ciao*." He left.

For a few seconds, both men were silent.

A chord was being plucked in the Conde subconscious. "Vargas . . . Vargas." He pounded the table. "Ramalho!" He looked eagerly at Barton. "The letter to his uncle, the judge? He mentioned a Vargas. In Para's office!" He grabbed the file once again. "I have a strong feeling my Antonio Rubio is Cooper's Antonio Vargas!"

"No doubt?"

"Not in my mind."

"What have you on this Rubio, a.k.a. Vargas?"

Conde sat up. "Colombian. Comes from a very good family, father a diplomat. Well-educated, studied law but find the wrong side of it much more interesting and much more, how you say . . . profitable. Known drugs trafficker, distributor, not cartel, but maintain with them good relation, each respect the other. Good contacts, especially in the U.S., Holland, U.K. and, Imperio. And, he was spotted in Santa Mosqueiro a few weeks ago. Which is why I know Cooper is right."

"You think this Rubio was in the same car pool as Mendoza, Para and, Possi?"

Conde nodded. "And more."

Barton indicated the envelope in Conde's hand. "Anything else new?"

"Oh." Conde opened the envelope leisurely. "It a fax. From the air ministry." He withdrew a second sheet. "Now we know what pilot Pepe Babenco look like." Reversing the page, he held it in front of Barton.

"Jesus H!" The American shot to his feet, in doing so scattering the table's contents. He pointed at the photocopy. "Him!" He pointed at Conde. "He was sitting in *that* chair, *your* chair, only minutes ago!"

Conde's eyes were darting hither and thither. "The Airport! Quick!"

The couple rushed out of the room, scattering anyone and anything in their way.

Kurt looked over a shoulder. "What d'you suppose that's all about?"

Cooper shrugged. "Didn't want to do the washing up, I guess."

SCENE 64. TAKE 9.

"Dumb, plain fucking . . . dumb!" Barton smacked the steering wheel. "Why didn't it occur to me when the guy said, '*my captain calls*'?"

"Dick, that the handbrake."

"Christ, when'd I last drive a stick shift?" The full thrusting power of the flat-four twelve hundred cubic centimetres of Volkswagen power surged into life, as Barton wrestled with the clutch, prompting the car to imitate a kangaroo. "And, wearing aircrew blue pants!" Despite VW having produced one of the very finest gearboxes of all time, Barton managed to crunch the gears when shifting from one to two.

"I always double declutch on a manual box."

Barton gave a quick sideways glance. "Double what?" He gave his attention to the road. "Double idiot more like. Me!"

The road to the airport was not very busy and whatever other traffic there was, Barton was able to pass without difficulty. "Jorge, when we get there, you head straight for the tower. If the plane's already left, get it recalled, and if the controller can't do that, you must know somebody in Alentejo who can? And, if God willing it's still on the ground . . ." He glanced at Conde. "We, I, we don't let it take off!"

Together with Pepe Babenco, Captain Huerta was going through the pre-flight checks. "Auto pilot?"

"Check."

"Flaps?"

"Check."

"Rudder?"

"Check."

"Transponder?"

"Check."

The ground power unit was coupled still to the aircraft. Wearing headphones, the operator was standing where he could be seen from the cockpit.

The 'Fasten Seat Belt' and 'No Smoking' signs were illuminated. Without passengers, the three attendants sat in the cabin instead of their usual jump seats.

"Start number two engine."

Pepe pressed the engine start switch to GRD, watching a dial. "Number two engine stable."

"Start one."

The same procedure. "Number one engine stable. Doors to automatic."

Huerta advanced the engines and then throttled back. Looking down, he spoke into his mike. "Disconnect G.P.U., chocks away."

Immediately, the operator disappeared under the fuselage to disengage the umbilical trunking between the G.P.U. and the aircraft. This done, he pulled away the chocks and signaled to the cockpit a thumbs up, which gesture was returned by Huerta.

"Tower, this is VASP alpha-lima-mike. Request taxi to runway."

"VASP alpha-lima-mike. Taxi via alpha one. Hold short runway two-seven."

"Roger, tower." Captain Huerta advanced the controls. Majestically, the Boeing 737-400 moved off the stand.

While traversing the narrow street of a village, Barton had slowed down but as clearing the built up area he accelerated, the car picking up speed.

Without warning, Conde screamed. "Look out! Look out!"

Frowning, Barton looked to his left. "I don't see anything?" But he felt it. "What the hell's that!" He braked hard.

"Dick, no, no! Don't stop! Don't stop!" Conde was hysterical. "Keep moving! Keep going!"

"Jorge, we gotta flat!"

"Dick! Drive! Just drive!" Conde looked behind him. "Keep going. They here!"

Barton hesitated. And then, in the rear-view mirror he saw them. About seven boys. Between the ages of ten and fourteen. Running fast.

"Dick! Faster, faster!"

Throwing a piece of two by four lumber, one kid smashed the rear screen, leaping on to a running board while another jumped on to the driver-side running board.

As best he could with the limping car, Barton accelerated. The kid reached in and grabbed the wheel, sending the car swerving. Punching the kid's hand, Barton opened his door suddenly. The boy lost his grip, falling by the wayside.

Attempting to avoid the punches raining down on him, Conde was crouching to his left, pushing on Barton, who found it almost impossible to steer properly.

Barton pressed the cigar lighter.

It ejected.

Grabbing it, the American leaned across Conde and rammed it into the back of the other boy's hand. The hand with which he was hanging on. Except he wasn't any more. Not now.

"What the hell was that!"

"I try to warn you." Conde checked himself for any possible injuries. "It an old *favela* trick. Kids. They put nails through a strip of plywood, attach a long piece of twine, place it nails upright in the road . . . and wait. A car comes along, it run over the nails and bang! A puncture. The boys pull away the ply, the driver gets out, checks the tire, they come up behind him, beat him, rob him and strip the car. Hubs, wheels, spare, seats, anything." Conde wiped his brow. "I see the ply and the nails at the very last minute." He turned. "That why I scream."

Barton rolled his eyes. "If I'd been by myself, I'd have got out, too." The car was lurching crazily. Barton checked the speedometer. "Not bad, only three good tires, but we're making fifty."

"Kilometers."

Barton's head spun to the right. "What's that in American?"

"Thirty-one miles per hour."

The car passed a sign. "*Aeroporto 2km.*"

"VASP alpha-lima-mike. Holding short runway alpha one. Ready for departure."

"VASP alpha-lima-mike, roger. Continue holding. This field is not radar equipped. We have to make a visual check first."

"Roger, tower." Heurta heaved frustration. "We can't even have a smoke."

"Jorge! We're in luck. It's still here!"

Barton steered for the tower, while all the time looking at the plane, willing it to remain. "Stay where you are baby, stay!"

Conde had the passenger door open. "What you gonna do?"

"I'll think of something." He tilted back his head. "*Eeh ahaaa!*"

Not attempting to close the door, Conde leapt from the moving car and ran to the tower as fast as his legs would carry him.

"Alpha-lima-mike, you are cleared for take off. Runway two-seven. Heading one six zero. *Bon voyage.*"

"Roger, San Gabriel tower. Thank you. *Ciao.*" Captain Huerta taxied on to the runway, and halted. He glanced at Pepe. "All A-Okay?"

"All A-Okay."

Huerta released the brakes and applied full power for take-off.

Above the clatter of the crippled car, Barton heard the scream of the two CFM56 engines. "Come on, Herbie, this is your moment, give it your all!"

In the tower, summoning his nearly exhausted breath and showing his I.D., Conde screamed *"Pare a avião! Pare! Não deve decolar!"*

The two controllers were confused. Two plane movements a day were stressful. But a Boeing-737, the first time the airport had ever handled one, a limping car on the airfield and a madman screaming at them to stop it taking-off? They looked at Conde, his I.D. and at each other, and at the aircraft. Which was moving . . .

"Stop it!" Screamed Conde in English. "Stop it, you imbeciles. Stop it!" Conde moved to the windows. Mortified, he watched the aircraft gather speed. And then. He saw a car limp on to the paving, drive to the centre of the runway and stop. Positioning it directly in the path of the rapidly-approaching aircraft.

Barton dived out of the vehicle and ran into the surrounding grass, heading for the tower.

"Abort take off! Abort!! Abort!!!"

Reverse thrust was applied, air brakes jammed on. Wheel brakes squealed, the noise deafening as the cockpit crew fought to halt the large aircraft which seconds earlier was accelerating under full power. To all on board, it felt as if the plane was standing on its nose.

The three cabin attendants blessed themselves repeatedly.

In a mass of noise and a fog of burning rubber, the aircraft slammed to a halt, some fifty feet short of the car, the two jet engines still screaming. Huerta roared into his mike. "Tower! Your visual check should include low flying Volkswagens as well as aircraft! Now, what the hell's going on!"

The controller was unsure as to what should be his response. "Eh, sorry, captain."

As a breathless and sweating Barton rushed into the room, Conde grabbed the mike. "Captain Huerta. *Fala Inglês?*"

Anxious to know what drama was being played out at the tiny airport, the cockpit was crowded, the three girls standing behind the flight crew.

Huerta looked at Pepe, and shrugged. "Yes, I speak English."

"Good, I like we conduct this conversation in English. My name is Jorge Conde, I represent the Imperio Department of Justice, answerable personally to the Office of the Chief Justice."

"I don't care, Sênhor Conde, I do *not* care. I care about my schedule, which does not include talking to you. Now, get that car off the runway!"

"Captain, I'm the driver of that car and I'm not moving it."

"And you, sir. Who the hell are you?"

"Special Agent Richard Barton, United States Drug Enforcement Administration."

Huerta killed his mike. "Pepe, get down there and move that car."

"Captain, we need steps", reasoned Pepe. "Even if I could get down, there's no way I could get back up?" He looked out of the cockpit. "And Captain, even unladen, we need most of this runway to get airborne? Until that car is moved, and I bet it has no key, we're trapped, we can't even get to a taxiway?"

Activating the mike, the irritated tones of Barton were heard. "Captain, do you copy? I am with the—"

"Yes, yes, Mr. Barton, I heard!" Huerta was angry. "But what's this got to do with me, my crew or my aircraft?"

"Are you going to come up here or shall we come down there?"

Grinning, Huerta looked at his crew. "Mr. Barton, this aircraft is Brasilian, Brasilian sovereign territory, manned by a Brasilian crew."

"Correction! You have on board first officer Pepe Babenco who is an Argentinian national, and it is with your Mr. Babenco that we wish to speak. Now, I repeat. You coming up here or do we come down there?"

Huerta glanced at his F.O. "Care telling me what this is all about?"

Pepe looked mystified. "I wish I knew, Captain. But I haven't a clue, not the faintest idea."

"Captain!" Barton's voice filled the cockpit. "What's it to be?"

"Barton, you have no authority of any kind to board this aircraft!" Adding, and nodding forcefully. "I am not going anywhere!"

Barton chuckled. "Now, isn't that the truth, captain?" Barton replaced the mike. "Stand-off time." He looked out to the plane. "Jorge, it's your country." He turned to his partner. "What do we do next?"

To the controller, Conde spoke in his native Portuguese. "You have such a thing as a fax? Or a telex?"

"Fax. In there."

Heading for the door, Conde spun around, pointing to the two controllers. "*Algum pedido da cabine do piloto? Negado! Compreendido?*" He spoke to Barton. "I tell them do nothing, *nothing* to help the plane."

URGENTE! In connection with Santa Mosqueiro murder of Boa Vista State Police Colonel R. Mendoza and related deaths of Police Captain V.Possi, citizens M.Para, Regina Possi and prison guard V.Presares. Have unofficially detained aircraft BR V-ALM of Brasilian airline VASP which is positioning back to Sao Paulo. No passengers. On board is crew member Argentinian national Babenco, P., person of interest crucial to ongoing investigation. Please obtain a.s.a.p. all warrants and/or detention orders necessary to legalize my position. Aircraft and crew can be released once we hold Babenco here in Imperio. He is First Officer on aircraft. If Babenco detained flight will require replacement F.O. Fax copies of orders to me at this number as soon as available. Liase all relevant sections Ministry Foreign Affairs. MEDIA BLACKOUT this event! No media release! J.Conde, Office of the Chief Justice.

Conde signed the paper and faxed copies to four different numbers in Alentejo. The Department of Justice, the Ministry for Foreign Affairs, the Ministry of the Interior and the Air Ministry.

"Alpha-lima-mike to tower."

A controller looked at the mike, which was picked up by Barton. "Yes, Captain."

"Tower, we request a G.P.U. It is getting very hot in here."

"Sorry, Captain. Not available."

"Barton! I can see them from here, two of them, standing idle!"

"Captain, I'm a civilian, I'm not authorized."

"Then put the controller on!"

"Eh, they're on siesta. Why not open the main door? Just make sure you don't fall out."

Despite the plea for expediency, it had all taken much longer than Conde had anticipated. It was mid-afternoon before he received facsimiles of the necessary documents, authorizing the detaining of Babenco. Imperiavia provided a First Officer, helicoptered in from Santa Mosqueiro.

Observed by crowds of onlookers at the perimeter fence, just before last light alpha-lima-mike made it away from San Gabriel. Finally.

From the Tower, Pepe watched the 737-400 climb into the evening sky, and turn south-eastwards. He stood staring for some time, even after the aircraft had long disappeared from view. "I know now how the English Captain Bligh feel as the 'Bounty' sail away."

Barton sounded cheerful. "Babenco, we'll try to have you outta here in no time."

Pepe turned, nodding. "It strange." He looked at Barton. "When I lived in Imperio, they kicked me out. Now I live in Brasil, they insist I stay." He rolled his eyes. "Imperio people?" He spun a forefinger around his right temple. "*Loco.*"

"Dick!" Came a call up the stairs. "The taxi is here."

They gazed at the forlorn Volkswagen. "Oh, Jesus . . . I'd completely forgotten about that." The rear screen smashed, the rear seat rent by shards of shattered glass, a rear tire in shreds, missing wheel trim, while the wheel rim itself was no longer circular. Barton spoke. "One of us should return it?"

"But, Dick. A square wheel?"

"We change it for the *spare* wheel."

"We cannot just leave it here?" Conde glanced at Barton. "Besides, you rented it."

"Toss you?" Barton produced a coin.

The observer Babenco was enjoying it. "Sênhor Conde, how do you know it is not a double-headed coin?"

Looking at Babenco, he indicated Barton. "He not do that to me. We are partners."

"Heads I take it back, tails . . ." He spun the coin, slapping it down on his wrist, which he held out to Conde. The coin was revealed. "Oh dear." He looked pityingly at Conde.

The Imperian held up a finger of pause. Barton and Pepe watched as Conde strode to the tower.

The controller was locking the door. "I need", said Conde in Portuguese. "I need to use the telephone."

The controller made no attempt to unlock the door.

"On federal government business!"

Keys were produced, the door unlocked. Promptly.

"Yes, I am calling for a Mr. Richard Barton . . . Yes, Barton. He has a car of yours . . . That's it . . . The VW . . . . Well, the car needs collecting . . . It is at the Airport . . . Damage? . . . Eh, some . . . Where at the Airport? It is parked beside the runway . . . Yes, the *runway* . . . Bill? Charge to his card and send receipt to Mr. Barton, at the Hotel Alburquerque. *Ciao.*"

He collected the room key from the clerk.

"Mr. Cooper?"

The director froze. "Barton. Leave me alone."

"I've someone I'd like you to meet."

The clerk stood back from the desk. Cooper turned, slowly.

"Malvinas!"

"My God! Pepe!"

Hugging each other, the two men did a little jig. With an arm around Pepe's waist, Cooper smiled at Barton. "Where'd the hell you find him? And so quickly?"

"Here," said Pepe.

"It was nothing." Barton appeared suitably humble. "Just that good old American know how."

"Plus a few Imperian phone calls," chipped in Conde.

Hugging Pepe, Cooper cocked an ear. "And speaking English, yet?" Cooper pinched a Pepe cheek. "The language of the enemy?"

Pepe laughed. "I fly now for VASP, Brasilian airline. English is the language of aviation. I took lessons."

"Now the reunion's over", said Barton caustically. "Can we get down to business?"

Cooper gave the DEA Agent a slow burn. "And Dick, what business is that?"

Barton lowered his voice. "The drugs business."

Cooper's arm was still around Pepe's waist. "Dick, last night? I told you everything I know, *everything*. Like the person you really needed was Pepe Babenco, and no sooner said than *voila!* He's here." Cooper patted Pepe on the back. "We get together before you leave?"

"Sure." Pepe grinned. "I bring the pinga."

"I'll drink to that!" Turning away, Cooper walked toward the stairs.

To feel an arm grabbed in a vice-like grip, himself being propelled right through the lounge and out on to the terrace.

"Look, you little Limey prick!" Slamming Cooper backwards against a wall, Barton put a hand on the Englishman's shoulder, the arm against his throat. "This is no fucking game, so don't fuck with me! Either you play ball or I'll have Conde arrest you!"

Cooper spoke with difficulty. "On what charge?"

Barton moved his face closer. "Cooper, he doesn't need a reason. Suspicion of drugs involvement? That is all he needs, man, just *that!*" He relaxed his grip.

Rubbing his throat, Cooper looked at the American. "How many *times* do I have to say it? I've told you *all I know!*" Said through clenched teeth.

"Possi's funeral."

"I told you! I've never even met the man."

"The wreaths? We had them all checked." Barton was smirking. "One was from you."

Cooper was stunned, overwhelmed. Circumstance was devouring him.

"So, to know he was dead, you had to have known him when he was alive, which to me means you know much more?" Barton put his face in Cooper's. "Much more than you've been telling us?"

The two just stared at each other.

"Leave me alone, Barton. I'm not your boy."

"They've killed Mendoza, they've killed Para, and when they killed Possi they also took out his wife *and* a prison guard. They don't care Cooper, they simply *don't* care!" Barton was prodding Cooper's chest. "I wonder who could be next?"

Cooper slumped. He regained his composure. "Dick, perhaps we could continue this conversation in the bar, where I can at least get a drink and a sandwich?"

They both munched ravenously. Barton had a cold beer, Cooper the inevitable large V and T.

"*You* know where their processing plant is." He leaned closer to Cooper. "Don't you want to find it before they find you? A movie company is very conspicuous, even in the Amazonian rain forest?"

Cooper finished his sandwich. He took a drink. Then he looked at Barton. "You have Babenco. What more d'you want from me? I've a movie to finish."

Barton caught the eye of the bartender. "Same again." He returned to Cooper. "You'll only get to finish your movie on my say so."

The drinks were served. Barton showed his room key. "Put it on my tab." Barton drank some of his fresh beer. "You finish off in L.A., right?"

"Right"

"So there's an H.1. visa application in the pipeline." Barton shook his head. "The I.N.S., the Immigration and Naturalization Service? Instructed already, 'Cooper, J., H.1. visa application, petitioner Tonnini International Pictures.' " As he drank, he spoke into his glass. "Denied!" Cooper felt the prodding forefinger again. "And that B.1. visa you hold already? Cancelled! You couldn't get into the United States even if you were God!" Barton swiveled on his stool, enjoying Cooper's visible shock and discomfort. "And forget about merry old England. Conde will see to it you stay here, in swinging Third World Imperio, with no job, no money, and if I recall, there is no extradition treaty with the U.K." Barton stared at the Brit. "So, Cooper? What's it to be?"

He sighed. "I have a choice?"

Barton nodded. "Yeah. Don't you guys call it 'Hobson's choice,' the option of taking what's on offer, however unpalatable, or nothing at all?"

"So what's on offer?"

"An H.1. visa."Adding quickly, "Maybe even your life. Who knows?"

The director looked in his glass.

"Cooper . . ." His tone was more affable. "I want that plant destroyed, I want the people running it and I want whoever is behind them . . . destroyed. You said so yourself, the airstrip is the *key*, and the only way I can think of finding it is to replicate that flight of yours?"

Cooper spoke quietly, and levelly. "You've got Pepe, he was the pilot." Sighing, Cooper shook his head. "I pilot movies, not planes."

A reminding finger was being pointed. "Your words, you said, '*Pepe was struggling to control a crippled plane.*' So, that as he had his hands full shall we say, isn't it more than likely *you're* the one who'd have recognized landmarks?"

Cooper felt jaded. "Possibly." He caught Barton's look. "Probably."

Barton made with his best Walter Matthau what-more-can-I-say expression.

Breathing-in deeply, he exhaled both slowly, and loudly. "Okay."

Barton gave him a resounding nudge. "It'll take a few days to set-up, similar plane, permission to fly into Colombia. Then we do it."

"When?"

"You get a day off, don't you?"

Cooper gave him his best you-must-be-joking look.

"Well, don't you?"

"Saturday."

"Great!" Barton opened his arms, expansively. "You don't have to suspend filming, hopefully we find the airstrip, and no schedules are interrupted."

Cooper eyed the American. "How quickly do I get the H.1.?"

"I'll call Monday."

"What's wrong with tomorrow?"

"You might change your mind." Barton smiled. "Before Saturday."

Cooper groaned. "Dick, my middle name's 'Hobson,' remember?"

"Nightcap?"

"Thanks. Cutty Sark. Triple. No ice."

Barton did a double-take.

"Jorge, can this all be set up for Saturday?"

"I would say so, yes." He studied Barton. "But, Dick. "It would no do any harm for the D.E.A. in Washington to liaise with the Colombian authorities, to back us up down there."

Before answering, Barton looked around the bedroom, as if fearing eavesdroppers. "This is our bust, Jorge, *ours*." He strived to sound not too pleading. "I don't want half the fucking agency taking the credit for it, so the fewer people who know, the better. *We've* done the leg work. *We* found Cooper, *we* found Babenco and *we'll* find the plant. Us!" He looked at Conde. "So screw Washington, okay? It's *you*. And *me!*"

Nodding agreement, Conde pressed delicately. "You don't think we should have a shadow plane with us, in case of trouble?"

"Like what?" Barton frowned. "What sort of trouble?"

"I dunno, Dick, but that my whole point, 'what sort'? So, should we not play it safe?"

Barton was pointing that much used forefinger. "Safety . . . is in secrecy. This is our bust, *ours*. I've done the groundwork on too many of these goddam cases." He pointed at himself. "And I'm not letting go now, so no, no shadow plane."

Conde fidgeted. "Whatever, Dick. As you say, it your bust."

SCENE 65. TAKE 4.

Cooper sat up front beside Pepe, Barton and Conde in the rear seats.

They had been flying for about thirty minutes. Pepe banked the plane into a shallow turn of one hundred-eighty degrees. "Okay, now we head for Santa Mosqueiro, just like before." The plane steadied. "James, what do you think? It seem about right?"

Cooper looked down, intently. "Ye. . . es." He rested his forehead on the plexiglass. "Yes, definitely! See that tree?" Cooper pointed. "That one there, look! The *green* one?" He pointed repeatedly. "I recognize it!"

Pepe giggled.

Barton leaned forward. "Y'know, Cooper, you don't have to live up to your flip reputation."

Cooper half turned. "Dick, I thought we were replicating the flight? Because I was much more glib, flip as you call it, then."

Sitting back, Barton mumbled. "Thank Christ I didn't know you then."

Pepe was pointing. "Santa Mosqueiro."

Cooper nodded. "That's it, that's how I remember it, only then it was under thick cloud."

Pepe checked the time. "Is only fourteen hundred now, too early for the daily downpour. That why we have sunshine and cumulus."

Looking at the city below, Cooper mused. *If we'd been able to land here that afternoon, would I be directing* Redmayne *now, the people who are dead, would they have still been alive?* Melancholia engulfed him. He wished he was alone.

Without warning, the plane banked steeply, and was losing height rapidly. Such were the G-forces created, everyone felt as if they were being pushed into their seat-backs.

Cooper studied the dials, particularly the fuel gauges.

"Don't worry. We have plenty of fuel", said Pepe, reassuringly. "But it was about here, this is where we turned that time, this where we start the run." He tapped Cooper's wrist. "Our record-setting glide."

"But we didn't make *The Guinness Book of Records*, did we?"

"I hate interrupting, but are we on course?"

Pepe took his hands off the controls, his mitts held aloft.

Barton was frustrated. "Surely you have *some* idea?"

"Sure, some, but that was when?" Pepe glanced at Cooper. "Nine, ten months ago?"

Cooper nodded. "All of that, and more."

"And, Mr. Dick, we had no reason then to remember, no reason to take notes." Pepe tapped his right temple. "And I don't have a black box recorder in here."

"Christ, this is like looking for a needle in the proverbial."

"No it's not, Dick, it's not." Cooper half turned again. "What we're looking for is a swathe, something long and straight cutting through the trees."

"How near do we have to be to see it?" Asked Conde.

Looking ahead, Pepe half turned. "Near? It depend on our altitude. The higher we are, the more we see."

Barton was scanning. "Then how high were you when you saw it?"

"Dick, we were out of fuel, running on fresh air. Pepe was willing the plane to stay up."

"How? High?"

Pepe continued his forward gaze. "Maybe sixty-meters. Just above tree top height." He scanned, and leaned. To the left and to the right. "If I have done correct, we are in the area now." He piloted a series of wide sweeps.

Cooper stiffened. "This going to be dangerous?"

Once again, Barton leaned forward. "Cooper, we're just the forward survey team, not the frigging Marines."

"Just checking."

As surreptitiously as possible, Conde scanned the skies, particularly those behind their plane . . .

Cirla was mesmerized. He watched the tiny blip on the radar screen, as the aircraft it represented made turns, runs, sweeps, more turns, more runs. "Antonio . . ." Without looking away from the screen, Cirla beckoned. "We have company."

Hands resting on the chair back, Rubio leaned over a Cirla shoulder. Both men watched the radar screen, absorbed totally.

"What d'you reckon?"

Cirla narrowed his eyes. "By the way it maneuvers, it's a small craft."

"Chopper or fixed wing?"

"Fixed wing." Cirla pointed. "Here it goes again."

"Crop spraying?"

Cirla spoke over his shoulder. "What, coca leaves?"

Rubio was silent.

"I think it's searching." Cirla leaned closer.

"How far away?"

Cirla concentrated on the screen. "About thirty kilometers. Just under nineteen miles." He scrutinized the image. "Though it doesn't seem to be getting any closer."

"Thirty kilometers is close enough. Which direction?"

"South east."

The aircraft leveled-off. Inconspicuously, Pepe nudged Cooper. "This could take months." He spoke just above the level of the engines. "Is not accurate enough."

Out of the corner of his left eye, Cooper looked, replying. "Should we be lower?"

Pepe was flying in a series of overlapping trapezoid paths, sweeping the same general area but moving always into new air space, covering a fresh part of the terrain.

"*Eee-aahhh!*" As Barton whooped, everybody was startled. "Look! There, over there!" He was jabbing forefingers. "That line? Straight through the trees!"

In a leisurely sweep, Pepe brought the plane lower, to obtain a clearer view. Of an electric power line, cutting through the jungle.

"Oh . . ." Said Barton.

"We fly now for three hours."

"How much more daylight?" Asked the American.

"About those same three hours."

"Well,"said Barton, looking out of the cockpit, but addressing the other three. "Until we find what we're looking for, we might just have to try again tomorrow, or the next day or the day after that."

Cooper spoke. "This plane's too small for histrionics, so I'll behave." He turned to Barton. "The running costs down here for Tonnini Pictures are in the region of one-hundred and twelve-thousand U.S. dollars *per day,* and for every day I'm away from the set and no shooting takes place, it'll cost. But I can rest assured, can't I Dick, that for every day I'm up here joy riding with you, the D.E.A. will compensate my company accordingly?"

Barton shifted in his seat. "Jim, I'm not empowered to answer that question." He looked at the director. "But I've a pretty good idea of what the answer would be."

"So have I," said Cooper, resignedly.

I wonder, thought Pepe, *I wonder.* He checked his watch. Fifteen-forty. Why not? I'll try it. He changed direction, albeit subtle, through only thirty-two lazy degrees, to the south east, towards Santa Mosqueiro, yet again . . .

For the first time in an hour, Roberto Cirla relaxed. He breathed in deeply, leaned back in the chair and exhaled loudly through puffed cheeks, watching the blip. Heading south south-east. Away from the hacienda. "That's it, you go home to mama baby, keep going . . . *adios.*"

The door opened. "I heard voices. Who you talking to?"

Cirla turned, gesturing to the screen. "Our friend? Like Peter, he fly away. I said, *adios.*"

Rubio lit a cigarette. "I asked Topete if he'd heard of anything."

"And?"

Rubio smiled. "No, nothing. Not a thing."

Cirla turned to the screen. "I wonder what they were looking for?"

Rubio nodded. "Whatever it was, they must have found it. Which reminds me," He looked at Cirla. "We've some looking of our own to do. Those flickering runway lights?"

"Oh, right." Recall dispelled the frown. "The drunk Cobb's complaint?"

"Correct. Apparently some are actually down now, so we'd better check them."

"But it's too light."

"Not this minute but say in a half hour?"

"Babenco, you jerking us off!" Barton was prodding Pepe on the upper arm. "Just 'cos I'm a gringo don't think I don't know Santa Mosqueiro when I see it!" With a thumb, he gestured over his shoulder. "Now, turn this thing around and get back out there!"

Pepe maintained his course, and his cool.

Which is more than Barton did, becoming more apoplectic by the second. "Goddammit Babenco! You heard me. Back!"

"Dick," whispered Cooper. "We all heard you."

"Mr. Dick," said Pepe evenly. "I am the pilot, I am the captain, and I am in charge. I will find your airstrip, *my* way." He glanced at Cooper, gestured ahead and winked. "*Chuva.*"

Cooper followed his gaze. "*Muito pesada?*"

Pepe grinned. "*Muito, muito!*" Winking again, he gestured Cooper to tighten his seatbelt.

The forward view was obscured as the windshield became mottled with heavy rain.

Pepe patted a Cooper thigh. Then pulled on the controls to the left. The aircraft banked steeply.

The turbulence started.

They were a Dinky Toy again, being tossed all over the place.

Cooper wondered if the two lines in *Daily Variety* and *The Hollywood Reporter* would credit him now with having directed *Redmayne West*?

Into the kamikaze dive they went.

"Pepe, it's, eh, okay. I didn't mean it and you're right, *you* are the boss and, eh, yes, you do it your way."

"*Si*, I do it *my . . . way.*" Pepe checked the instruments, scanned all horizons, patted Cooper on the thigh and . . . killed the engines. They were above the river. Like before.

Barton's words came out in jerks. Loudly. "Have, have we. . . stalled!?" His voice became more strained. "Lost power?" He looked at his fellow passengers. "We, we gonna crash?!"

Looking ahead, Cooper shook his head. "Dick, we're the forward survey team, not the frigging Marines!" He shrugged. "Remember?"

Barton pointed silently at Pepe's back, whispering. "Does he know what he's doing?"

"He certainly knows what he's doing. And in case he's got it right . . ." Cooper gestured. "Shouldn't you be ready with those cameras?"

Cooper glanced at Conde, doing a double take as the Imperian seemed more interested in what might be behind them. "Eh, *Sênhor*? If we find it, it'll be in front of us."

Conde smiled, weakly. "Excuse me."

"And *sênhor*, you'll need to get the co-ordinates from Pepe, to pinpoint the place."

In his lap, Barton had a Nikon, and a camcorder.

"Need any help?" asked Cooper.

"You know how to handle one of these?"

"Could Bogart act?" As Cooper tut-tutted, they were thrown about. "Updraught?"

"Yeah," replied Pepe. "But I need power now, otherwise we lose height too quick." Firing the engines, he pulled away from the river to the north-west, and under power, began a gentle descent.

It had stopped raining.

Still the sky was overcast heavily, with not much daylight available. All four men were silent, each searching their respective range.

And all the time, the small aircraft was descending . . .

Rubio looked at the darkening sky. "Now's as good a time as any." He delegated. "Topete, you wait here with the jeep, Roberto, you go into the operations room. I'll drive to the far end of the runway and when in position, I'll radio for the lights to be switched on. If any are out Topete, I'll guide you to them, and you mark them with the paint spray." He checked with his colleagues. "Understood?" They nodded.

Together with the spray can and walkie-talkie, Topete placed his Uzi automatic assault rifle on the passenger seat of the jeep.

Rubio climbed into the Range Rover, and drove away.

Cirla walked into the operations room. He glanced at the radar screen. No blips. No activity. He walked across to the radio, his back to the radar.

Which is when a blip appeared on the screen. At a heading of five o'clock. The image was creeping directly for the plant.

Rubio positioned the Range Rover in the direction of the hacienda. "Roberto, you read me? Over."

"Loud and clear."

Rubio looked about him. "Okay. Switch on the runway lights. Over."

On the console in front of him, Cirla flipped four switches.

Rubio saw the lights come on.

So did Pepe.

So did Barton. "There! Look, over there!"

"I see . . . I see." Pepe banked through forty-five degrees.

"Topete. The whole center section is out, both sides. Don't bother to mark them, there's too many and besides, nothing's due in tonight. We'll do it early tomorrow morning."

"Right, boss." Topete relaxed, taking a cigarette break while awaiting orders.

"Roberto? You hear me?"

"*Sí.*"

"Kill the lights."

"What happened? Where'd it go?" Yelled Barton. "We lost it!"

"No, no", said Pepe quietly. "I think I have a fix but please, no talking, don't distract me." Pepe kept his eyes on the spot, that spot some eight-to-nine kilometers away where they had just seen the lights.

Everybody quietened, each looking to their own horizon, where they could have sworn they had seen something. And praying it wasn't a mirage.

Conde. Now and then he looked. Behind.

Rolling along in the Range Rover and to overcome the noise of the A/C fan on full blast, Rubio had on the stereo. Loudly. He could not hear the approaching plane.

In the kitchen, Cirla was grinding coffee beans. He could not hear the approaching plane.

Topete was in the jeep, with the engine running. He could not hear the approaching plane. But. The jeep was facing the runway threshold. Topete saw the Range Rover approaching and beyond it, in the sky . . .

A dot.

Getting nearer.

"Target in sight!" Shrieked Barton. "*Eeee aahhh!*" He could hardly keep his seat, with excitement. "*Eeee ahhh!* There's the fucking runway!"

Cooper nudged the pilot. "How did you *do* it?"

Wordlessly, while looking sideways at Cooper, Pepe fumbled inside his shirt and held forth the Crucifix hanging around his neck. He winked.

Cooper felt his eyes moisten. He punched Pepe, playfully.

"Pepe?" From the rear seat came Conde's voice. "The co-ordinates please!"

In Portuguese, Pepe shouted out the latitude and longitude in degrees and minutes. Conde wrote frenziedly.

"*Eee aahhh!*" Yelled Barton. "*A-Fucking-Pocalypse-Now!*"

Why, Rubio wondered, why is Topete jumping up-and-down like a demented chimpanzee, and pointing to the sky?

And then. Topete spread wide his arms horizontally, making a diving motion. And pointed again. Skywards.

"No!" Screamed Rubio. He slammed on the brakes, the SUV slewing to a halt. Pushing open the door, Rubio stood on the sill, looking up. To see a small twin-engined Piper off to the right, some three kilometers away. Rubio grabbed the radio. "Topete! One chance, you have only one chance. For all our sakes, make sure you hit it!"

Using the camcorder, Cooper was filming in the advancing direction, while Barton was standing above Pepe, the pilot having leaned forward to help the agent take his photos.

With Pepe hunched over the controls, Conde looking increasingly to the rear and the other two men each looking through an image-reducing viewfinder prism, no one had noticed him . . .

Topete.

Standing in the jeep. With the Uzi at the ready. For steadiness, resting the weapon on the top of the windshield as he lined up on the aircraft. It was in his sights. Topete eased off the safety. His radio crackled into life with Rubio's voice, cool, calm and collected. "Topete, you may only get the one chance, one chance to bring it down." Rubio's voice rose. "Don't . . . miss!"

At some three-hundred-and-seventy meters, Topete fired two volleys, spraying within a narrow arc.

Simultaneously:

Thick black smoke poured from the starboard engine.
    Cooper ducked as the windshield shattered.
    Barton slumped, his whole weight falling on Pepe.
    The aircraft slewed.

"Get him off me, off!" Pepe was trying to extricate himself from under the inert mass of Barton. "I can no fly the *fooking* plane!"

Cooper leapt up, to be jerked stationary by his harness. Unlatching it, he pushed Barton off Pepe, Conde dumping the American back into his seat and fastening his safety belt.

Cooper inspected Barton. "He's been hit in the shoulder and upper arm." Cooper looked off. "There's blood everywhere He *is* human after all!"

Pepe shut down the smoking engine. "Come on baby, fly, fly, stay up, you are an *air*plane!"

As Cooper moved from Barton, once again Conde was looking out, rearwards. Cooper regained his seat. "Can we make it?"

Pepe blessed himself. "I hope."

"Santa Mosqueiro?"

"No way!"

Cooper was confused. "Then, where?"

"Here!" Pepe was pointing downwards. "Here!"

"Here? Pepe, that's where the bloody bullets are coming from!"

Pepe was fighting the controls. "James, we gonna crash. What you prefer? We crash in the jungle?" He shook his head. "Is better we make a crash land here. No trees on the runway." Pepe put the plane into as tight a turn as he dared.

Cooper found himself worrying. Had he put on clean underpants?

Still Conde was looking behind, checking both port and starboard, while Barton was unconscious.

The loud noise, the heat, the smell of burning. All were oppressive.

Almost parallel to the plane, the jeep sped along the runway, a euphoric Rubio at the wheel now, shouting. "Topete! Brilliant! You got him!" He was thumping the horn. "Now finish him off." Rubio halted the jeep.

Looking at the runway over his left shoulder, somehow Pepe coaxed the stricken aircraft through a turn, the plane losing height speedily. The Piper came around. Pepe leveled off. He had the plane lined up. For the runway.

Standing, Topete had the plane lined up. For the kill. The Uzi once again resting on the top of the windshield. The plane was in his sights.

The aircraft was slewing almost uncontrollably. Pepe's method of applying some control over the plane was done by advancing and then retarding the throttle of the one remaining engine. The groaning of the wounded Barton added to the mayhem of noise.

"James!" Pepe was pointing to the jeep, Rubio now at the wheel, Topete poised, behind the Uzi.

Cooper forced himself to look. "Christ! We're a sitting duck!"

"They're a sitting duck," said Topete to himself. He was relaxed, he was ready, the plane locked in his sights. As the craft slewed, Topete panned with it. He never took his eyes off the dropping plane. He fired off another volley.

Struggling frantically to control the unpredictable aircraft, Pepe looked on in horror as, seemingly in slow-motion, bullets ripped through the port wing.

Agonizingly, Cooper watched Topete take aim yet again. "Pepe! There must be *something* we can do!"

"We pray!"

As the plane neared the jeep, a transfixed Cooper stared at it, seeing Topete and then . . . the driver. "Conde! It's Vargas! Rubio, whatever you call him!"

More bullets ripped into the aircraft.

Boom! Bang went the other engine, bits exploding into space.

Rubio was jubilant. "Bullseye! Bullseye!"

Pepe was fighting a losing battle. The plane lurched violently. "I put the plane down on this runway if it the last thing I ever do!"

Now only a few feet off the ground, the plane almost fell out of the sky. Dipping, a landing wheel clipped the jeep. Killing instantly the standing Topete.

The aircraft dropped on to the runway like a wounded bird. Somehow, the landing gear held.

The noise was deafening.

So deafening, Cirla wondered what the hell was going on? He thought he'd heard a plane, the sound of automatic gunfire but now? All was ominously quiet.

Exiting the hacienda, Cirla jumped into a truck. As he cleared the buildings and drove on to the ramp, he was horrified to be confronted by a plane, powerless and fast sliding out of control, smoke streaming from both engines.

Neither the plane nor the truck had a chance of avoiding each other.

The aircraft slammed into the pick-up, the impact of which spun the vehicle, upturning it. The plane slewed, rocked, almost tipped over and then rolled . . . to a soundless halt.

All of them had collected bruises. There was no time to check if the blood was theirs or Barton's.

Cooper offered a hand to Pepe. "No time, James! Out, quick!"

Barton was slumped against the door. In Portuguese, Pepe yelled at Conde. Who climbed over Barton, opened the door, fell out, and then hauled Barton unceremoniously on to the tarmac.

Pepe was the last man out of the aircraft. "Get away from the plane!"

Conde and Cooper supported Barton. Cooper looked off. "Uh, uh. Company."

Advancing slowly, a phalanx of peasants confronted them, armed with an assortment of weapons—shovels, hay rakes, machetes.

"Pepe, you're the Spanish speaker. Tell 'em we mean no harm."

Pepe shook his head. "Anyone who take away their living, that means harm."

The jeep was bearing down on them.

And then a plane could be heard. And a chopper. Conde was scanning the sky. "There!"

When could be seen a small military aircraft and a helicopter gunship. The plane buzzed the strip as the helicopter came into land.

The peasant army fled.

"The Cavalry!" Cried Cooper. "Where'd they—"

"I call them," said Conde, quietly. "Colombian paratroopers. I request shadow plane when I get permission to fly in here."

Grabbing Conde's hand, Pepe pumped it furiously. "*Gracias, senor. Mucho gracias!*"

The group watched as the jeep was surrounded, Topete pulled out, Rubio apprehended. The Colombian was made to place his hands behind his head, whereupon his wrists were bound. An officer drove the jeep to where stood the group.

He looked at them. "*Senor Conde?*"

Conde stepped forward. "*Hola.*"

"*Capitain Lopez.*" The two men shook hands.

"*Capitain, su habla Inglês?*"

Lopez nodded. "Yes."

"Because my Spanish is no very good," admitted Conde.

Looking around, Lopez shook his head. "Your plane? I guess we were a little too late?"

Cooper was looking at Rubio, sitting in the back of the jeep, an armed soldier beside him, another up front. "Oh, no, Captain, oh . . . no." Watched warily by the soldiers, Cooper walked over to the jeep, observed also by Rubio. For several seconds, Cooper just stood, staring at the man. Then he spoke, very quietly. "You. You're a cold-blooded animal. And like that animal, hopefully you will be shot. In cold blood."

"Cooper . . . " Rubio spat. "The blind man."

"You rot in hell."

Capitan Lopez spoke to Conde. "I believe the arrangement is Imperio gets Rubio first." He looked around him. "In return for us getting the plant, and destroying it." Lopez indicated Rubio. "He will be handed over to the Imperian authorities at the Valdivia border crossing once the necessary orders have been finalized."

Conde nodded in the direction of Barton. "He hurt pretty bad. We need to get him to the hospital."

"The chopper will fly you all to Valdivia, where transportation to Santa Mosqueiro will be waiting. You'll be on your way very shortly." The soldier up front was ordered out of the jeep. "Put him in here."

Conde and Cooper walked Barton to the jeep, helping him in. He winced. "Y'know, I don't remember this being in the manual."

Conde stood beside Barton. "Soon be in Santa Mosqueiro."

Barton eyed him. "You had to do it, didn't you, Jorge, you had to get your back-up?" He looked at Conde. "Did you call Washington?"

"No, I did not. It still your bust."

"*Our* bust." He gestured to Pepe and Cooper. "All of us." He touched a Conde hand. "And thank God you did it, Jorge, thank God you didn't listen to me."

"Amen to that."

Looking at Cooper, Barton shook his head. "And I guess I was wrong about you?"

"Think nothing of it, Dick. Like Joe E. Brown said, '*Nobody's perfect.*' "

"I'll take him to the chopper. Then I'll come back for you guys." Lopez drove away.

At Santa Mosqueiro an ambulance was waiting to receive Barton. He was placed on a gurney and wheeled across the apron.

"Dick!" Cooper ran over, walking beside the gurney. "Dick, at the risk of seeming heartless, eh, what about my visa?" He looked down at the recumbent Barton. "What happens about my H.1. while you're in hospital?

Barton moved only his eyes. "Should be cleared within a coupla days, three max."

"How can you be so sure?"

Barton forced a smile. "I called the other night. As soon as you'd said 'yes' to today."

Pepe was waiting for him. "You okay?"

Cooper sighed. "I've got to get back to San Gabriel. But there are no more flights today and I'm working tomorrow."

Pepe put an arm around Cooper's shoulder. "I fly you up early in the morning, air taxi." He produced a small bottle, holding it in front of Cooper.

"*Pinga?*"

"*Malvinas!*"

Cooper giggled. "Just like the old days!"

"How about dinner and more *pinga*?" asked Pepe.

"*Malvinas!*"

SCENE 66. TAKE 2.

The intercom buzzed. "*Si*?"

"It's the editor, John Lincoln," said Kay. "D'you want to take it?"

"Put him through." Tonnini picked up a phone. "Yes, John?"

"I need a director."

Tonnini shrugged towards Seidelman. "What you mean, you *need* a director? An' I thought you the Stuart Baird of Tonnini Pictures?"

"Franco, I can't work miracles. I can edit, I can cut, but the fine honing? That can only come from a director. I came into this cold."

"Is why I bring you in."

"But I'm still *learning* the script. I need someone totally familiar with the material, someone with an overview, someone who can analyze what's on the screen, otherwise I'll be here for months, or stuck. Until this Cooper guy gets here."

Tonnini was level. "John, I hear you, okay? Leave it with me. *Ciao*."

Seidelman frowned. "Problems?"

Tonnini nodded.

"*Redmayne?*"

From the raised desk sitting on a plinth, Tonnini looked over his reading glasses. "We get problems with any other show?"

Seidelman smiled, shaking his head.

Having risen from his chair, with hands behind his back, Tonnini was pacing slowly, in the process of deliberating.

"What, exactly, *is* the problem?"

"Lincoln say he need director input." Pausing, Tonnini looked at his V.P. Business Affairs. "Or, more time."

Seidelman watched the pacing Italian. "And there's no way we can't wait until Cooper arrives?"

On the move, Tonnini was perusing his cuticles. "Don, I hope Lincoln *finish* cutting by the time Cooper get here, so then he free to work *with* Cooper." He paused. "On the video release—Director's Special Edition—while the pick up version for A.E.C. pass on to the sound, ADR, Foley, and music editors." He continued his pacing. Up and down, up and down, up and down . . . To stop. Grinning, he turned to Seidelman.

"What?"

Nodding like a shy girl, the grin grew coyly wider.

"Franco! What?"

Tonnini seemed like the schoolboy bursting to answer the teacher's question. "Anthony . . . Leef."

Closing his eyes, with outstretched arms Seidelman flopped back on the sofa. Inert. "You jest." He opened his eyes. "Yes?"

"Don, you know me." Tonnini flapped a hand. "I no joke."

Seidelman retained his pose. "Then what are you? A sadomasochist?"

"No, I a businessman. I have a movie I need edited quick. Leef? He direct some of that movie. The editor? He need help. An' Leef need work, need money. To me, is a simple equation. Leef's knowledge equal solving editor's problem." A forefinger pointed Seidelman-wards. "An' mine."

Seidelman sat up. "What about Cooper?"

"What about him?"

"Well, it's his movie."

Tonnini repeated the phrase, quietly. "It *his* . . . movie?" He leaned on his desk. "What you mean, 'it his movie'?" A Tonnini thumb jabbed his own chest. "It my movie. *Mine! I* buy the script, *I* finance the shooting an' post. *I* carry the bond! It *my* movie. Nobody else. An' certainly not Mr. Cooper's!" He thumped the desk. "*Mine!*"

"Franco." Seidelman raised an arm. "I'm not deaf."

"Sometimes, Don, sometimes I think you are."

Seidelman disregarded the remark. "You know what I mean. Cooper's directed the bulk of it, so in those terms it's 'his' movie?" Seidelman studied the marble floor. "Christ! Bringing back the director who walked." He glanced up at Tonnini. "What about professional etiquette?"

"Etiquette, *schmettiquette*! There you go again, Don." Tonnini could not believe his ears. "Fuck etiquette!" The remonstrating finger was in action. "You think etiquette a consideration in a multi-million dollar negative pick up, a deal which benefit you, an officer of this company an' a stockholder? What price this etiquette, eh, Don? What price!"

"Franco, I was merely playing devil's advocate."

"Then take your brief someplace else!"

"Okay, okay." Seidelman was shaking his head yet again, in resignation. "But you're skating on thin ice here. Cooper won't want his material screwed around with."

"What this, '*Sanctum Sanctorum*'?" Tonnini lowered his voice. "An' since when, Don Seidelman, since when you care about Mr. James Cooper, eh?"

His eyes closed, Seidelman put his head in both hands. In exasperation. "Pretend I never spoke."

Tonnini had sat down at his desk. "Leef. Who his agent?"

"Irving Resnick." Seidelman felt he should make a stand, argue against Tonnini's dangerous impetuosity. "Want me to call him?"

Tonnini flicked the intercom. "Kay, get me Irving Resnick right away, wherever he is. You have his car phone?"

Seidelman eyed his boss. "What screen credit would you give him?"

"When they ask, I answer."

"They'll ask."

The Lazio charm oozed like lava out of Mount Etna. "Irving, how are you? I just say here to Don Seidelman, I wonder what Anthony Leef up to? Such a talent . . . Do I have a movie for him to direct? Well, Irving, it funny you say that, but you know, he put this company in a very difficult position. He an' his fag short fuse, he screw us big time . . . What he have to do to get another movie from us?" He winked at Seidelman. "Well, what he do now? . . . Oh, considering offers. For what? His car, his house? Irving, Irving, no bullshit a bullshitter. He get no offers, he unemployable. I know this, you know this, the *whole* town know this! He hungry, no? Well, I need a job done an' Anthony Leef may be the man for it . . . No, no, not directing. *Redmayne West* still shoot, in Imperio, but I want a cut done of the movie within three weeks. Start now, I pay thirty-thousand dollars . . . Irving, Irving, listen. director's fee? Sure, he can have director's fee. By staying at home. Or, he can be working, making thirty grand, which is no bad money for three weeks' work? An' I tell you what, T.I.P. pay *you* his three grand commission, he get full thirty gees, okay? Screen credit?" Tonnini rolled his eyes. "How about 'creative associate'? No, no, Irving, don' put it to Anthony, say yes or no, man to man . . . Yes? Fine. I fax over a deal memo right away but he start tomorrow, *capis*? Call Don Seidelman to complete the deal. *Ciao*, Irving, *ciao*."

Tonnini replaced the phone. "How that for etiquette?"

SCENE 67. TAKE 1.

"Jimmer, do you know how many times you've done that?"

"Done what?"

"Read that friggin' call sheet?"

Cooper did so once more. "I still can't believe it." From the sheet he read aloud. *"Number ninety-five, bracket, last day of Principal Photography, end bracket."* Cooper looked at his friend. "Kurt, the *very* last one."

"Jeez, Jimmer, what are you going to do for reading tomorrow?"

"Well may you mock, Kurt Greene. Oh, and by the way, when we last worked together your surname was spelled G-R-E-E-N. Whence came the last 'E'?"

"It sounded like a bus terminal, y'know, *number Eighty-six, Kurt Green*? The last 'E' added class." Cooper eyed him through slitted lids. "Jimmer, my agent's idea, not mine. Scout's honor." Kurt winked.

David Langley called through his bull horn. "No tears now, folks, but we're ready for the very last shot. Stand by."

"Come on, Jimmer, they're playing our tune."

Two takes. Two prints.

"Check the gate!" First A.D. Langley looked at the director. "Do I get to say the magic words?"

"David, it's all yours." Cooper handed his script to a runner. "Put this in my car, please."

Langley bellowed through the bull horn. "Ladies and Gentlemen, sênhoras y sênhors . . . It's a wrap! *Adios . . . Redmayne West, adios Imperio!*"

The next thing Cooper knew his chair was being hoisted aloft with him in it, was carried to the river bank and tipped over, throwing him into the water. He surfaced. To see on the river bank, facing him, the whole crew singing *For He's A Jolly Good Fellow*.

Cooper stood, dripping wet, his clothes clinging to him as one and all clapped and cheered. Champagne was being poured, Barry Gillette and his team undertaking bartender duties. Wading in, Gillette placed into Cooper's hand a styrofoam cupful of bubbly. "Thanks, Ba. Who's doing the honors?"

"Kurt." Gillette put an arm around Cooper. "Till the next one?"

Cooper raised his cup. "To the next one, china." The cups didn't clink. They scraped. Like chalk on a blackboard. Cooper and Gillette shook hands and drank the wine.

Another splash into the water. Golda, styrofoam cup in hand, waded to Cooper and plonked on his lips the kiss of all kisses, so strong that the couple submerged, Golda on top. And surfaced. To even more cheers. She grabbed a Cooper arm, holding it high.

"What's this for?"

"I'll think of something."

"We need to talk. My suite. Breakfast tomorrow. Seven-thirty."

"Copy that."

Cooper raised a Golda arm. More cheers.

"Speech, speech!" Was the cry from the crew.

Cooper waded nearer to the bank. And raised his voice. "I know at the end of shooting, every director says 'I couldn't have done it without you.' But believe me, it's true. I couldn't . . ." Emotion got the better of him. He raised his cup. "But. It's true. *Obrigado, gracias*, and, thank you!"

The crew applauded Cooper's little homily.

In the evening light, sitting on the river bank, paddling in the cool shallow waters of the upper Amazon, with arms around each other, a movie director and his leading man polished off a bottle of champagne.

"Jimmer, Carole and me. We will get an invite?"

Scene 68. Take 2.

The breakfast trolley was wheeled in. By Golda. *"Bom dia!"*

"Besides the breakfast, got a pad and pen?"

"Never leave home without it."

"Okay, after breakfast I want you to do some shopping."

"Stores don't open until ten."

"Then check the hotel shop."

"For what?" A pause. "Coffee?"

"No, not for coffee!"

"I mean, do you *want* a cup!"

"Oh, yes. Please." It was passed to him.

Taking one for herself, Golda sat, waiting with pad and pen. "Poised."

"Presents. Charged to me personally. Give all the receipts to Con and he can deduct cost from my per diem. And I trust you to make the appropriate choices. By the way, when does the charter leave for Alentejo?"

"Demain. Zero-eight-hundred hours."

"Okay, I'll ride on that. Then book me on to L.A., First Class, one-way."

"Copy that. Now, presents?"

Cooper picked up a handwritten list. "Eh, Elaine, the camera crew, the three A.D.s, Barry Gillette, the sound recordist and boom man, and . . ." he smiled at Golda ". . . you."

She nodded, graciously. "James, being promoted to production supervisor was enough of a gift. I don't need another present."

"For once on this show, do as your bloody well told!"

"Copy that." She re-checked the list. "What about your chauffeur? And Pat Corcoran?"

"I'll take care of Rafael. And Pat will be with me in L.A. I'll look after him there."

Golda detected a mood change. "What?"

"Was Ramalho married, had he a family, dependents?"

"I'll check."

"I want them looked after."

SCENE 69. TAKE 1.

Taking Cooper to the Sovereign Hotel in Santa Monica, the limo chauffeur had routed sensibly via Lincoln Boulevard, rather than the four-o-five and then the ten.

Checking-in, he was handed a room key and two envelopes. He opened one, and read. *"Mr. Cooper. Welcome. If you wish to keep the limo for the rest of the day, feel free. A car will pick you up tomorrow morning at nine-thirty, for a meeting here with Mr. Tonnini, Mr. Seidelman and Mr. Lincoln. Yours truly, Kay Meyers. Executive personal secretary to Mr. Francesco Tonnini."* Cooper studied the note, thinking, *Who the hell's Mr.Lincoln? Surely not Abraham?* Then the second envelope. *But how would she know where I was staying? She'd call a secretary, dummy!'*

Trembling hands opened the envelope. Dollars. Lots and lots of dollars. His per diem.

Tipping the chauffeur, Cooper dismissed him and signed the register.

John Lincoln sat. "I thought the director was going to be here?"

"He will be," replied Tonnini. "But I wan' the three of us to talk first." He arose from his desk and gazed out of the large panoramic window. "How the edit going?"

"It's, eh, it's coming along."

Tonnini turned to the editor. "How many reels you cut so far?"

Glancing at Seidelman, Lincoln then studied the floor. "Three."

"Three?" Tonnini was visibly shocked. "Three!" Open-mouthed, he glanced at Seidelman. "I hear right? Three?"

"You hear right. Three."

Lincoln looked up. "Franco, your Mr. Leef? He's not the world's fastest, and if he could just get in before ten it would help."

"*Ten!*" Tonnini frowned. "What time he leave?"

"You mean at the end of the day?"

Tonnini sighed. "What else?"

"Lunch," said Lincoln. "He takes a leisurely lunch, and not just around the corner on Melrose."

"What time he go to lunch?"

"Around twelve-thirty."

Tonnini rolled his eyes. "When he come back?" The producer again looked to Seidelman, he sitting on the edge of the sofa, fascinated.

"As I said, he likes a leisurely—"

"How leisurely!" Snapped Seidelman. "What *time* does he return?"

"Around two-thirty."

Shaking his head in disbelief, Seidelman continued. "Then tell us, John. What time does he usually go home?"

Lincoln was floor gazing again. "He's always gone by five."

"*Five!*" Tonnini had fingers to temples. "I no believe this!"

Seidelman spoke, quietly. "It works out at some four-hundred dollars per *hour*."

"And sometimes," added Lincoln. "He just naps."

An angry Tonnini pressed the intercom. "Kay, get me Irving Resnick!"

He shook his head, sighing deeply. "Three reels . . ." He eyed Lincoln. "We neg cut them yet?"

"How can we? None of the sound editors are on, so we've recorded no tracks, done no track-laying, no Foley, no ADR, so, no premixes." He trod cautiously. "There's no way we can neg-cut until an approved fine cut and an answer print?" He eyed his inquisitors. "Approved by the director?"

The intercom squawked. "Mr. Resnick, line two."

Dispensing with pleasantries, Tonnini switched up the phone. "Irving, you on the speaker, okay?"

"Okay, Franco. And good morning to you too."

"I have with me Don Seidelman and the editor. Now, when you speak to your client, Mr. Leef, what hours you say to him?"

"Hours?"

"*Si*, hours! You know, like when he come, when he go?"

"I, eh, I didn't mention any hours to him. I guess whatever is normal industry practise."

"You call five hours a day *normal?*" Covering the speaker, Tonnini spoke to Lincoln. "Where you based?"

"Reverb. It's on Cahuenga."

"They a time clock there?"

Lincoln nodded. "I guess."

Tonnini cleared the speaker. "Franco, you still there?"

"Irving." A Tonnini digit stabbed the desk top, in sync with each and every word. "Tell your client the hours are eight-thirty to six. One hour— one! For lunch, an' he punch in and out with a time card!"

"A time card? Franco, this could be a deal breaker."

"Fine, Irving, it the deal breaker," said Tonnini reasonably. "I look forward to your client's next movie." He smacked the switch. He spoke to nobody in particular. "He be there, don't worry."

"How do I keep them apart?" asked Lincoln.

"Who we talking about?" replied Seidelman.

"Leef, and the director, what's 'is name?"

"Cooper. James Cooper."

"They in separate rooms, no?" Tonnini squinted. "So worry more about getting the work done."

Lincoln looked from one to the other. "But what if they meet?"

"So they meet!" The Italian was losing his patience. "They say 'hello' or 'fuck you,' who care?"

The debate was interrupted by the intercom. "Mr. Cooper is here."

Tonnini glanced at the desk clock. "Right on cue. The English? They *have* to be on time, to remind us Italians we Italian."

Cooper entered.

"So, the prodigal son, he return." They shook hands.

"I don't see the fatted calf." Then he noticed Seidelman. "Oh, I don't know though . . ."

Seidelman rose, shaking hands with Cooper. "Hi, James. On schedule and even slightly under budget. Good deal."

"Thank you, Don."

Lincoln stood. "John Lincoln, editor." He smiled at Cooper.

Cooper was confused. "Editor? " In turn, he glanced at both Tonnini, and Seidelman. "*My* editor is Pat Corcoran, who'll be here the day after tomorrow?"

Tonnini nodded at Seidelman. Who got the message. "He won't."

Frowning, Cooper faced Seidelman. "Why not?"

"Because he was taken ill. Stomach trouble. As he'd dispatched all of the material here, we figured it better to send him directly back to London."

Like Queen Victoria, Cooper was not amused. "It would have been nice to have been told?"

"You were *en route.*"

Cooper returned to the editor. "Nice to meet you, John."

They shook hands. Cooper sat. Lincoln relaxed. Visibly. "I was about to ask you, James, when can we expect the final footage?"

"The U.P.M. arranged for it to travel on the same flight as me. It made last night's bath, so it should be off around now, and, the quarter inch sound tapes, for transfer."

"Terrific."

"You get all Pat's notes, logs?"

"Yup." Lincoln nodded forcefully. "Everything. He's a very meticulous guy."

"And a not half bad editor." Cooper smiled at Lincoln. "I guess you're itching to get started?"

"Well, actually I've already—"

Tonnini jumped in. "He have difficulty in keeping his hands off the material, don't you, John?" Added Tonnini. Pointedly. "But he wait, he wait till you get here." Tonnini spread his hands, as if on that balcony overlooking the piazza of St.Peter's. "Now, James . . ."

Cooper did a surreptitious scan of the Italian. No ring, no wedding band but as Cooper thought to himself, *Do Italian men wear a wedding ring? So, for all I know, the two of them may be married by now? How the hell do I find out, who can I ask? It's simple, Cooper. You can't.* "Yes, Franco?"

"How long, to fine cut?"

"Franco, I've only just got off the plane, but, that'll be after my director's cut."

"Not D.G.A. James." It was Seidelman. "We've discussed this before, you and me?"

"I thought you'd granted me director's—"

"James, we very busy at Tonnini International now, an' we need to finish *Redmayne* a.s.a.p. So, any way you can help us . . . ?"

Cooper nodded at the editor. "It depends more on John than me. He's the one to get familiarized with the material."

"I'm okay with the footage, I know it fine."

"I thought you said you *hadn't* touched it," said Cooper, tersely.

"Eh, no, I haven't." Said Lincoln, sheepishly. "I, eh, I've run the cutting copy a few times, yeah, the cutting copy." Lincoln glanced at Tonnini briefly, disliking intensely the deception being perpetrated, not so much for Cooper's sake but more for his own, as it made him extremely uncomfortable trying to remember what, and what not, to say.

"When do we start?" Asked Cooper, looking around the room.

"Tomorrow, first thing."

"James, you familiar with L.A.?"

"Nothing a *Thomas' Guide* can't show me."

"We're at Reverb, Cahuenga and Franklin. The dailies will be synched.

You okay with viewing them on the Kem?"

"Sure."

"Great. Then straight into editing?"

"You bet." Cooper stood. "Franco, you've seen the footage?"

"Of course!" Said without batting an eyelid. "Every frame."

"And?"

Tonnini scanned the room. "What can I say?"

Cooper chuckled. "I think you've just said it." He nodded to himself. "Okay, eight-thirty it is." He crossed to the door.

"James, you no tell me?"

"What?"

"Fine cut?"

Cooper looked at the editor. "Three, four weeks, max?"

"Should be do-able."

Tonnini was like a fussing hen. "Now, James, you go see Kay, she look after your rental car, you go relax, prepare yourself for tomorrow."

Cooper said his farewells.

Tonnini stared at the closed door, willing Cooper *not* to return. He didn't. Rubbing his hands gleefully, Tonnini pointed at Lincoln. "You think he serious?"

"About what?"

"Fine cut." Tonnini beamed. "Three or four weeks?"

Lincoln was non-committal. "He knows his capacity better than anyone."

Tonnini looked at Seidelman. "Is fantastic, no?"

No one else seemed fired with Tonnini's excitement. "It is?"

Tonnini nodded, energetically. "*Si!* If Cooper do it in three weeks, four max, then it solve the problem. Looping, Foley, effects, all that shit." He looked at the two men. "It mean we do it all at once."

"Franco." Seidelman made a face. "Once Leef's gone, who supervises that version, the pick-up? Who directs the actors at looping?"

"Cooper!"

Seidelman studied the Italian. He deliberated. Has he flipped, finally? "But, Franco—"

"Don, is *so* simple." He looked from one to the other. "Theatrical will be picture cut by Leef . . ." He gestured to Lincoln. "Together with John, per the pick up deal, one a hundred minutes. But as it shorter, Cooper supervise the sound effects, Foley, A.D.R., music." He rounded on Seidleman. "We a composer booked, an' a fixer?"

Seidelman was subdued. "We need to talk about that later."

"Where was I?"

Lincoln chipped in. "Post. Cooper."

"Right. Whatever looping Cooper do, it has to fit the shorter version."

"And," interjected Lincoln, "The dialogue editor will have selected those speeches which need looping."

"Right. So Cooper none the wiser? He think he cut for theatrical, while what he actually cut is the Director's Special Edition video release." Tonnini waved an indifferent hand. "An' if Cooper find out there a shorter version, we say *that* is the network TV version. He buy it, you see, an' we get all our sound done *by* him, within the one post schedule, an' on time to deliver the pick up." He looked at each of them. "*Perfecto?*"

Lincoln nudged the business affairs chief. "If I submit a p.o. for a set of roller blades, will you okay it?"

A quizzical look on his visage, Seidelman turned to face Lincoln. "What *are* you talking about?"

"Well, as I see it, that's what I'll need to zoom silently between Cooper's editing room and Leef's?"

"I got it!" Tonnini smacked a palm. "We split the shift! Cooper by day, Leef at night!"

Lincoln's head snapped up. The shock on his demeanor was evident.

"What? What I say?"

"When do I *sleep*?"

Tonnini giggled. "During a Leef meal break. That plenty enough time?"

Cooper decided on lunch, and then back to the hotel, read through the script once more checking his notes along the way, and as Tonnini suggested, an early night, the long flight from Imperio having left him jet lagged.

He parked at the hotel, and took a cab downtown. *Ivy at the Shore* was his lunch venue, followed by a brisk walk along the length of Santa Monica pier, to aid the digestion, and, lungs-full of ocean air would make him sleep more readily. He hoped.

While reading his script notes, he recalled the morning conversation in Tonnini's office. He had to find out. He dialed International.

"Golda?"

A sleep-laden reply. "Who is it?

"Your favorite director."

"James, d'you know what bloody time it is down here!"

"Yes, Golda, I do and I apologize. Sincerely. But I wouldn't have called if it wasn't important."

"Okay, so what's so *bloody* important?"

"Pat Corcoran. Was he sent back to London because he was ill?"

"Ill? James, what are you talking about? He wasn't ill. I had a fax from Seidelman saying that Pat wasn't needed in L.A., and that I should send him back to London together with the rest of the U.K. crew. Why, what's up?"

Livid, Cooper kept his cool. "Sorry to disturb you, Golda. Sweet dreams. *Ciao.*"

From the minibar, Cooper fixed himself a large V and T with ice 'n slice. What, he wondered, what game is being played by Tonnini and Seidelman, the Leopold and Loeb of movie-making, because as sure as God made little apples, they are up to . . . something?

"My, I've been in an airport many times, but Nessa, I don't see nothing like this." Despite being in the United States for over forty years, the German background of Mrs. Or, 'Frau' Preiss. was very evident in her heavily-accented speech, as she marveled at the perceived opulence.

Nessa smiled, awkwardly. "Mom, it's just the First-Class lounge."

Mrs. Preiss looked adoringly at her daughter. "Nessa, you know I love seeing you, but . . ." Her gesture to the room was one of wonderment. "A phone call would have been cheaper?"

"I know, but I not only wanted to hear you say it . . ." She smiled at her mother, "I wanted to *see* you say it."

"That important, huh?"

Nessa was nodding and smiling at the same time. "Yes, *that* important." She squeezed her mother's hand, as Mrs.Preiss placed a hand on top of that of her daughter's.

"All worked out, no regrets?"

Nessa smiled. "I never realized before how certain parts of my life lacked direction, like you know, *you* have to make things happen, even role models in you and daddy."

"Miss Preiss? Excuse me." An airline agent was standing beside them. "The L.A. flight is boarding."

"Thank you." She turned to her mother. "Once I'm settled, I'll call you."

Mrs.Preiss had tears in her eyes.

"Mom, it's a time to be happy, not sad." Nessa took both of her mother's hands in hers. "And I owe it to you, for pointing the way."

The handkerchief of Mrs.Preiss alternated between the dual activities of eye dabbing and nose blowing. "Nessa, you know it is the father of the bride what pays for the wedding, but with your papa gone . . ."

"Mom." Nessa giggled. "He's always been okay for money. I don't think it'll be a problem."

They hugged their goodbyes.

Apart from her mother, Nessa had not told a soul when she was arriving at LAX, so there wasn't waiting for her a Hoffman lady nor a Music Express car and driver. She considered her next move. And to Nessa came a clear decision. Move is what she had to do now, while there was still time, while the way ahead was still simple.

A taxi? Take the Blue Van? Or rent a car? Rent? Why do that when my beloved Mercedes convertible is sitting in the garage of the Siena Way house? A further thought struck her. ***My** Mercedes? In who's name is* it? She stood in line for the Hertz courtesy bus.

"Welcome to the Radisson Bel Air Summit, Miss Preiss. Upper level, lower level, smoking, non?"

"Non smoking, upper level," thinking, *That way I don't have to run the gaunlet of the public areas.*

"O . . . kay. Just complete the registration card."

Nessa did so, giving as her address 237, Morrisey Street, Madison, N.J. 07940.

Settled in the room, Nessa stood by the phone, thinking. She snapped her fingers. *Thursday! Her day off!* She dialed the direct line of the housekeeper. And as she had hoped, there was no reply. She picked up the keys of the rental car.

Nessa stared at the closed gates, remembering her gate-opener was clipped to the sun visor of the Mercedes, which was in the garage. She looked at the security phone set in the pillar. "Come on, Nessa," she whispered. "It was six numbers, Franco's birthday, one twenty-six, and his ex-wife's, but what was Sofia's birthday, *what* are the other damn three entry code numbers?"

Reckoning there was something in the order of five-thousand permutations to punch in on the dial of the touch phone before she might luck out and get the month and day of the ex-wife's birthday, the prospect daunted her. Then she remembered. The little gate hidden in the foliage for emergency use by the gardeners.

It took her less than fifty minutes to pack, less than fifty minutes to remove all and any signs that Nessa Preiss had ever resided in this house.

As she reactivated the alarm system, Nessa looked at the keys on her Gucci gold chain. *Do I leave them or . . .* Pocketing the keys, a few minutes later she was driving away from the house. She never looked back.

The following morning.

Tonnini was reading the *Calendar* section of the *L.A. Times*. The hall clock chimed eight. Looking both at a small phone book and dialing, he waited for the phone to be answered.

"Yes?"

"Anthony?"

"Who's this?"

"Francesco Tonnini."

There was a vocal standing to attention. "Oh, Franco, yes, good morning, *bon giorno*. Eh, what, what can I do for you?"

Tonnini was glancing at the newspaper. "What you work on now?"

"Eh, I . . . I don't quite understand?"

"You do a job for me but it *not Redmayne West*. Now you understand?"

"Oh, eh, yes. Perfectly."

He turned pages. "Anthony, where you live?"

"Brentwood. Canyon View Drive."

"Ummm . . ." Tonnini checked his watch. "That give you only twenty minutes to get to the editing rooms at Cahuenga. An' all that traffic on Sunset? Twenty minutes!" As he slammed down the phone, already he was into *Daily Variety*.

Having placed on the table a freshly brewed *caffettiera* of coffee, housekeeper Gina was fiddling with plates and cutlery, movements guaranteed to irritate Tonnini. In their native Italian, he spoke from behind the journal.

"Gina, what's on your mind?"

"Nothing, Signor Franco. Just tidying."

Tonnini lowered the paper. "Why tidy an already immaculate table?" They looked at each other. "Gina, we've been together longer than me and all of my wives put together."

She clasped her hands, twisting them constantly. "I don't know how to say it."

"Then try?"

"It's Signorina Nessa."

"What about her?"

"She's gone."

With exasperation, Tonnini regarded his housekeeper. "Gina, I know she's gone. She's been gone for a week, to her mother's, remember?" He resumed his reading.

"Signor Franco, I mean she's gone, left, gone for good? Her clothes, all her things, gone, all gone. It's like she was never here."

Tonnini lowered the magazine. "Show me."

He followed her into a guest room. She slid open the closet doors, revealing the wardrobe space. Empty. Except for a few clothes hangers, some with plastic gown covers dangling from them.

Gina opened drawers. All empty.

The bathroom was the same.

"So maybe her things are back in the master bedroom? We should look in there."

"Signor Franco." She disliked having to be the one. "I have. Already. They are *not* there. Even the laundry has been cleared."

Tonnini wondered if he was supposed react like Charles Foster Kane, when Susan Alexander walked out of Xanadu. But there weren't any props with which to play the scene.

Skipping down the back stairs, Tonnini hurried through the large kitchen and outside to the garage block. He barged in. The Mercedes convertible was still there.

Having returned to the breakfast room, Tonnini poured a cup of coffee, checked the speed dial on the phone, and pressed seven.

"Hal . . . low?"

His eyes went up into their lids. "Mrs.Preiss, is Francesco Tonnini. I wish to speak to Nessa."

"I am sorry, Mr. Tonnini, but she has left. Yesterday."

He frowned. "An' where she go?"

Mrs. Preiss hesitated. "She did not say."

"Well then, does she come back to Los Angeles?" Asked testily.

"Possibly. I really don't know." She was deliberately vague.

"Thank you." For nothing, he thought. "If she call, have her call me. *Danke*." Ugh! Germans! Tonnini sipped his coffee, wondering, trying to recall the last time a woman had walked out on him. If ever at all.

Scene 72. Take 1.

The post schedule had been published.

Specialist facilities had been booked for the recording and premixing of ADR, sound FX, Foley, music, and then, the final mix.

With Lincoln sitting beside him at the Kem flatbed editing machine, Cooper ran the scene, the two men watching the action unfold. Cooper repeated the operation thrice.

He stared at the now-blank screen. "That arsehole Leef . . ."

"Shhh!" Lincoln was scared visibly.

Turning, Cooper studied his editor. "What's up with you?"

"Oh, eh, nothing, nothing. But you never know who's listening?"

Cooper was amused. "Like who?"

"That's just it. You never know?"

Cooper did a double-take, the action of the editor confirming in his own mind that all Californian's are paranoid. He pondered if it had anything to do with earthquakes? Cooper returned to the Kem. "As I was saying," his eyes darting rapidly hither and thither, Cooper whispered, "that arsehole Leef." He resumed normal speech. "Would forget his head if it wasn't screwed on to his neck." The director ran the scene yet again and again, saying nothing, but shaking his head and sighing, constantly.

Lincoln studied the screen. "I think I know what's bugging you?" With a wax pencil, he tapped the prism. "Would it be the tying together of Ruth *and* the alligator at one and the same time, in the same frame?"

Cooper smiled. "Seidelman said you're a good editor." He sipped coffee. "When I first saw an assembly of this sequence, I knew then, and *I* wasn't directing, but I knew then we were light about three or four shots, cuts." He shrugged. "I wanted to give Leef the benefit of the doubt and put it down to first day jitters, reckoning it could always be picked up later, but, who was to know the fate of Susan Chase? Even so, fundamentally, Leef fucked up."

Lincoln flinched.

Another Cooper double-take. "You got a built-in Richter Scale, you know when the big one's coming?" Shaking his head, he glanced at the Editor. "Anyway, we picked up a couple of shots down there using a double, but as Susan Chase had left, I never got that one all important linking shot." With a forefinger, Cooper stabbed the screen. "And I know more than ever now, we need it—we *absolutely* need it."

Lincoln nodded agreement. "And not only dramatically but to establish the geography of the scene?" The editor took a sly glance at his watch. "Would you excuse me?"

"You screwing someone's wife?"

Not replying, Lincoln departed. Cooper thought it odd the editor took with him a notebook, especially as he left behind the one marked *Redmayne West.*

When Lincoln returned, Cooper was on the phone. "Thanks, Kay. See you shortly." Replacing the device, Cooper gestured to Lincoln. "I've a meeting with Franco. I'd like you to come with me."

"Sure, no problem." He pointed to the Kem. "I guess you want to run the sequence?"

"I dunno." Cooper chuckled. "My experience of the Tonnini's of this world and studio and creative executives in general is they're incapable of analyzing a piece of film unless it has been looped, contains all necessary edits and opticals and has a fully mixed track of dialogue, sound effects and music."

Lincoln laughed aloud.

"Can they run double-head in the Tonnini screening room?"

"Sure, they show dailies there for the old man."

Cooper indicated the two small cans of film. "Did you cut in the *Scene Missing* insert for the Susan Chase shot?" Lincoln nodded. "Bring it, but we use the sequence only as a last line of defence."

Ushered in to the Tonnini office, Cooper and Lincoln sat.

"So, how it go? How near to a *Redmayne* fine cut?"

"We're almost there", said Cooper. "Just a few more days."

Tonnini nodded. "You do well." Tonnini looked at Lincoln. "An' you, you do *well*?" He asked, pointedly.

The editor snatched a sidelong glance at Cooper. "On schedule."

Clapping his hands then rubbing them briskly, Tonnini beamed. "This is . . . *great*." From his raised desk, he looked down on the two men. "But. What so important you 'ave to drop everything an' come here?"

Cooper inhaled deeply, held it . . . and exhaled, at the same time speaking rapidly. "I need to shoot one more day!"

Tonnini jerked taut. "Shoot! Shoot?" He looked at each man in turn. "What nonsense this?" He flipped the intercom. "Don, step into my office." He stood, eyeing the two men. "What you think this is! *Bladerunner*? *Fatal Attraction*? *Heaven's Gate!!!*" Tonnini looked to Cooper, to Lincoln, and back to Cooper.

Seidelman entered.

Tonnini pointed to the two silent men. "Sacco and Vincetti here give me both good news an' a bad."

Seidelman remained standing. "Okay, I'm a big boy. What's the bad news?"

Tonnini pointed to Cooper. "You tell. You tell Don, in case I no hear right first time."

"I need to shoot one more day."

Seidelman looked at the ceiling, nodding his head in sync to the spoken words. "One. More. Day." His head moved down from the ceiling.

Turning slowly, he looked at Cooper. "Why?"

"The Susan Chase alligator shot? We don't need to go to Imperio, it can be shot here on a studio back lot. With minimum set dressing. So, minimum crew." He looked pleadingly at Seidelman. "But, Don. We need it, desperately."

Frowning at Cooper, Seidelman turned to Lincoln. "You agree?"

"One hundred percent."

"Who miss it if it not there?" asked Tonnini, dismissively. He eyed Cooper. "How much it cost?"

"Gimme a few minutes and maybe a drink?"

The intercom. "Kay, send in some ice, please."

While Cooper calculated, each did and had his own. Sparkling water for Tonnini, bourbon on the rocks for Seidelman, iced tea for Lincoln and a large Scotch for Cooper. *Sans* ice, of course.

The calculations were finished. Cooper looked at both Tonnini, and Seidleman. "No interruptions, okay?" They nodded an affirmative. "A normal L.A. day for us would be around one hundred twenty-five thousand dollars. As I need only Susan Chase and a stand in, and a minimal crew, this'll be about a third of that cost, if not less."

"You no want none of the crew you 'ave down there? The D.P.?"

"No. Any lighting variations can be fixed when we time the print." He gestured to both Tonnini and Seidelman. "The only crew I want from previously is the animals wrangler, Joe Tors, and his team, all of whom are L.A.-based."

Seidelman stood, gesturing to Tonnini. "While we're both familiar with creative accounting, I don't follow your math?"

He looked from one to the other. "Leefe needed video assist. I don't. I elbowed it and sent it, and the crew, packing. The production designer? Once he was shipped back to the U.K., I stopped his salary. Those two items alone are a cost saving of over a hundred grand."

"But he went back by air ambulance. What was the cost of that?"

"In the claim for the Fort set, which was approved, I padded some of the accounts. His air ambulance costs and those of Susan Chase? They were that padding."

Seidelman was smiling. "O . . . kay." He looked directly at Cooper. "But the Brasilian art assistant? You were going to promote him. Wasn't any of the designer money used for that?"

"I only gave him a different title. I didn't give him a different salary."

Tonnini was becoming impatient. "When?"

Seidelman turned to his boss. "When *what*!"

"When we shoot this day?"

Cooper couldn't believe his luck. He decided Scotch, a theatrical swallow thereof, was needed. All eyes were on him. "Subject to Susan Chase's availability, as soon as possible."

Tonnini checked his nails. And his palms. "You have your one day but, it only *one* day." He shrugged. "If it rain or snow that day, too bad. One day. Not a second more!"

Seidelman looked around the office. "We done?"

As papers were being gathered and shuffled, Tonnini held aloft a sheet. "No." He waved the paper above his head. "The post schedule? I no see anything here about music?"

Cooper frowned. Crossing to the Tonnini dais with outstretched hand, he read the schedule. And looked at Seidelman. "I thought we had a deal?"

"What are you talking about?"

"Santa Mosqueiro? You pleading for a doctor, me saying in return you allow me choice of composer, remember?"

Seidelman stiffened.

"He right? What James say?"

He nodded.

"Then what happen?" asked an incredulous Tonnini.

"I forgot."

A backhand rested on Tonnini's shaking brow. "I no believe this."

At the drinks cabinet, Seidelman fixed himself a very large bourbon, with less ice. Drinking, he continued studying the wall.

Cooper broke the impasse. "Franco, may I suggest we get Kay in here to take notes, and I'll map a way out."

By now, a silent and subdued Seidelman had resumed his seat, lost in his thoughts.

"Kay, head this *Redmayne Music*." He looked to the secretary. "D'you take shorthand by any chance?"

She smiled. "I guess this gives away my age, but yes, I do shorthand."

"Great. Now, one. Music editor, on board a.s.a.p. Once fine cut's done, I sit with him and plot music. Two. Find an L.A. recording studio that also has a dependable affiliate in Sao Paulo, Brasil. Three. T.I.P. makes a deal with my choice, Eduardo Homrich. No residuals, full buyout, all media, in perpetuity. He speaks clear English and will be glad of the money, preferably dollars U.S. Four. Send music editor to Sao Paulo to go through plots with Homrich. Allow three weeks for Homrich to compose, book fixer and Sao Paulo recording studio accordingly. To be paid in dollars. Then have tapes couriered up here, in time for the final mix." He gestured to Kay. "You get all that?" She nodded. Cooper looked around him. "Any questions?"

Tonnini chuckled. "Just one. fine cut. *When?*"

Cooper eyed Lincoln. "Five days?"

The editor nodded.

"Okay, it settled. Kay type up the memo an' we struggle on." He gestured to Cooper. "James, tell me, can you read music?"

"As a matter of fact, yes, I can. I also play piano. Why?"

"Just curious."

Sensing another Tonnini trap, Cooper withdrew, with Lincoln in his wake.

"You hear that, Don? Cooper can read music and play piano."

"Limey know all. I bet he copulates standing up. In a hammock."

What, Cooper wondered, *what does she look like now? Has the experience scarred her? What about the continuity? Is she still 'Ruth'? Has she got over it or does she look little better than when I saw her last, crammed into a crate, terrified out of her wits?*

"The Finney residence."

"Is Mrs.Finney available?"

"May I say who is calling?"

"James Cooper. I'm the producer of *Redmayne West.* Oh, and the director. Of *Redmayne West.*" He waited.

"Hello?"

"Susan?"

Hesitation. Followed by a gasp. "Rubenstein? And has my maid got it right? *Director?*"

"She has it right."

"What happened?"

"It's a long story, a very long story, but you were instrumental in it's happening."

"I was?" said in a tone of surprise mixed with disbelief. "Are you in L.A.?"

"Santa Monica."

"You know Beverly Hills?"

Dead pan defense time. "Sure. She's an opera singer."

"That's Beverly *Sills!*" shrieked Susan. "Well, do you? Know Beverly Hills?"

"Pretty well."

"Why not come up for cocktails?"

"Love to."

"You have the address? We're up behind the Beverly Hills Hotel. In about an hour?"

"Just like Lens Crafters."

All the time Susan was chatting, Cooper could not but help looking at Victor Finney, sitting in his wheelchair. Once or twice their eyes met, and Finney smiled, adding considerably to the Englishman's discomfort and self-loathing, knowing he had made a cuckold of the man.

"And . . ." said Susan. "There just aren't any meaningful roles for women, not anymore."

"Television?" asked Cooper.

Susan grimaced. "Same old story. Sponsors want the youth market, the networks are angling for a younger audience, *everything's* oriented to them."

"We're all dinosaurs, at thirty-plus onwards."

Susan smiled. "There's a lot of truth in Victor's words." She looked at Cooper. "The studio creative executives are all so young they think Cary Grant is a double malt and Orson Welles a desert spa resort . . ."

They sipped their drinks.

Finney nodded to Cooper. "So, what are you doing here in L.A.?"

"Post. I'm busily editing." He studied Susan. "And the reason I called Mrs.Finney here . . ." Cooper wished he could see behind the veiling sunglasses. "I need to shoot a couple of extra shots overlooked by Anthony Leef."

Finney nearly choked on his martini. "Don't you just love that British understatement . . . *'overlooked'* by Anthony Leef?"

Susan was happy. Because her husband was happy. "What are these shots? Not Imperio?"

Cooper shook his head. "No, no, here in L.A. A studio back lot." Leaning forward, he rested forearms on thighs. "Remember the first day of shooting, Ruth in the water just before the alligator attacks?" Susan nodded. "I need—the sequence needs—a shot seeing you and the reptile in the *one* frame, *at* the same time."

She absorbed what had been said. "How will you do it?"

Cooper sat-up, arms outspread. "On a wide angle. We see the alligator short-sided right of frame. It starts moving towards camera, then your dripping wet head raises up into left of frame, facing out left, your back to the alligator, which *you* can't see but the audience *can*! And as you're drying yourself off, *they* know *you* haven't seen it!"

"Eh, how many places does Maria lay for dinner that night?" asked a deadpan Finney. "Two. Or one?" They all laughed. Finney continued. "I know I should be just the spectator here, but as you're obviously not doing this process, how'd you prevent the reptile from gobbling up my old lady?"

More mirth. Cooper waited for the laughter to subside. "Simple. Camera and Susan will be in the water. But on a rostrum. We'll be on the eighteen, able to split the focal point to cover both foreground and background. If the gator gets adventurous, he'll get a mouthful of tubular steel and four by two planking. And dinner for two can be laid. Here." Cooper sipped his cocktail.

"When?" The second time in less than twelve hours Cooper had been asked that same direct question. Susan made it sound much more agreeable than did Tonnini.

Cooper looked at her long and hard. "Would you think me impertinent if I asked you to remove the sunglasses?"

Wordlessly, Susan glanced at him. She put a hand to each side of the glasses and slipped them off, slowly . . .

Finding the move incredibly sexy, Cooper reckoned he'd been in the jungle too long. "Look up to the light. And, to me." No trace of trauma, no anxiety lines, no stress rings, no crow's feet. "Thank you."

Replacing the sunglasses, Susan tapped home the bridge. "So. When?"

"How tied up are you at the moment?"

Smiling, Susan turned to her husband. "My, doesn't he know how to make a girl feel important?" She returned to Cooper. "I am, what you Brits call, *resting*."

"Today's Thursday. How about Friday of next week?"

"You got it." She offered him canapés. "But, James, I left *Redmayne* some five months ago. Is there any chance of me seeing the sequence, especially the edits either side of what we're going to be shooting, so's I can recall the scene and how I played it?"

"Of course! I should've thought of that." He held his hands in supplication. "D'you need to see it on a large screen or will an editing machine suffice?"

"An editing machine will be fine."

"Well. . ." Cooper looked at the two of them. "How about tomorrow morning? Around ten?"

"Fine. Where?"

"We're on Cahuenga, at Franklin. The place is called Reverb. There's a small parking lot with a couple of visitor spaces."

"What more could a girl ask?"

Taking his leave of Finney, he was walked to the front door, by Susan.

As she opened it, Cooper spoke. "Susan. May I ask a question?"

"James, Victor and I have reconciled our differences," said hurriedly. "We're very happy." She looked at him. "I'm not the same person you knew in Imperio."

He gazed at her for some moments. "And I hope I'm not that same person you knew either, believe me." He smiled. "What I was going to ask is. When you left, did the money stop?" Her look to him was unblinking. "Because you were on a picture deal?"

Susan nodded. "Yes, it stopped. Why?"

"Understand, this is the producer in me talking."

"Ohhh, and don't I know that producer!" Was the laughing reply. "But James, you know as well as I. Money? You talk to my agent—"

"Pretend you don't have an agent, pretend a friend is asking, no, presuming, that friend is *presuming* your play or pay has been honored in full and so he was going to ask for this one day . . . gratis."

She looked down. "Did you make an insurance claim on me?"

Cooper nodded.

"Was the claim met?"

"Denied."

Still she looked down. "Did I cost you a lot?"

Images of Imperio flashed into his mind. Ugly images. "Let's just say . . . you cost us. And leave it at that."

She looked up. "No, let's not leave it at that, let's say 'yes,' I do do it. *Gratis*." She smiled. "That's a nice word, *gratis*."

"I like it."

"Music to your ears, right?" He laughed. She moved back, as if to get a better look at him. "Directing seems to have mellowed you."

"*Do not step on anyone on the way to the top.*" In the half light, he hoped she could not see his moistened eyes.

"That's very profound. Who taught you that?"

"It was in a fortune cookie."

She looked at him, for seconds. "You never did tell me how come you're the director?" She leaned forward. "Whatever happened to the talentless Mr. Leef?"

Cooper blew his nose. "Anthony Augustus Leef maintained he'd signed on to direct Susan Chase and when it became obvious you were out, he huffed and puffed, got on his high horse and galloped off. In other words, he walked." He shrugged. "For all I know, he's still walking?"

"What a pompous old fart!" She smiled at Cooper. "Must've made you feel proud to be British?" She held her look. "What's he doing now?"

"I've no idea Susan, none at all. Maybe importuning young sun-kissed Adonis's on Venice Beach?"

They both laughed. Holding her hand, he kissed it. "*A demain.*"

Susan walked back through the house to the patio, to where Finney was making a fresh pitcher of dry martini. "Charming guy, and bright, too."

"James was telling me, that old queen, Leef?" She shook her head in disbelief. "When he heard I wasn't fit to finish the shoot, he upped sticks, and walked. Can you believe that? He *just* walked."

"Some people never know when they're well off." He taste-tested-the cocktail, handing a glass to Susan. "So what's Leef doing now?"

"I asked James. Said he doesn't know."

Nodding in the direction of the recently departed Cooper, he sat. "He, eh, he one of them?"

An almost whispered, "Yes." Susan looked into her glass. "Victor, there's been enough hurt, enough lies, deception, cheating." Their eyes met. "But, you know, in cheating, in betraying you—betraying *us*—I was only really cheating on myself, interested only in . . . escaping." An index finger moved around the rim of the glass, creating a ghostly sound. "And d'you know what? In losing my self-respect, self-esteem, I nearly lost . . ." She looked at her husband. "Everything." She touched his cheek. "And, you're my everything."

He held her hand to his cheek. "Then we're two very lucky people, honey. Two people who surfaced at the same time, intelligent enough to recognize their good fortune." He kissed her hand.

"What would you like for dinner?"

He eyed her suspiciously. "Who's cooking?"

"That's important?"

Finney fretted. "I fancy chicken pot pie."

"And you don't like Maria's?"

He considered the question. "My darling, let me put it this way. I've never gotten used to chicken pot pie Salvadoran. Don't they understand? They're meant to *kill* the bird first?"

SCENE 74. TAKE 3.

The switchboard girl looked up. "Don't I know you?"

"I'm Susan Chase. I'm looking for the *Redmayne West* editing room?"

"D'you have a photograph I could have? For my collection?"

"Sorry . . ."

With a pencil, the girl pointed skywards. "Second floor."

Walking the corridor, Susan couldn't find a door marked either *Redmayne West* or *James Cooper*. She retraced her steps, but nothing. Out of sheer frustration, she chose a door and knocked.

"Enter."

"I'm looking for a James Cooper?"

"Su-san!" Leef stood up from the Kem. "Darling! What a wonderful and lovely surprise, and how well you look . . . considering?" He held her hand. "And such a gorgeous frock!" Gently, but deliberately, he guided her to the door. "Mr. Cooper, you say?" She found herself back in the corridor. "Third door on the left, sweetie." Leef blew her a kiss and closed the door. Susan heard a bolt rammed home.

For Susan, the scene was run several times and to reassure her further, Cooper drew a small plan, showing the camera rostrum and its true proximity to the alligator. "We'll have Joe Tors, the same animals wrangler we had in Imperio, plus on the rostrum a marksmen with a rifle." He nudged her. "We don't want to lose you a second time."

"Which could be for good!" She drank some coffee. "By the way, I thought you said you'd no idea what Anthony Leef was up to?"

"I don't."

"You are *kidding* me?"

"No I'm not." He smiled, warily. "Why? Why would I kid you?"

"Because . . ." Susan gestured over a shoulder. "He's just down the corridor."

"Anthony Leef?" Cooper frowned. "You sure?"

"Positively."

Cooper's bewilderment intensified. "Doing what, I wonder?"

Susan gestured around her. "Well, judging by the fact he's in a room much like this . . ." She turned to him. "I guess he must be editing?"

An unyielding bolt in the Moviola was being tapped, by the wrench in Lincoln's hand.

"Eh, John? Maybe some WD 40?"

Without a word but with a clatter, Lincoln dropped the tools, moved to the flatbed and rewound film.

Nodding towards Lincoln, Cooper whispered to Susan. "How's your house insurance?"

Susan tried to muffle both her surprise, and a laugh. "What!"

Cooper put a finger to lips. "Shhh." He whispered. "He has a built-in Richter Scale and right now, it must be under heavy seismic pressure." Lowering his head, Cooper scanned from left to right, and then to Susan. "Could be the big one." Nodding, he winked. "Insurance. Increase cover."

Having accompanied Susan to her car, Cooper returned upstairs. Pausing by the door, *that* door, he tried the handle. Locked. He stood back. The lock was built in to the doorknob. No key hole. Kneeling, Cooper put an ear right up to the door.

"Hear anything interesting?"

Cooper felt as if he'd jumped three feet into the air. He stood. To face Anthony Augustus Leef, him with a supercilious smirk creasing his flaccid face.

"Spying for the I.R.S., dear?"

"I'd uh, I'd heard . . . That, that you were here."

"And now, you've seen." Disregarding Cooper, Leef held out a key, aiming it dramatically at the lock.

Cooper moved aside. "Um, eh, what, what are you doing?"

"Minding my own business." Leef walked into the room, slamming shut the door behind him.

Trance like, Cooper stood in the empty corridor, the sounds around him of a thousand Kems and Moviolas spewing forth dialogue and sound effects. Why, he couldn't fathom, why did he feel so angry, so very angry? Gut instinct told him it was to do with the Leopold and Loeb of movie-making, Tonnini and Seidelman. He wandered back to his own room.

Cooper got his all-important Ruth cover, the new shots being edited into the cutting copy, and together with the additional inserts he'd shot, an interesting sequence became an exciting sequence, editorially fast paced and highly cinematic, due entirely to director tenacity and vision.

"The Finney residence."

"Susan?"

"Rubenstein! What's up?"

"We've edited the whole sequence. I thought you might like to see it?"

"Same place?"

"D'you have a VCR machine?"

"Sure."

"I've had a copy transferred to VHS tape, so I thought I might bring it up and show both you and Victor the result?"

"We're about to have a light lunch. Care to join us?"

"Be there in about twenty minutes."

On the way, he stopped off at a Liquor Barn, purchasing a bottle of Gavi de Gavi *La Scolca*. Chilled.

36c

The tape ended. As nobody said a word, Cooper feared the worst. Finney broke the pregnant silence. "James, that sequence?" He pointed to the VCR. "You've out-jawed *Jaws*. I particularly like the framing on the wide angle, with Susan short-sided left, the gator short-sided right and then that cut to the animal's silent, moving P.O.V. Good stuff." He turned to his wife. "Honey?"

She took her time in answering. "Even without the sound effects, I think it's terrific, I really do." Leaning, Susan kissed Cooper on the cheek. "Congratulations. And thank you."

"Susan, it's me who should be thanking you. Your help made it all possible."

"I must go see how Maria's doing." She gestured to Finney. "James, would you mind wheeling Victor outside?"

"My pleasure."

As they reached the patio, Cooper enquired. "Any favorite spot?"

"As near as possible to the drinks cart." They both laughed, with Finney passing to Cooper a large vodka martini. He proposed a toast. "To the next one."

"And may there be many more of them. For all of us."

As Finney sipped his cocktail, he gazed at Cooper. "Yesterday, Susan and Maria went shopping. I house sat. During that time there was a call, which I answered. It was for Susan, from her agent. He wanted to thank her for the commission on her freebie day on *Redmayne West*." He leaned towards Cooper. "Apparently, the cheque wasn't from Tonnini International but from, and signed by, you. Why?" Maintaining his position, Finney awaited a reply.

Cooper swallowed his martini. "Victor, you and I both know Susan's gone through a hell of lot recently. She was gracious enough to forfeit a fee for that day's shoot. I thought the least I could do was to pay the agent his fee, especially as she didn't need that hassle. If it's a problem . . ."

"No, no, no problem, none at all." Finney relaxed. "Just curious." He offered his hand. "And thank you." Noticing Cooper's glass, he emptied into it the pitcher of remaining vodka martini. And set about immediately on creating another jug-full.

Lunch was finished. Cooper looked to his hosts. "An elegant sufficiency. Thank you."

Finney studied his glass. "I never knew Italy produced such a great Chardonnay."

Susan turned to Cooper. "So tell me, James. Who is she?"

He looked bewildered. "Pardon me?"

Susan laughed, in turn looking at her husband, and then to Cooper. "Y'know, ever since the Garden of Eden the male species has never been able to perceive feminine intuition." She returned her attention to Cooper. "James, you're love sick. And it shows."

"It does?" He shrugged. "P.P.S.?"

She frowned. "Don't you mean P.*M*.S.?"

"No, P.*P*.S. Post production stress."

SCENE 75. TAKE 2.

Driving back to the hotel, Cooper acknowledged mentally how correct had been Susan in her assessment. He thought of Nessa often, but no more than first thing in the morning and last thing at night. He went to sleep thinking of her, he awoke with a vision of her in front of him. *"Cooper, it **must** be resolved!"* Thus was opened Cooper's *The Nessa File.*

He dialed. The call was answered. By a feminine voice. *"Pronto."*

"Nessa Preiss, please."

"She no 'ere'!" The line was disconnected.

Cooper studied the receiver, speaking aloud. "She no 'ere.' Then where? On honeymoon? No, Tonnini is here, in L.A. So, 'no 'ere' at the moment, no 'ere today' or 'no 'ere' at all? Which?"

"Tonnini International Pictures. How may I help you?"

Cooper bit the bullet. With the best American accent he could muster.

"Eh, yeah, Nessa Preiss there?"

"One moment, please."

His heart was pounding.

"'Allo? Who this?"

Cooper slammed down the phone.

He reviewed 'The Nessa File'. He had two local leads, neither of which had proved positive. He was no further forward.

Think, Cooper. Think! What about that time in New York? Didn't she have parents somewhere in that area? Where'd ex-pat Germans live? Milwaukee, Wisconsin? They're hardly New York? Connecticut? No. Long Island? No. New Jersey? He reflected. *New . . . Jersey?*

He called the concierge. "George, does the hotel have a map of the northeast, like New Jersey?"

A few minutes later and courtesy of Rand McNally, Cooper was poring over a map of The Garden State. "Perth Amboy?" Cooper spoke and laughed aloud. "Who'd forget a town with a name like that?" His finger moved over the page. "Hackensack. Ditto memory. Too much like Groucho's 'Dr. Hackinbush.' Montclair?" Cooper frowned. 'No, but I remember now. It starts with an 'm'. He checked the index. Maplewood . . . Madison . . . Millburn . . . Morristown. He paused. On Morristown. "Morristown?"

Directory assistance revealed no Preiss listings in Morristown. Nor at Maplewood. Madison had two. 'Oren' and 'Helga'. In a palm, Cooper held a coin. "Heads . . . for Helga."

"Hal . . . low?"

He jumped in with both feet. "Mrs. Preiss? Hi. I'm a friend of Nessa's. D'you know where I can contact her?"

"Who are you?"

"Cooper." He was fit to burst. "James Cooper!"

"You say . . . James Cooper?"

"Yes! *James* Cooper!"

"And maybe you have been in the jungle lately, like Tarzan?"

"Yes! Yes!" The thumping of his heart reminded Cooper of the opening bars of *Also sprach Zarathustra*. "Yes, Mrs. Preiss, the jungle. And I love your daughter!"

"Well," said reprimandingly. "What took you so long, what sort of courting is this?"

"Mrs. Preiss, put me out of my misery, please, one way or the other." It was better he knew sooner rather than later. "Is she, is she . . . Mrs.*Tonnini?*"

Helga Preiss was enjoying his torment. "Let me see now. When we last spoke, she was still Nessa Preiss." The voice was very definite. "Yes, Nessa Waltraud Preiss, but, of course, who knows what has happened since then?"

Cooper was frantic. "Where? Where is she!"

"Nessa said not to give out her number. To anyone."

Cooper forced himself to keep his cool. "Mrs.Preiss, I've just spent over two hours trying to find you. If you won't give me her number, what sort of courting is this?"

Helga Preiss laughed. "You truly love her?"

"Truly."

"You like children? I *vish* to be a grandmother."

"I like children", said Cooper. He had none, nor liked them particularly.

"Area code, three one zero, four seven six . . ."

Cooper drove directly to the hotel.

"No, sir, Miss Preiss has not returned yet."

"What's her room number?"

"I'm not at liberty to divulge that, sir."

Cooper gestured to the lobby. "This the best place to wait?"

"The hotel is on two levels, sir."

"On which one is Miss Preiss?"

"I'm not at liberty to say, sir."

"You ever work for the C.I.A.? I know, I know—you're not at liberty . . ."

Purchasing a newspaper, Cooper walked out to the street. Sunset Boulevard. Cooper smiled at the sign. "Two magical words." *You're Norma Desmond, you used to be in silent pictures. You used to be big.*

I am big. It's the pictures that got small! Sunset Boulevard. Two magical words. 'Nessa Preiss.' Two more magical words. "Much more," said Cooper aloud

He looked around. The only suitable vantage point was the hotel sign, set on a plinth. Hoisting himself up, he sat atop it. From where he could see into and be seen by, every vehicle entering the Radisson Bel Air Summit Hotel.

Having been perched there for some two hours, Cooper reckoned his backside was harder now than the concrete on which it was seated. He leaned to his right and to restore circulation rubbed his left cheek, energetically. Having completed his posterial massage, he resumed his surveillance. Which is when he saw her. Nessa. At the exact self-same moment she saw him.

Stopping her car dead in its tracks, Nessa jumped out, running, and at the same time crying "James! James!" Despite the fact there were four other cars behind hers, all trying to turn into the hotel from Sunset.

And then she was in his arms. Cooper held her tightly, smelt the closeness of her, held her tighter in case she was a mirage and might disappear. He tilted her head so that their lips were aligned. Nessa closed her eyes, Cooper bent to kiss her. Which is when he noticed the traffic stretching back to Church Lane, and also the outer lane to the four-o-five overpass. "You'd better move the car."

Nessa's head was tilted still, with eyes closed in eager anticipation. "Is that the most romantic line you can come up with?" She opened her eyes. "After *all* this time?"

"No. But it's the most practical."

Giggling hysterically, they ran the gauntlet of horn-honking and shouting.

Cooper leaned against the door of Nessa's room, shutting out the world. "Let me look at you."

They drank-in each other.

Nessa reached-up, brushing hair off his forehead. And then they kissed, the kiss that each had craved from the other for so long, so very, very . . . long.

"James, it is you? Isn't it?"

The Cooper throwaway knew no bounds, not even in love. "No, I'm a hologram."

"You . . ." She hugged him tighter. "Don't ever, *ever*, leave me again."

They kissed. "Can we stay like this forever", whispered Nessa.

"Until *rigor mortis* sets in?"

"Until then."

"For how long have you booked the room?"

They looked at each other, and giggled.

"James, however did you find me?"

"Interpol. Plus *Rockford, Perry Mason, Magnum P.I.*, oh, and directory assistance." He gazed at her. "Actually, sheer bloody determination." He looked at her once again. "By the way, your mother? She ever work for the *Stasi*?"

"Whaaat?"

"Well, she was very good at protecting her sources. Like not giving out your number."

"I told her not to." She smiled. "But the important thing is, you found me, you're here, *we're* here. So, what do we do now?"

"Lunch?"

Abruptly, Nessa pulled away. "I was thinking in terms of us? Something more . . . *personal*?"

"Darling, I wasn't planning on eating alone."

"Ohhh . . . you!"

He held her tighter. "Nessa, we've so much to say to each other, so much to catch up on." He gestured to the room. "And there are too many temptations here, for me, anyway. And I don't want us to get ahead of ourselves. I want to savor every milli-second of the relationship." He smiled. "Our new, and, lasting relationship. The courtship? I don't want to drink the champagne before the cork's off. You understand what I'm trying to say?"

Nessa kissed him once more "You? You're a revelation. And I love you so much, that yes, I want to take the same measured steps, but you're right." She looked around the room. "Too many temptations here. So lunch." She laughed. "A good idea."

Cooper held her left hand. One by one he spread the fingers. He rubbed the third digit. "Doesn't feel as if there's been a ring there for some time?"

Nessa eyed her left hand. "There hasn't."

"Should I ask why?"

"You don't have to."

Still holding her left hand, Cooper held the right, feeling the bulk of the engagement ring. Looking at her, he held it aloft.

"Diamonds are a girl's best friend," said matter-of-factly.

Cooper shook his head. "Not any more, Nessa. I'm your best friend now. And forever."

The lunch was at Malibu. *Geoffrey's*. It was a long drawn-out meal.

They ate little.

They talked a lot.

And looked at each other, more.

"And, that's where we are now, waiting for the answer print."

A Cooper hand was held by both of Nessa's. "You must be feeling pretty excited right now?"

"You're right, I should be, but d'you know how I *really* feel?" She frowned. "I feel decidedly uneasy." He raised his free hand. "Something's not right." He gazed off at the Pacific Ocean, the azure of the water. And the curtain of smog above it.

Nessa was studying their clasped hands. "D'you still intend keeping those things to yourself or am I to be included?"

"Of course you are." All hands were now entwined. Not knowing quite where to start, he nodded. "A few weeks back, when Susan Chase came in? She said she'd bumped into Anthony Leef in one of our editing rooms.

So I checked, and she was right. He was there."

"So, he was there." Said neither as a question nor a challenge.

"At Reverb, the whole of the second floor, every cutting room, editing room, is rented by Tonnini International." He leaned forward. "You don't think it strange, the very guy who walked out on *Redmayne*, leaving Franco high and dry, that very guy is now working in a Tonnini editing room, presumably on a Tonnini movie?"

Nessa nodded, sagaciously. "Franco never forgets a bad deed, a cross. As an Italian, he's not one to forgive and forget. But." She eyed Cooper. "He's also an astute businessman, and if a business opportunity presents itself that'll benefit *him*, he'll exploit it, whether it comes from somebody who crossed him or not." She lifted his hands, kissing them. "But what about us, James. Where are we in all of this?"

"Nessa, I love you, I cannot be without you and I shudder to think of a future without you. I could go on and on, but the dialogue would end up on the editing room floor."

"*I love you*, is dialogue, just that." She was looking again at their hands. "But, how do I *know* that?" Their eyes met. "How do I know this isn't just take two?"

"Take *two*? Of what?"

"New York City, several years ago? Where your service found you and suddenly I was left behind in your rush to a new movie assignment. How do I know, *really* know, that I won't come second again to a movie?"

"Because I cannot contemplate life without you. It's that simple. And for what it's worth, and thanks to you, I have an agent. I'll be guided by the suggestions and choices of John Hess, not fear."

"Fear?" She frowned. "Fear of what?"

"Of the phone never ringing again." Looking at Nessa, he kissed her hds. "No one thing has ever dominated my thoughts in the way that you do." Cooper moved his head from side-to-side. "Except, except perhaps that . . . that opening sequence of *Touch of Evil*?"

Nessa laughed loudly. With relief. "I guess a girl can't complain when she's getting as much Cooper thought time as Orson Welles?"

He gazed at her. "I couldn't have got through this movie if you hadn't been there."

"But you don't know that James. Because I was there."

"There were times you *weren't* there, when you *were* there."

"Meaning?"

"Meaning such as when you were on the phone to Tonnini, or the numerous times I couldn't tell you how I really felt because you . . . you were his. I ached for you." He shrugged. "Is any of you still his?"

She looked at Cooper. Then to her right hand. Removing the engagement band, she opened her purse and dropped in the ring. Holding out her hands, Nessa spread her fingers for inspection. "And, not done to match the moment."

Cooper smiled, his eyes fixed on the marriage finger. "What *did* happen?"

"You did."

"When?"

"Despite your shitty behavior in New York, maybe subconsciously you were there, always there, all the time."

"And Tonnini?"

"A chance to bury you, a chance to advance myself. You?"

He never took his eyes off her. "When I took this show, I'd been home less than twenty-four hours after thirteen hellish months in India. I was in my bedroom repacking. I opened a drawer and there was this photo. Of you. At the time I couldn't recall you, but it was *you*, and me on a tour boat trip of New York. I stared at it for ages, *trying* to remember your name. Which I couldn't recall until you said it to Claudia Klein."

"Where's that photograph now?"

"In my London house. On the bedside table. Facing my bed."

Nessa studied Cooper for what to him seemed like an eternity. "Might I get to see the London house one day?"

"I'll book the trip now!" Cooper wiped his eyes. "Nessa, does this mean we're, eh, dating?"

Nessa looked at him, coyly. "Yes, we're dating."

"Dating." Cooper savored the word. "Dating . . ." He looked at her. "Sounds like we're harvesting palm trees?"

Nessa burst out laughing.

"And what happens once we've picked all the dates?"

Her mirthful outburst was tempered. "Well, I think we should leave one date till the end, the very end, one very special, very *particular* date?"

Cooper leaned back. "Ohhh, this sounds serious." He placed both hands over his heart. "Serious enough to get the check!" He signaled a server.

"James?" He turned to her. "Would you mind if we didn't broadcast 'us' to the world, not just yet?" She held his hands. "With that uneasy feeling of yours and my knowledge of Franco, I think we need to be cautious?"

Cooper nodded. "You're absolutely right. Prudence before valor."

SCENE 76. TAKE 1.

"How long have I been your agent?"

Leef turned. "I don't know, Irving dear," said uninterestedly. "Why?"

"Because whenever we meet, it's always here, in the Polo Lounge."

"This is convenient." Leef swept an arm across the table. "I just get on to Sunset and whoosh! I'm here."

Resnick sipped his water. "It ever occur to you to throw a right and come down to *my* office." He eyed his client. "If only for a change of scenery?"

"Beverly Hills is impossible to park in," said Leef, testily.

"There's parking underneath the agency."

"Maybe, but you stingy buggers don't validate." Adding, indignantly. "Even Tonnini Pictures validates."

Resnick nodded to a Leef hand, holding the inevitable glass of champagne. "You could park for a month on what that costs."

"Perhaps so, but hardly as convivially." Leef sipped the wine.

"We here just to discuss parking facilities?"

Leef twisted his Asprey swizzle stick. "Irving, what's the positioning of my screen credit on *Redmayne West*?"

"Creative Associate."

"That can be changed." He ordered another glass of *Kristal*. And turned to Resnick. "If my little plan works, I'll soon be able to order this stuff by the bottle again." He looked at the glass. "Maybe by the shipload?" Leef had Resnick's full attention. "The people who are doing the negative pick up on *Redmayne*. Are they a signatory to the Guild Basic Contract?"

"Yes."

"Oh, goody!"

Resnick's lids narrowed. "Anth-ony, what are you up to?"

"Good, Irving, I'm up to good." Leef drank some wine. "And I think you'll be proud of me."

Resnick leaned closer. "You care to make your agent privy to what's on your mind?"

Leaning back, Leef studied his glass. "Irving, it's a little shall we say, premature?" He nodded to Resnick. "But patience is a virtue, so don't kiss your commission goodbye. Not just yet." Raising his glass, he held it poised in a silent toast. "I think, no! I'm *sure*, I'm sure I can get us our just rewards. My directing fee *and* your commission on it." He drank.

"Legally?"

Leef nearly choked on the champagne. "Irving dear, don't tar me with that brush. Everything above board." He smiled at his agent. "Like I just said, you'll be proud of me."

And, thought Resnick, *not before time.*

"As a result, there'll be other offers. Directing assignments." Leef gestured to Resnick. He patted his agent's left hand. "You . . . are going to make a lot of money out of me."

SCENE 77. TAKE 1.

"**D**'you feel okay?" Asked solicitously.

"Trepidation is the name of the game."

Stepping back, she studied him. "Aw, come on, James, it's a big day, *your* big day." Nessa kissed him lightly. "The first running of the completed movie, James Cooper's *Redmayne West*, the first screening of the answer print."

He gazed at her.

"What?"

"I love you."

And perhaps Nessa didn't realize just how much. The breast-pocket handkerchief. On those rare occasions he wore a suit, of which he had only two, the dress handkerchief had to be positioned perfectly. By him. Yet here he was uncomplaining, letting Nessa flick it, pull it, tug it. True love.

"I love you, too." She leaned back, studying her hankie handywork. "You know, you can get these already made up, you just clip them—" She caught his look. "Besides the obvious, who else is going to be there?"

"Feldman and his marketing people, all of the editors, Jay Baxter, the lab contact man, eh, the person who'll be compiling the release script, oh, and I've invited Kurt." Holding her chin, he kissed her. "You know better than anyone. Will Franco be truthful?"

"About the movie? You better believe it."

"I was afraid you'd say that." He managed a weak smile. "Wish me good luck."

Crossing her wrists around his neck, she kissed him, passionately. And whispered in an ear. "Good luck."

To the emotionally-arousing strains of the Mussorgsky-piano/Ravel-orchestrated piece *La Grande Porte de Kiev*, the drapes closed, the house lights illuminated.

He had to know, he had to. He could not contain himself. Cooper turned to Tonnini. Who was crying. "Christ, it's that bad?"

To the screen, Tonnini simply gestured with a hand, trying to find his voice, struggling for words. "James? Is wonnerful." He patted a Cooper hand. "Wonnerful!"

"You seem surprised?"

"I am, James." Tonnini blew his nose. "I very surprised."

"But why? Not that I'm not flattered, because I truly am. But why?" Cooper pointed to the screen. "After all, you've seen it all before. The dailies?"

Tonnini was shame-faced. "Not since Leef walked."

Cooper was astounded. "But you said? You said you'd seen every frame?"

"I lie."

"Franco . . ." Cooper could not help but laugh. "Then what did you expect?"

Tonnini shrugged. "I no know what to expect?" To the screen he extended both arms. "But I no expect this, this . . . this wonnerful movie." He turned to Seidelman. "Don who thought? From that script?" He slapped a Cooper thigh.

"Any changes?"

Tonnini pointed to himself. "Changes? Me?" In unison with his speech, he thumped the back of the seat in front of him. "No! No!! *No!!!*" He looked Cooper up-and-down, as if seeing him for the very first time. "You make a purse out of a sow's ear." Tonnini stood. "Congratulations. You pay your dues."

"Yes, James", said Seidelman, rising. "A job well-done." He gestured to the screen. "But the music? I thought we'd agreed? Everything would be the Homrich indigenous music. But the end bit. Source music?"

"Don, it's only a temp track. I added it as I thought it appropriate. But it can be ereased."

"No, no, keep it! It wonderful! How long is it?"

Music editor Denise Phelps answered. "Exactly eighty-six seconds."

Tonnini gestured to Seidelman. "Buy it. All media, in perpetuity."

"Done." Glancing at his watch, Seidelman spoke quietly. "Franco. Our meeting?" A sly thumb was gesturing. "We should go."

Tonnini and Seidelman departed.

Followed by Feldman and all the marketing staff.

Lincoln gestured all of the editing crew to leave.

Kurt Greene looked at Cooper. "Jimmer, I hate to tempt Providence, but I think we've got a hit here?" He nodded to the screen. "And Franco's right. You've worked wonders."

Cooper bear hugged his leading man. "Like I said before Kurt, not without a little help from my friends."

Kurt looked at Cooper, concernedly. "Everything else okay?"

Cooper smiled. "More than I could ever have hoped for."

"Great." He mock punched Cooper. "Dinner. Next week?"

"Love to. Wednesday?"

"You're on. How many do I make the reservation for?" He eyed Cooper. "Three? Or . . . four?"

Cooper was both smiling and nodding. "Four."

"Via con Dios!"

Cooper flopped back in his seat, a happy man. At that moment. He turned to Lincoln. "Thank you, John. We seem to have satisfied them."

"You're very welcome," said Lincoln. Who wished more than ever he onscould come clean, and tell the truth. Both for his sake and for that of Cooper.

"James," asked lab contact man Jay Baxter. "You happy with the print?"

"That's a timed print, yes? Off the grading I suggested earlier?"

Baxter nodded forcefully. *"It* is."

Cooper considered. "Well, it's a bit warm in places, but what concerns me more is the density." He glanced at Baxter. "It's all over the place." He gestured to the screen, the now dim and blank screen. "Also, it's very grainy in parts, parts where I *know* there's good resolution on the negative."

Fidgeting in his seat, Lincoln stood. And left. Without a word.

Baxter wiped his spectacles. "Well, I guess that's unavoidable, with all those dupe sections."

"Dupe sections?" Cooper leaned to one side, to confront Baxter. "Jay, what are you talking about? Apart from the titles and a couple of opticals, there aren't *any* dupe sections. None." He shook his head.

Baxter pulled a face. "Have I said something I shouldn't have?"

"I dunno, you tell me, you tell me all about dupe sections?" A thought struck Cooper. "Or are you talking about the trailer, I.P. sections for that?"

Baxter shook his head. "Only if the trailer's some fifty minutes long."

Cooper's eyes flicked to the screen. "You mean to tell me there's fifty-minutes worth of duping in there, I.P. sections from an internegative?" He frowned at Baxter. "In an answer print?"

Baxter nodded. "Yup."

"But why? Is there anything wrong with the original negative?" His eyelids narrowed. "Or has there been a screw-up in the lab?"

"No, there hasn't been a screw-up in the lab, and no, there's nothing wrong with the original neg."

Cooper thought aloud. "Then, what *is* with the original neg?

Baxter spoke, as if he thought Cooper knew. "It's in the other version."

"Other version? *What* other version? What are you talking about?"

Baxter both looked and felt extremely uncomfortable. "Look, I'm just the lab contact guy." He glanced at Cooper. "You better talk to John Lincoln about this."

Cooper looked around the otherwise deserted screening room. "John seems conveniently to be a.w.o.l." He turned back to Baxter. "So, Jay, I ask again. *What* other version?"

"The shorter version." Baxter shrugged. "The TV version, I guess?"

Cooper studied the lab man. "Jay, you know as well as I do, that makes no sense at all. You don't use original negative as the source for a TV version that's only going to play via a telecine machine while for the theatrical version, which by the way, is going to be projected through some two hundred feet or so several times daily on to a large screen, not for theatrical are used dupe sections, second generation internegative? That's crazy! " Leaning back, Cooper shook his head. "It makes no sense Jay, none at all."

"Hey, I'm with you, but like I said, speak to John Lincoln." Baxter stood. "He's the one who ordered the dupe sections, it's his signature on the P.O.s."

"How long have you known?"

"James, I do what I'm told."

With his chair reversed, Cooper sat astride it, his chin resting on the seat back. "Cut many movies for Franco, have you John?"

Lincoln had his back to Cooper. "It's fine for you directors, you make enough on one show to last you three years, but there's an awful lot of editors in this town and an awful lot of them are out of work. I don't plan on being one of them." Turning, he faced Cooper. But did not look him in the eye. "I've done well with Tonnini." Finally, his eyes met Cooper's. "He's been very loyal to me."

Cooper studied the floor. "Ah, yes, loyalty. *Steadfast in allegiance.* Then why the secrecy?" He looked up. "It's to do with Leef, isn't it, him being here?" He shook his head. "And to think I wondered where you used to disappear to."

Lincoln remained silent.

"John, tell me this." Cooper sat erect. "Why are we using a mass of dupe sections in the theatrical, but coming off the original neg for the TV version?" He leaned forward. "Why?"

Remaining silent, Lincoln lowered his eyes once more.

"John, give me the courtesy of an answer. Loyalty? You owe me that much?"

Lincoln spoke so quietly his reply was almost inaudible. "It isn't a TV version."

His hands on the chair back, Cooper stood. "Say again."

"It *isn't* a TV version."

"Then what sort of bloody version is it?"

Sighing deeply, Lincoln eyed Cooper. "Look, I've said enough as it is."

The Cooper voice went quiet, very quiet. "Wrong, John. Wrong. You haven't said half enough, not *nearly* enough!"

"Oh yes I have, way too much." He grabbed his jacket. "You want to know the rest? Ask Tonnini!" He walked out, slamming the door.

Looking at the door, Cooper allowed his anger to wane. "Ask Tonnini," he said aloud. And grunted. "And what would he tell me?"

He dialed Nessa. "Hi."

"How'd it go?" He could almost feel her jumping-up-and-down. "Tell me!"

"Too much to tell right now. I need to shower. Meet me at my hotel, in forty-five minutes. *Ciao.*"

Shirtless, he was still-drying-off his hair when were heard two gentle knocks. "It's open."

Nessa rushed in, and kissed him, lustfully. "So tell me! How'd it go?"

He combed his hair, his back to her. "It went okay," he said levely. "Better than I expected. I think he likes it."

"I hope he showed more enthusiasm than you do." Her tone changed. "What's wrong?"

He turned, placing hands on her shoulders. "We have a problem."

"What sort of problem?"

"That's the trouble, I'm not sure. But remember that uneasy feeling of mine?"

"Yes."

"Well, I think the chickens have come home to roost."

Watching him put on a shirt, it was a moment before Nessa spoke. "Tell me."

He nodded. "Let me fix us a couple of drinks, and then, a game plan, a strategy."

Sipping their cocktails, they sat on the sofa, feet on the coffee table, either side of a phone. "Well, obviously you were right about Leef, him being there on the Tonnini editing floor." She paused, thinking, *And there's no smoke without fire.* She kissed Cooper. "And you're sure, sure he's *not* editing the TV version?"

"That's it, Nessa." Said frustratingly. "No, I'm *not* sure, not sure of *anything*." He leaned into her. "But. My director's contract? Contractually I supervise both the TV version and the video release. I do both."

"Plus, the all-important theatrical version, right?" Nessa sipped her cocktail, contemplatively. "You say Franco left, for a meeting?"

He nodded. "Him and the shadow, Slydelman."

Picking up the phone, Nessa dialed. She placed a forefinger and thumb on her nostrils. "Hi, has Mr. Tonnini returned yet? No? Thank you." Removing her hand and ignoring Cooper's quizzical expression, she redialed. "Kay? Hi, this is Nessa—oh, I'm great, terrific, thank you and yes, it was a good trip. Kay, are there scheduled any screenings of *Redmayne West*? Tomorrow? At what time? . . . Okay, thanks. G'bye." Replacing the receiver, she stared at the instrument and then turned to Cooper. "Did you know there's another screening tomorrow?"

A frowning Cooper shook his head.

"And you don't think that's odd?" She nudged Cooper. "That the director, *you*, hasn't been told of another screening?"

"Now you mention it, yes."

"James, it stinks!" A mischievous smile lit-up Nessa's face. "Are we going?"

As the thought flourished, so did Cooper's smile. "Wouldn't miss it for all the tea in China."

"Okay. But strategy." She sipped while strategizing. "We don't enter together, we don't sit together."

"Not until we know the play."

"Right. And, we don't show our hand until we want *them* to see it."

He smiled. His turn to dial. "James Cooper for John Hess." He winked at Nessa. "John, hi. By any chance, would you be free tomorrow afternoon to attend a screening with me? Time?" Nessa wagged fingers. "Three. Tonnini offices. Just around the corner from you. But John, we must talk first. How's two-thirty? Good. There's a Hamburger Hamlet on the corner of Little Santa Monica and Century Park East. See you there. Bye . . . and thanks." Replacing the phone, an arm held Nessa, tightly. "Thank God you checked."

SCENE 79. TAKE 5.

Leef had checked, too. The screening was confirmed. Three P.M He dialed. "Irving?"

"Anth-ony?"

"The very one." As a precaution, Leef scanned the deserted editing room. "Now, Irving dear, remember our little *tête-à-tête* of the other day, the don't-kiss-goodbye-to-your-commission chat?"

"Sure."

"Tomorrow . . ." Leef had difficulty in containing his excitement. "Should be bingo day! There's a screening of *Redmayne* at three P.M, Tonnini offices. I shall be there, and so should you."

"Let me check the diary."

"No, Irving!" The geniality evaporated. "Stuff the diary. Be there!"

Cooper sipped his coffee. "I'd not been told of this screening, hence not invited." He looked at his agent. "Which is why I smell a rat."

"Any idea who's going to be there?"

"Apart from the usual suspects, no." Cooper rested his cup. "John, if it's alright with you, I'd like to slip in at the last moment, just as the movie's about to roll and everybody's looking at the screen and not at the door."

Hess beamed. "Oh, how I love intrigue and subterfuge."

"John, this might be all for nothing, y'know" He pointed to his chest. "Maybe just Cooper paranoia?"

Hess winked. "Beat's the weekly staff meeting."

As Cooper collected the check, Hess pointed to it. "Don't forget to have that validated for me."

Cooper frowned. "Park under the Tonnini offices. They validate."

Hess shook his head. "I resent being beholden to producers."

Leading Hess towards the screening room, Cooper heard the receptionist exclaim. "Why, Miss Preiss. What a nice surprise." Smiling to himself, he nodded to Hess. "Wait here."

The door to the room was closed. But unlocked. Cooper entered and ascended the small flight of stairs to the projection booth.

The projectionist was lacing up, that precise part of threading the leader through the gate. "Hi, Stan."

"That you, Mr. Cooper? Come to see your masterpiece again?"

Cooper surveyed the booth. "Stan really, two carbon-arc projectors? When are you going to get up to date, one projector, cake stand, no changeovers?"

Stan chuckled. "Ask Mr. Tonnini that, but he says there's plenty of life left in these two." He looked at Cooper. "Besides, what would we get for them. Scrap value?" He shook his head. "Not worth it."

Cooper looked through the projectionist's window, down into the auditorium. He felt like Raymond Shaw in *The Manchurian Candidate*. Except Cooper hadn't a rifle, he wasn't out to murder. Just maim.

He scanned the screening room. From above and behind it was difficult to distinguish one head from another, although it was obvious beside the squawk box was John Lincoln, and the Executive Vice President Business Affairs was recognized readily, although Cooper could not place the two 'suits' sitting to the right of Seidelman. *Now, there's a surprise*, said Cooper to himself, looking down mockingly on the Friar Tuck-like pate of Anthony Augustus Leef. Intuition told him that the man next to Leef was most likely his agent. Cooper saw then the familiar head of Tonnini, and Kay Meyers, pencil and notebook in hand, entering with her boss and sitting beside him. Cooper cursed the sound proofing of the projection booth.

"Franco!"

"Sol!"

The two men shook hands, animatedly.

"Oh, and Franco, this is my partner, Mel Sokoloff."

More handshakes.

Tonnini gestured to Seidelman. "Don, you meet Sol Levy and Mel Sokoloff, American Entertainment Cinema?"

"We've met already."

As Tonnini looked around the theatre, Nessa slid down in her seat. "Ah, Anthony, you here. Good." The Italian looked to the man from A.E.C. "Shall we?"

"Roll 'em!" said Mel, with the authority of one just about familiar with movie parlance.

Lincoln pressed the squawk box.

His voice filled the projection booth. "Stan? Roll it."

As Stan fired up projector number one, Cooper dashed downstairs, grabbed Hess and made for the two seats he'd earmarked from the projection room.

With a mixture of bewilderment, bemusement, frustration, indignation and tedium, Cooper watched intently. "I don't fucking believe this", he said to himself quietly. But not sufficiently quietly that Hess didn't hear. "Oh, no . . ."

"James!" Hess was whispering. "Shut up!"

"There's huge chunks missing!" While whispering, Cooper squirmed. "And projected in one-eight-five spherical widescreen, not TV. Nothing makes any sense!"

Hess put his mouth to a Cooper ear. "James, when the lights go up, say nothing, say sweet fuck *nothing*. Understand?"

Without taking his eyes off the screen, Cooper nodded.

"It's important we hear what's said and find out what the hell's going on."

"Okay!" Whispered Cooper, in an irritated reply. "Okay, okay!"

The screen dissolved into blackness, the house lights glowed.

Cooper clicked off his watch. "One hundred minutes," he whispered. "But ninety-six-minutes of screen time. Of what?"

"Listen up," murmured Hess. "And you might find out."

Mel Sokoloff turned to Tonnini. "It's rough, but . . ."

"It's only a work-in-progress print," advised Lincoln.

"That's what all those squiggly lines are, right?" Lincoln nodded. He turned to Tonnini. "Franco, perfect. What's the running time?"

Cooper. "One hundred min—*Ouch!*" As he felt an ankle hacked.

Tonnini was looking to Lincoln, but it was Leef who spoke. "One hundred minutes, Mel, to the precise frame, including front credits and end roller."

In a squeaky whisper and shaking his lowered head, Cooper aped Leef. "*One hundred minutes, Mel . . .*" Before he could finish, another shin kick.

"Music?" Asked Sol Levy.

"We simply lift tracks," replied Leef. "From one to—"

"We prepare the music right now, we try an interesting formula."

Tonnini turned to Leef. "Right, Anthony?"

"Eh, yes, Franco, right. Absolutely. Yes."

"Will it make an album?"

"An album?" Pressed heavily was the Lazio charm button. "Of course! We contact Sarabande Varese already."

Smiling, Sokoloff stood. "The movie? It's fine, change not a frame." He looked around him. "*Not a frame!*" And focused finally on one man. "Well done, Mr. Leef, good job. You should feel . . ." He extended his open hand. "Mighty proud!"

Through clenched teeth, Cooper hissed. "He should feel my boot up his fucking poofter arse. Ouch!" Cooper nursed his ankle. Again.

Sokoloff and Levy headed for the exit.

"Mel, Sol?" Seidelman was on his feet. He gestured to Tonnini. "Are we right to think you like the movie?"

"Like it?" Stopping, he spread open his arms. "We *love* it!"

"Still the same release date?"

"Yes, oh, and . . ." He leaned forward. "We need trailers and teasers. Like yesterday!"

Seidelman looked around him. "Then, with that time schedule can we take '*we love it*' in lieu of an immediate letter of confirmation, as formal acceptance and authorization, to complete and to deliver?"

"Don, time is of the essence, so yes, you can." Sokoloff gestured grandly. "And you have the witnesses here to what I've just said."

Tonnini stood. "*Va bene, va bene.*" He bowed. "*Y grazie.*"

Seidelman embraced Tonnini. "Franco, a master stroke." He broke the hug. "Perfect!" Which is when he noticed the tops of two heads. Seidelman cleared his throat, "Eh, fellas, your two guys, Mel and Sol? They left already."

"Now!" Said Hess.

The two men stood, as did Nessa.

Open mouthed, Tonnini looked from Cooper, to Hess, to Nessa, and back to Cooper. He indicated Hess. "James, who your friend?"

"I'm John Hess, James's agent." He looked at Seidelman. "We spoke one time, remember?"

The pain showed on Seidelman's face. "Only too well."

Hess gestured to the screen. "Do you gentlemen mind telling me, and my client, what's going on?"

"It none of your business."

"Mr. Tonnini. With your industry experience? You really surprise me."

Kay Meyers made muffled apologies and almost sprinted out of the theatre. John Lincoln saw this as an opportunity to escape. As he moved, he was spotted. By Cooper.

"Don't you dare John." Said *very* quietly. "You stay, right . . . there."

"Now," said Hess. "As for it being none of my business Mr. Tonnini, I contest that." The agent indicated Cooper. "My client's current project is *Redmayne West. That* makes it *my* business." He stared at Tonnini. "So, I repeat. What is going on and what is it we've just seen?"

"What you have just seen, Mr. Hess, an' I no remember inviting you or your client to this screening?"

"Time takes its toll on the aged . . ." said by Hess, sadly. "Standard industry practise is no such screenings take place without the director being present, *si*?"

Tonnini controlled his rage. "What you just see is a final cut of *Redmayne West*, theatrical."

"What!" Exploded Cooper. "Theatrical? Ouch!" For support, Cooper grabbed a seatback

Inclining his head, the words were repeated slowly by Hess. "A the . . . atrical version?"

"Mr. Hess, I a busy man. I say again, it none of your business." The Italian looked around, smiling graciously. "But I tell *you*. I nothing to hide. What you just see is a negative pick up sale." Graciousness was replaced by smugness. "*Redmayne West* has been sold to American Entertainment Cinema. They take it world-wide, all territories."

"Except five," was the reminder from Seidelman.

"Except five," parroted Tonnini.

Resnick was becoming impatient. "Anth-ony," he whispered. "Where's this leading to?"

Whispering back, Leef rubbed his hands excitedly. "To us, dear, to us.

The moment will be upon us in a flash!" He was smiling. "Everything comes to them wot waits."

"Negative pick up, you say?"

Tonnini nodded, retaining his smug expression.

Hess cocked his head screenwards. "And that's the theatrical release?"

"*Si.*"

"Then what the heck has my client been editing these past few months?"

Tonnini was looking directly at Hess. "What your client has been editing will become the video release, the Director's Special Edition."

"But theatrical in five territories," added Seidelman.

"*Si*, that right," remembered Tonnini. "It play five important territories theatrical. Japan, Italy, France, Germany an' the U.K." He pointed to Cooper. "Your client, it play in his home country, in cinemas, multiplexes." He addressed Hess. "Cooper's name will be on the paid advertising, posters, the Underground, buses, billboards . . . he be on *The Parkinson Show*. He a lucky guy."

"Lucky!" Shouted Cooper. "Lucky?" Looking at Tonnini while shaking his head, his voice quietened. "Franco, you ingrate. Your movie was in tatters, a shambles." He pointed to Leef. "Thanks to that indolent talentless prick!" Cooper's tone became more confrontational. "And who stepped in at a moment's notice and saved your bacon?" His voice rose. "Who?"

"The very same person," said Seidelman, dryly. "Who's being paid handsomely for it."

"But not without a fight," reminded Hess.

Again, a Cooper finger was pointed at Leef. "And, no more than you would have paid to that inept pariah! Less! Actually less, when you count fringes."

"I no know why *I* have to defend myself!" Tonnini was shouting, and all the time gesticulating wildly. "This *my* offices! This *my* screening room." In unison, two arms were aimed at the screen. "An' that? That *my* movie, to do with what *I* like!" Turning, he scanned the group. "We work in the movie *business*. I a *business* man! I see a business deal, a negative pick up deal. *I* make that deal. Is my movie! Is my deal!" Becoming calmer, Tonnini eyed Cooper. "James, you a very talented man, but you make that mistake, the same mistake all you directors make." He nodded. "You think the moment you first say, '*action,*' the movie belong to you. Wrong! The day you raise twenty-million-dollars for a movie, that the day the movie is yours!" He leaned forward. "How much you raise for *Redmayne West*, eh?" Tonnini cocked an ear. "Eh?"

Cooper was silent.

"Right . . ." Tonnini scanned the room. "So, who's movie is it?"

Cooper was matter-of-fact, neither unctuous nor wheedling. "Franco, *I* did the grafting, the heavy lifting. *I* wrote many new scenes, but what I've just seen up there, that's not my movie. It's a travesty, that's what it is. A muddled travesty."

"James, what you care? You want to be known as a director, no? So what you care if it a travesty? It a screen credit. It still have your name on it, as director?"

Leef nudged Resnick. "That's our cue." Leef stood, coughing affectedly. "Eh, Franco, may I just make a teeny point here?"

Exasperation was in Tonnini's voice. "Anthony, it important, it relevant?"

Leef was smiling sweetly. "Well, yes, I think it is, yes indeed, so I'll come straight to the point. The directing credit?" He was tapping his chest. "I think you'll find that's rightfully mine."

Cooper's jaw sagged. "Am I supposed to laugh? Or cry? Or both?" He scowled at Leef. "You? You couldn't bloody direct a guided missile!"

Leef regarded Cooper disdainfully. "Sticks and stones, dear boy, sticks and stones" He smiled at Seidelman. "Don, am I correct in saying that both Tonnini Pictures and A.E.C. are signatories to my Guild contract?"

Seidelman nodded. "Yes, both are."

"As I thought," smiled Leef. "As I thought." He scanned about him. "Now, Don." He looked at both agents. "And Irving here, and Mr. Hess." Leef showed a booklet. "I'm sure you are all familiar with this tome?" The booklet was waved above his head. "This is the Guild Basic Agreement, and I'm equally sure you're all familiar with the procedure when a movie has two directors and the screen credit is in contention?"

Hess frowned. "Since when has the screen credit been in contention?"

Leef gestured to the Italian. "Since Franco indicated that it would be accorded to Mr. Cooper here, he of the florid phrase."

Hess whispered to Cooper. "This guy breaks me up." Regaining his composure, Hess questioned Leef. "And why wouldn't he, of the florid phrase, be accorded screen credit as director?" He spoke quietly but firmly. To Leef. "After all, he directed the major part of it, virtually all of the movie?"

Leef brandished a finger. "Correction. He directed *some* of it while I—"

"Directed less than a tenth?" Came the Hess rejoinder.

"Not! Mr. Hess, not. *Not* less than a tenth, more than half!"

Hess studied Leef, and then he was shaking his head. "So that's it?"

Cooper felt helpless. "John, tell me, what is *'it'*? Please?"

Leef smiled at Cooper. "James, you seem lost. And you have. You see, *you* were editing for a screen time between one-hundred thirty minutes to one-forty, while my brief was one-hundred-minutes—less titles—a total of ninety-six screentime minutes. That reduction presented me the opportunity to use more of *my* material." Leef pointed to Lincoln. "Ask the editor. He has all the cuts logged, coded. He can tell you which director has the greater proportion . . ." With both arms, he gestured to the screen. "Of his work up *there*."

Cooper looked from Leef, to Hess. And did a double take. Suddenly it all flooded back. Santa Mosqueiro, Mendoza, Rubio, Para, Ramalho, Boscoli, the drugs threat, the visa threat, the crash at the airstrip, and now . . . this? It all boiled over. For several moments, Cooper held his head in his hands. When he looked up, it was to Tonnini. "I went through hell for you. Yes, I was ecstatic at the chance you gave me. You, *you* gave me *Redmayne West* to direct. Which I did. It *is* my movie. So, I ask you humbly. Let me re-edit *my* movie."

"James, you no hear." In contrast to Cooper's final outburst, Tonnini was the epitome of calm. "It *my* movie, *mine*. You no have contractual final cut." A finger stabbed his Lazio chest. "I do! An' if you think I risk a multi-million-dollar deal to satisfy your dreams, think again."

"But, Franco. You *know* it's my work?" Cooper pointed at Leef. "That multi-untalented excuse for a director walked out—on you! *I* was the suture. I stitched it all together again, and more." His voice faded, "Me . . ."

Tonnini was nodding. "You absolutely right, James. But Mr. Sokoloff, who just buy this movie." All eyes were on him. "We all hear him say *no change a frame, not a frame.*" He gestured to Cooper. "James, my hands? They are tied."

Cooper remained silent, head in hands, studying the floor.

Hess addressed Lincoln. "Is it correct what Mr. Leef is saying, that there's a greater proportion of his material in the pick-up version?"

Lincoln avoided looking Hess in the eye. "Yes."

"What sort of ratio?"

Still no eye contact. "About six-to-four, Leef to Cooper."

Cooper studied the editor. "John? You need change your first name. To Judas."

"Welcome to Hollywood, James." Hess had an arm around a Cooper shoulder. "From one jungle to another."

Leef was grinning. "I've never looked a gifthorse in the mouth. Wherever possible, *I* used *my* material. Not difficult?" Leef looked to his agent. "Why, Irving dear, you're smiling. I don't believe you've done that since Israel won the Six Days War?"

Resnick was even chuckling. "Can I presume we're agreed on this or do I take my client's case to arbitration?"

Cooper looked up. "Franco, I have director's cut in my contract."

Leef was his patronizing self. "It's as Franco said James, you no listen. I—*I*—am the director. And that?" He pointed to the screen. "*That* is *my* director's cut!"

Hess looked at Tonnini, and Seidelman. "We don't dispute my client did the physical act of the greater part of directing, that's not in contention?"

Seidelman shook his head. "No."

"Good," said Hess. "Final payment is due on delivery." He looked again at both Tonnini and Seidelman. "Yesterday you saw an answer print of my client's work, and I believe it was accepted?"

"*Si.*"

Hess spoke to Seidelman. "I look forward to the early receipt of a final payment check."

"Hold on, Hess. Not so fast." Seidelman looked around. "The director credit is settled, yes. But it's *not* Cooper. So, no direct, no director's fee?"

Hess smiled. "Don . . . may I call you Don?"

Seidelman nodded.

"Tonnini International Pictures has signed a contract for my client to direct *Redmayne West*, for a mutually agreed fee. That contract is watertight. Play . . . or pay?" He gestured to Cooper. "He play." And looked at Seidelman. "You pay. Or do we settle this in court?"

Tonnini looked daggers. At Hess. At Cooper. At Nessa. At Seidelman. "You have an offer?"

"I hoped you'd see reason. Cooper's full directing fee, plus, you agree to grandfather him into the D.G.A. Immediately. But by doing it now, you save on the fringes. Then the five territories *not* part of the A.E.C pick up deal? My client to be accorded director credit on that version. Which is sure to confuse Siskel and Ebert." He looked around him, his gaze resting on Leef. "That'll also confuse the Academy?" He eyed Cooper. "That cover it?" Grinning, Cooper nodded. "Oh, and ten VHS copies of the Director's Special Edition." Hess grinned at Tonnini, and then to Seidelman. "That . . . *director* being my client, Mr. James Cooper, who's name will be on all paid advertising associated with it." He looked at Tonnini. "*Capis*?"

Tonnini sighed a reluctant sigh. "Understood."

Seidelman spoke. "The loose ends. Your client has a rental car, paid for by us. No more. Your client is on a generous per diem. Finished."

Cooper fumbled in a pocket, producing car keys, which he handed to Seidelman. "It's parked below."

It was Resnick's turn. "Don, we need to discuss some things, things like renegotiation, substantial renegotiation?"

Seidelman was in no mood for more appeasement. "Irving, you'll have made a lot of money by us, from the Pebble Beach gig."

Resnick smiled. "And now, I'm gonna make a whole lot more."

"Oh, and Don." Nessa was speaking. "We need to discuss some things, like fees, *my* substantial fee?"

"What fee? What the hell are you talking about?"

"Associate producer fees." Even knowing Seidelman was immune to it, Nessa radiated *that* smile. "Remember? Of which I have yet to receive a *single* penny and as it is agreed the movie is delivered, I'd like payment immediately. In full," she added sweetly.

"I'll look into it later."

"No, Don, not later . . ." The tone went from agreeable to acerbic. "Now!" Nessa walked between a row of seats.

Tonnini studied her every move. "Nessa. You back?"

Reaching the aisle, she paused. "Back?" Watched by Cooper, Nessa replied to the question. "Sure, I'm back." Stared at intently by both the Italian and the Englishman, Nessa walked up the aisle to stand beside Cooper, slipping an arm through his. "Like Dolly Levi, I'm back. Back where I belong." She smiled at Cooper. "Home, James?" As they turned, Nessa halted. "Ooops, nearly forgot." She looked at Tonnini. "You were kind enough to lend me these." Opening his hand, she dropped into it a bunch of house keys, and a diamond engagement ring. "*Arrive'derci*."

EPILOGUE

Tipping the porter, with her shapely behind Nessa nudged close the door. She looked at the large envelope. The label, headed *Amalgamated Creative Talent,* was addressed to "Ms. Nessa Preiss and Mr. James Cooper." Nessa smiled. "I like that."

Cooper was on the phone. "So, there you have it, Kurt. They screwed us. What? You're going on the Letterman Show?" Cooper laughed. "You wouldn't? . . . Tell all?" Cooper was nodding and laughing. "I know . . . what buddies are for! Okay, dinner Wednesday. Where? *Tiramasu*. Where's that? . . . Corner Ventura and Woodman. Seven thirty. Got it. See you then. Bye."

Nessa held out the envelope. "This came. For both of us." Sitting on his knees, Nessa kissed him. "You open it, you're the man."

"Ladies first."

She slit open the envelope. Within was a smaller envelope, addressed to 'Ms. Nessa Preiss', and a script, with a buck slip addressed to "James Cooper. From the desk of John Hess."

Cooper flipped through the script, as Nessa read aloud her letter. *"Dear Nessa. Nothing will give me greater pleasure than to pursue both Mr. Tonnini and Mr. Seidelman not only for your two-hundred-thousand dollar fee for associate producer services on* Redmayne West, *but also for the per diem payments for the period you were in Imperio, which I gather have never been paid? Any agency commission will be covered by a ten percent late payment penalty. Oh, and paid advertising as A.P. Best personal regards, John Hess."* Nessa looked at Cooper. "Your turn."

He read audibly. *"James, we have to get it behind us! The most important thing for you right now is to be on to your next movie, your next directing assignment, pronto! And, before the release of* Redmayne West. *The enclosed script is out to directors. I think you would be perfect for it as long as you don't mind California, as it shoots entirely in L.A., to which you would bring a fresh cinematic eye, much the way Boorman did with* Point Blank *and Schlesinger with* Day of the Locust. *Call me when you have read it and we'll discuss but as you read, keep uppermost in your mind the imperative need to be going straight on to your next show, not any shortcomings you might feel the script has. They can always be fixed. But we must maintain <u>momentum</u>. Truly, John."*

"Why are you looking at me like that?" Nessa asked.

"You know where the Santa Monica Court House is?"

"Sure."

"Can you be there Wednesday, eleven A.M.?"

"Why?"

"I thought we'd get married."

FADE TO BLACK.

GLOSSARY (Alphabetical)

Title Page. "Check the Gate". Film runs between the lens and a pressure plate, known as the 'gate'. Film passes through the gate at 24 frames-per-second, 90-feet per minute. This speed can create static in the felt-lined film magazines, sometimes causing dirt/tiny hairs to adhere to the film itself and carried thereon; if left unchecked, these hairs would appear as small tree branches when enlarged by projection on to a theater screen. Once a print/prints has/have been confirmed by the director, the gate has to be checked to ensure it is clear of any such debris.

Page 1. B.S.T. British Summer Time.

Page 2. ". . . biscuits." Plate of cookies.

Page 3. Ploughman's (*Plowman's*). Traditional English yeoman's lunch. Hunks of bread, buttered, generous portions of Chedder cheese and sweet pickle, served daily in most English pubs.

Page 3. Junket. Sweetened blancmange of flavored milk curds. Boarding School staple.

Page 3. Semolina. Pudding of hard round grains of wheat. Another Boarding School basic. 'Orrible!'

Page 4. First A.D. First Assistant Director. Director's right hand person , schedules each day's work, runs the set.

Page 5. Pinewood or Shepperton. U.K. major movie studios.

Page 7. Lazio. A region of Italy, the capital of which is Rome.

Page 10. Play-or-Pay. A contractual deal where, if, for any reason a movie is cancelled, the nominted actor/technician receives the whole contracted fee.

Page 10. Negative Pick Up. Company 'A' sells a complete movie to another company. The Movie Industry equivalent to buying a DVD/Blu-Ray.

Page 10, cont. Development, First Look, Overheads. These are all various financial agreements made to independents by a major studio, where the studio is reimbursed subsequently from any Box Office take.

Page 10, cont. Agency Packaging. Where a major Agency will put together the packaging of an A-Team-Director, Screenwriter and major stars, offering as a whole the bundle to a studio at a lesser group rate, in return for the guarenteed use of that talent, and their inclusive fees.

Page 11. Principal. Principal (Main Unit) photography, the actual shooting period.

Page 12. Green-lit. The official go-ahead.

Page 16. Federales. National police force.

Page 18. A.T.F. U.S. Agency: Alcohol, Tobacco and Firearms.

Page 18. F.B.I. U.S. Agency: Federal Bureau of Investigation.

Page 18. C.I.A. U.S. Agency: Central Intelligence Agency.

Page 20. Adam and Eve it. Rhyming slang—'Believe It.'

Page 23. North-and-South. Rhyming slang—'Mouth.'

Page 26. "Brigade." Abbrevation of 'Obrigado'—'Thank you.'

Page 27. Siskel and Ebert. Famed U.S. movie critics.

Page 28. Coca-Cola. The beverages company purchased Columbia Pictures in 1982: the company sold it on to Sony, in 1989. Sony Pictures is based now at the former M.G.M. Lot, in Culver City, California. Thus was a fabrication, the MGM end roller claim *"Made in Hollywood."*

Page 29. M.O. 'Modus Operandi'.

Page 30. C.A.A. Creative Artist's Agency.

Page 31. Below-the-Line. A movie budget is in four sections. 'Above-the-Line,' major Creative personnel. Writer, Producer, Director, Major Stars. Their salaries, contractual expenses, travel costs, etc., etc. 'Below-the-Line' covers all Production personnel and equipment. Accounts, Art Dept., Camera, Construction, Costume, Location fees, etc., etc. Then there is 'Post Production' and 'Other,' the latter covering Legal, Studio Overhead, etc., etc.

Page 31. Chasen's. A one-time famous upscale Hollywood restaurant, beloved of the movie coterie.

Page 32. 'Porky.' Rhyming slang. 'Pork Pie'—'Lie,' abbreviated to 'porky.'

Page 33. Production Board. Pre-computerization method of scheduling a movie. Laborious. (Been there, done that . . .)

Page 35. D.P. Director of Photography. Known previously as Lighting Cameraman.

Page 35. Deferment. To help in the financing, this is where an Above-the-Line person defers an amount of their total, to be paid subsequently at an agreed point down the line.

Page 36. N.T.S.C. U.S. National TV System Committee. NTSC is the TV transmission standard for North America, Central America, The Philippines and Japan, etc., etc.

Page 36. Secam. French system. 'Sequential Coleur avec Memoire.' This transmission system is used in a number of European countries plus those once in the Soviet bloc, including modern-day Russia.

Page 36. P.A.L. German system, 'Phase Alternation Line.' The standard in Germany, the U.K., Ireland, Brasil ('PAL-M') and anywhere in the world where neither are used NTSC nor SECAM. Considered generally to be the best system. NTSC is a 525-line 60-cycle system, the other two are 625-line, 50-cycle systems; better picture quality and more amenable to being shot on, and linked to, film.

Page 39. Fringes. Additional payments to a Guild/Union, to cover Health and Welfare, Pensions, etc.

Page 39. D.G.A. Director's Guild of America.

Page 39. S.A.G. Screen Actors Guild.

Page 39. W.G.A. Writer's Guild of America.

Page 42. Major. One of the major studios—Columbia, Disney, MGM, Orion, Paramount, Tri-Star, Twentieth Century Fox, Universal, United Artists, etc., etc.

Page 42. Sacha Torte. Tart made famous by the Hotel Sacha, Vienna.

Page 44. Possessory Credit. Where the Director's name appears before/end of the film's title. Such as, 'A Film by John Boorman.'

Page 47. F.A.A. U.S. Agency: Federal Aviation Administration.

Page 50. Chippies. Carpenters.

Page 52. Geared Head. The camera is mounted on a head, as on the book's cover. The geared head, manufactured either by Moy (UK) or Worrell (US), has two handles, which engage cogs, enabling the camera operator to both pan and tilt, simultaneously. A less sophisticated piece of equipment is the 'Friction Head,' whereby the operator moves the camera non-geared head via a pan bar.

Page 52. Dollies. Known sometimes as 'velocilators,' these are specially-made vehicles that permit the camera to track, on rails or, per an Elemak, or a Crab Dolly, on 10 x 8 sheets of strong plywood. The Elemak has two sets of detachable wheels, grooved for use on metal track, or rubber tyred, when on tracking boards.

Page 52. Steadicam. To all intents and purposes, this is a hand-held dolly which permits greater freedom in tracking. Specially-trained operators are used for this wonderful piece of equipment, which has revolutionized the movie-making process making possible set-ups/shots for which previously, director's could only dream.

Page 67. Strike the set. Dismantle.

Page 70. 'Joanna.' Rhyming slang—'piano.' (Lingo— *'pianner'*.)

Page 74. U.C.L.A. University of California at Los Angeles.

Page 78. Rushes, Dailies. The viewing of the previous day's shooting.

Page 83. Production Reports. A total daily record of each day's shooting, showing scenes completed, actors on call, film stock used, any untoward events, happenings, etc.

Page 85. Treed out. Using foliage to hide unwanted items in a set-up.

Page 92. Rurales. Rural area local police.

Page 98. Tartar con Cuidado. Spanish; 'Handle with care.'

Page 98. U.S.C. University of Southern California.

Page 100. I.L.M. Industrial Light & Magic. San Rafael-based (Calif.) Optical Effects company founded by George Lucas.

Page 100. Rotoscope. An optical technique whereby frame-by-frame can be transferred, enhanced or diminished specific imagery. Last time your author considered using this process was in 1990, at which time the price **per frame** was $1300.

Page 105. Answer Print. The final offering, but subject to further editing.

Page 105. Paid Advertising. Contractual agreement for name to be included on **all** forms/types of advertising, world-wide.

Page 105. A/C. Air-conditioning.

Page 106. Cutting Copy. Work-in-Progress template during picture/sound editing.

Page 106. I.A.T.S.E. International Alliance of Theatrical Stage Employees. The union covering also motion picture technicians, artistes and allied crafts, such as camera, sound, make-up, wardrobe, grips, electricians, etc., etc. It's jurisdiction covers the U.S.A., its territories, and, Canada.

Page 106. Foley. If an actor walks from long-shot up to camera, the footfall cannot be recorded on shooting as the mike boom would be in picture on the long-shot position. Known previously as 'Footsteps', they are recreated during Post in a specially-equipped Sound Recording Studio.

Page 106. A.D.R. Automated Dialogue Replacement. Known previously as Looping (U.S.) or Post Synching (U.K.). Where poor/unclear recording of dialog is reproduced perfectly in a sound recording studio. Actors generally loathe the process, as they're not interacting with other characters, regarding it as a necessary evil.

Page 106. Loan-Out. For purposes mainly of tax reasons, individuals will form their own corporation, which 'loans' them out to a studio for a movie.

Page 109. Dripping toast. 'Dripping' is the congealed fat melted from a roast. Dee-licious; and about a million calories per slice of toast...

Page 110. Second Eleven. Stand-ins. They stand in for the principals, when lighting, etc.

Page 112. Tewe. Pronounced 'chewy.' this is a German-manufactured viewfinder, holding a wide range of lens sizes. Not 100% accurate. More a toy than a tool. Worn/used mostly by insecure directors. Watch 'Argo'.

Page 112. Arri. Abbreviation of Arriflex, the German camera developed for use in WWII and refined subsequently to be a very versatile piece of equipment, sound-proofed eventually.

Page 112. Frankenheimer. John Frankenheimer, famed movie director.

Page 115. Blue Screen. A matte process, such as being able to make Superman fly. Superseded now by 'Green Screen.' More efficient.

Page 121. Flatbed. Editing machine. See also page 206, 'Kem.'

Page 123. P.S.T. Pacific Standard Time, such as Los Angeles, etc.

Page 127. Moviola. An editing/viewing machine. Runs Picture and Sound in synch. The type has been superseded by the much-more refined flatbed version.

Page 128. P.O.V. Point-of-View.

Page 129. Two Three Five to One. The screen is divided into Aspect Ratios. The original was 'Academy,' one three three to one. For every 100 units vertical, there were 133 units horizontal. 2.35:1 is full anarmorphic widescreen, a.k.a. 'letterbox'; one hundred units vertical, 235 units horizontal.

Page 135. George Kaplan. The phantom character in Hitchcock's *North by Northwest*.

Page 137. Verna Fields, Anne Coates. Award-winning renowned film editors. Author worked with Anne on 'The Legacy', 1978.

Page 137. Bob. Colloquial English for coins. A 'bob' was a shilling, which now is the decimal five pence.

Page 141. Eastmancolor. The original Technicolor process involved the use of three separate negatives (tri-pack) in the camera, each reacting to a specific color, blue, red, yellow. Eastmancolor is a multi-layer monopack negative, named after George Eastman, the founder of Kodak.

Page 142. Magazine. Houses the film. Fitted to all and detachable from, every camera.

Page 142. N.G. No good.

Page 159. VARIG. One-time national airline of Brasil. Pronounced '*vareegee.*'

Page 169. Dicky bird. Rhyming slang, 'word.'

Page 176. Agincourt salute. At that famous battle, whenever the English archers fired a volley of arrows, they showed to the French the two fingers used on the bow, for if captured, the French cut-off those very two fingers of their foes. Today, the two finger salute means 'Fuck Off!'

Page 184. Trouble. Rhyming slang. 'Trouble 'n Strife'—'wife'

Page 184. Saucepans. Rhyming slang. 'Saucepan Lids'—'kids.'

Page 184. Cead mille failte. Gaelic/Irish. 'A hundred thousand welcomes.' '*Ced miller faultcher.*'

Page 184. Go raibh mile maight agat. 'A thousand thank yous.' '*Go rave miller ma'hagut.*'

Page 184. Sea. 'Yes.' '*Sha.*'

Page 184. Ros Comàin. Roscommon. '*Ross Cumoyne.*'

Page 187. Bapty's. London-based Bapty & Co. rents/supplies arms and weapons to movie companies and stage productions. An employee, 'The

Armourer' is the custodian of the weapons, which are released only when required; overnight storage usually is in a local Police Station or Military facility. Also, the Armourer stands-by on Set whenever weapons are in use, including the loading of blank ammunition, which is held by him, under lock-and-key.

Page 187. Bird. British slang—'girl.'

Page 188. Slàn. 'Health' (Irish), 'Cheerio', colloquial. *'Shlarn.'*

Page 188. Sin a bhuil. 'That's all' or 'That's it'. *'Shin a will.'*

Page 211. Fine Cut. Where all the excess has been trimmed from the Cutting Copy. But *not* Final Cut.

Page 218. *Jefe.* Spanish. 'Chief'.

Page 222. BAe. British Aerospace.

Page 246. Khazi. British slang, bathroom/lavatory/privy/toilet.

Page 265. Pan glass. Essentially a small piece of smoked glass mounted in a retractable frame, used by D.P.s to look directly at the sun to check for proximity of clouds obscuring sun when shooting exteriors.

Page 268. I.A.T.A. International Air Transport Association.

Page 268. F.O. No, no, not that, but First Officer.

Page 274. H.R.H. His Royal Highness.

Page 277. I.N.S. U.S. Agency; Immigration and Naturalization Service. **D.E.A..** U.S. Agency; Drug Enforcement Administration.

Page 280. Continuity Sheets. A log kept by the Continuity Lady/Script Clerk of each and every set-up shot, containing all relevant info., for the departments Editing, Accounts and Production, etc.

Page 286. Cafezinho. Very, *very* strong black coffee laced liberally with sugar, served in deni-tasse cups.

Page 286. VASP. Pronounced *'Vashpee.'* A one-time Brasilian airline based in Sao Paulo.

Page 288. Austin Reed. A once-famous chain of U.K. high-end gents' outfitters.

Page 289. Video Assist. Whereby a video camera records exactly the images photographed by the movie camera, which then can be played-back to allow the director (and usually half the crew) to see if the take is a 'print' or not. A real time-waster if ever there was one . . .

Page 292. Jock and Snowy. Two characters in a famous BBC radio serial, 'Dick Barton—Special Agent'.

Page 301. butchers.'Rhyming slang. 'Butcher's Hook'—'a look.'

Page 303. G.P.U. Ground Power Unit.

Page 329. Stuart Baird. Leading U.K. Editor, and Director, the savior of many a movie.

Page 333. Runner. Production 'Gofer,' to be found in both Production Office and On-Set.

Page 333. It's a wrap. Finished. Previously '. . . a rap!'—'Report and Print!'

Page 339. Synched. Throughout both Production and Post, the picture track and sound track are separate. Thus when screened, the two have to be synchronized.

Page 340. Kem. Together with the Steenbeck, refined, modern flatbed editing machine, which has more-or-less replaced the Moviola.

Page 341. P.O. Purchase Order.

Page 349. Double-Head. The screening simultaneously of the separated picture and sound tracks.

Page 349. Scene Missing. A few hand-written frames inserted into an edited scene, to identify just that, and that the scene will be included when shot or supplied by a film library.

Page 350. Dressing. Décor, Props, mock scenery, etc.

Page 355. Process. Front or Rear Projection. A pre-shot scene becomes a background/foreground 'plate', against which is played a scene, such as a dialogue two-shot in a bus, car, train, plane, etc., etc.

Page 355. Short-sided. Within the framing, where an actor is placed either extreme left, or, extreme right.

Page 355. The Eighteen. Wide-angle lens. The designation reflects the number of millimetres between the back element and the front element, of the lens. An 18mm lens.

Page 360. Inserts. For instance. A character looks at his watch, followed by a close-up of the watch. This latter shot is the 'insert.'

Page 372. Release Script. Book with original scene numbers of the final dialogue/edited version of the film, mostly for foreign distributors, for when they are preparing sub-titles, etc.

Page 373. Source Music. Existing music, in the public domain.

Page 374. Timed Print. Where the Director and D.P. sit with the Lab Contact, to screen and iron-out any faults/flaws, inconsistencies, the Timed Print becoming the final template for the subsequent Release Prints.

Page 374. Dupe Sections, InterPositive, InterNegative. Once the original negative is cut/edited, from that is struck in Interpositive, which in turn creates an Internegative. It is from multiple Internegatives that the Release Prints (as seen in movie theaters) are made. Once these systems have been created, the original neg is not used again, being stored then in a vault.

Page 375. Telecine. Projection system, film to television.

Page 380. Squawk Box. The intercom between the Screening Room and Projection Booth.

Page 382. Sarabande Varese. Record label specializing in movie music scores.

Page 388. Academy. The Academy of Motion Picture Arts & Sciences.

NOTA BENE

Within the book are quoted fragments of lyrics from three popular songs. The author wishes both to acknowledge and confirm that copyright of said lyrics is vested in the rights of the lyricist and/or publisher or both.

ACKNOWLEDGEMENTS

The spur for the book came from my long-time friend, mentor, and movie-making partner, John Boorman. Very many years ago (more than I care to mention here), it was John who chided me about my constant complaints that Producing was not 'truly creative'. "Then do something about it!" was the immediate riposte. John, thank you for your encouragement and our enduring friendship. And any serious student of the process of movie-making should read John's book, *Money Into Light*– that is, if you're lucky enough to find a copy!

Another long-time friend with whom I've made some small movies in Sacramento is Mike Carroll. A devoted movie-buff, Mike is another 'helper,' in that for publication he has formatted the book both diligently, tolerantly and patiently. Also, Mike designed the covers.

Emmett Corcoran is a friend from 'The Emerald Isle,' and his Brasilian wife Larissa is another who helped with the English-to-Portuguese translations. Larissa, *go raibh mille maight agut*!

To another Brasilian, Antonia Crafford, also for the many invaluable English-to-Portuguese translations she has provided for the piece. Antonia, *Obrigado*!

Antonia's husband, Ian, is a former movie-making partner. An Editor *par excellence*, Ian and I have worked together on some four major movies, and he was nominated for his work on 'Field of Dreams.' He has helped considerably in refreshing my Post Production knowledge. His son Paul provided the English-to-Spanish translations. *Gracias*, to you both!

For the Boeing 737-400 cockpit drill, my thanks to Jim Poots and particularly his son Sam, a pilot with Irish airline, Ryanair.

And then there are those Irish phrases and words, which unless you are a student of the Gaelic/Irish tongue, you'll never be able to pronounce correctly, as the Irish language is not phonetic. So for the Hibernian input, my profound thanks to friend Michael Farrell, of Clondra, Co.Longford, Ireland.

Thanks are due also to my *Oxford Dictionary*, my *Oxford Thesaurus* and, my *New American Webster Dictionary*.

That's a wrap!

Michael Dryhurst
Hot Springs Village, Arkansas, U.S.A.
March 2020